THE LUCKY HAT MINE

The Lucky Hat Mine

A Novel

J.v.L. Bell

HANSEN PUBLISHING GROUP, LLC

This is a work of historical fiction. All of the characters, organizations, and events portrayed in this novel are either a product of the author's imagination or are used fictitiously.

The Lucky Hat Mine

21 20 19 18 17 10 9 8 7 6 5

ISBN: (PAPER) 978-1-60182-334-2
ISBN: (EBOOK) 978-1-60182-335-9

Cover design by Jeffry A. DeCola
Title page artwork by Annie Carter
Book interior design by Jon Hansen

Hansen Publishing Group, LLC
302 Ryders Lane
East Brunswick, NJ 08816
http://hansenpublishing.com

Author site: www.jvlbell.com

For my parents, Joyce and Cleve…

Thanks for your encouragement and for helping me to believe I could do anything.

In memory of the amazing women in my family who shared their stories with me: Jeanne Hereford, Goldie Bell, and Mable Knight.

THE LUCKY HAT MINE

ONE

August 8, 1863
Denver City

Gunfire rent the air, tearing Millie from her restless slumber. Two more shots broke the pre-dawn calm followed by the whine of a ricochet. Millie scrambled to find her calico dress, knowing the filthy canopy covering their prairie schooner offered no protection against six-shooters and lead balls. Biting back a curse, she fumbled into her clothing. If she was going to be scalped by savages or shot by outlaws, she'd at least die dressed like a proper Southern lady.

Nearby, angry swearing replaced the gunfire as Millie crept from the packed wagon. She nervously fingered her pocket watch, stole around her companion's lean-to, and squinted in the shadowed light at a group of figures huddled around an unmoving, dark form. Their heads were bowed, but the foul language issuing from their mouths was far from a prayer. Millie took a quiet step closer, straining to see how many bodies littered the prairie dog colony that Denver City called the Elephant Corral.

The still form was a horse, Millie realized with surprise. Why had these settlers shot their horse? Two men stepped away from the dead animal and picked up what Millie thought might be a thick branch, although trees in this rolling prairie were rare. The wood sagged between them.

"A snake," she whispered, her Southern accent rolled and rounded her *a*'s, stretching each word.

One man glanced at her and shook the snake's body, producing a sound like brittle branches tumbling across the empty Nebraska plain. "Damn rattlesnake killed our horse," he growled, calling the creature several vile names.

Millie looked down, carefully backing up until she felt the wagon and quickly climbed in. In the crowded, confined space, she crawled onto her sleeping quilt and pulled her legs up against her chest, resting her head on her knees. The musty smell of canvas and worn leather pressed in on her as she wondered how her life had gotten so out of kilter.

In the past three months—since she left New Orleans—everything had changed, but not in the ways she'd imagined. Traveling in the paddleboat *Sultana* up the Mississippi to St. Louis had been exciting, although tending the horrendous wounds of the Yankee soldiers had stretched her limited medical expertise and personal fortitude. But it was the months spent crossing the Great Plains in this prairie schooner that demonstrated the irrevocable changes in her life. During those months she endured the never-ending howl of wind, encountered savages, and buried several of her traveling companions.

Looking back, she could see the imprudence of her decision, yet coming west was her only chance to escape a life of servitude. She left New Orleans besieged with Northern aggressors, the War for Southern Independence raging around it. She was twenty-three—almost a spinster—and miserably employed by the dreadful LeGrand family. An orphan with no dowry, money, or prospects. Closing her eyes in the dark recesses of the covered wagon, Millie thought back to that morning as if she were still in New Orleans.

Waiting for her tea water to boil, she thumbed through her well-worn copy of Eliza Acton's *Modern Cookery in All its Branches*, finding the pigeon soup recipe. Pigeon soup wasn't one of her favorite recipes—she'd never found a dish that made pigeon taste like anything but pigeon—but the birds had been specially priced at the French market. After plucking and rinsing the carcasses, she placed them in boiling water, added spices, and began slicing vegetables. She'd just begun chopping an onion when the LeGrands' four children arrived.

"Illie," asked Anna, the four year old. "Where's Pawpaw?"

Sighing, Millie repeated the answer she'd given at least ten times the day before. "Pawpaw is dead, sweet pea. He lives in Heaven now."

"God live in Heaven?" asked the little girl, her expression serious.

Millie wasn't too sure if there was a God or if he lived in Heaven, but she was happy to leave religious education to the priest. "Yes, sweat pea," she said, her eyes tearing from the onion. "God's in Heaven."

The child nodded and began eating, her expression thoughtful. Of all the LeGrand children, Anna was Millie's favorite, although her never-ending curiosity sometimes gave Millie a headache. The little girl looked up, her brown eyes confused, and asked, "God dead, too?"

A knock on the back door interrupted any reply Millie might have given, assuming she could have thought of one. The door flew open and her best friend, Carissa, bounded in, her blond hair disheveled, green bonnet askew. "Miss Millie," she said, giving Millie a breathless hug and a kiss on each cheek, "I've found something you hafta see."

Lor' Almighty it was good to see her friend, but what was she doing here? "How wonderful to see you, Miss Carissa," she said, trying to hide her alarm. The youngest LeGrand child, a toddler just over a year old, balled his little fists and brought them down on his bowl. Millie grabbed for it, missed, and felt sticky grits slide down her skirt.

"Mrs. MacIntyre is not allowed in my house," said the oldest girl in a voice that came shudderingly close to her mother's shrill tones. "My mama said so."

Carissa bent down until she was eye to eye with the impertinent girl. "That, young lady, is *not* ladylike behavior." Adopting the strict voice of a schoolmarm, she added, "The American Lady says to: 'Cultivate a soft tone of voice and a courteous mode of expression.'"

Millie burst out laughing, reminded of the many times she'd reprimanded Carissa for improper ladylike etiquette—or at least what she thought was improper. They'd been nine or maybe ten—sharing a bed in the Annunciation and Calliope Girls' House of Refuge—when they'd discovered a copy of *True Politeness, A Hand-Book of Etiquette for Ladies,* written in 1847 by An American Lady. From then on, they were either quoting rules of politeness or scolding other girls for unladylike behavior.

"I'm gonna tell Mama," screamed the girl, knocking grits to the floor as she squirmed from her chair and ran from the room.

"Papa said Mrs. MacIntyre married a common Irishman. He said she lives in a dirty hovel on the wrong side of Canal Street," added Rufus, the oldest boy. "It's filled with cholera, yellow fever, and other diseases. She shouldn't be in our kitchen."

Carissa's face fell. Millie cuffed Rufus for his cruel words, earning a barrage of insults before he too lurched from his chair and ran to find his mother. Watching his retreating figure, Millie knew she was in for a serious dressing-down. Might as well earn it honestly.

"Let's go outside, Miss Carissa," Millie said. "It'll take Mrs. LeGrand a few minutes to rise from bed and come down." After double-checking that the toddler was strapped safely in his chair, Millie admonished Anna to keep an eye on him before she hurried outside. "I'm sorry Miss Carissa. The children didn't mean what they said." Millie kissed her friend on both cheeks.

"Of course they do. They're becoming just as horrid as their parents. That's why I brought you this!" She waved a copy of New Orleans' *Daily Picayune*, fanning humid air across Millie's face. "I'd ruther you stay than leave, but I hate you working for the LeGrands. I want you happily married, like me. Have your own home. Even if it is a *hovel*." She spat out the word. "I want you to do all the things we dreamed about. It'll *never* happen if you stay here with those dreadful LeGrands."

"Hush, Miss Carissa!" Millie said, dragging her name out in a long breath. It was one thing to dream about changing her life, but quite another to be dismissed for impertinence. With Northern aggressors occupying New Orleans, hungry war widows roamed the streets scraping out a living in ways Millie had no desire to experience.

"Just listen," Carissa said, dancing back as she lifted the newspaper. She peeked over the top and added, "Remember how much you hate working for the LeGrands. Think how you'll feel when Miss Anna starts treating you like a white slave. Like the older two."

Millie winced. Mr. and Mrs. LeGrand's treatment was demeaning, but when the children Millie raised began imitating their parents and treating her like a servant, it was insufferable. Carissa was right. In a year or two, Anna would also begin to emulate her mother and older sister.

"Listen," Carissa insisted, reading from the paper.

> **WANTED, A WIFE.** PROSPECTOR, AGE 30, OWNER OF A CABIN WITH A COOKSTOVE, WANTS A WIFE, AGED 19 TO 24, OF LIBERAL EDUCATION, A GOOD COOK, ABLE TO WITHSTAND COLD WINTERS IN THE COLORADO TERRITORY. ANY LADY, POSSESSING THE ABOVE ACCOMPLISHMENTS AND WISHING TO MARRY, SHOULD SEND A LETTER OF INTRODUCTION AND A PHOTOGRAPH. J. W. DROUILLARD, IDAHO SPRINGS, TERRITORY OF COLORADO.

"You want me to answer a wife-wanted advertisement, Miss Carissa?" Millie asked. "To travel to the Colorado Territory? To marry a *Yankee*?"

"No." Carissa shook her head in frustration. "Well, yes, Miss Millie. I want you happy. To live the life you've dreamed about. You're an orphan. You've no prospects here but to remain a common servant."

Millie knew it was true, but would answering an advertisement and marrying a stranger make her happy? The idea both terrified and thrilled her. That evening—after a day filled with the LeGrand's reprimands—Millie wrote a letter of introduction. Two correspondences later she became engaged to Mr. Drouillard—a Yankee prospector living in the mining community of Idaho Springs. He sent her a paddleboat ticket, five dollars of travel money, and a carte-de-viste—his photographic calling card. It had been all the enticement she needed. In a whirlwind of activity, she'd left her employment and traveled to a world as different from New Orleans as night was to day. A world where gunfire, rattlesnakes, and death were commonplace.

The first rays of dawn illuminated the prairie schooner's cluttered interior, and Millie lifted her head and shook it trying to clear away New Orleans and her past. Looking through the wagon's back flap, the white-capped Rocky Mountains rose before her like a terror. Later, Millie would leave Sarah Ouellette and her husband, the farmers who'd brought her across the Great Plains, and begin the last leg of her journey. The thought terrified her.

After two days of travel by stagecoach into that rocky abyss, Millie would arrive in the mining settlement of Idaho Springs, and there she would marry a rough, bearded stranger—if he agreed to have her.

In New Orleans her decision seemed like such a silly thing. She'd been in a hurry, still needing to stop at the butcher and baker shop, but wanting to post her reply to

Mr. Drouillard. All she lacked was a picture. Mr. J.W. Petty, the proprietor of the photographic store, had shown her the carte-de-viste of a cream-faced young woman with delicate features, pouting lips, and long straight hair. He'd meant it as an example, to show what hers might look like, but when he laughingly offered to sell it for five cents, Millie quickly agreed. The forty cents savings constituted two full day's wages, and after all, the advertisement asked for a photograph, not specifically one of the applicant.

Besides, Millie's complexion *was* creamy, except for her freckles. And Carissa said her features were pleasant and pretty, although definitely not delicate. Unfortunately, her thick curly hair had never lain smooth down her back, but that's why she kept it contained in a long braid.

The closer they got to the Rocky Mountains, the more that picture haunted her. Since reaching the California Crossing, where they'd separated from the Mormon wagon train and headed toward Denver City, Millie had begun re-reading Mr. Drouillard's correspondences. By now she had his letters memorized, especially one sentence. *You sound like an accomplished young lady and well-liked by your current employer, but if I must be honest, your picture separated you from the other women and captured my heart.*

Oh Lor'. When he discovered she wasn't the woman in the picture, would her fiancé refuse to marry her?

TWO

August 8, 1863
A Catalogue Woman

Millie cleaned breakfast dishes and watched her unfortunate neighbors morosely jury-rig a harness for their milk cow and place it beside their second horse. Leaving the dead horse where it lay, the sorry contraption slowly pulled out of the Elephant Corral and away from Denver City, the skin of the dead rattlesnake nailed to the side of the wagon. These settlers, like many they'd spoken with on the plains, were heading back to the States, disillusioned from the dream of striking it rich in this Pikes Peak gold rush. Millie wished she too could leave. The more she saw of the rugged Rocky Mountains and uncivilized miners, the more she regretted her foolish decision.

"Ready?" asked Sarah, handing Millie the lead of two goats.

Sarah Ouellette and her husband were farmers, hoping to make their fortune not with discoveries of gold, but by "mining the miners" as Mr. Ouellette was fond of saying. In the States, Mr. Ouellette had heard miners were willing to pay upward of fifteen dollars in gold dust for a bushel of potatoes and almost fifty dollars for a hundred pounds of flour. "I'll plant potatoes," Mr. Ouellette once told Millie, "but also sow a field of wheat." They'd been paid to bring

Millie across the Great Plains, but today, in Denver City, they would leave her at the Larimer Street Post Office.

"Walk, muttonheads," Millie mumbled, jerking on the goats' leads.

During their first hour of acquaintance, Sarah had proudly introduced Millie to her goats. They were the strangest looking animals Millie had ever seen, with bulging eyes and floppy ears, no bigger than a knee-high dog. They would have been simple oddities but for their abnormal habit of hopping on stiff legs and falling over whenever they were startled. In Millie's mind, that made them downright peculiar, although she'd never hurt Sarah's feelings by saying so. Mr. Ouellette called them fainting goats and often threatened to roast them or turn them loose for the prairie wolves. Millie agreed the goats weren't worth the trouble, but after almost two months of travel, Sarah had become like a sister. Millie knew how much the girl loved her goats, so she kept her dislike to herself.

She and Sarah followed the wagon down the dusty road into Denver City. They passed weather-worn, ramshackle buildings, drooping Indian tepees, new emigrants with covered wagons as travel-weary as theirs, and many, many men. Filthy, smelly men. The more Millie saw, the more her anxiety grew.

An unusually disgusting male specimen staggered by, his long beard and greasy hair making Millie cringe. His appearance caused Millie to ask Sarah the question that had plagued her for months. "Miss Sarah. May I ask? I mean. It's improper, but…What happened after you married Mr. Ouellette?"

"After?" Sarah scratched her head and pulled absently on the leads of her goats. "After Mr. O and Pa finalized the trade? Well. We all gone ta the courtplace. Mr. O and first Mrs. O filled out a paper ta break up. Law like. After Pa and first Mrs. O tied the knot, we signed them papers and then Mr. O and me married, and they signed papers for us."

During their journey, Sarah had told Millie stories about her Pa—an ugly man who used his fists freely, even on his daughter. Despite this wickedness, Millie had trouble believing any father would trade his sixteen-year-old daughter for another man's wife.

"Yes. But after you were married, what happened?"

"At the courtplace, 'fore Mr. O and I go, I says I want ma goats, a milk cow, five hens, and a cock. First Mrs. O ain't too happy, but ma Pa don't care. He drug first Mrs. O toward our shack. Said he want his husband rights. I snuck into ma barn and took ma critters."

Millie pulled on her braid, flinched, and jerked on the goat's lead instead. Sarah wasn't understanding her question. What did it mean, a *husband's rights*? Millie gazed at the merchant stores intermixed with saloons, boarding houses, liveries, blacksmith, shops, and taverns. Sour smells blended with cigarette smoke and alcohol, making the city smell as bad as its occupants.

How did she politely ask something so indelicate? Her former boss, Mrs. LeGrand complained bitterly about "a wife's duty," but her friend Carissa had smiled when she mentioned the "joys of marriage." What exactly did that duty or that joy involve?

Mr. Ouellette jerked the wagon to the center of the road as a man tumbled out of swinging doors, creating an explosion of dust as he landed face-down in the street. His hat rolled to a stop at Millie's feet.

"That's whot happens ta men who don't pay for a lady's favors after 'cepting them favors," yelled a big-busted woman from the door, her eyes and face painted, her hands planted on her round hips. "Don't ya come back now, ya hear?"

Millie swallowed, guiding the goats around the prone man. For all she knew, he could be her future husband. Oh, Lor'. What was she doing here? Several men staggered out the swinging doors, six-shooters strapped to their hips, their arms around the bare shoulders of working women.

Millie looked away, embarrassed by where the men's large hands were resting.

She had to ask, indelicate or not. "Miss Sarah. W-what I want to know. Is…Well, what happened after you were married? That night, I mean."

"Oh," Sarah said, pausing, her face reddening. "You know. Mr. O tell me it be okay. A husband's right, he says, just like Pa." She shrugged. "It ain't so bad, now I's getting use to it."

"Well yes, but what *is* a husband's right?"

Sarah's blush deepened. "You know. Like the he-goat."

Like the he-goat?

They turned a corner and stopped beside the Larimer Street Post Office. Millie swallowed, her question momentarily forgotten as she looked up at the rickety building. This was it. In a few short minutes Sarah would leave. Millie grabbed her friend's hand. "Miss Sarah. W-will you come inside with me?"

"Course," Sarah said. "We be family."

After tying the goats, Sarah took Millie's arm and together they entered the poorly lit building. In one corner, a balding, middle-aged man sat behind a desk; faded posters covered the walls surrounding him. Several were enrollment notices that described President Lincoln's March 3 Enrollment Act requiring all eligible men to enroll for possible military service. Other posters showed the faces of rough-looking men with "WANTED" written below and a price for their crime: $500 for train robbery or killing a man, $200 for stealing a horse, $50 for lewd behavior.

"May I help you?"

Millie jumped and turned to face the man. "I'm Millie Virginia, I'm…" She hesitated. What exactly was she?

"Ah. Miss Virginia. We've been awaiting your delivery."

Delivery? Millie bristled.

The clerk stood, his pot-belly sagging on his desk. "Elliot," he yelled. "Go fetch Mr. Gould. Tell him Miss Virginia has finally been delivered." A boy dashed from the back room and disappeared out the door. The clerk returned his attention to Millie, eyeing her. "Most catalogue women don't make it this far. Your fiancé will be pleased."

"What, sir, is a catalogue woman?" Millie asked tartly.

"You," he said chuckling. "One who's been ordered. A mail-order bride."

She was *not* a piece of merchandise! Only good manners kept her from giving him a well-deserved tongue-lashing. Instead, she asked coldly, "*Why* don't most women make it this far?"

He laughed. "Most get snatched away by other men while in transport. Miss-delivered, we call 'em. But not you. I'm surprised. I'm sure that soft Southern accent could melt many a Yankee heart. That mean you have a temper matching your fiery red hair?"

"My hair is auburn with a few red streaks!" Millie responded, her Southern accent neither soft nor polite. "And I made it this far because I promised to marry Mr. Drull, ah, Mr. Drool." How did one pronounce Drouillard? "I mean. I promised to marry my fiancé."

"I see. Nobody else would have you, huh?"

"Have me? That sir, is impertinent! If you must know, on the paddleboat *Sultana*, injured Yankee soldiers accosted me several times a day, begging for my hand in marriage." She raised her eyebrows. "And not just the soldiers, mind you. First Engineer Wolff, the shipman who'd escorted me while I was on the ship, proposed after apologizing for the impropriety of his actions." First Engineer Wolff had been a gentleman with a fine sense of humor, and Millie might have said yes, but she'd foolishly set her sights on adventure in the Colorado Territory. Plus, Mr. Drouillard had paid for her travels.

"I'm sure Mr. Wolff enjoyed those inappropriate actions. No matter. Your fiancé won't care if you're damaged goods. Out here, a man takes what makes it across the plains—"

"*Damaged Goods!?* Sir!" Millie blushed. "*I* am a lady. First Engineer Wolff was *always* a gentleman. I left him because I promised to marry another. A lady keeps her word." And she would, unless Mr. Drouillard had been that drunk in the street. Or one of these wanted men. Or...

A thin, almost weedy man with a receding hairline, a tangled gray beard, and stringy mustache swaggered into the post office, ending Millie's tirade. He wore a ruffled shirt, a low-cut weskit, and a brightly colored silk scarf tied around his chicken neck, looking like an aged and slightly used dandy—although Southern dandies never wore two oversized six-shooters strapped to their hips. Everything about the newcomer, from his leering eyes to his arrogant stance, made Millie uneasy.

"Miss Virginia," he said, stretching out her name unnaturally as his eyes made an improper tour of her body. "I'm Mr. Gould. A business associate of Mr. Ferris, your fiancé's solicitor."

Flustered, it took Millie a moment to recognize the name. Ferris. In his last letter, Mr. Drouillard had included a handwritten document—he'd called it a holographic will—along with some legal papers. A gesture Millie had found reassuring and gentlemanly. The name Ferris might have been on the legal papers.

"It's a pleasure to make your acquaintance, sir," Millie lied. "Are you assisting me with stagecoach travel from here?"

"Yes." His smile was vulgar. "I'm to escort you to Idaho Springs." He offered an arm and a bony hand. "Come with me."

Millie hesitated, glad she'd donned gloves. The man felt as disagreeable as this morning's rattlesnake. Sarah tightened her hold on the arm Mr. Gould hoped to claim.

"You, girl. Bring Miss Virginia's bags," he said, snapping his fingers at Sarah.

"They with ma husband, sir. We comin' to the coach office with Miss Millie."

The man glared at her, gave Millie a disapproving look, and dropped his arm. "This way," he said, rudely turning his back on them and striding out.

Outside, Sarah turned to her husband who had waited by the wagon. "Mr. O, we needing the wagon this way, please." Her strong East Kentucky accent stressed the first part of most words, making "wagon" sound like "wahgon."

Millie clung to Sarah, feeling cowardly, following the disagreeable man down the dusty road, already dreading spending any time alone with him. Several turns later, on the corner of Blake and G streets, Mr. Gould entered a building marked with the sign "The Overland Stage Line—Ben Holladay Proprietor." The door slammed behind him, leaving Millie, Sarah, and Mr. Ouellette in the street.

"I donna like that one. He feel like ma Pa," Sarah whispered.

"How could my fiancé send such a wretched man?" Millie muttered. "What am I going to do if he is anything like Mr. Gould?"

THREE

August 8, 1863
Millie's Pocket Watch

Millie released Sarah and nervously fingered her pocket watch, waiting for Mr. Gould to reappear. Two days in the crowded confines of a stagecoach sounded dreadful, especially if Mr. Gould continued to stare at her in that scandalous way. And what would she do if he tried anything improper? Mr. Gould emerged with two tickets pinched between his bony fingers. He ogled Millie as if reading her mind about indecorous behavior, his tangled mustache quivering like the tail of a rat.

No! Millie couldn't travel with this man. Just looking at him made her skin crawl. He stepped into the street and smirked, obviously aware of Millie's distress.

"Mr. Gould?!"

Millie jumped. She'd been so focused on the unpleasant man she hadn't heard anyone else approach. Spinning around, she found a respectable-looking couple striding toward them. The woman lifted her full skirt up from the street's filth, showing the lace tatting of her petticoat. Her puffy pagoda sleeves, high neckline, and oversized bonnet were the picture of a respectable matron. The man on her arm was dressed in a fashionable double-breasted frock coat, black wool trousers, a beaver fur top hat, and tan gloves. In one hand, he carried a fine walking stick.

The woman's eyes swept over Millie, the Ouellette's wagon, and Mr. Gould before returning to the dandy with a look of distaste. "Mr. Gould. Has another man entrusted you with his future wife? After what happened last time?"

"Mrs. Adriance. This is none—"

"Last time?" The gentleman turned to the woman. "Pray tell, Mrs. Adriance. What are you talking about?"

"Reverend Adriance. This man is Mr. Gould. I don't know his profession. Four months ago he was hired by Mr. Ferris to escort Mr. Martin's fiancé from Denver City to Mountain City."

Reverend Adriance's thick eyebrows rose. "Our Mr. Martin? From church? But I thought his fiancé never arrived?"

"There was a miscommunication—" began Mr. Gould.

"Miscommunication? I understand Mr. Martin's fiancé arrived in Denver City. I believe you lost her, didn't you? She was found a month later working in an establishment on McGaa Street."

"Madam. *I* am not responsible for the morality of a woman who answers a wife-wanted advertisement."

Millie blushed all the way down to her toes. Before she could respond to this unfair statement, the lady stepped forward and turned to Millie, her back to Mr. Gould. "Good morning, Miss…?"

"Miss Virginia, ma'am."

"Miss Virginia. I'm Mrs. Adriance and this is my husband, Reverend Adriance."

"It's a pleasure to make your acquaintance," Millie said, remembering the American Lady's advice on proper introductions. She stole a glance behind the matron. Mr. Gould watched, his eyes sparked daggers and his fingers twitched over his gun.

"May I ask your destination?" asked the lady.

"Idaho Springs. I'm engaged—"

"Excellent. We're on our way to Mountain City. We insist you accompany us. We'll chaperone you, so this…this man," she flicked a hand at Mr. Gould, "doesn't misplace you. Tonight you'll be our guest and tomorrow we'll see you safely to Idaho Springs." She winked and smiled at Millie. "We might even accompany you. I just *love* weddings."

Millie sagged with relief. "That is most kind of you, I—"

"No thanks necessary. It's our Christian duty." She turned and gave Mr. Gould a hard look. "We want to make sure Miss Virginia is delivered safely to *her* fiancé."

"That's quite unnecessary, madam," Mr. Gould snarled. "I—"

"I assure you, it is," interrupted Mrs. Adriance, plucking a ticket from Mr. Gould's hand. "Return the other one, won't you." She turned to Millie, her expression softening. "You must be excited. Your fiancé will want to marry immediately. With so few women out West, a wife is a precious commodity. You know how men are."

After Sarah's words, Millie was more confused than ever about men. How did they behave like he-goats? No, she had no idea how men were, and she doubted she would enjoy finding out.

"Thank you, ma'am." Millie glanced back at Mr. Gould. "It would be my pleasure and honor to be your guest."

"Then it's settled." Mrs. Adriance ignored Mr. Gould and turned to her husband. "Reverend, shouldn't our stagecoach be here any minute?"

Reverend Adriance opened his frock-coat and pulled on the chain attached to his weskit, withdrawing a gold pocket watch. He clicked open the cover, glanced down, and sighed. "We'll have to return it to Mr. Howard," he said. "It appears to have stopped again."

"I have a watch," Millie said, reaching into her apron. The silver pocket watch was her only family possession. The nuns had given it to her on her fifteenth birthday, when she'd left the Annunciation and Calliope Girls' House of Refuge to work for the LeGrands. It—along with a slip of paper with Abingdon Virginia written in block letters—

had been wrapped inside her baby blanket. Fortunately, the nuns decided Abingdon was not an appropriate name for a Southern child so they named her Permelia. Permelia Abingdon Virginia.

"It's quarter to seven," Millie said, her eyes drawn to the daguerreotype of a man, woman, and child mounted in the inside cover. They were her parents—or at least the woman looked like Millie—and a sibling, maybe a brother? Why had they left her—a helpless infant wrapped in a blanket—on the steps of an orphanage in New Orleans? Had they named her Abingdon after the town in Virginia? Maybe she'd been born there. It really didn't matter. Whatever their reasons, they didn't wait around to see if anyone found her.

"Nice daguerreotype. May I see?"

Millie jumped, bumping into Sarah. Mr. Gould now stood directly behind her—so close she could smell his sour sweat. He peered over her shoulder and snatched the watch from her hand without waiting for a response. Millie turned and stepped away, itching to take her watch back. It wasn't much, but it was all she had from her past.

Mr. Gould stared intently at the picture, turning it into the light, and spending more time than was polite. Finally, he snapped the cover closed and stepped to Millie's side, digging his bony fingers into her shoulder. "I have been hired to accompany Miss Virginia. I cannot shirk my duty. Besides, you are only able to chaperone her as far as Mountain City, correct?"

"Nonsense," said Mrs. Adriance. "We'll make sure she arrives safely in Idaho Springs."

Millie tried to pull away, but Mr. Gould tightened his grip. "I feel—"

"Don't trouble yourself, sir," said the Reverend. "Miss Virginia is safe in our hands."

Pounding hooves interrupted the discourse as four pawing horses pulled a stagecoach up beside Mr. Ouellette's wagon. Millie snatched her pocket watch from Mr. Gould's hand and jerked free of his fingers. She hurried to stand on the far side of Sarah, covering her mouth with her handkerchief as the horses stirred up dust.

"Thank you, Mr. Gould," Millie said, tearing her eyes from the egg-shaped coach with its leather curtains, belts, braces, and matching horses. "But I'm sure I'll be well cared for. I'll inform Mr. Ferris of my decision."

"Excellent," said Mrs. Adriance, beaming. "There's our luggage." Two men carried a large trunk from the stagecoach office and hefted it into the boot of the coach. Millie turned to grab her carpetbags and found Mr. Ouellette already carrying them toward the coach. Mrs. Adriance unfolded a long, light linen cape and slipped into it. "My apology, dear, but I only have one duster." She patted Millie on the arm.

"Duster?"

"This," she said, lifting the linen cape. "It protects your clothes from the blowing dirt. Stagecoach travel is rather unpleasant." With that, her husband handed her into the coach and followed her inside.

They were leaving. Now, tears stung Millie's eyes as she turned to hug Sarah, but the girl wasn't there. Sarah walked toward her, leading one of her goats.

"I want you to have Buttercup, Miss Millie. She be ma favorite."

"Gracious sakes, Miss Sarah! I can't take Buttercup." What in the world would she do with a goat? Especially one of Sarah's odd goats? "I don't—"

"Sure you can!" Mr. Ouellette said enthusiastically, picking up the goat and tossing it to the man tying down the luggage. "One down, five to go," he added, grinning. "Bet your husband will love it every time she faints at him. They make me feel like a stupe every time I come near." He smiled with satisfaction as the driver roped the bleating animal down on top of the luggage.

Millie was quite certain, no matter what kind of man Mr. Drouillard might be, he would not enjoy Buttercup, but she couldn't refuse Sarah's gift.

Sarah hugged her. "I's gonna miss you, Miss Millie." Tears streamed down her friend's cheeks.

"Oh, Lor'. Miss Sarah, I'm going to miss you too. Terribly." Millie hugged her friend, kissing her on either cheek. "After you settle, you'll write? You have the address?" Sarah nodded hesitantly. "Promise?" Millie added desperately.

"Course, but I donna spell so good."

"No matter. We're family now. You be careful." She looked at Mr. Ouellette. "You take good care of her."

He grinned. "I won't be trading her. Not now that you taught her to cook."

The unhappy cries from Buttercup echoed around them as Millie glanced at a scowling Mr. Gould and quickly climbed into the stagecoach. She took the seat opposite the Reverend and his wife, her knees bumping theirs in the tight space. Millie looked out the window, caught a glimpse of Sarah waving frantically, but with the crack of a whip, the stagecoach jerked into motion.

And what an awful motion it was!

Dust poured in through the windows, making it difficult to breathe. The coach rocked and creaked like a ship about to capsize. Millie choked down a couple foul breaths as she was knocked to one side and thrown forward, landing in the Reverend's lap. Mortified, she scrambled to her feet and stumbled backward, groping for the side grip. Clutching it with both hands, Millie wondered how anyone rode in a stagecoach.

"Your first coach ride?" yelled Mrs. Adriance. She'd tied a bandana around her face and held the side grip with practiced hands. "Unfortunately, it doesn't improve with time or experience."

Millie nodded miserably, unable to answer. The awful motion was making her sick. Breathing as deeply as the dusty air allowed, she focused on keeping her morning meal in her stomach and her seat on the bench.

"Shall we begin our journey with a prayer for safe travel?" Reverend Adriance asked in his deep voice.

"Safe travel?" Millie caught a glimpse of the mountains' ridges looking sharp as a kitchen knife. "Are…are we in danger?"

"Always," said the couple in unison.

FOUR

August 8, 1863

Into the Dark and Dangerous Rocky Mountains

Millie grasped the handle of the stagecoach in dismay. She'd endured the difficult paddle-boat trip up the Mississippi through the war-torn South. Spent months with shot sewed in her skirt, struggling to survive violent windstorms, river crossings, Indian encounters, and other dangers of the Great Plains. She was sick and tired of fearing for her life.

"What kinds of trouble might we encounter?" she asked, her stomach roiling.

"The savages are always worrisome," said Mrs. Adriance. "And this summer we've been plagued by the dreadful Espinosas."

"The dreadful Espinosas?"

"Fearful Spaniards. The *Rocky Mountain News* said they've killed at least twenty white settlers—some with knives and axes. The paper described the murder scenes as *grisly*."

Millie swallowed. "Where?"

"All over the territory."

"With all the dangers in this unforgiving frontier," added Reverend Adriance, "we always begin a journey with a prayer." He lowered his head; his wife quickly followed suit.

"Have they caught the Espinosas?" Millie asked, her stomach giving an ominous lurch.

"No!" answered the couple in unison.

Millie stared at their bowed heads. She'd been raised by Catholic nuns, but she'd always questioned why God gave so much to a few, leaving most barely surviving. Trying to answer this fundamental question, she'd read pamphlets and even attended different churches. Instead of clarity, her confusion only increased. Which answer should she believe? The Catholic nuns? The austere Calvinists? The Deists who relied on reason? The Baptists or Methodists? Joseph Smith and the Mormons?

Reverend Adriance cleared his throat and Millie's stomach gurgled. With worries about killers, Indians, and marriage, Millie would take any help she could get. She lowered her face.

"Lord, hear our prayer," Reverend Adriance began, his voice loud enough for the driver to hear over the noises of the stagecoach and Buttercup's unhappy bleating. "As is written in the Psalms, God is our refuge and our strength. He will not abandon us in moments of trouble and fear, for we always remember, no matter what happens here on Earth—torture, scalping, knifings, robbery, shootings, landslides, cave-ins, savage attacks, avalanches, runaway stagecoaches, or even death. Our Lord awaits us in heaven."

Millie raised her head as a shiver ran up her spine. If the prayer was meant to calm and reassure, it failed. The Reverend paused to take a breath and Mrs. Adriance shouted, "Amen! Hallelujah!"

"Do I say such terrible things to scare you? No, my child. I say them only as warnings. Even when terrible things happen, God's will cannot be questioned. For he sent his only son to be tempted and punished so *we* may have eternal life."

"Amen! Hallelujah!"

"Yes, my child, in this life you may be punished, experience terrible pain, feel the sharp edge of a knife cut deep into your skin, and watch as your blood spills to the dusty ground…"

Millie clenched her teeth, trying to swallow her rising bile. Reverend Adriance's reference to bloodshed didn't help in keeping her unhappy stomach in check. The coach made a sharp turn and went over a rise.

Millie gagged. She stuck her head out the tiny window and yelled for the driver to stop. The coach slowed, but Millie couldn't wait. Knocking the door open, she stumbled out, landing hard, but on her feet. She staggered over to a shrub, bent over, and lost her pork and bean breakfast and maybe even last night's ox tail stew.

Her system was empty when she finally stood up. She wiped her face with a dusty handkerchief and turned to face the coach. Reverend Adriance and his wife watched from the window, looking decidedly unhappy.

"I'd better ride in the open air, beside the driver," Millie said.

"Pray, please do," said Mrs. Adriance.

"I'll pray for you," Reverend Adriance added, slamming the coach door.

Millie scrambled onto the driver's box and the coachman urged the horses back into a gallop. Cool air fanned her face, helping to calm her raw stomach. As long as Millie gazed at the nearby rolling hills and flower strewn meadows she felt okay, but every time she glanced toward the mountains, her stomach churned.

Beside her, the rough-looking driver sat hunched over, a whip and leather straps laced through his fingers. A cigarette dangled from his mouth and his eyes roamed from the countryside to the horses and the trail. Millie asked him about the weather, the scruffy trees, the red flowers, and even a bird that flew by, but to each question he answered "donno," "s'pose so," or "s'pose not." After a quiet period she asked, "What kind of stagecoach is this?" She hadn't expected a response, but suddenly the quiet driver became as talkative as poor Buttercup.

"This here's a Concord coach. It's got leather strap braces 'stead of springs. That's what causes the swinging motion stead of a nasty jumping up and down. People call it a cradle on wheels."

"I guess my mama never rocked me in a cradle," Millie responded dryly.

"S'pose not."

"How do you control the horses?"

"They's easy. The wheelers—thems the big, strong ones right below us—control the stopping and turning and the leaders, the two littler-ones up front, thems the smart ones. Old Joe and Molly got lots of 'sperience leading and watching for trouble."

Millie didn't ask what kind of trouble. She didn't want to know. "How do the wheelers know when you want them to turn or stop?"

Enthusiastically, the driver demonstrated, but Millie became confused how the traces, hames, breeches, backbands, terrets, ribbons, and other equipment helped the horse understand the driver's commands. When Millie admitted her confusion, the man repeated his demonstration, sticking to simple words and sentences, like he was explaining it to a slow-witted child. "See here. Thems are ribbons. Thems control the horses. I pull on 'em to slow the horses." He demonstrated and the horses' steady gallop slowed. "Pull on one," he continued, snapping his whip to encourage the horses into a faster gallop, "and thems turn the horses."

They turned, following the curve in the narrow path, and a small town came into view.

"That there's Golden," said the driver. "The Colorado Territorial capital. We'll trade out Joe and Molly there."

The trail into Golden was dotted with wood frame homes, horse corrals, and cow pastures, but as they entered town, cabins were replaced by saloons, liveries, saloons, general stores, and more saloons. Every other building appeared to be a watering hole! Dismayed, Millie watched men of all colors stagger in and out. This was the Colorado Territorial capital?

It took less than ten minutes to change horses and leave Golden behind. The stagecoach wound through low hills, always climbing, following the path of a stream that tumbled over rocks, gently twirling and bubbling. Millie's unease grew as the trail and scenery became mountainous and massive stone cliffs grew beside them, closing in from both sides. The confined space made her feel dizzy. She tried to calm her racing heart by taking slow, calming breaths, but her efforts only made her feel light-headed.

Finally they stopped at a rough cabin—called the Guy House by the coach driver. The driver climbed down, mumbling he would help change the team before joining them for a quick meal.

Millie climbed from the stage, her legs unsteady, and tottered over to a horse trough, the tank coated in green and brown slime. She closed her eyes and dipped her hands into the water, splashing her face and neck. The cold revived her, and she breathed deeply and opened her eyes. In the water, long-legged bugs ran across the surface, dimpling it with their spidery legs. Jesus bugs. Their familiarity was somehow comforting. Millie dried her hands and face with her apron and headed into the rough cabin.

Mr. Guy, the station caretaker, served a surprisingly good meal of potted chicken and bread, but too soon the driver was herding them back into the coach. From the shotgun seat beside the driver, Millie had a clear view of the narrow, impossibly steep trail they were following. She gripped her seat and held on until they paused at the top of what the driver called "Big Hill." Millie took one look at the abrupt path downward and blurted out "Oh, Lor'. We can't do that!"

"You rather walk?"

Millie nodded and scrambled off the coach. The Adriances joined her and together they slipped and slid down the treacherous incline. Behind them, Millie heard Buttercup's desperate bleats—it sounded like the goat knew what was coming.

She and the Adriances made it to the bottom without mishap and climbed off the road, looking back up at the stagecoach.

"They'll surely crash," Millie said as the driver perilously drove over the rim.

"Won't be the first time," said Mrs. Adriance.

The horses stampeded down the hill, the stagecoach rocking violently behind. The wheel struck a rut and momentarily went airborne, almost knocking the driver from his seat. Millie saw the man desperately gripping his hold, all control lost, not even trying to use the brake.

The coach bounced by and Millie gasped as she caught sight of the coach's boot. Buttercup no longer bleated. Instead, the goat flopped around like a yarn doll, her ears and tail popping every time the coach bumped over a rock.

"Buttercup!" Millie yelled, lifting her skirt and chasing after the coach. "Buttercup!"

The trail leveled and the coach rolled to a stop, still upright and on all four wheels. Millie hurried up from behind and reached into the boot, resting a hand on Buttercup's side, which rose and fell steadily.

"Is the poor animal dead, Miss Virginia?"

"No, ma'am," Millie said, quickly turning to face Mrs. Adriance. "She just fainted." Millie opened the coach's door, hoping the couple hadn't noticed the stream of goat pee dripping down their trunk.

After Big Hill, shadowed evergreens and jagged rocks closed in around them like a tightening noose. Just when

Millie thought she might crack, the suffocating surroundings opened into a beautiful meadow with stunning views of white-capped mountains. Never had Millie seen such a diverse and wonderfully terrible landscape.

From the meadow, the trail wound into a relatively narrow canyon and the wide blue sky was reduced to a thin ribbon. Millie glanced upward, chilled from the shadows of the canyon. She turned to ask the driver how long the narrow canyon would last when the wooden brace near her head exploded.

She screamed, grabbed her neck, and felt splinters cut into her skin.

The horses neighed shrilly and jerked the stagecoach forward, breaking into a wild gallop. The violent movement knocked Millie backwards, almost dislodging her. Her flailing arms struck something solid and she grabbed on. The stagecoach lurched and pitched dangerously. Gasping, Millie dragged herself back onto her seat, looked up, and screamed again. The horses were stampeding down the narrow canyon, totally out of control. Beside her, the stagecoach driver was gone.

The coach pitched from side to side, banking dangerously as the horses made another sharp turn. They broke from the confines of the narrow canyon and two riders—their faces hidden behind bandanas—galloped by, one on each side.

Shocked, Millie watched the rider on the left urge his horse up beside the frightened stagecoach horses and lean over. His mount galloped wildly as he wrapped his long fingers around the ribbons and began to pull.

The lead horse shied sideways, jerking the unbalanced outlaw off his horse and onto the stagecoach horse's back.

The outlaw bounced belly down on the stagecoach horse, the straps and harness tangling around him. For an instant, he glanced up. Millie saw the whites of his eyes and a rattail mustache slithered out from beneath his bandana. The horses turned and the man bounced off, the wheels of the coach popped as they rolled over him.

The second outlaw, obviously unwilling to make the same mistake as his partner, pulled out his six-shooter and aimed at the lead horses. Millie screamed, imagining too clearly an injured horse stumbling and dragging the other animals down, overturning the coach.

The bandit steadied his aim. A shot rang out behind them. The outlaw's horse stumbled off the trail. Straining around in her seat, Millie saw Reverend Adriance, his handkerchief covering his lower face, a derringer in his hand.

Millie spun back around at the coaches' violent lurch. The bandana-clad outlaws were gone, but the horses continued their wild rampage. Millie grasped her seat and remembered the wagon train stampede described by Captain Budge, the leader of their wagon train. At the time she thought he'd exaggerated the damage and loss of life. No longer. If the horses didn't stop, they would crash.

Tightly grasping a wooden bar with her outside hand, Millie edged her other hand over and scooted toward the driver's side of the coach. They hit a rut and the coach bounced sideways, knocking Millie over to the driver's side and almost off the seat. Her fumbling hand found the wooden handhold and she slowly regained her balance. Gasping for breath, she reached for the ribbons. They were looped around a metal ring and after two tries, she finally managed to grab them and sit up.

She looked up and almost dropped them again.

In front of them, a giant man—his beard jerking wildly with his frantic waving—stood in the middle of their path. His tiny burro blocked the road.

Millie hauled back on the ribbons. The horses slowed, but not fast enough.

They thundered toward the man. His eyes grew as large as the prospecting pan tied to his burro. His arms wavered and stopped. Scrambling off the path, he jerked wildly on his burro's lead. The poor creature appeared paralyzed by fear, unable to move.

Millie pulled desperately on the ribbons as the stagecoach bore down on man and beast. Just before they collided, the man released his burro and dove out of the way. Millie dropped the ribbons and covered her face.

The stagecoach shuddered violently, knocking Millie off her seat. She landed on the footrest, her shoulders flopping in the air, her face bouncing against a leather strap. Floundering backwards, she dragged herself back until she was sitting in the footrest. In front of her, the two back horses sat on their haunches, dust billowing around them like a thick fog. The stagecoach rocked dangerously.

Finally, all motion stopped. Everything was eerily silent.

Millie gingerly fumbled back onto the seat as an apparition emerged beside the back horses. She rubbed her eyes. The dust settled and the ghost transformed into a man.

An unkempt, impossibly filthy man.

His hair and beard were yellow from grime, his clothes had animal fur protruding in messy tuffs, scorch marks striped his worn hat, and a blackish bandanna hung lopsided around his neck.

He took a couple of uneven steps forward, his blue eyes wide. "Why in tarnation does the stage company allow woman drivers?" he bellowed.

FIVE

August 8, 1863

A Most Unkempt, Uncouth, Ungrateful Man

The ill-bred man added several more uncomplimentary comments about women and their place in society with his grimy beard swaying, his arms flailing wildly. Millie sucked down several deep breaths, trying to calm her racing heart, but she couldn't smother her rising temper. The audacity of the man! She'd managed to stop the coach, yet he was blaming her for nearly trampling his donkey. Brushing back her loose hair, Millie sat up straight and, for the first time in her travels, entirely forgot ladylike behavior.

"Sir, you are the rudest, most unsavory male I have ever had the misfortune of laying eyes on. Are you blind, or just a muttonhead? How can you not comprehend that I am a *passenger* on this stagecoach? We were accosted by bandits. The driver was lost. I just saved your life and the life of your worthless ass."

The man narrowed his eyes. "Where'd you learn to drive a coach? Never mind, I don't want to know." Shaking his head, he turned and disappeared in front of the horses, mumbling about strong-willed females. He emerged leading his burro, but Millie could barely see the poor creature buried beneath its dusty bundles.

"No wonder it refused to move," Millie said, goaded by the man's uncomplimentary mutterings. "Did you ever consider carrying some of the load yourself?"

The man glared at her. "I've yet to meet a redhead that ain't a pain in the ass."

"*MY HAIR IS AUBURN WITH A FEW RED STREAKS!*"

He paused for a long moment and burst into laughter. His booming mirth echoed through the valley as he bent at the waist and slapped his knee.

"I see nothing…" Millie said, but his loud bellowing drowned out her words. What an uncouth, unpleasant male. She questioned which one was the ass. Picking up the ribbons, Millie gently slapped them against the flanks of the horses, just as she'd seen the driver do, repeating the words he'd used. "Git up, Turk. G'wan, Clothesline."

The horses jerked the stagecoach forward.

The man's laughter abruptly died, replaced by a loud oath and cry. "Wait one blasted minute, Red!"

Millie seethed and urged the horses to go faster. Growing up, she'd hated her hair and the nicknames it caused. Most of her pranks, like coating the Nun's outhouse seat with molasses or sprinkling hot peppers in their supper, were childish ways to discourage nicknames. A battle she'd lost. One Sister called her Flame, another Carrot-top, but Mama Angelica—while punishing Millie with her strap—preferred Red. Millie hated that nickname.

Despite Millie's encouragement, the horses refused to move faster than a walk. From behind, Millie heard the man's creative cussing before his head appeared. The stagecoach groaned as he climbed into the driver's box.

"Where the heck are you going, Red? Gimme those ribbons!" He jerked them out of her hands. "Mountain City's just over the rise. I'll drive so you don't kill nobody. We'll send the sheriff back for the driver."

"I only want to murder one man right now," Millie uttered between gritted teeth. "Unfortunately, I missed my chance."

"True, but you'd regret running over my Columbine. Killing a man's one thing, killing a prospector's burro. That's just plain mean."

Fortunately, Mountain City came into view, removing the need for Millie to respond. If this man was an example of a miner, she'd never marry. Better to become a spinster or die young.

The uncouth man drove the team down the middle of the rustic settlement and stopped in front of a small wooden building, tying the ribbons to their ring. "Hey, sheriff," he bellowed. "You got trouble. Not sure which is worse, the bandits who attacked the coach or the redhead on it."

The coach groaned as he climbed down and his head bobbed in front of the horses.

"What you got, Dom?" asked a man emerging from one building.

The large man used his hands and loud voice to tell the tale, as if he'd witnessed it. He described the runaway stagecoach, making Millie sound like the real problem, almost forgetting to mention the bandits. Millie reached to untie the ribbons so she could run him down, but paused when Mrs. Adriance interrupted the brute and gave her version of events.

The sheriff immediately turned to the gathering crowd and announced, "I need a posse!" Shouts erupted around them.

"Maybe it's the Espinosas."

"Let's get the varmints."

"Saddle up boys."

"Bring a rope. There's plenty of tall trees."

The area burst into chaos as each man scrambled to find gun, horse, and gear.

Millie climbed from the wagon, feeling aches and twinges of pain that hadn't been there this morning.

"Red. The dead goat belong to you?"

Buttercup! Hurrying behind the stagecoach, Millie found the uncouth man had his burro's lead in one hand and Buttercup cradled against his other arm. The goat looked tiny compared to the man's large stature. Buttercup lay still, head lolling to one side, eyes open.

"I think she fainted," Millie said, gently resting her hand on the goat's flank. She felt Buttercup's heartbeat and sighed with relief. Awkwardly, she lifted the goat from the man's arm, failing to avoid touching him. She'd have to scrub off his filth.

"Fainted? Goats more of a lady than you, Red. Maybe you should take some lessons."

Millie opened her mouth to respond, but Mrs. Adriance hurried over. The respectable matron's bonnet was askew, her hair in disarray, and her bandana still covered part of her face. "You poor, poor child. What a dreadful experience. We need a bath. And a hot meal."

A bath? A real bath? Millie hadn't bathed proper in two months. She forgot about the awful man and eagerly followed Mrs. Adriance to a pleasant clapboard house with all the comforts of society: hot food prepared by a hired girl, an extra bed—a real one covered with a bright quilt—and most important, a tin tub for a bath. At Mrs. Adriance's urging, the hired girl heated water for the bath, and Millie moaned as she sank into the steaming liquid.

Millie scrubbed places that hadn't been clean in months, donned clean clothes, and ate a hearty meal. Exhausted but content, she climbed into bed and sank beneath the quilt. Maybe life in the Colorado Territory wouldn't be so terrible.

She closed her eyes but thoughts of the morrow slowly eroded her contentment. By this time tomorrow evening, she'd be married to Mr. Drouillard. Images of the uncouth mountain man and the Denver City drunk caused her to thrash about in her comfortable bed. Finally, Millie gave up and lit a candle. From her carpetbag, she removed Mr. Drouillard's letter.

February 10, 1863
Dear Miss Virginia,

Thank-you for your letter and carte-de-viste. You sound like an accomplished young lady and well-liked by your current employer, but if I must be honest, your picture separated you from the other women and captured my heart. You are a beautiful woman and I fell in love when I saw your face.

Millie stopped reading, as she always did at this point, and felt her stomach lurch. *Fell in love with her face.* When she'd first read the letter, she'd assumed a few well-cooked meals would easily solve this problem. Now, she wasn't so certain.

Therefore, I would be honored if you would accept my proposal of marriage. Please write as soon as possible if you are agreeable.

As you know, the journey west will be difficult. I wish I could accompany you, but with the present conflict it is impossible. If you accept my proposal, I will arrange your travel by riverboat to St. Louis where a ticket will be waiting for the overnight steam locomotive to St. Joseph. At the St. Joe station, my representative will meet you and arrange your passage west with a wagon train to Denver City. From there, you will be met and escorted by stagecoach to Idaho Springs. I will arrange and pay for all travel with your comfort and safety as my priority, but do not underestimate the difficulty of the journey. It will be demanding and you will be forced to travel mostly unescorted.

Millie thought about the journey she'd almost completed. When she'd first read Mr. Drouillard's description, she'd been excited about a new adventure, imagining herself traveling west with Natty Bumppo, the main character in James Fenimore Cooper's *Leatherstocking Tales* that she favored. Looking back, she realized how naive she'd been. Mr. Drouillard's final paragraph drew her eyes, even though she could almost recite it without reading.

With last year's Homestead Act, a woman may now own land in the Colorado Territory. As a gentlelady, I wish to assure your comfort upon arrival, even if, God forbid, something should happen to me. Therefore, I will request my solicitor, Mr. Ferris, to prepare documents to deed my cabin and gold mine to you as a precaution. This document, and my holographic will, shall be included with my next letter if you accept, as I hope, my marriage proposal.

The legal papers had been a thoughtful gesture, convincing her Mr. Drouillard was a gentleman. Considerate. A man she could marry. Not anything like the ill-bred mountain man she'd encountered today.

I have enclosed my carte-de-viste and anxiously await your response.

With greatest respect and the highest of hopes,

Mr. Johannes Drouillard
Idaho Springs, Colorado Territory

Millie sighed and looked at Mr. Drouillard's carte-de-viste. Round gray eyes looked out from a face hidden behind a bushy black beard and mustache. Curly black hair fell almost to his shoulder, mingling with his generous facial hair. It was difficult to tell what he really looked like, but his eyes were kind, at least Millie thought they were.

Tomorrow the wait would be over. She'd become the wife of this stranger or…

Well, she didn't want to think about any other options.

SIX

August 9, 1863

Idaho Springs in the Colorado Rockies

After a hearty morning meal—and the lengthy prayers accompanying it—the Adriances escorted Millie to the stagecoach and introduced her to her new driver, a Mr. Updike. He promised to "keep good care of her" as he tied Buttercup once again into the boot of the coach. Relieved that there was no sign of the unpleasant man from yesterday, Millie climbed up beside the driver and bowed her head as Reverend and Mrs. Adriance began a farewell prayer. She hid her smile when the driver said "G'wan, Chuck-a-luck. Get, Bummer," forcing Reverend Adriance to abruptly end and yell a hasty "Amen."

The trail from town wound through a beautiful mountain meadow and unlike her previous driver, Mr. Updike, with his drooping hat and amused gray eyes, happily chatted about the countryside. He used his whip to point out a whitetail deer with her fawn, a pair of bald eagles, and flocks of geese flying in wedge formations.

They stopped in Central City and picked up a well-dressed man who looked out of place in this rough mining community. He climbed into the coach, his features hidden under a broad hat, without offering Millie and the driver even a friendly, "Good Morning." Mr. Updike urged the horses on, and they soon entered a mountainous valley dotted with mine tailings. These unnatural yellow mounds spilled out from dark, forbidding holes, forming a distinct marker at each mine.

Millie pointed out the mines, commenting on their high numbers.

"We're in Hamlin Gulch," said Mr. Updike, "an area prevalent with color."

"Color?"

The driver laughed, the sound rough with tobacco smoke. "The reason we're all here, Little Lady. Color. Gold!"

Gold! Millie had spent her life poor, an orphan, and then a servant. What would it be like to find gold and suddenly become rich? She understood the allure.

Had her fiancé struck it rich before he advertised for a wife?

Millie imagined a fine two- or maybe even three-bedroom house. After their marriage, she'd become one of Idaho Springs' prominent society ladies, inviting her neighbors to tea. Maybe she would even have her own servant. Lost in the daydream, Millie saw herself visiting New Orleans, driving by the LeGrand household in her own stylish buggy with Carissa beside her.

"Used to be a big geyser in Idaho Springs." Mr. Updike's rough voice interrupted Millie's daydream. "It attracted all sorts of critters like that bruin. The Arapahoe called the geyser Edanhau Edauhoe which means 'Gem in the Mountain.' It used to throw up a beautiful bluish spray. That's where the name Idahoe come from, or so they say. The geyser sank in '60 or '61. Now all we got are hot springs and vapor caves. Probably for the best. Once I saw a beaver climb up and peek into the geyser." He glanced at Millie, his eyes dancing. "Being curious ain't always good. That beaver lost his head over it."

Millie shuddered, but noticed the steam rising from a side valley. "Are we almost there?" Her stomach tightened as she glanced around anxiously.

"Yep. Just over the hill."

This was it. She was about to meet Mr. Drouillard. They'd marry before the sun set. Oh, Lor', what would she do if he were anything like the oversized galoot with the burro? Or if he refused to marry her and insisted she pay for her travel costs? Her heart pounded wildly. Her head felt light.

"That's Idaho Springs," said the driver as they topped a rise, pointing to a cluster of log buildings and dusty tents. "The river's all tore up from the placer mining, but it's still purdy."

Millie stared. And stared. *That* was Idaho Springs? Mountain City and Central City had at least looked like towns, but this? Shabby cabins were spread out across the valley, each located near a mine tailing or ripped up section of river. A few of the structures had roofs, but many were log piles with canvas covers or just well-worn tents. In the center of this hodgepodge was a cluster of larger buildings located haphazardly along the dusty path.

"*That's* Idaho Springs?" Millie repeated, unable to hide her dismay.

"Yup. People here are real friendly."

This was her new home? She'd be lucky if Mr. Drouillard owned a cabin with a real roof. Oh, Lor'. She didn't have to worry about rejection. Her fiancé wouldn't care if she wasn't the woman in the picture. He wouldn't care what she looked like. Any man who lived in such desolation *couldn't* be picky.

"You the mail-order bride Mr. D ordered?" the driver asked, giving her a side-glance. "Course you are. No other white woman be coming here unchaperoned. Tonight Mr. D's gonna be one happy man."

Millie swallowed, her attention drawn to a crowd of silent people standing near a tilting building with "Theobald and Shafter, General Mercantile" painted in slanted letters across its false front. Millie searched each face, frantically looking for the hairy face she'd memorized. She couldn't find him. Maybe he'd shaved. Maybe it hadn't been him in the picture after all. Would he dare to be that dishonest?

The coach stopped and Millie climbed from the dusty stagecoach, her hands shaking. She turned and stared at the silent crowd. No man stepped forward to claim her.

Hesitantly, wishing she knew how to pronounce the name she'd soon acquire, she asked, "Is Mr. Drool…I mean Mr. Droil—"

"Dead," screamed a shrill voice. "He's dead! You poor, poor girl. So young, and already a widow."

SEVEN

August 9, 1863
Widow Drouillard

A widow? Millie stared at the woman in confusion. "Where is Mr. Drou…Ah Drool…" Blast it, how did one pronounce Drouillard? "Mr. D?"

Over the wailing of the woman, a well-dressed man solemnly replied, "I'm sorry ma'am. Mr. D is dead."

"*Dead*?"

"Dead. Mr. D died in a mining accident last week."

"*Died in a mining accident?*" Millie repeated stupidly. "Last week?"

The man stepped forward, the weeping woman clasped to his side. "I'm Mr. Henry Ferris, his solicitor." The man had no beard, but his waxed mustache curved around his sharp chin, almost circling it.

Dumbly, Millie stared at the crowd of fifteen or twenty silent strangers, totally at a loss. Mr. D was dead? How? If she had survived her journey, the least he could do was to live until after their marriage.

Millie cringed at her own callousness. A man had died. It was a tragedy, but she was too flustered to feel sad. For one of the few times in her life, Millie had no idea what to do or say.

A short, portly man with a tight-cropped mustache and a small, triangular beard stepped forward. "Don't worry none,

Widow D. I'm Lewis N. Tappan the Third. You mourn a bit, as is proper. A day, maybe two. Then we can marry." He waved toward a smaller building down the street. "We'll live behind my shop. As the Bard once wrote," he pitched his voice deep, "A heaven on Earth I have won by wooing thee." Lifting his hand so she could see he carried a book, he added, "You'll find me a learned man. Brother Bunce'll say so."

"Brother Bunce?" Millie echoed.

"Hold on one gosh darn minute, Old Shakespeare," said a thin man dressed in black and white striped coveralls, reminding Millie of a scarecrow wearing chain gang cast-offs. He stepped forward, giving Millie a better view of just how many patches covered his faded overalls. "I'll be marrying her, after a proper mourning." He grinned, and through his thick beard Millie saw numerous gaps between his rotting teeth. "I'm Asa Poor, but I ain't poor. My prospecting found me plenty of gold." He pulled a long narrow sack from his pocket. "See, my poke's full." He lifted his eyebrows. "Want to see my nuggets?"

"Your nuggets?" Millie felt like a puppet with someone else pulling the strings.

"Nay. I'm to marry the lassie," said a beefy man in a strong Scottish brogue. He wore a buckskin vest with several round holes burned through it. "Me mate, Johannes, said I was to care for his lassie when he weren't around." A streak of soot ran down one cheek. His was one of the few clean-shaven faces in the bunch, although more facial hair might have concealed his prominent nose. "I'm James Shumate, the town blacksmith. Me mates call me Sooty. Johannes was me best mate."

"She don't want you," snarled a dark-haired man, his facial hair braided into two stringy ropes. He elbowed Mr. Shumate aside and stepped forward to present himself. "What lady would want to marry a stubborn Scot?" He gripped his braided beard—one massive fist surrounding each braid—and squeezed nervously as he spoke, the motion reminded Millie of the milking of a cow. "I'm the man for you, Widow D. Name's Titus Turck." He made an awkward bow and added, "I'm a prospector, just like Mr. D." He turned and sneered at Mr. Poor. "One day I'm gonna strike it big, Asa Poor, and when I do, my nuggets will be bigger than yours."

Several more shouts filled the air, each new miner insisting he would be the best husband. Millie's eyes bounced from man to man, feeling like a bone being fought over by a pack of hungry dogs.

"Please," said a short, stocky man with a round, pudgy face hidden beneath snow-white side whiskers and a long beard. "Widow D will decide later who to marry. For now she has endured a long trip and experienced a dreadful shock. She's a tenderfoot. Probably experiencing some problems with our light air." He stepped forward and patted Millie lightly on the shoulder. "I'm Brother Bunce, the Baptist minister, though most round here call me the Arkansas Traveler. Mr. D had asked me to marry you; I mean, to marry him to you. Don't mind the men none. A single woman round here is rarer than, well, than a one-inch nugget." He turned and waved to one of the women in the crowd. "Mrs. Beebee. Why don't we take Widow D to the Beebee House? She's looking a bit peaked."

"Didn't Mr. D have a home? A cabin?" Millie lifted her voice over the sobbing woman and belligerent suitors. She hoped the cabin wasn't one of the canvas-covered woodpiles she'd seen, but at the moment, she didn't care. Anywhere away from this crowd would be an improvement.

"Of course, Widow D. It's your cabin now," said Mr. Ferris, twirling his mustache with his fingers. "You did receive Mr. D's legal documents, didn't you?"

"Uh, yes."

"Mr. D's place is a mile up Spring Gulch," said Brother Bunce. "Too far for a lone woman."

"Why's that, Brother Bunce? I do just fine." A good looking woman wearing men's trousers pushed forward through the crowd. "Charlotte Card," she said, vigorously shaking Millie's hand. "Sorry about Mr. D. He was a good sort."

"Thank you, ma'am. I—"

"Yes, but Miss Card," interrupted Brother Bunce, "You're well…You're one of the prospectors. Widow D comes from the South where ladies are genteel. She couldn't possibly survive alone, so far from town."

Millie smothered a hysterical laugh. This place. This town. These suitors. None of it was civilized. A mile away couldn't be worse. "I can walk. I'd like to see Mr. D's cabin." She frowned, hoping she looked sad. "Please. I just lost my husband. I need some time to mourn. In private."

"If she ain't tough, she won't survive here," said a middle-aged woman, her handspun dress covered by a colorful red shawl. She stepped forward, carrying a large basket. "I'm Mrs. Euphrasia Gilson. I got a place just outside town. Made you some food. Tomorrow, or the day after, I'll bring you some miner's laundry. Teach you how to earn a bit of gold dust. Give you some breathing space to figure out which one of these—" she gestured toward the arguing men, "you might want." In a quieter tone she added, "But let me tell you, none but Sooty are good for nothing."

"Thank you, ma'am," Millie said. The woman handed the basket to Brother Bunce and Millie turned to the solicitor, Mr. Ferris. "How did he…? I mean. What happened?"

"Cave in. At his mine. Mr. Shumate, the blacksmith, found him. A real shame."

"Here's your bags, ma'am. And your goat." The stagecoach driver placed Millie's carpetbags at her feet and handed her Buttercup's lead. "I'll come back through on the morrow. Could take you back to the Adriances, if you like." He tipped his hat. "Sorry about your loss, ma'am."

"Thank you, Mr. Updike." Millie bent down and patted Buttercup, trying to reassure herself as much as the goat. Should she go back to the Adriances? They were kind people, but they'd find her a husband, and she'd have little to say about it. Could she return to Denver City and find Sarah?

Her thoughts were interrupted by the man in the overalls, the poor one who wasn't poor. He stepped forward and pointed at Buttercup. "We can roast that critter at our wedding—for a wedding feast." He leaned so close, Millie could smell his foul breath. Licking his chapped lips, he rubbed his hands together. "I like roasted goat. A lot."

Buttercup lifted her head, her bulging eyes focused on the man. Instantly her legs stiffened and she tumbled over. The man grinned. "Look, she's ready for the spit. Shall I break her neck?"

Millie quickly picked up the goat and hugged her tightly.

"Widow D needs some time to mourn," said Brother Bunce. "I'll escort her to her cabin."

"My wife and I will accompany you," insisted Mr. Ferris. "I'm sure Widow D would appreciate female companionship. I can carry her bags." He stepped forward and picked up Millie's carpetbags.

Relieved they were leaving, Millie turned to the crowd and fumbled an awkward bow. The American Lady advised to "Always bow when meeting acquaintances in the street. To curtsy is not gracefully consistent with locomotion." These were hardly acquaintances and calling this rutted trail a street was putting on airs, but she refused to forget proper manners. "Thank you all..." The suitors' angry voices drowned out her words.

Brother Bunce led them down the dusty trail through the center of town, passing by two saloons, a dry-goods shop, a livery, and a guest house. Each looked so run-down, they made the buildings in Denver look luxurious.

Like a tour guide, Brother Bunce pointed out Clear Creek as they crossed it on a rough-hewn bridge and led them towards a smaller stream he called Chicago Creek.

He kept up a steady monologue, even after they left Chicago Creek, and began climbing a steep trail, crisscrossing the hill.

"This here's Spring Gulch," said Brother Bunce, indicating the smaller brook. "Mr. D's homestead is up yonder."

The trail rose up and disappeared into shadowy woods. Millie paused to catch her breath and steady her nerves. She was not fond of cold, dark places. Buttercup, who'd woken and now walked quietly behind Millie, butted her forward.

"Are you tired, child?" Brother Bunce offered his arm which Millie gratefully accepted. Together, they walked under the shadowy evergreen canopy and trudged over rocks and around fallen timber. Cold air caused goose pimples to rise on her skin. Millie clung to the minister's arm until an open meadow appeared and bright sunshine filtered through the thinning trees.

They emerged into the large meadow where the meandering stream twisted around three nearby deer. Buttercup bleated and the deer took flight, bounding away and disappearing behind a small log cabin. A second cabin sat on the far side of the open space with a fenced garden out front and smoke rising from its chimney.

"This way," said Brother Bunce, pulling Millie toward the empty-looking cabin. They crossed a small footbridge and Millie had to stop and stare. This was her cabin. Her own home. It was made from rough, notched logs, and on the closest wall a stone chimney climbed up to the roof. In front of the door, an uneven log porch kept the mud out and two rectangular windows were closed, both shuttered on the inside.

Millie felt tears prick her eyes. Her own home. Never in her twenty-three years of life had she owned *anything* of consequence.

Mr. Ferris strode ahead and pushed open the door. Turning, he glanced from Millie to Buttercup. "Mrs. Ferris, why don't you take the, uh, goat and put it in the barn out back."

The woman had stopped her wailing, but her eyes were still red and puffy. "Will Buttercup be safe there?" Millie asked.

"Should be," Mr. Ferris said with a shrug. "The town pigs roam free until just before sunset. Rocky Mountain lions, bears, wolves, and such aren't usually out until dusk."

"Lions and bears and wolves? Oh my!" Millie picked up the goat and squeezed Buttercup tight against her chest. "I'll bring her inside."

A disdainful look crossed Mr. Ferris' long face but he said nothing. Millie hurried past him, stepped through the door and froze, shocked by the civilized comfort surrounding her. Instead of a dirt floor, the main room had uneven worn wooden boards with protruding dark knots. A large river rock fireplace filled one wall. Two rough wood rocking chairs faced the fireplace, a coarsely woven rag rug between them. On the opposite side of the room stood a table with three chairs and behind it was an iron cookstove.

A *real* cookstove!?

Eyes wide, Millie crossed the room, set Buttercup down, and laid a reverent hand on the cold metal. "Oh Lor'!" she whispered. "It's a Charter Oak."

"He bought it as soon as he got your letter," said Mrs. Ferris, gently reaching out to squeeze Millie's hand. "He was so looking forward to marrying."

Mr. D had bought her a Charter Oak stove. Brought it across the plains and up to this tiny mountain town! Just for her. The sound of running water caused her to look over. Water gushed from a hollowed-out white log into a basin, filling it two-thirds full. At the bottom of the basin, a similar hollowed out log poked through the wall, allowing the water to flow out. Millie stepped over and ran her fingers through the water. It was icy cold.

"Mr. D liked creating crazy stuff like that," said Mrs. Ferris. "Runs year-round. Can't imagine it won't make the cabin cold and clammy. I'm sure Mr. Ferris could find a way to turn it off."

"Thank you, but I'd like to leave it for now." A bit of cold was well worth not having to haul water by hand from the stream.

Continuing her exploration, Millie spotted two wooden plank shelves holding a coal oil lamp, two frying pans, four pots of different sizes, a water kettle, a coffee pot, and an odd assortment of tin cups, tin plates, spoons, forks, and even a butcher knife.

"It's so modern," Millie whispered. Tears of exhaustion and amazement flowed down her cheeks. Sadness filled her. She was truly sorry Mr. D was dead. Any man who had equipped a kitchen like this, in a place as remote as Idaho Springs, would have been a man she could have loved, or at least happily married.

"Poor Widow D. Don't you cry none. Mr. D died quickly and without pain." Mrs. Ferris hugged Millie before glancing at her husband. "Didn't he?"

"Course. Mrs. Ferris, why don't you start the stove and make tea?" Mr. Ferris nodded Millie toward the rocking chairs. "Sit down ma'am. We need to talk." Turning to the minister he added, "Brother Bunce, please light the fire. I'll put her bags in back."

"Talk?" Millie felt a pang of guilt. She had a home, but Mr. D was dead. "Of course." She walked to the rocking chair, sank down in it and immediately stood up. "I'd like to visit Mr. D's grave and pay my respects."

"Can't do that 'til we give him a proper burying," said Brother Bunce.

"He's not buried? But you said he died…" Millie hesitated. "When did he die?"

"Over a week ago, but—"

"A week ago!?" Millie cringed. In New Orleans, a body not buried within a day stunk atrociously, not to mention it attracted deadly diseases. Mr. Drouillard died a week ago. She felt sick to her stomach but also indignant for this man who had given her so much. "Why hasn't my husband been buried?"

"Well," the preacher shuffled back and forth. "You have to understand, this is gold country. Mr. Poor, you remember the man with the nuggets, and Mr. Turck, the one with the beard braids. Well, they were digging Mr. D's grave, but—" He lifted his hands.

"But what? Mr. D should have had a proper Christian burial." Millie might question Christian beliefs but a burial was a burial.

"Yes, but. Well, while digging his grave, they...Well. They discovered a bit of color."

"They discovered gold in the town graveyard?"

"Yes, a thin but promising vein. It presents quite a problem, as you can imagine," added Mr. Ferris, returning to the room. "Mr. D's grave wasn't the first in our Old Chief Mountain Graveyard. How do you determine ownership? I've been working on the legalities with the miners' court—"

"They cannot dig up existing, consecrated graves," insisted Brother Bunce. "That would be sacrilegious!"

The solicitor had the good grace to look embarrassed, but Millie had other concerns. "So where is he? I mean, what did they do with Mr. D? Did he have a coffin?"

"Not to worry, Widow D. We took care of him. It's too warm to leave the, well, him exposed to air."

"Quite right. He's resting in the river."

EIGHT

August 9, 1863
Resting Ten Feet Under

Resting in the river?!

For a moment Millie had the hideous vision of walking out to the stream, looking down, and seeing Mr. D's dead face fluttering just beneath the surface. Her knees felt weak and she dropped back into her seat. She actually felt faint. Oh, Lor', she was never faint. Women like Mrs. LeGrand fainted. Her former boss had swooned weekly, usually in dramatic fashion. She'd place her hand on her forehead, theatrically announce she was going to swoon, and then gracefully collapse into her divan. If Millie ever acted that way, she'd have to kill herself.

"Is he safe?" Millie asked, trying to regain her composure. "What about wild animals?"

"Of course he's safe. We weighed his coffin down with stones. He's resting about ten feet under."

Millie took a deep breath and thought of the man who'd brought her here. He'd been considerate, leaving her a cabin and a mine. He'd even bought her a Charter Oak cookstove! Rising, she realized there was no time to be faint. She had to right a terrible wrong. Putting her hands on her hips, she turned to Brother Bunce. "That will not do. Tomorrow we dig a grave behind this cabin and bury him proper."

"Yes," agreed Brother Bunce, his beard swaying as he nodded. "Yes. Now his widow is here, it's time. Mr. Ferris, you make the arrangements. Tell the townsfolk the service will be at, shall we say, ten. Afterwards, Widow D can catch the afternoon coach back to Central City, if that's her wish."

Millie glanced around the modest room. Her cabin.

Could she survive alone here? She had no idea.

Where else was there to go?

Even if she knew where Sarah and her husband had settled, what would she do on their farm? She could sell the cabin and mine and perhaps make enough to return to St. Louis or New Orleans.

"I'm staying," she said slowly, deciding as she spoke. "This is my home now." Somehow she'd find a way to survive.

"Quite right," said Mr. Ferris. "But I feel obliged to make the following offer. If you decide to leave Idaho Springs, something all the townsfolk would understand, I'd be pleased to purchase this homestead and your mine. I'd offer a fair price for the cabin and although the mine never produced, being a gentleman, I'd be willing to give you, say, two hundred dollars for the claim. That way you'd have funds to live on, until you remarry."

Two hundred dollars! That would pay for a stagecoach ride to St. Louis.

"That's very generous," said Brother Bunce, quickly stepping between Mr. Ferris and Millie. "But I'll purchase the mining claim. Mr. and Mrs. Ferris have done enough. Shall we say two hundred and fifty dollars? It's my Christian nature, you understand, making sure you have money to live on."

Millie shook her head, overwhelmed by their generosity. "That's very kind—"

"Brother Bunce's Christian nature is noble, but I couldn't let him make such a sacrifice." Mr. Ferris stepped beside the man of God. "I'll offer three hundred dollars for the mine."

Millie looked from one man's strained face to the other. Why were they fighting like dogs, albeit polite dogs, over Mr. D's mine? She was too exhausted to understand.

"I appreciate your offers," she said, hoping her smile looked as tired as she felt. "But I won't make any decisions until after Mr. D's funeral."

"You look exhausted, my dear." Mrs. Ferris stepped in front of the men and handed Millie a cup of tea. "Drink this. Afterwards you can lay down. I'll stay with you tonight."

Millie choked on the weak tea. Having the weepy woman as company sounded dreadful.

"That's very kind, but I'll be fine. I have food from Mrs. Gilson and I need a bit of time…" She glanced at the minister, "To mourn and pray."

After making sure the fire was banked, the wood box filled, and the kettle hot, the three finally took their leave. Millie sighed into the silence. For a long time she sat, rocking and sipping her tea, petting Buttercup as she watched the fire burn. For the past week her restless slumber had been filled with nightmares about Indians, rattlesnakes, and marriage. Now her mind felt blank. Only when nature called did Millie find the energy to light a candle and stumble to the privy. She returned and peeked into the two closed doors at the back of the cabin. Both were tiny bedrooms, although only one had been recently occupied.

Feeling embarrassed but curious, Millie entered what had been Mr. D's bedroom. A pole bedstead filled most of the room, packed with a thick layer of pine boughs covered by a deerskin. Near the bed, rough-hewn boxes lined one wall and over each protruded a coarsely forged nail. Two nails were empty, but a red shirt hung on a third. Wool pants with reinforced buckskin patches in bad need of repair hung on the forth, and on the fifth, a worn coat almost hid a dirty cloth hat.

A tin washbasin sat on top of one wood box and mounted on the wall were two twisted metal brackets that held candles, one by the door and the other by the window above the bed. The room was rough but somehow felt homey. Millie could live here and be happy, if she didn't starve. How long would three hundred dollars last? Long enough to choose one of her suitors. And if she didn't want to marry? She yawned. Tomorrow she'd worry—tonight she needed sleep.

Her bags had been opened and her sleeping quilt removed, a thoughtful gesture she hadn't expected of the weepy Mrs. Ferris. Millie wrapped herself in it and lay down on the bed, but immediately stood up when something sharp dug into her shoulder. Cautiously she felt between the folds of the deerskin.

Who knew what a single man might hide in his bed.

Her fingers brushed against something hard. Warily she withdrew a small, narrow buckskin bag that resembled Mr. Poor's poke, although this one had the initials JD on top. Millie worked the leather thong free and poured a bit of the bag's contents into her hand. Small tear-shaped nuggets and flakes of gold sparkled in the moonlight.

Gold. Honest to goodness, real gold. Once again Mr. D had provided for her. She had no idea how much the gold was worth, but it gave her a means of living independently until she decided what to do. Hugging the poke to her, Millie lay down and cried herself to sleep.

The following morning, her quiet meadow erupted into noise as men dug a grave under a tall pine tree and women arrived with food and drink. When the men finished, they all accompanied Brother Bunce to the grave and stared solemnly into the empty hole. The preacher placed a comforting hand on Millie's arm.

"Where's Mr. D?"

"Still taking a swim."

Murmurs filled the air and the crowd migrated from the grave to a deep pool in the stream. Millie followed her neighbors to the riverbank and stared at the wooden box resting in the deep water. Four large boulders weighed it down.

"How do we retrieve the lad?" asked Mr. Shumate.

Mr. Turck snorted, his fists wrapped around each beard braid, squeezing in a milking rhythm as he spoke. "Some fools got to go swimming."

Everyone took a step back. The morning was chilly and the water was fresh snowmelt. After much discussion, Brother Bunce coerced Mr. Shumate and Mr. Poor to take the plunge.

Millie joined the other women and politely looked away as the men stripped to their drawers. Curses rung out as they splashed into the water, and Mr. Turck's voice echoed across the pasture as he described the two men's attempts to retrieve the coffin.

"That scrawny Mr. Poor ain't got the mettle to knock that big stone off. Good thing blacksmith Shumate is down there." Millie rolled her eyes. Mr. Turck had not only *not* volunteered, he'd called Mr. Poor and Mr. Shumate fools.

Buttercup had obediently followed Millie around all morning, but at the sound of the men splashing in the water, her ears twitched and she turned toward the river. Millie grabbed out, missed, and the goat bounded toward the pool and the ring of men that surrounded it. In the center of the group, Mr. Turck stood balanced on a boulder, calling out insults as he described the men's labors.

"Buttercup. No!"

The goat skidded to a stop but Mr. Turck, who'd pivoted toward Millie at the sound of her yell, lost his footing. Letting out an unmanly yelp, he slipped and tumbled into the pool. His sputtered curses were lost in the hoots of the townsfolk's laughter.

Much later, Mr. D's dripping pinewood casket was gently lowered into the grave and covered with dirt. A hundred or so people milled around, listening to the surprisingly short, but emotional service by Brother Bunce. Millie tried to listen. She really did want to learn about the man who had given her so much, but her attention wandered to the people surrounding her.

From what she could see, beneath their shaggy beards, the men had lined, brown faces. They wore well-patched wool pants and dull red shirts, similar to the clothing she'd found in Mr. D's bedroom. The women, the eight or ten in attendance, wore sprigged calico or dark-colored dresses with full skirts and oversized sun bonnets—clothing she'd seen on the wagon train—although here in Idaho Springs, dressy paisley shawls were popular. Just as she'd found in the wagon train, silks, lace, chemisettes, hoop petticoats, and fashionable gloves were luxuries left behind.

The service ended and the men buried the casket before heading back to Mr. D's cabin for his wake. Millie hesitated, wanting a silent minute alone. Kneeling, she inhaled the earthy scents and laid a bouquet of blue and white columbines on Mr. D's grave. Buttercup nudged forward, eyeing the colorful blossoms, but Millie grabbed her before she could eat them.

After the unfortunate incident at the river, Millie had tied a bandana around Buttercup's neck and kept a solid hold. After silently thanking this stranger for her home and new life, Millie rose and pulled Buttercup toward the cabin. The goat followed meekly until they passed the small barn behind the cabin. Here Buttercup bleated and dug in her heels.

Millie glanced around, trying to see what had alarmed Buttercup. Her gaze froze when it settled on Mr. D's grave.

Kneeling in the fresh dirt, a black woman laid bright red and white flowers beside those of Millie's. The woman's dark head was bowed, but Millie saw tears reflecting the sun on her ebony cheeks. Buttercup bleated and the woman looked up, her eyes widening as they met Millie's. Like a frightened deer, she shot to her feet and fled into the woods.

NINE

August 10, 1863

Did Mr. Drouillard Find the Mother Lode?

Millie watched the black woman disappear into the forest, turning only when she heard the voices of Mr. and Mrs. Ferris.

"Did Mr. D own a servant?" Millie asked.

"Of course not!" Mrs. Ferris looked offended. "We're a Union territory. We don't own slaves. That woman was Mary Randolph. Mr. D allowed her to live in his cabin across the pasture. They had some kind of arrangement." Her tone indicated she thought their arrangement quite improper. "You now own the homestead and can insist she leave."

"The women are serving the food," said Brother Bunce, walking out to join them. "Come eat Widow D, and I'll introduce you to your neighbors."

Her neighbors filled her cabin and spilled out onto the meadow, overwhelming Millie with their offers of condolence and assistance. Inside, her table was loaded with dishes of stewed rabbit, corn dodger, fried redbelly dace, meat pies, fresh bread, and, if she wasn't mistaken, tapioca pudding.

Millie loved to cook. Besides a book on lady's etiquette, her only other important possessions were two cookbooks:

Eliza Acton's 1845 edition of *Modern Cookery in All its Branches* and the more modern 1860 edition of Miss Randolph's *The Virginia Housewife*. She'd taught Sarah to cook as they traveled across the plains, but with an open fire and single pot, there'd been few opportunities to cook anything but basic meat stews and vegetable soups. Glancing from the food to her cookstove, Millie couldn't wait to make her own favorite recipes. Maybe, after a proper mourning period, she could even invite her *own* guests to supper.

To her delight, the atmosphere both inside and out soon turned from mourning to celebration, reminding her of an Irish wake she'd once attended. Young children chased Buttercup around, laughing each time they made her faint. Women gathered in small circles, introducing themselves and chatting about quilting, cooking, children, and gardening. Outside, the men began a horseshoe game and loud shouts erupted at each successful throw. Is this what Mr. D would want for a wake? Millie hoped so.

"May I have a word with you, Widow D?"

Millie turned and almost dropped her plate. In front of her, a short, portly man removed his top hat and bowed low. "I'm Mr. Tappan the Third. We met yesterday."

Nodding, Millie set down her plate and coughed into her handkerchief to hide her laughter.

"Are you sick?" asked Mr. Tappan, his white-gloved hands pausing mid-air as he reached for her hand.

"No," Millie choked out, "Just, ah, grieving." She didn't want to be impolite, but his outfit looked, well, ridiculous. His dark, oversized coat hung down almost to his knees and clashed terribly with his tiny-print, white-checkered pants. A white shirt peeked out beneath the coat, held by a stiff-looking horse-hair stock which hung lopsided around his neck, the bow so crooked Millie had to stop herself from reaching down to straighten it. To top it off, literally, he wore a top hat made of straw. It barely reached Millie's nose.

He must have decided grieving wasn't contagious because he took her hand, swept off his top hat, and bowed a second time. When he stood back up, he held her hand tightly, apparently afraid it might get away. Looking up—he was a full head shorter than Millie—he cleared his throat and began what was obviously a well-practiced speech. "I am but an amateur with words compared to the great Bard, so I rely on his verses." He cleared his throat and spoke in a deep, pleasing baritone:

Doubt thou the stars are fire;
Doubt that the sun doth move;
Doubt truth to be a liar;
But never doubt I love.

He pulled her closer, his expression hopeful. "That's from Shakespeare's *Hamlet*. What do you say, Widow D? Shall we be like Romeo and Juliet and sweep each other off our feet? Brother Bunce is outside. I could move in and start exploring your mine tomorrow." His gaze dropped to her chest and his voice became husky. "Of course, there's no rush. I could start working the day after tomorrow."

"That's terribly kind of you, Mr. Tappan," Millie said, trying unsuccessfully to regain custody of her hand, "but unfortunately, I'm in mourning." Thank the dear Lor' for her experiences on the *Sultana* where she'd become an expert at refusing proposals diplomatically.

Reluctantly, his eyes rose from her chest to her face. "How long do you plan to mourn?"

"Until Christmas, or maybe longer." Millie had no idea how long Mr. D's gold would last, but she'd be willing to live like a pauper to keep her independence. Mr. Tappan seemed sweet, but definitely not husband material. Plus, if *this* was his formal wear, what would he wear to his wedding?

"Christmas, huh?" He frowned. "That's too long. How about I buy the mine today and we can settle other matters in a week or two. Shall we say," he narrowed his eyes, looking like a shrewd merchant, "a hundred and fifty dollars?"

"Mr. Ferris offered three hundred dollars. Brother Bunce two hundred fifty." Millie finally pulled her hand free. "Mr. Tappan, did Mr. D discover gold in his mine?"

"Ah, well, he never said. Course, last Christmas when he advertised for you, he did seem to have his share of gold nuggets. I'll give you three hundred twenty-five for the mine. After all, I'm practically your husband."

An older man with friendly eyes stepped forward and removed his hat as he bowed to Millie. "Now Old Shakespeare, there ain't a man here in town who don't want her mine. And not a single one who ain't willing to marry Widow D to get it." Returning his attention to Millie, he added, "I'm Elder Griswold. I believe you've met my wife."

"It's a pleasure to make your acquaintance, Elder Griswold."

"That was a fine funeral you had for Mr. D." Elder Griswold nodded thoughtfully. "He'd be right proud. It was far better than the first funeral we had here in '61. Long before the Arkansas Traveler arrived. Mr. D helped me officiate that one."

Millie was impatient to ask about her mine, but she could see Elder Griswold had a story to tell. "What was that first one like, sir?"

"Well you see, we found a dead man up Chicago Creek. He'd been shot, although we weren't sure if he done it himself or had a bit of help. It was January, colder than a..." he paused and coughed. "Well, anyway, it was cold. We used the gold dust he had on his person and Mr. D went and bought a bottle—to help with the cold you understand." He paused a moment and took a pull from his drink. After a long draft, he continued. "We used a litter to drag the body to the burying site—it was 'fore we had the town graveyard. I, of course, put my hat under the fellow's head. Wouldn't want it banging about. We also wrapped him in a blanket.

He didn't look so good and we weren't so keen to see what we were hauling.

"When we reached the grave, Mr. Barnes—one of the original fifty-niners—made a rough box of boards, though not nearly as nice as Mr. D's. We had some waiting to do while the fire warmed the ground, so we passed the bottle and imbibed a bit. After digging a hole we put him in and I was asked to say a few words, being an Elder and all. Course, I ain't so good with prayers, not like the Arkansas Traveler, but I did know all the words to 'Now I Lay Me Down to Sleep.' A fitting benediction, I thought, for a man like that one. After my prayer, we thought we should sing a hymn, but none of us knew the words to none. Fortunately, we all knew 'Old Rosin the Beau,' so we sung it. After the burial, we used his surplus gold dust for a bit of bibulous jollification. I reckon the fella didn't mind none, but I think Mr. D would have been right proud of today's funeral."

"I hope so," Millie said, wondering if "Old Rosin the Beau" was the saloon tune she and Carissa used to sing to annoy the nuns. "Thank you."

"My pleasure. Now, back to your mine. None is saying it Widow D, but we all think Mr. D hit pay dirt. Old Shakespeare just offered three twenty-five. I'm already married, so I can't marry you to get the mine, but I'll offer three-fifty."

Millie turned to the short man and put her hands on her hips. "Mr. Tappan, did you offer to marry me for my mine?"

"Well, not just for the mine. This cabin's a fine place to live. Plus, I don't mind redheads."

"My hair is auburn with a *few* red streaks!"

Both men took a step backward as Millie blew out a long breath. Brushing back loose strands of hair, Millie reminded herself she was now a proper lady and needed to act like one.

In New Orleans, Mrs. LeGrand made sure Millie knew her place, but on the *Sultana*, she'd learned if she acted like a lady, she was treated like one. In a quieter tone she added,

"I thank you both kindly for your offers, but I'm not ready to sell the mine."

"Widow D, are you still decided to stay here?" asked Mr. Ferris, hurrying in from outside. "Do you have means?"

"Some." Tomorrow Millie would take one of the tear-shaped nuggets from Mr. D's poke and see what it would buy.

"I've drawn up a bill of sale for the mine," Mr. Ferris said, pulling out a folded paper. "I'll pay you four hundred dollars." For emphasis, he pulled out his poke.

Millie looked from Mr. Ferris, to the bill of sale, to the money. She glanced at Elder Griswold for help.

"It's a fair offer. Not sure you'll get better. No one's certain what Mr. D found. He kept his cards so none could see."

"Are we making offers on Mr. D's mine?" asked a tall, good-looking man with the greenest eyes Millie had ever seen. He swaggered in from outside. "I'm James Whitlatch, Widow D. I serve as justice of the peace in the miners' court. I can't outbid the four hundred dollars Mr. Ferris just made, but I know Sheriff Reynolds could. He's joined the posse searching for the Espinosa killers but should be back in a couple weeks, if you're willing to wait."

"The miners' court?" Millie asked.

"We solve property disputes and, when necessary, deal with criminals." He tipped his hat to her. "You'd come to us if anyone tried to jump your claim." Scratching his head, he added, "Not that anyone could, mind you. Not unless they hauled away the rubble from the landslide."

"About my offer," interrupted Mr. Ferris.

"No need to rush the lady, Ferris," said Mr. Whitlatch, looping an arm around the lawyer's shoulder and dragging him outside. The lawman looked back and gave Millie an insolent wink.

Millie blushed and looked down, surprised to find Mr. Ferris' contract still in her hand. She slipped it into her apron. It wouldn't hurt to see what a proper bill of sale looked like.

Early that evening, Millie sat at the table and emptied Mr. D's poke into a tin cup, filling it almost a third full. She poked at the yellow flakes and picked up one of the tear-shaped nuggets, carrying it to the window for better light. It was round, almost a perfect sphere on one end, but the other tapered down to a rounded point, like a water drop just before it fell. How had it formed such a strange shape? How much would one nugget buy? Millie had no idea.

Dropping the nugget back into the cup, Millie retrieved her book, *The Ladies' Book of Etiquette, and Manual of Politeness.* Carissa's farewell gift was a modern edition of their childhood handbook and written by a real American Lady, Florence Hartley. The front page touted the book as "A complete handbook for the use of the lady in polite society" and contained full instructions for "correct manners, dress, deportment and conversation" and "useful receipts for the complexion, hair, and with hints and directions for the care of the wardrobe." Flipping to the chapter on health, Millie eagerly read Mrs. Hartley's advice.

"The universal remark of travelers visiting America, as well as the universal complaint of Americans themselves, relates to the ill health of the fairer portion of the community." Millie suspected Mrs. Hartley had never met the women who traveled west. Wagon train women had no chance at ill health—not if they wanted to survive. Reading further, Millie nodded in agreement at Mrs. Hartley's comments on the healthful effects of daily bathing, fresh air, clean clothes, and neat housekeeping, but when she reached the advice on hot drinks, she paused in indignation. "Cocoa is cheaper and much more nourishing than tea," Mrs. Hartley advised. "None of these liquids should be taken hot, but lukewarm; when hot they inflame the stomach, and produce indigestion."

Millie shuttered at the thought of lukewarm tea. Obviously Miss Hartley had never woken to a howling windstorm on the Great Plains. Without steaming hot tea to warm her hands and belly, Millie might not have survived her journey west.

The fire banked lower and Millie yawned. Rising, she left her book on the table beside the cup holding Mr. D's gold. With Buttercup at her heels, she headed to bed.

At first Millie thought the wild cry was part of her dream, but an ugly swear-word and a loud thud brought her fully awake. Struggling to rise, Millie's legs tangled in her quilt and she fell to the floor. Her own cursing filled the darkness as she thrashed at the material, struggling until she found her feet.

Heart pounding, she listened intently, standing in darkness so deep she couldn't see her own shaking hands. Boots thudded against the floor and a door slammed.

Someone had been inside the cabin.

Was he still inside?

Millie stood, frozen in indecision, hating how vulnerable she felt. Growing up, the orphanage nuns thrived on making their wards feel helpless and powerless. Only after Carissa came, as Millie tried to comfort her new friend, had she learned the only way not to feel helpless was to not *be* helpless. Act confidently, even if you aren't. Taking a deep breath, Millie squared her shoulders and crept from her room.

The cabin was deathly still.

"Buttercup?" she whispered. Nothing. As she stepped into the living area, the flicker of firelight revealed an empty room except for a dark lump on the floor.

"Buttercup?!"

Rushing over, Millie felt the goat's sides, relieved to feel breathing. Buttercup must have interrupted whoever had been in the cabin, but in her fright she'd fainted. Leaving the goat, Millie hurried to the fireplace and lit a candle. The intruder was gone but the hair at the nape of Millie's neck rose as she looked around. A chair was knocked over and on the table a long, curved knife protruded from the wooden surface.

Cautiously Millie approached. A white sheet of paper was speared by the knife. Big bold lettering covered the paper.

LEAVE IDAHO SPRINGS OR DIE!

Worse, the tin cup and all of Mr. D's gold was gone.

TEN

August 11, 1863
Mr. Poor's Proposal

Millie rocked, biting her lower lip, watching the cloudy morning sky turn a brilliant red as the sun poked up over the mountains. In New Orleans, a red sky boded stormy weather, a day better spent cooking inside. What did such weather mean in these towering Rocky Mountains?

LEAVE IDAHO SPRINGS OR DIE!

Millie shuddered. Did the intruder want her gone, or was he just trying to scare her into selling the mine? Did it matter? Without Mr. D's gold, she had to do something.

She could marry—for protection—but the thought turned her stomach. None of the men she'd met here appealed to her, no matter how desperate or unsafe she felt. Buttercup butted her, and Millie scratched her behind the ears.

"No way we're letting some muttonhead scare us into leaving," she said to the goat. "This is our home." It was true. After only a day, the cabin felt more like a home than anywhere else she'd lived. Selling the mine was the easiest course of action, but would it appease the intruder?

While pondering this unanswerable question, a new thought intruded. If Mr. D indeed did strike it rich, surely he'd hidden some of his wealth somewhere in the cabin. If she could find it, she'd no longer be destitute.

"If it's here," she told Buttercup as she jumped to her feet, "We'll find it." She started looking in her bedroom, rifling through clothing and sorting through Mr. D's belongings. When she found an ornate box, Millie was certain she'd found Mr. D's treasure, but instead, inside were her letters and the picture of the cream-faced woman. The girl really was quite pretty. Millie tossed the picture into the fire and returned to her search. Under the bed she found a disgusting trap with a dead rat; Mr. D had been tidy, but he still cleaned like a man.

In the box closest to the door, Millie paused when she found a knife sheath, but no knife. Unpleasant tingles ran up her spine as she carried the sheath to the kitchen and compared it to the knife protruding from her table. They matched in size and shape. It took rocking the knife back and forth to free it from the note and wooden table, but when free, it neatly slid into the sheath. How did the person threatening her have Mr. D's knife?

Returning to her chair, she rocked and pondered this new problem.

Maybe Mr. D wasn't really dead. Had he watched as she climbed from the stagecoach, decided she wasn't the woman in the picture, and pretended to be dead? But why? He could have just said he didn't want to marry her. There were plenty of men happy to take his place. Plus, the whole town attended his funeral. They'd buried a dripping casket. Surely the townsfolk wouldn't join in such a crazy hoax. Or would they?

Millie was reminded of numerous pranks reported in the newspaper. Just last year there'd been an uproar about the Petrified Man found in Nevada. Samuel Clemens, a young reporter, published a detailed story about a petrified man who had every feature perfect except a wooden left leg. The details had been published in Nevada's *Territorial Enterprise* and picked up by numerous papers, creating quite the stir. Only later did Mr. Clemens admit the story was fabricated, calling it "a string of roaring absurdities." Millie shook her head. She couldn't believe the hard-working men and women of Idaho Springs would agree to fake Mr. D's death. They didn't have time for such hogwash.

Mr. D had to be dead! So how did the intruder have Mr. D's knife? The possible answers raised the hairs on the nape of her neck.

After a tasteless breakfast of tea and hardtack, Millie opened the door to the second bedroom. Dust covered everything in the room except for the wooden boxes near the door. In them, Millie discovered bags of corn, flour, beans, peas, sugar, and a box with more hardtack. If the root cellar yielded enough salted meat, vegetables, and other foodstuff, she might make it through half the winter. Then all she'd have to worry about was someone trying to kill her.

Leaving the food for later exploration, Millie began searching the room. On a shelf she found rocks set up as if on display. A fist-sized rock turned a remarkable blue-green after she wiped off the layer of dust and grime. Under it was a slip of paper with "AZURITE AND MALACHITE" written in bold capitals. The printing didn't match that of the threatening note—or Mr. D's handwriting. Another rock, milk-white in color, had a perfectly square red stone poking out of it. Millie fingered the sides, wondering how Mr. D had gotten it so smooth. The paper underneath read "RHODOCHROSITE CRYSTAL." She found a silver rock called "HEMATITE," a gray rock with two blue pin-sized protrusions called "AQUAMARINE," and an ugly brown rock with startling blue faces labeled "TURQUOISE." Unfortunately, not one rock was identified as gold or silver. Sighing, Millie left the shelf and bent down to search the crate below.

Much to her surprise it was filled with books. On top sat the *Principles of Geology, being an attempt to explain the former changes of the Earth's surface, by reference to causes now in operation*, by Charles Lyell. Beneath it was the *Report on the Geology, Mineralogy, Botany, and Zoology of Massachusetts* by Edward Hitchcock. Digging deeper, she discovered *Observations on the Geology of the United States of America* by William Maclure and a chemistry textbook. Mr. D had been well educated; unfortunately, his books, like his rock collection, wouldn't keep Millie fed. She sneezed as she returned the dusty books to the crate.

The box near the dust-covered bed yielded more interesting and useful items. Extra flint, a smaller knife and sheath, and best of all, a six-shooter with a bag of lead balls, a horn of black powder, caps, and wads of felt. Millie stared. She owned a six-shooter! Next time the intruder came to threaten her, she'd shoot him.

While following her favorite hero, Natty Bumppo, in his many adventures with Chief Chingachgook, Millie had read all about guns, although she'd never actually shot one. Deciding a bit of practice might be useful, she carried the gun to the front porch and looked it over, trying to decide how to load it. The slots in front had to hold the shot and powder, but to pour the powder into these holes, she had to look right down the barrel. Not the most pleasant sight. Clumsily, she held the gun at arm's length and spilled enough powder over the gun to fill all the openings. Next, she stuffed felt wads into the holes, managing to spill most of the powder onto the ground before she'd plugged each hole. Finally, she took a lead ball and tried to shove it in on top of one felt wad.

It didn't fit.

Shoving as hard as she could, Millie only managed to get the ball stuck part way, but as soon as she turned the gun, the ball fell out. How did one load a six shooter? After trying a second ball with the same results, Millie gave up and returned powder, felt wads, balls, and caps to the spare bedroom. She slipped the six-shooter into her apron beside her watch.

If someone threatened her, she'd pull it out. Her adversary wouldn't know it wasn't loaded.

Millie scoured the rest of the cabin and found several useful items, but no fortune in gold nuggets. The only places not searched were the root cellar, privy, and barn. Oh, Lor'! She hated root cellars. They were cold, dark, and nasty. Taking a deep breath, she reached for the back door, bracing herself for the unpleasant search. A knock on the front door froze her motion.

Was it the intruder? She reached into her apron and gripped the handle of her six-shooter. Silently she tiptoed to the front door, opening it a crack.

"Widow D, I'm Asa Poor. We met when you arrived. I'd like a word."

Millie recognized the stripped coveralls, thick facial hair, and rotting teeth. Deciding politeness required it, she opened the door and a slightly unpleasant odor wafted in. Her suitor followed it inside.

"Mr. Poor, what a pleasure," Millie lied. She could feel her heart pounding and her hand ached from clutching the six-shooter. Buttercup, who'd been sniffing around the kitchen for something to eat, bounded over, took one look at Mr. Poor, and fainted. Millie understood the sentiment. After last night's threat, having Mr. Poor inside her cabin was decidedly disagreeable. "What can I do for you, sir?"

He glanced from her to the goat. "How 'bout we roast her? She'd be easy to catch. I could break her neck before she woke up." He licked his chapped lips. "I like roasted goat."

"We are *not* roasting Buttercup." Millie stepped protectively between the man and the comatose goat.

"Okay, no roasted goat. I'll shoot us a deer for our wedding feast."

"Wedding feast?" Millie asked, stepping backward and stumbling over Buttercup.

"Oh, I forgot. You and the goat got me sidetracked." He dropped to one knee and grabbed Millie's hand, pulling her back toward him. "Widow D, you need a husband to protect you. To hunt and provide for you." He used his free hand to pull a six-shooter from inside his coveralls. "I got a gun."

Millie inhaled sharply. Would he use the gun if she refused his proposal? Mr. Poor sneered, as if reading her thoughts, and slid the gun back into his coveralls. "No reason to be worried, Widow D. I use it *mostly* to hunt."

Millie swallowed. *Mostly?*

He pulled on her hand, forcing her closer. Millie wished there was a polite way to cover her nose with her free hand. The smell was so unpleasant she breathed through her mouth.

"I forgot where I was," he said, scratching his head. "Let me try again. Widow D, you need a husband to protect you. To hunt and provide for you. You also need a miner to tend to your mine. I'm a good miner." He pulled his poke from his pocket. "Want to see my nuggets?"

"No, Mr. Poor, I do not want to see your nuggets. I believe you're a good miner." Millie noticed Mr. Poor's poke sagged. Mr. D's poke had been so full it stood right up.

"Okay." He sounded disappointed, paused, and scratched his head. "Forgot where I was." Clearing his throat, he began again. "Widow D, you need a husband to protect you. To hunt and provide for you. You also need a miner to tend to your mine." He paused to breathe but Millie didn't interrupt. She didn't think another hearing would improve the proposal and the smell was beginning to make her ill. "You also need a husband to chop and carry wood. And do chores you can't do. I need a wife to cook for me. Plus you don't have to pay a wife, like I pay Tit Bit. Each crib visit costs me two dollars in gold dust. Marrying you will save money. What do you think?"

Save money? Tit Bit? Millie had a good idea who Tit Bit might be, although she wasn't exactly sure what a woman of ill-repute did to earn her two dollars. The thought caused Millie to miss her opportunity to respond. Mr. Poor continued, obviously taking her silence for agreement.

"Good. We'll be needing Brother Bunce, so we'll have to wait a day or two. The Arkansas Traveler went off to Empire this morning. But," he lifted his eyebrows suggestively, "I could move into the cabin today and we could celebrate marriage bliss a bit early."

He rose and looked down at Buttercup. "Sure you don't want roasted goat? Just thinking about Tit Bit put me in the mood for some marriage bliss, and afterwards, a good meal."

"No," Millie sputtered, more flabbergasted than scared.

Mr. Poor's hopeful expression sagged. "You want a deer, huh?"

"No," Millie repeated and finally found her voice. "Mr. Poor, I thank you kindly for your offer, but I'm in mourning. I cannot marry right now."

"But you need a husband. To protect you. And for all the other reasons I said."

"I'm sorry, but I cannot marry right now."

He frowned and looked out her window. Millie glanced in the same direction and saw a figure near the trees.

"That's Titus Turck. He wants your mine, and he's decided a wife might save him money too." Mr. Poor scratched his head. "Okay, I don't want to wait, but if I have to." He shrugged, looking far less friendly. "When you're done mourning, will you promise to marry me? And before the marriage, I want to prospect in Mr. D's mine. I think he found a rich lode. In exchange for my mining, I'll protect you. Long as I get to keep everything I find." He stepped forward and pulled out his gun, giving Millie a hard look. "If you're staying around here, you'll be needing protecting."

Stepping back, Millie picked up Buttercup and hugged her, wondering if Mr. Poor had been her night visitor. Did he think to scare her into marriage? Or to just scare her.

After a deep, calming breath, Millie said, "Mr. Poor. I am sorry but I cannot make such a promise. And Mr. D's mine *will* remain closed until spring."

Mr. Poor's thick eyebrows lowered, making him look downright mean. "That ain't a good decision, Widow D. I'll wait a week, maybe two, but then we'll talk again. You stay inside. I don't want Turck finding you. He ain't like me. He gets mean when he don't get what he wants." He turned, pulled open the door, and left, slamming it in his wake.

Millie didn't wait to see what happened with Mr. Poor and Mr. Turck. She rushed out her back door, passed Mr. D's grave, and disappeared into the trees. Her neighbor, Mary Randolph, might not like to make her acquaintance, but Millie didn't care. No way was she waiting alone for another suitor.

ELEVEN

August 11, 1863
Life Among the Lowly

With Buttercup cradled in her arms, Millie followed a game trail until she saw her neighbor's cabin through the underbrush. Sneaking from tree to tree, she stopped behind a fence surrounding a beautiful garden. Silently Millie caught her breath and watched the woman working inside. Mary Randolph had the ebony skin of a Southern slave and the build of a woman who worked to survive. Her garden was flourishing and Millie was pleased to see potatoes, beans, onions, carrots, garlic, and mustard greens along with medicinal plants like yarrow, hollyhock, horehound, boneset, and tansy. Next year Millie would plant her own garden, if she survived that long.

Harvesting cucumbers, the woman didn't notice Millie until Buttercup woke and cried out weakly. Mary stood up, her eyes narrowing as she spotted Millie.

"Hello, ma'am," Millie said, gripping Buttercup tighter. Mary Randolph was several inches shorter than Millie, but she looked strong and her expression was far from friendly. "I'm Miss Virginia."

"Mr. D's mail-order bride," the woman responded in a harsh Northern accent. Her tone softened slightly. "Thank you, for getting him buried proper."

"You're welcome. You knew him?"

"Yes, ma'am. He be a good man. The best." She looked away, but not before Millie saw grief tighten her face. What had been Mr. D's relationship with this woman? She'd obviously cared for him.

"You here, looking to make me leave?"

Millie glanced from the garden to Mary Randolph's dark, expressive face. If Mary left, this garden and all its produce would belong to her. She'd have plenty of food for the winter. Self-reproach and a feeling of disgrace filled her. Such thoughts were unworthy of a lady.

"What was your arrangement with Mr. D?" Millie asked, blushing.

"We have no arrangement, least not what you mean." The woman's eyes flashed, even as they teared. "When I come to Idaho Springs, I don't know nobody. Didn't have the know-how to homestead. Even if I did, winter be fast approaching. Mr. D, he help me. He ask for nothing back." Shaking her head, she wiped a tear off her cheek. "At first I don't believe him, but I got no choice. He bring me here and let me live in this here cabin. He chop wood. Bring me meat." She waved her hand at the garden. "He don't ask for nothing but I cook, clean, wash. Nothing improper. Next year, I grow me a garden. That man, he *love* potatoes." She stretched the word love and smiled weakly. "He eat 'em every day."

Millie glanced around and realized half the garden contained potato plants.

She looked away and saw Mr. Poor and Mr. Turck together on the far side of the meadow, obviously engrossed in an argument. Turning toward Mary Randolph, she thought again of her fiancé. He'd been a good man, one who might have made her happy. She would have at least felt safe. Sighing loudly, Millie looked up at the towering mountains. Surviving here, even without someone threatening her, would never be easy.

Mary Randolph shook her head and dropped the produce she'd been carrying. She turned toward her cabin. "I pack up. Be gone 'fore sundown."

Millie started. "I'd druther you stay, Miss Randolph. And I'd be obliged if you'd help me just as Mr. D helped you."

The woman spun around, her large brown eyes widening. "You gonna let me stay?"

"Yes ma'am. Mr. D would have wanted me to. But I'd be obliged for your help."

The woman paused, considering, but suddenly scowled. "When you marry, your husband drive me off. Might as well leave now."

"I don't intend to marry, Miss Randolph. Especially not to a man who'd insist you leave."

"Why? Lots of single men'll have you. Surviving with no man be hard. I know."

Millie thought of Mr. Tappan and Mr. Poor's proposals. "I'd druther not marry, if I don't hafta. The men I've met so far aren't to my liking."

"Me neither. I don't got no husband no more." She pulled a six-shooter from her apron. "But I knows how to protect meself."

Millie smiled, setting down Buttercup so she could pull out her own gun. "I'd be right pleased if you teach me to load and shoot."

The woman tilted her head to the side and gave Millie a baffled look. "Ma'am, you not like other Southern ladies. Not that I knows any. You ain't like the white ladies in town neither. They buy from me, but never ask for help. Why you different?"

"I…I was raised in an orphanage. When I was fifteen, I went to work for the LeGrand family. Mrs. LeGrand treated me like a servant. Made sure I knew my place. For years, I considered myself no better than a slave." Mary's disbelieving snort caused Millie to pause. "I know. I was free, but still." She shrugged. "Anyway, after I accepted Mr. D's proposal, I traveled by riverboat up the Mississippi. All my life I've dreamed of being a lady, and suddenly there I was, with a boatload of Yankee soldiers, treating me like a high-society Southern belle." Millie knew she was babbling, but she couldn't seem to stop. Mr. Poor had rattled her and she truly wanted this black woman to understand. "I became a lady, at least I tried."

"Even 'fore that, you weren't no slave."

"No. I learned that too. The Captain asked me to read to the injured soldiers. Said most were ignorant and it would be a great kindness. So I sat in this awful room, men younger than me sprawled all over the floor. Most more dead than alive. First Engineer Wolff—my escort on the ship—asked if anyone had a book for me to read."

Millie closed her eyes, remembering. "This man, a soldier with a bandaged stump below his right shoulder and his eyes bound closed. He was a mess, but he calls out, 'I got a book.' Said his 'missus' sent it. She liked it. Didn't know what it was, since it arrived after his injury. I'll live my whole life and never forget that soldier's words. He said, 'If you read it, ma'am, maybe she and me can talk about it. After I get home. Maybe that way she'll want me back. Probably not. Can't farm if I can't handle a plow or see the field. Probably she won't want what's left of me.'"

"What book?" Mary asked, stepping closer.

Millie rubbed Buttercup's ears and smiled. "That half dead soldier gave me a book no self-respecting Southern lady would ever read. Abolitionist newspapers in St. Louis hailed it a masterpiece that humanized the horrors of slavery, but in my home in New Orleans, the book was outlawed. Branded irresponsible and touted to be full of distortions and lies."

Mary doubled over and slapped her thigh. "Gracious sakes, ma'am," she said breathlessly, "You spend your whole trip reading *Uncle Tom's Cabin* writ by Miss Harriet Beecher Stowe?" Tears streamed from her eyes. "Them Northern boys must a laughed and laughed."

"Have you read it?" Millie asked. She blushed, realizing the rudeness of the question. Black people couldn't read. "I mean…You've heard of it. Right?"

"I read it," Mary said, wiping tears from her face. "Me Mama work for a white lady. She teach me and Mama to read. But you got one purdy accent. Bet you make it sound good."

Relieved she hadn't offered an insult, Millie put on her strongest Southern accent and quoted Prue, an abused slave who Uncle Tom was trying to convince to live a Christian life. The words from the book had burned themselves into Millie's mind when she'd first read them. "'I looks like gwine to heaven,' said the woman; 'an't thar where white folks is gwine? S'pose they'd have me thar? I'd rather go to torment, and get away from Mas'r and Missus.'"

Mary clapped her hands appreciatively.

"Reading *Uncle Tom's Cabin.*" Millie paused, trying to find the right words. "It was difficult, but I…It taught me my life hadn't been so hard. Not like a slave. My work was difficult. Mrs. LeGrand unpleasant. But still—"

"Your white skin mean your husband not got sold," Mary said sharply. "Your master never take you to his bed. Sell his kid next year."

"No," Millie said soberly. "Are you war contraband? Did you escape from the South?"

"No. I born a free woman. In New York." She looked away, her expression distant. "But free blacks, even in Union states, ain't got it so easy. We ain't slaves, but we ain't treated so good."

Mary quit speaking and the silence that followed made Millie uncomfortable. She was acutely aware of bees buzzing in the garden, Buttercup ripping at the grass nearby, and the strong smell of the mint patch near her feet.

"I'm sorry. In New Orleans, I didn't know any slaves. Or any free blacks for that matter." It would have been highly improper for her to even speak with one, but she didn't need to tell Mary that. "New Orleans has its Code Noir, a French law that requires slave owners to feed, clothe, house, and provide religious instruction and basic medical care to their slaves. Slavery is awful, but in my hometown, white immigrants—Irish, Italian, and such—were treated far worse."

"Worse than a slave?"

"Yes, ma'am. Immigrants, like my friend's husband, were considered an expendable workforce, brought over to dig the city canals. Didn't matter if they were exposed to bilious fever, chorea, dock fever, and other ailments. When an immigrant died, they just brought over another one. They'd never let slaves do that kind of labor. Slaves cost money. *They* were considered valuable property."

"Humph," said Mary, scratching her head. She shrugged. "Miss Virginia, I think I gonna like being your neighbor."

"Maybe we can become friends," Millie blurted out and then blushed at the ridiculousness of her statement. A white Southern woman and a free black could never be friends. Or could they? Mr. D had befriended Mary. Maybe in this untamed country, the unimaginable was possible. If she wanted to survive, Millie would need all the help she could get. Hesitantly, she asked, "Do you mind if we're a bit informal? I'm Miss Millie."

The woman shook her head. "You and Mr. D. You woulda been good. He never mind none, me being colored. I'm Miss Mary. Miss Mary Randolph."

"It is a pleasure to meet you, Miss Mary. How did you end up in Idaho Springs, if I might ask?"

"I born in New York. Come to the Colorado Territory in '61."

"Whatever for?"

The woman looked down and her voice thickened. "In New York, I marry a free man. Adam and me, we be real happy." She paused and blew her nose. "Day of our first anniversary, Adam get killed by white men. New York ain't so friendly. So I come here."

"I am so sorry, Miss Mary." Millie was sure there was more to the story, but politeness demanded she change the subject. "Did you join a wagon train to get here?"

"Naw," said Mary, wiping her eyes. "I come by train to St. Louis. Afterwards, I pay me fare by stagecoach. They say I ride on top cause no colored folk 'lowed inside. So I ride on top. Went good 'til we near Fort Riley. Some white passenger complain. No colored folks 'lowed. So they put me off in the empty plains. That night it got bad. Real bad. Prairie wolves come round to eat me. But they's scared when I's snap me umbrella." She grinned. "I snap me umbrella all night long. Next morning, new stagecoach pick me up. In Auraria, Denver City now, I got me a gun. I start walking. Ended here."

A gunshot punctuated her words. Millie spun around and shaded her eyes. On the far side of the pasture, Mr. Poor—distinct in his striped overalls—waved a gun at Mr. Turck. The other miner was stumbling down the trail toward town.

"You might not want a man, Miss Millie, but they want you. And you mine. Maybe we should make us scarce. Less you want to talk with 'em?"

"I'd druther slit my throat," Millie said and blushed. "Sorry, that wasn't polite."

Mary laughed. "Tit Bit say the same, but she ain't got no choice. A woman got to eat."

"You know Tit Bit? Mr. Poor made her sound like some kind of fancy girl."

"Fancy girl. She like that name. She and Smooth Bore share a crib. They be town girls. Town ladies don't talk to them none, but they don't talk to me neither. So I talk to the public women. They ain't so bad. They got money." She glanced toward the men. "Mr. Turck ain't me favorite. He got one mean temper. Mr. D never like him and told me to stay clear. How 'bout we go raspberry picking?" She turned and headed toward her cabin. Millie hurried around the fence after her, hoping raspberry picking was someplace far away.

They gathered baskets and left, skirting the meadow until they reached a path behind Millie's cabin. Raspberry patches lined the creek and in a couple of hours they'd picked enough fruit for several pies. As they meandered toward home, Mary showed Millie patches of wild onions and mushrooms. When they reached her cabin, Mary shyly invited Millie to share a supper of fried potatoes and sourdough bread. Afterwards, she insisted Millie go through the garden and add tomatoes, green beans, and cucumbers to the raspberries in her basket.

"If you want," Mary said, opening the garden gate for Millie, "tomorrow we can pickle cucumbers."

"I'd like that awfully much, Miss Mary. Thank you."

"You like sourdough bread? I carry me starter from New York and Mr. D build me a shelf—right by the stove—so the sourdoughies stay warm. Mr. D, he love sourdough bread almost like taters."

"I've never cooked with sourdough, but I would love to learn."

"Tomorrow I make you a starter."

They parted ways and Millie trudged across the field, carrying enough produce to last a week. With Mary's help, Millie might be able to dry, pickle, and preserve enough food to survive the winter. Her spirits were high and she was looking forward to a quiet evening when she spotted Mr. Shumate, the town blacksmith, waiting on her front porch. He held a dead rabbit in one hand, a rifle in the other.

Millie's pace faltered. Before she could turn around, Mr. Shumate spied her, let out a hearty yell, and lumbered over, his long legs eating up the short distance. He was a large man, his blacksmith muscles bulged under his hole-bitten buckskin vest, soot darkened one side of his short blond hair and his left cheek.

"Lassie," he said, halting in front of her and shifting his rifle under the arm that held the rabbit. "I come to ask you a question." Enveloping her hand in his hefty fist, he dropped to one knee. The head of the dead rabbit swung back and struck the butt of his rifle. "Will you marry me, lassie?"

Millie's eyes darted between the man's soot-smeared face and his rifle. The barrel now pointed directly at her heart.

TWELVE

August 11, 1863
Firing a Six-Shooter

Looking into the action end of his rifle, Millie couldn't find her voice. They remained like statues—her staring mutely at the rifle, him kneeling on the wet ground. Finally he groaned and stood, the motion moving the rifle barrel. "I prefer an answer, lassie, but I hear you still be mourning for Mr. D." Millie nodded mutely. "Och aye the noo! I can wait a day or two." He laid the dead rabbit in the basket on top of her produce, his singed eyebrows rising. "And what time tomorrow should I be coming to supper?"

"Uh. Two?"

"Aye. That'll do, lassie." He turned, resting his rifle on his shoulder and strode away. Millie didn't move until he'd disappeared into the trees.

When she reached her cabin, she dropped the basket on the floor and quickly barred the doors and shuttered the windows. Leaning back, she took a long, deep breath. She was through with unexpected visitors.

The following morning, anxious to brighten the gloom inside her cabin, Millie unbarred her shutters but left her doors securely locked. Her breakfast was interrupted by a loud pounding that rattled her front door. Cautiously she peeked through a half-opened shutter. The woman in trousers, Charlotte Card, stood on her stoop.

"Miss Card," Millie said, opening the door. "It's a pleasure to see you. Won't you come in and join me for some tea?"

"Nope. Got to get to work. Glad to see you got sense enough to check before opening the door. You didn't seem like the silly sort. We ain't back in the States no more. Out here, a lady, 'specially a lone one, got to be careful."

"I thank you kindly for the reminder. Is there something you're needing from me?"

"Doubt it. Heard you weren't selling your mine, or are you? I'd offer four twenty-five. Twenty-five more than Ferris."

Word did get around. Millie considered. Would there be trouble if she sold the mine to Miss Card? Would her intruder turn his attention toward her? "That is a generous offer, Miss Card, but I haven't decided to sell Mr. D's mine."

"Smart. You could mine it yourself or wait to see if the price goes up."

Millie blanched. No way would she ever set foot inside a dark, closed-in mine.

"I come to teach you to shoot," said the woman, interrupting Millie's thoughts. "A lady got to protect herself. 'Specially ones like us, without a man."

"That's kind of you, Miss Card," Millie said. The woman's accent was Northern, but a bit softer than Mary's. Midwest. Ohio, maybe?

"Call me Charlotte. I don't hang on formality. This here's my gun." She pulled a six-shooter from her hip holster. "Mr. D had a Colt revolver just like this but in better shape. He always carried it when prospecting. Heard it weren't found when they dug him out. Probably got buried under the rubble." She handed Millie her gun. "I can show you with mine, but you'll need to buy your own real soon."

"Actually I found this six-shooter in the cabin." Millie removed the gun from her apron.

"That's odd." Charlotte pulled on her braid. "Never known Mr. D to mine without his Colt." She shrugged and took her own weapon back. "Find his shot and powder too?" Millie nodded. "Good. Go get it. I'll show you how to load and shoot." She glanced at Buttercup who peeked out curiously from behind Millie. "And lock the goat in the house. Wouldn't want to accidently shoot her."

"Thank you kindly," Millie said, amused by the woman's brusque manner. Retrieving the shot and powder, she shut Buttercup inside and joined Charlotte on the front porch. Curiosity won over manners and Millie asked, "You're not married, Miss Charlotte?"

"Not really," the woman mumbled, her sunburnt face darkening. She reached over and pointed at Millie's gun. "This here is the wedge pin. You push it like this to take the gun apart." The weapon broke into three pieces. "You need to keep your Colt dry and clean. Wouldn't want it to jam when you need it."

Millie wanted to ask what "not really" meant, but she never got the chance. Using brisk commands, Charlotte had Millie clean the cylinders and lubricate all the moving parts with lard. After reassembling the gun, Charlotte showed how to hold the grip and pull down the hammer.

"This is now half-cocked," she said, "Always load it half-cocked. It lets the cylinder turn freely." She spun the cylinder. "Plus the gun shouldn't fire accidently if you pull the trigger. Pour black powder into the chamber, filling it to here." She pointed.

Using the powder horn, Millie poured until Charlotte told her to stop. "Now push one of those felt wads in to keep the powder from falling out. That's right. Good. Now put a ball over the chamber."

"I forgot. The balls here are too large. One got stuck when I tried yesterday. I'll buy some of the proper size in town."

"Too big?" Retrieving a lead ball, Charlotte glanced at it and shook her head. "Nope. These are fine. You just didn't ram it."

"Ram it?"

"Use the gun's rammer." She took the Colt, added a ball, and cocked the hammer back. The motion caused the chamber to rotate one notch, placing the ball and loaded chamber directly under the barrel. "Hold the gun tightly by the grip, like this. Unhook the rammer, and ram the ball into the chamber." She demonstrated and handed the gun back to Millie. "Now you try."

Under Charlotte's sharp eye, Millie repeated the process, loading four more chambers. "That's all you need," said Charlotte. "I always leave one unloaded, the dead man. For safety. Leave the hammer against the unloaded chamber." Grabbing two caps, she handed one to Millie. "Now, cap each loaded nipple, like this." She demonstrated, making it look easy. Millie tried and dropped the tiny cap, but Charlotte just handed it back. She quietly watched until Millie successfully capped each loaded chamber.

With the gun ready, Charlotte took it from Millie. "To fire," she said, looking as comfortable with the six-shooter as Millie was with a frying pan, "you aim, cock the hammer all the way, and pull the trigger."

She demonstrated, aiming at a young evergreen sapling.

"Aim like you're shooting a no-good, worthless husband," Charlotte said, pulling the trigger. The top of the sapling burst into several pieces.

"Was your husband worthless?" Millie couldn't hide her smile.

Charlotte aimed and fired again. The next section of the sapling exploded. "He was worse than worthless. You try."

Worse than worthless? Millie took the gun, gripped the stock in both hands, and aimed at the evergreen. Fleetingly she imagined the person who'd stolen Mr. D's gold. She cocked the hammer and pulled the trigger. The gun jerked her arms up and back, knocking her off balance. Millie cried out, tumbled backwards and landed on her backside. Her ears rang as white smoke puffed from the gun's barrel, surrounding her with the smell of burnt powder.

Charlotte grinned down at her. "I fell too," she said offering her hand and helping Millie stand, "first time I fired my Colt."

After an hour of practice, Millie's arms were sore, but she felt comfortable loading and firing the weapon. She also felt safer. "I can't thank you enough, Miss Charlotte. Won't you come in for a cup of tea before you leave?"

"I need to get to work," answered her guest, shuffling her feet from side to side. She looked shyly up at Millie and added, "But maybe one cup."

Buttercup greeted Charlotte, butting her in the thigh as Millie heated water. Millie knew it was none of her business, but her curiosity got the better of her. "If I'm not being too bold Miss Charlotte, may I ask what you meant by not really married?"

Charlotte flushed. "I'm married, but don't got no man."

"Did your husband pass?"

"Hope so."

Millie lifted her eyebrows and Charlotte scowled. "You weren't the only one to answer a wife-wanted advertisement."

THIRTEEN

August 12, 1863
A Not Really Married Mail-Order Bride

"Miss Charlotte. You answered a wife-wanted advertisement?" Millie hoped her voice didn't betray her incredulity.

"I did. Louis Driebel. We corresponded. I thought I knew him. Said he was a shop owner in Santa Fe." She shook her head. "Never trust a man!"

"He didn't own a shop?" Millie asked.

"Might have. But it weren't how he made his living. I didn't figure it out until after we were wed." She gave Millie a sour look and sighed. "I traveled by stagecoach across the Kansas Territory from Fort Dodge to Fort Union. Didn't know it, but the coach was carrying a strongbox. Four thousand dollars in gold. Pay for Fort Union soldiers. Just after we crossed the Cimarron River, four men wearing gunnysacks held up the stagecoach. They—"

"Gunnysack?" Millie asked.

"A croker sack. Or maybe you call it a crocus sack."

"They wore these sacks on their heads, with eye holes?"

"Yes. So no one could see their faces." When Millie nodded, Charlotte continued. "The outlaws couldn't get into the strongbox, so they decided to blow the lock. I noticed my trousseau sitting right beside the strongbox. It was all I had. I hurried over and asked one outlaw to remove it. Surprisingly, he did. As he lifted it, I saw a long, jagged scar on the back of his hand. Afterward, they blew the box, took the gold, and left. The coachman cussed, but he tossed my luggage back into the boot."

She paused to take a sip of tea and Millie couldn't help adding, "That was brave of you, Miss Charlotte, to save your trousseau."

"Not so brave. That chest held everything I owned. My Pa was clear: he told me not to return. I got four other sisters, but no brothers." She shrugged. "When we reached Santa Fe, my fiancé's landlady helped me prepare for the wedding. I bathed, dressed in an actual white wedding dress like Queen Victoria, and went downstairs. Found Louis there with a preacher. He looked just like his carte-de-viste. Tall, light hair, kinda shy looking. I was real nervous. The landlady handed me over to him. No introductions or nothing. Preacher just said his bit, we said ours, and a few minutes later we were pronounced man and wife."

"You married him?"

Charlotte gave her a sour look. "It's why I traveled to this god-forsaken place, ain't it? You would have done the same, if Mr. D hadn't died."

"So what happened? How long did you stay married?"

"We're still married, for all I know. But I only stayed with him for a couple minutes. After we was married, my husband leaned over and kissed me. I was shaking and scared. Not exactly sure what come next, but he knowed what he want. He said we were going back to his room. Wedded bliss, he called it. But the preacher asked us to sign the marriage paperwork. That's when I saw it. The jagged scar on his hand."

"Your husband was the outlaw who robbed the stagecoach?"

"Yes." She stretched the word out angrily. "I was so mad I took the preacher's Bible and hit my husband over the head.

The landlady and the preacher thought I'd gone crazy. They called the sheriff. I was still beating on that man when the sheriff showed up." She grinned sheepishly. "I had to buy the parson a new Bible. It was shredded by the time I were done. Anyway, I explained and the sheriff arrested Louis, removed his Colt and belt. I grabbed them. The sheriff took one look at the Bible and removed the firing caps. Guess he thought I might shoot Louis. I didn't. Just wrapped the holster round my wedding dress, jammed the gun in, and left. Never heard what happened to him. Don't care. I'm done with men!"

Millie thought about Charlotte as she pickled cucumbers later that morning with Mary. Could she have survived without Mr. D's cabin and Mary's help? Charlotte was basically living like a man, prospecting gold and surviving on her own. Millie shuddered. She'd rather marry than put one foot inside Mr. D's mine. The face of Mr. Poor popped into her head. Well...maybe she could overcome her fear of dark places.

That afternoon she roasted Mr. Shumate's rabbit, following one of her favorite recipes from *Modern Cookery in All its Branches*. After skinning and removing the animal's back-bone, she lined the rabbit's inside with bacon, filled the cavity with forcemeat, and sewed it up before roasting it over the fire. Delicious smells filled the cabin by the time Mr. Shumate knocked on the door. Millie opened the door and immediately tried to close it. A foot blocked the way.

Her visitor wasn't Mr. Shumate.

Mr. Gould, his hair disheveled and his rat-tailed mustache drooping, shoved the door open and stepped inside. The dandy from Denver city had lost his shine, although he still carried his six-shooters. One was in his hand, aimed at Millie.

"Mr. Gould," she said slowly, "What a...surprise."

FOURTEEN

August 12, 1863
Mr. Gould

It is, isn't it." Mr. Gould pushed Millie backward and limped inside before slamming the door. He hobbled over to the table and sat down, sniffing the air as he glanced around. "Looks like you're not missing your fiancé." He licked his lips. "What are you cooking? I haven't smelled anything that good since I came west."

Slowly, Millie backed up until she hit her rocking chair. Mr. Gould's clothing was dirty and his mustache drooped so badly the ends tangled with his tousled beard. "W-what do you want, Mr. Gould?"

Like a cat inspecting a mouse before it pounced, Mr. Gould stared at her for a long moment. "Food," he said, banging his revolver down on the table in easy reach, "and your watch."

Millie swallowed. This morning she hadn't managed to actually hit the evergreen sapling, but she'd seen the damage from Charlotte's balls. She didn't want to imagine what a ball fired this close would do to her. Cursing her stupidity—her Colt sat cleaned, loaded, and useless on the shelf above her bed—Millie pulled her watch from her apron.

"Give it to me and fix my plate. Are you slow? I've been on the run for days. I'm starving. Coffee, too."

"Why?" Millie nervously slid the watch across the table. "You were one of the outlaws. The ones who tried to rob the stagecoach." Bewildered, she looked at her watch. "For this? It's cheap. Not even worth a Liberty half-dollar."

"Thought you might have recognized me. Too bad for you."

Too bad for you? Millie grimaced.

He snatched the watch off the table and stared at it. "Never thought I'd ever see this thing again. Couldn't believe it, when you pulled it out." He popped open the cover and gave the picture a look of pure hatred. "It was a gift. My dear partner, William Saul, gave it to his wife a year or two before he disappeared. I was there when they made the daguerreotype." He pulled out a nasty-looking knife and scraped it under the picture.

Millie wanted to grab it back and make him stop, but she was too shocked. "Y-you knew my daddy and mama?" she asked. "How? I-I was raised in an orphanage. In New Orleans."

"New Orleans, huh? Figures. Your daddy, mama, and brother disappeared from New York on Christmas Day of '38. They took my two thousand dollars in silver coin with them." He pried the daguerreotype out of the cover and watched it flutter to the table. "Took me a year, but I tracked William down to Knoxville, Tennessee. Heard his wife died there in childbirth."

A heavy weight pressed on Millie's heart. Her mama was dead. She'd been abandoned, yet, as a child, she'd dreamed about having parents. Someday they would return and she'd have a family. A *real* home. Even as an adult, it was difficult to abandon those dreams.

"Your daddy and I, we worked for the Bowe brothers in New York. Were partners, of a sort. One night, we liberated a hefty sack of silver coins from a ship anchored off the East River. Thought we might increase our personal profits. Cut the Bowe brothers out. That's why William had the loot."

"My daddy was a criminal?" Millie blurted out. Her hand covered her mouth. "He...he couldn't have been."

"Your father was a thief. A no-count thug who'd beat up his own mother for a Liberty half-dollar."

Millie gasped. It couldn't be true, but she saw the truth in his eyes.

"We decided to hide the coins with his wife and kid so the Bowes wouldn't find them. They didn't. Didn't have a clue until William disappeared. Loot, wife, kid, and all. But after William took off, the Bowes started asking questions. They had an unpleasant way of asking questions." He lifted his left hand to show his missing pinky. "I was lucky to get out of New York with my life. Had to start again without a Liberty half-dollar to my name."

Millie felt tears sting her eyes. It was silly and she knew it, but she'd always imagined her parents as special. An English lord down on his luck. A lady with a family who disapproved of her secret love. Instead, her daddy was a crook. A partner to this awful man. And her mama was dead.

"Food!" Mr. Gould struck the table with his fist, making Millie jump. She quickly turned to make him a plate, but listened as Mr. Gould carried on a crazy monologue—as if he were talking to Millie's daddy. "You were a fool William, to leave this with your daughter. Planned on returning, huh? Never planned on me finding you."

Millie jerked and spun back around. "You found my daddy? After he left me?"

Mr. Gould ignored her and poked the sharp point of his knife into the watch. Millie heard it scrape against the metal cover as the man mumbled incoherently. He sounded insane.

"There it is, William," he said, laughing as a folded piece of paper fluttered to the table. "Jammed it in behind the daguerreotype, just like you said. Thought you were being smart. But I'm smarter. Always was." Unceremoniously he dropped the watch and carefully unfolded the paper, pressing it flat against the table. "Looks like you told me the truth, just before I killed you."

"You killed my daddy?"

"Yep. Right after he told me about this map. His final words were the coins were hidden right under the X." He looked from the map to Millie. "What does Boone Dogs' Cave mean?"

"I…I don't know." Millie stared at the map numbly. Her daddy was dead. This man had killed him. There was a treasure map in her watch? How could any of this be real?

"Food, woman!" snapped Mr. Gould, his eyes never leaving the map. "I haven't had a decent meal in days."

Millie's hands shook as she took a tin plate from the shelf, the one she'd intended for Mr. Shumate. Where was he? Slicing off a slab of meat from the roasted rabbit, Millie cut off the end of the sourdough loaf and dished up some sweet carrots. Cautiously she approached Mr. Gould and placed the food on the table. From where she stood, she could clearly see the paper. It looked like a rough map.

Mr. Gould pushed the map to one side, his eyes never leaving it, stabbed the meat with his knife and bit off a chunk. "Mumm," he mumbled, picking up the plate and using his knife to shove carrots into his already full mouth. "Think I'll take you with me. Seems a waste to kill you."

Millie sucked down a breath. Getting killed sounded bad; going anywhere with Mr. Gould sounded worse.

He laughed, spraying the table with food and spit. "That'd be a bit ironic, don't you think? Having my partner's little girl as my woman." He sopped up the meat's sauce with the bread and ate half the slice in a single bite. "This *is* good. Definitely taking you with me." He pulled one side of his mustache into his mouth and sucked it clean.

Millie cringed. She'd always prided herself in her cooking, but she'd make sure the next meal she made—if she ever made another—would taste truly awful.

Using the last of the bread to wipe the plate clean, Mr. Gould pushed it aside, sucked clean the other side of his mustache, and pulled the map closer. "So, William, where's my silver?" He rotated the map and flipped it over. On the back were a series of curved lines with another large X. "Bet these are the tunnels in the cave... But where the hell is the cave?" He shoved the map at Millie. "Where?"

Where indeed. Where was Mr. Shumate? What town was depicted by the map? In the center of the paper was "Main Street" and on either side were rough squares. One marked James Field, another Francis Preston, a third Armstrong farm, and another Frank Blair. There was the Gibson store, the Tavern, and a square with a cross marked Sheffey/Methodist church. A large X had been drawn above Main Street with the words Boone Dogs' Cave written beside it. It could have been a small town anywhere in the States. Field. Preston. Armstrong. Boone. Sheffey. None of the names meant anything to her.

"I don't know. Didn't my daddy tell you?" *Before you killed him?*

"No. Said he didn't remember. Claimed he found a cave near some little town, made the map, buried the coins, and hurried on. He knew I was trailing him." Mr. Gould looked up at Millie, his rat-tail mustache twitching. "He was lying. He knew where he hid it. But he refused to tell me. Unfortunately, I got a little over eager. My shot missed his knee and hit an artery. He bled out without telling me anything more." He glared at Millie. "He left the map with you. There had to be another clue."

Millie looked again at the map. She had no idea.

Mr. Gould stood and picked up his revolver causing Millie to step away. The heat from the cookstove warmed her back as Mr. Gould slowly cocked the hammer back. "What else was left at the orphanage with you?"

"Nothing," Millie said, her heart pounding. Drops of sweat trickled down her back. "I swear. He left the watch and a piece of paper with my name."

"There must be more!" He turned the muzzle toward Buttercup. The goat looked up innocently.

"No!" Millie pleaded, taking a step toward Buttercup. They both froze at the sound of a loud knock.

"Who's that?" whispered Mr. Gould.

"One of my suitors," Millie said, a crazy, desperate idea forming in her head. "He's who I cooked dinner for."

"Well then. Open the door and let him in."

"Please come in, Mr. Shumate," Millie called out. Mr. Gould scowled as he swung his revolver toward the door. The latch clicked up and the door swung open.

"Widow D," said Mr. Shumate in his strong Scottish burr. "You bonny lass. What have you cooked? Och! It smells—" He stepped through the door, grinning, a line of soot running down his chin like drool. His eyes widened when he saw Mr. Gould.

"Too bad you won't get to enjoy it," Mr. Gould said, his gun pointed at the man. "It was quite good."

In one swift movement, Millie grabbed the handle of her cast iron frying pan and swung. The flat bottom struck Mr. Gould's skull with a sickening thud.

"Yes," Millie said as Mr. Gould crumpled to the ground. "He will."

FIFTEEN

August 13, 1863
Life in Idaho Springs

"You knock him out? With a frying pan?" Mary asked, her eyes wide.

"I did." Millie couldn't help but smile at Mary's astonished expression. "Mr. Shumate tied him up and hurried to town to get the sheriff. He's still hunting the Espinosas, so Mr. Shumate brought back Mr. Whitlatch, Mr. Poor, and Mr. Turck."

"The Grouse and Mr. Turck? Gracious sakes. Them two hate each other."

"The Grouse?" Millie asked.

"Mr. Whitlatch. Tit Bit call him that. Say he swagger about, all fancy. Lively like them grouse you see across the plains."

Millie laughed. On the wagon train, they'd run across male grouse strutting around with their tails open and their wings extended. She could well appreciate the nickname.

"Where they take Mr. Gould?"

"To Denver City. For the stagecoach robbery. But when they arrived at my cabin, they left Mr. Gould tied up and insisted on eating before they took him. He'd come around and if looks could kill, Mr. Gould would be a murderer."

"From what you say, he already a killer." Mary stood up and looked out the window. "I best leave. People be visiting soon."

"People?" Millie glanced behind Mary. She'd had more than enough unexpected company. "What people?"

"Townsfolk. Only thing here more valuable than gold be scuttlebutt and gossip. Course, stories ain't bad."

She was right. Within an hour, Mrs. Gilson arrived carrying a basket load of dirty clothes. While they washed, Millie recounted her story, unable to answer the question everyone asked: "Where were the coins buried?" Millie showed the map to Mrs. Gilson, but like Mr. Turck, Mr. Shumate, Mr. Poor, and Mr. Whitlatch, no one recognized any of the names or landmarks.

"You bring your map to supper tonight," Mrs. Gilson said. "Maybe Mr. Gilson will recognize something."

"Supper, ma'am?"

"Don't you worry none. Mr. Shumate is coming. He'll walk you home afterwards. I imagine you're feeling a bit skittish."

They finished the washing and hung the clothes to dry and Millie asked what Mrs. Gilson charged for the work. "Four bits, or two pinches of gold dust, for a white shirt, two bits or one pinch of dust for a colored one," she explained, "but the real trick to making money washing miner's clothes is carefully emptying the washtub."

"Emptying the washtub?"

"Yes, dear. See." Mrs. Gilson slowly poured the murky water from the tub. She stopped when Millie could see the dirt and grime on the bottom. "Look here." She turned the tub into the sun, and Millie gasped. Flakes of gold glittered in the light.

"I call it washtub panning!"

The following day, Mrs. Beebee, who ran the Beebee House and was known for her excellent cuisine, invited Millie to supper to hear the story. Mr. Poor escorted her home that evening, carrying his six-shooter in his hand "to protect her." Mrs. Gardner, who ran Payne's Bar House, couldn't be outdone by her neighbors and invited Millie two days later. Her escort choice was Mr. Tappan. The man quoted Shakespeare love sonnets the entire walk, which wasn't too bad until they reached the cabin and he tried to kiss her. Fortunately, all Millie had to do was stand up straight and he couldn't reach.

Matchmaking, it appeared, was also a favored diversion for the townswomen, not that Millie needed their help. Over the next few weeks, an unending supply of single men stopped by—sometimes in pairs so she'd have a choice—to propose or offer to buy her mine. Since she felt safe again in her cabin, Millie didn't mind the attention. Her intruder, Mr. Gould, was in the calaboose in Denver City, locked up tight and being fed bread and water.

Just like the other town ladies, Mrs. Ferris eventually invited Millie over for a noonday meal, although Millie suspected it was her husband's idea. She'd barely settled herself at the table before Mr. Ferris offered seven hundred and fifty dollars for her mine.

"That is a generous offer, Mr. Ferris, but I've not decided to sell just yet," Millie said. With Mary's garden, gifts of wild game from suitors who'd heard about her cooking, and an income from washing clothes, Millie no longer worried as much about money, although selling the mine would make her life easier. Problem was, she'd received offers from suitors, married townsmen, strangers, and even Charlotte Card. She didn't know who she should sell it to. Mr. Ferris' offer was highest.

Mrs. Ferris bustled about and served a tasteless mock turtle soup, an unseasoned boiled chicken with pickled onions on the side, and opened a can of peaches for dessert. To Millie's mind, the peaches were the only thing worth eating although Mr. Turck—Mrs. Ferris' favored suitor—ate the entire meal with gusto.

Since her arrival, Mr. Turck had become Millie's least favorite suitor. Most of the men had taken her refusals graciously; not so with Mr. Turck. He'd cursed and spat at her feet, calling her an ignoramus and threatening her with "unpleasant actions." Millie tried to avoid him and would have refused Mrs. Ferris' offer if she'd known he was coming. It was a relief to finally escape the Ferris house and head home.

A month passed and the excitement over Mr. Gould and his treasure map waned, although her suitors' continued to persist. Millie suspected their vigilance was due as much to her cooking—they all managed to time their proposals before mealtime—as to a true desire for matrimony. Still, their regularity had certain advantages. One morning Millie casually mentioned she could make hotcakes if she had eggs, and the next day Mr. Tappan ordered six chickens from Denver City. Mr. Poor and Mr. Shumate, their eyes gleaming at the thought of hotcakes, helped her build a coop, attaching it to the back wall of the cabin.

"We'll build the nesting box inside, lassie," explained Mr. Shumate. "In Mr. D's bedroom. The cocks will freeze during the winter if you don't keep them warm, but during really bad storms, you'll be needing a box to bring them inside. I'll make you one."

"It gets *real* cold during a blizzard," added Mr. Poor, lifting his thick eyebrows suggestively. "A woman needs a man in her bed, else she might freeze. I'd be happy to oblige until you're done mourning." Millie politely refused.

The night the chickens arrived she dreamed of a howling wind, snow so deep she couldn't reach her privy, and cold so bitter her fingers, toes, and nose froze. She tossed and turned, dreaming about hail and sleet thrashing her roof and walls. A loud rattling woke her. Heart pounding, she realized the noise wasn't from her dream.

Her back door groaned.

Someone was trying to get inside!

Millie scrambled to her feet, and reached out blindly for the shelf with her six-shooter. The groaning of the back door quieted as her fingers closed around the grip of her gun.

Her heart raced.

Boots crunched by her bedroom wall. Who was out there? Mr. Gould was in Denver City, locked up in the calaboose. A crack made her jump and she tripped over Buttercup's prostrate form. Ignoring her skinned knees, Millie huddled on the floor, hugged her gun, and waited for a door or window to give under the intruder's harsh attack. Outside, someone smacked the window shutter above her bed a second time.

The intruder went from window to window, searching for any weakness. Each time he struck a shutter, Millie jumped, but it was worse when she couldn't hear him.

After a long, noiseless minute, Millie slowly stood, trying to calm her harsh breathing as she crept through the blackness. Stifling a sob, she felt for her candle and flint. It took several tries—her hands were trembling badly—but finally she managed to light the candle. Clutching the gun in one hand, the candle in another, Millie crept from her room, lighting candles as she worked her way to the fireplace.

Her breathing and racing heart were the only sounds she could hear. Perhaps he'd decided he couldn't get in and left. Who was he? Why was he trying to get in?

In answer, Millie's chickens erupted with squawks and cries, sounding like they had a fox in the pen. Millie rushed to the back room, sitting down on the nesting box lid. Could someone crawl through the coop and enter the cabin? Surely the opening was too small. The chickens screeched, wildly flapping against the wood, sounding desperate. The intruder was killing her chickens! Without chickens, no fresh eggs. A winter without fresh eggs would be unbearable.

Hurrying to the shuttered window closest to the coop, Millie blew out her candle, cocked her six-shooter, and quietly removed the bar. Cracking the shutter open just enough to stick the muzzle through, Millie peeked outside. A dark form crouched in the coop, arms swinging. Millie's hand shook as she aimed the gun, closed her eyes, and pulled the trigger.

Obscene cursing erupted like a thunderbolt, emphasized by thrashing and thudding. Millie dropped her gun in her hurry to slam the shutter closed, but she couldn't find the bar. Frantically she searched, cursing her stupidity, expecting any moment to have the shutter knocked open and a groping hand grasp her.

She stepped back, her foot landing on the bar, and fell again. Ignoring the pain shooting through her hip, Millie grabbed the bar, scrambled to her feet, and slid it into its slot. Panting, she took two steps back, her whole body shaking.

Where was her gun?

Dropping to her knees, she scrambled around, banging into walls and boxes until she located the Colt. Despite the cold, Millie felt drenched in sweat. Gulping down air, she froze and listened, trying to locate the intruder. The chickens clucked unhappily but no longer sounded distressed. Buttercup bleated. Millie crawled to the fireplace, followed by the goat. She gathered Buttercup into her lap. Together they waited until sunlight slipped through the cracks between the shutters.

Hours after dawn, Millie finally worked up her courage, unbarred the back door, and peeked out. Cool air struck her face, making her shiver as she furtively searched the area. The door to the chicken coop was open, and four of her hens and the rooster scratched in the grass nearby. Millie cracked her door wider, her gun grasped in both hands, and stepped outside. Cautiously she inched around the cabin, searching behind wild current bushes and thick junipers. In the dry grass, she saw the imprint of a large boot, but the owner of the print was nowhere to be seen.

Millie inched open the door of the privy and pointed her gun down the hole. The smell quickly drove her out. Continuing her search, she found no sign of her midnight visitor until she reached the barn. Her missing hen lay dead on the ground. Above her body, written in blood on the barn wall, were the words Millie had seen before.

LEAVE IDAHO SPRINGS OR DIE!

SIXTEEN

October 9, 1863

Oh Brother!

Millie took her morning tea outside to admire the transformation of her meadow. Overnight the reds, yellows, and greens of autumn had changed to a sparkling white. In the crisp morning air, misty clouds formed when she exhaled and snowflakes swirled around her head. She stuck out her tongue, trying to catch a snowflake, but as soon as she stepped into the fluffy snow, cold penetrated her knit slippers. For the past two months, she'd come to know every corner of her meadow, exploring the meandering river, admiring patches of blue columbine and red Indian paintbrush, harvesting tiny wild strawberries, and watching spellbound as the quaking aspen leaves changed from green to gold to a brilliant crimson. October had ushered in chilly nights, but not until this morning had she seen snow.

Buttercup rushed past and jumped into the air, landing in an explosion of white. She let out a high, bleating cry, as if shocked by the cold, twisted around and charged back onto the porch. Millie laughed out loud. Obviously the goat had never seen snow either. Bending down, she picked up a handful of snow, packed it into a snowball, and threw it at Buttercup. The goat jumped sideways and fainted dead. Snow puffed around her as she hit the ground.

Shaking her head, Millie picked up the goat, shivering as snow from Buttercup's fur soaked her bodice and chilled her chin. In the cabin, she set Buttercup on her quilt and barred the door.

The women in town had told her once the snow arrived, it stayed until spring. Millie stared out her window, wondering if she was ready, hoping whoever had threatened her was long gone. After a quiet month, she'd come to hope he'd been frightened off, either because he now knew she was armed or because of the protective attentions of the townsfolk.

The morning she'd found the dead chicken, Millie knew she needed help. In town, she found Mr. Whitlatch and the other members of the miners' court in Mr. Diefendorf's saloon discussing the Espinosas' latest killing. Desperation drove her into the establishment, but she stopped short when she noticed the lawman's arm in a sling. Silently she tried to back out, but Mr. Whitlatch spotted her and waved her over. After he introduced her to the other men, Millie politely asked about his arm.

"An unfortunate hunting accident."

Hunting chickens, Millie wondered?

Millie was too flustered to lie so she recounted the intruder's two visits, watching Mr. Whitlatch for any sign of guilt. He acted incensed, as did the other men and by the time she returned to her cabin, every person in town knew of her troubles. She'd been home less than an hour when Mr. Poor arrived with his belongings, ready to protect her "in bed and out." Mr. Shumate, Mr. Turck, and Mr. Tappan helped dissuade Mr. Poor, but all four, along with several of the married men, Mary, and Charlotte Card began visiting Millie several times a day. From that day on Millie barred her doors, even during the day, and waited for a guest's visit before fetching anything from her root cellar.

Millie pulled down ingredients for sourdough bread, enjoying the feel of the dough as she kneaded it. While the bread baked, Millie fed the chickens and Buttercup, brought firewood in to dry, and completed other morning chores until the sweet smell of fresh bread filled the cabin. Setting out two plates—wondering which suitor she'd see this morning—Millie removed the sourdough loaf and set it on the table. Within a minute someone knocked on the door. The men loved her bread-making habit, but Millie had no idea how they managed to arrive precisely when the hot bread came out of the oven. Maybe they stood outside until they could smell it? Opening the door, Millie found Mr. Shumate waiting, soot smeared across his chin and neck.

"I come to see, lassie, if you be done mourning yet?" he asked, as he did every time they met. He glanced into the cabin and sniffed loudly. "I've made some nails, to fix the loose shelf you mentioned, and brought some oats for the chickens and wee goat." Of all her suitors, Buttercup liked Mr. Shumate the best, probably because he alone brought her treats. Millie wasn't certain if the man liked Buttercup, or if bringing her food was some sort of Scottish tradition. More likely, he wanted to fatten "the wee goat" for a future meal.

"How kind of you, Mr. Shumate, and I *am* still in mourning." She knew if she didn't say it immediately, he'd drop to his knees and propose. "But it would please me if you would join me for a slice of bread and some raspberry preserves."

"Aye, I'd like that, lassie." He stepped inside and reached into a pocket, handing Millie a package. "Mrs. Gilson sent butter. Says her cows are drying up and this may be the last for the season." From another pocket he removed a newspaper. "Mr. Tappan sent this *Daily Rocky Mountain News*. It's a wee bit old, but he knew you'd want it. Said there were also pages from a *Harper's Weekly*. Used as wrapping round some goods he received, so they're a bit mangled."

"Thank you kindly, Mr. Shumate." Eager for any news, even weeks old and torn up, Millie happily took the newspapers. During her first month in Idaho Springs, she'd hiked to Mr. Tappan's store just to read whatever paper he'd received. Old Shakespeare was always happy to give her his older Denver City newspapers—*The Daily Commonwealth* or *The Rocky Mountain News*. Every once in a while, like now, he'd get a couple pages of *Harper's Weekly*, the so-called "Journal of Civilization," or *Frank Leslie's Illustrated Newspaper*. Once her suitors caught on to her "newspaper obsession," as they called it, they began bringing newspapers with them when they visited.

She flattened out the pages of the *Harper's Weekly* while Mr. Shumate removed his boots, coat, hat, and gloves. Later with Mary she'd read every page, but for now Millie satisfied her curiosity by scanning the headlines. The British had used another pirate vessel to prey on American commerce. Knoxville had been captured and Charleston was still under siege. Mr. Tappan had circled a story about England celebrating Shakespeare's tercentenary birthday. Only he would consider *that* important news.

Known for its illustrations, this *Harper's Weekly* showed the horrors of the war with a picture of a battle-torn town accompanying a story about the destruction of Lawrence, Kansas. The War had not improved for the South, but both sides were suffering terribly. *How much longer could it last*, Millie wondered? *What kind of resolution was possible with so much hate on both sides?*

Millie's thoughts were interrupted as Mr. Shumate sat down and, without preamble, slathered a generous helping of butter and preserves on a thick slice of bread. Putting the newspapers aside, Millie joined him at the table. Mr. Shumate didn't read the news—Millie wasn't sure he could read, which was in his favor. Only a literate man could have written those threats. Even without this, Millie felt certain Mr. Shumate couldn't be her intruder. He was too kind and she loved listening to him tell stories with his strong Scottish burr.

"Did I mention, lassie, the Indian fight I witnessed while traveling west?"

On other visits Mr. Shumate had told her about his family. They'd arrived from Scotland when he was thirteen and immediately migrated to Ray County, Missouri. Before they could settle, both his parents died of cholera, leaving him and his five siblings to fend for themselves. He—because of his size—found work as a blacksmith's apprentice and helped support his siblings until his sisters were married. In 1860, he traveled to the Colorado territory, driving a team of six yoke of cattle, eventually ending up here.

"An Indian fight? No indeed, you have not, sir." Millie cut two thick slices from the loaf, refilled her tea and his coffee, and settled down expectantly.

"Aye. It was spring of 1860, while I was traveling west. On the way I stopped in Little Blue River, Nebraska, to visit an Indian village." He paused to enjoy another mouthful of bread and butter.

"Why, Mr. Shumate, were you visiting an Indian village?"

"Thought I might do some trading, lassie. But I wasn't actually in the village, just standing in a grove of trees nearby. Always best to determine if Indians be friendly."

Mr. Shumate took another bite, allowing Millie to ask a question. "How do you tell if they're friendly? I've heard most aren't." Newspapers described terrible massacres and killings, leaving Millie, like most white settlers, terrified of the West's *red devils*.

Mr. Shumate shrugged. "Don't know, lassie. That's why I was standing there. Good thing I'm slow at deciding, since all of a sudden eight or ten bucks charged out of the trees opposite me. They was whooping and hollering, riding them horses round the tepees, shooting arrows. Not a one of them boys held their horses' ribbons—they needed both hands to shoot them bows—but them Indian ponies seemed to go just where the rider wanted." He shook his head. "Them bucks didn't look like Indians I'd seen before, like the ones hanging round the settlements. These had faces painted spooky-like; even the horse's faces were painted."

"The horse's faces were painted?"

He looked at her earnestly. "Och aye, lassie. War paint. And you wouldn't believe the noise them bucks made. Horses running everywhere, arrows flying in both directions. Seems to me both sides were in total confusion, but that weren't the case.

"Suddenly, one of the bucks charged straight into the center of the tepees, his horse jumping over anything in his path. He grabs a squaw, pulls her up beside him, and dashes out, letting out a blood-curdling cry. Och! The lad could yell! Sounded almost like a wolf's howl. Poor squaw flopped around on his horse like an empty gunnysack, probably fainted just from the buck's howl." He sipped his coffee and grinned. "After he grabs her, all the painted bucks waved their arms, hollered their war cry, and charged after their leader into the woods and out of sight."

"Oh, my. Did the villagers go after her? To rescue her?"

"I don't know, lassie. After they disappeared, I decided the village might not be so friendly. But I always wondered. Did the buck rescue the squaw or steal her?" He looked up at Millie, helping himself to another slice of bread. "What do you think, lassie?"

Millie wanted to say, "I don't know, laddie," but didn't want to poke fun. Instead, she shrugged her shoulders and helped herself to more bread.

After eating half the loaf, Mr. Shumate fixed her shelf before reluctantly donning his heavy deerskin coat and boots. "Winter's here now, lassie. Will you be needing money for supplies? Och! I'll buy the mine. How about five hundred dollars?"

His price had risen by fifty dollars, but was nowhere near the eight hundred and fifty dollars now offered by

Mr. Ferris. Millie smiled and shook her head. "I thank you kindly, Mr. Shumate, but no. You have a safe day now."

Mary arrived mid-afternoon and they shared a dinner of venison stew—the meat compliments of Mr. Poor. To it they added boiled onions with a cream sauce, and, for a treat, a wild plum pudding, a new recipe from *The Great Western Cook Book* by Mrs. A. M. Collins. The cookbook was a gift from Mrs. Ferris, a quiet bribe in her husband's quest to buy the mine. Still, the cookbook was something Millie was truly pleased to have.

After the meal, Millie and Mary settled down to peruse the newspapers and gossip. Millie had noticed at the funeral Mary was the town outcast, and this reminded Millie of the many times she'd been left out because good society looked down on orphans and servants. This, and Mary's daily assistance, had solidified their friendship.

Absorbed in their conversation, Millie shot to her feet, her heart skipping a beat when the front door flew open. She berated herself for not barring the door as a large man stomped in. He was bundled in a heavy coat, gloves, hat, scarf, and carried an oversized backpack. He dumped his pack on the floor, sending snow everywhere, slammed the door, and unceremoniously began to remove his winter garments.

Millie watched, too shocked at the man's impropriety to immediately voice her displeasure. His large frame filled the space and even though his face was hidden behind a ragged scarf, Millie recognized him. How could she forget the rude man with the tiny ass—burro—she'd almost run over with the stagecoach.

But what was he doing here? Stomping into her home like he owned it. The man looked up at her, grunted something, and bent down to unlace his boots.

Hearing the word "Red" in his grunt, Millie finally found her voice. "What...what, sir, are you doing?"

"Taking off my boots," the man responded gruffly. "My feet are as cold as a rat's—" He paused, glanced at her, and shrugged. "They're cold."

He walked in stocking feet—his big toe protruding from a hole in one sock—and paused to warm his hands over the stove's hot surface. Millie couldn't believe it. None of her suitors had ever behaved so improperly. She stomped her foot indignantly. "Sir, you hafta leave. Immediately!"

He turned and leveled a steady gaze at her. "I knew you were the one when I met you. Still, it wasn't your carte-de-viste you sent. Bet that surprised Johannes!" He shook his head. "Advertising for a wife. Served him right."

Johannes? Her carte-de-viste? Millie was trying to understand his words when he turned, picked up his pack, and strode to the back of the cabin, disappearing into the second bedroom. As if to emphasize he didn't want to be disturbed, he slammed the door behind him.

"I don't believe. I mean. Who does he think he is? He walked in like he owns the place! Who is he?"

"That be Mr. D," Mary said, rising and slipping into her coat.

Millie felt her head spin. Slowly she turned and faced her friend. "Mr. D is dead. We both laid flowers on his grave."

"Mr. D be dead, but he be the other Mr. D."

"The other Mr. D?" *How many Mr. D's were there?*

"He be Mr. Dominic Drouillard. Your Mr. D's younger brother. He built me cabin."

Millie sat down, missed the chair, and tumbled to the ground. Buttercup's eyes widened and rolled back, her legs stiffened and she tipped over, her head landing with a thud on Millie's stomach.

SEVENTEEN

October 9, 1863

He Can't Stay Here

"Mr. Dominic Drouillard? Gracious sakes! My Mr. D didn't have a brother. Did he?" Millie looked at the closed door, her panic rising, and whispered, "Everyone says such nice things about Mr. D. How can *that* man be his brother?"

"Ah, Mr. Double D's all right," Mary said, slipping on her boots. "He bark be worse than he bite. Well, most times."

"How do you know?" In a shriller tone, as realization sunk in, Millie asked, "How do you know that man?"

"He live here last winter," Mary said, grinning as she gathered up her quilting material. "He build me cabin. But since I come, he stay here, with he brother."

"No. Noo. Nooo!" With each word, Millie's voice rose an octave higher and the no's stretched longer. "That is not possible! He can't live here!" Millie looked around wildly. "This is my cabin. That man is no gentleman. He's not even a nice man. Plus, we're not married. We can't share a cabin. It just wouldn't be proper."

"Miss Millie," Mary said in a quiet whisper. "He ain't be here all summer. Mr. D say he brother don't like settle none. He travel all over. Assay ore for miners. He only come here, when weather be cold." She touched Millie's arm. "He don't know Mr. D dead."

Millie's indignation, panic, and alarm instantly died. The man didn't know his brother was dead. That was awful. Worse, Millie would have to tell him. How? Even if he did have the manners of a jackanapes, how could she tell him his brother was dead? Before she had time to consider, the bedroom door opened and he strode into the room.

"I need a bath," he said, stretching. "Been on the road for a good many weeks. Why don't you ladies retire to Mary's and give me a bit of privacy." He nodded to Millie. "I'll send Johannes to fetch you when he gets back from the mine, Red."

Red? Red! Millie almost forgot she felt sorry for the man. He was incorrigible.

"Nice to see you, Mr. D. I best leave. Miss Millie be needing to talk." Mary fled the house.

"Coward," Millie hissed.

"What was that about?" Mr. D asked, poking around the kitchen until he found the left over bread and raspberry preserves. He sliced himself a piece and smeared on preserves. In four quick bites, the slice was gone. "This sure beats pilot bread. At least you didn't lie about being a good cook."

"I never lied."

He looked at her, raising one of his bushy black eyebrows. "Sweetheart, you are *not* the cream-faced darling in that picture you sent. Ah well. Johannes seems to have adjusted. He even bought you a fancy cookstove. Must of found his gold. Heavy stove like this costs a fortune bringing it across the plains."

Every time he mentioned his brother, Millie's indignation died. Still, at some point, she'd need to discuss how he addressed her. She was not Red, nor was she his sweetheart. Clearing her throat, she said, "Mr. D. There's something. I mean, well. I don't know how to say this. It's just—"

"Spit it out woman. I don't remember you having any issue saying exactly what was on your mind. What did you call me?" He paused, his eyes sparkling as he laughed at the memory. "I remember. You said I was the rudest, most unsavory male you ever had the misfortune of laying eyes on." He cut himself another slice of bread and grinned at her. "Bet you never expected me to be the brother Johannes talked about."

"Actually, sir. I'm sorry but Mr. D never mentioned he had a brother. I don't know how to say this, but—"

"Johannes didn't tell you about me? I can't believe it. He can't still be sore. I told him he was a fool to advertise for a wife." He added preserves to a new slice of bread and took a bite. "For once, I believe I was wrong. This is darn good grub. Ah well. I don't hang on formality. We're family. Call me Dom."

"I couldn't possibly, sir. I mean. It wouldn't be proper. We are *not* family!"

The man eyed her, both bushy eyebrows rising. "You're living with Johannes, so he must have married you...Despite the red hair and prickly temper. Makes us family. Brother and sister or some such nonsense."

"Hush up, would you. Mr. D never married me. He died the week before I arrived!" Millie gasped for a breath, immediately regretting her harsh words.

"What did you say?" He stepped toward her, the bread slipping from his fingers.

"I'm so sorry, Mr. D. I was trying to tell you gently, but—"

"What did you say!" he thundered, taking two large strides until he stood directly in front of her.

Millie stepped backward and Buttercup, who'd woken from her faint at his arrival, immediately collapsed again. Picking up the goat, Millie felt safer with the familiar form in her arms. Quietly, she said, "Mr. D I am sorry to inform you your brother is dead."

"Dead?" The thunder in his voice quieted, replaced with a soft disbelief Millie found much harder to hear. "How? How did Johannes die?"

"He died in a mining accident. A cave-in, I was told."

"A mining accident? That can't be possible." The man lowered his head into his hands and rubbed his face. Finally he looked up, his eyes narrowing. "My brother knew how to mine. He always double-checked everything. Shored up walls so they were safe." He violently shook his head back and forth. "Johannes didn't die in a mining accident!"

"I'm sorry, Mr. D. Your brother died the week before I arrived."

The spark of anger died as quickly as it had appeared. Slowly, the big man shrank before her.

"Johannes can't be dead," he whispered, his voice cracking. He covered his face with his hands, turned, and stumbled back to his room. Gone were his powerful movements and overpowering presence. He walked slowly, his shoulders hunched, his feet dragging like an old man. An old, wounded man.

Closing the door with a soft click, he left Millie alone.

Sighing, Millie laid Buttercup on her quilt and did the only thing she knew to do. She cooked. From the root cellar she retrieved the boiled calf's head she'd started earlier in the week and, as it heated on the stove, she mixed butter, sage, pepper, and salt. Once everything was cooked, she chopped the brains and added them to the spicing, skinned the tongue, and trimmed off the roots. Finally, she placed the tongue in the middle of the dish with the brains around it, adding a baked potato and boiled carrots. It wasn't much, but food was the only comfort she knew to offer her grieving guest.

When he finally came out of his room, Millie tried not to notice the puffiness around his red eyes, but there was no way to avoid it. Men like him didn't cry. But he had. He had obviously cared deeply for his brother. She didn't want to, but she couldn't help liking him just a little for it. He sat at the table and ate the food she set in front of him, breaking the silence only to say, "A gourmet meal. Johannes would have liked that."

Normally, Millie loved getting compliments on her cooking, but any man who thought boiled calf's head was a gourmet meal obviously had no refined tastes.

Buttercup, who'd woken from her swoon, timidly approached and head-butted the newcomer in the hip. The man rested a big hand on her tiny head and gently stroked her.

"What happened?" he asked quietly, not looking at Millie.

"I can't tell you much. He died before I arrived." She told him all she knew, finishing with his burial.

"Thanks for making sure he was buried proper."

After eating, he rose and wandered to the fire, settling into the larger rocking chair like it was his. It probably was. Buttercup, as if realizing her importance in providing comfort, followed him over and made sure her head was beneath his hand. Millie cleaned the dishes and put away the food, surprised the silence wasn't more uncomfortable. When dishes were done, she returned to her seat, retrieved her darning mushroom, and began repairing a stocking. It was over an hour later when he broke the silence. "Did they recover his hat and candle holder?"

"His what?"

"His mining hat. It was made of canvas but had a metal candleholder mounted in front. It belonged to our father. Do you know if they found it?"

"Your brother had a coat and hat hanging in his bedroom. I found them when I arrived."

"In the cabin? No, Johannes would never enter the mine without his hat." He paused for a moment and then looked up at her, his voice rising. "Show me what you found."

"One moment, sir," Millie said cautiously, not liking how his voice had changed. She remembered his hair-trigger temper. "His hat was hanging on a nail by my—I mean his—bed." She set her darning aside and rose. "Do you also want to see the clothing I found?" She thought about the knife and sheath and wondered if he could identify them.

"No. Just the hat."

Millie returned with the hat and the carte-de-viste Mr. D had sent her. Her guest spent a long time staring at the image of his brother. "May I have this?" he asked, his voice hoarse.

"Of course, sir."

After several minutes, he set the picture on the floor and looked at the hat. Millie quickly picked up the picture and put it on the table, out of Buttercup's reach. The goat would devour any of Millie's newspapers if she could get hold of them. When Millie returned to her chair, Mr. D was fingering the hat, tapping his finger on the metal bracket as he carefully examined it.

"This was in the bedroom? Hanging on the wall by his bed?"

"Yes, sir," Millie said nervously, not liking his tone.

"Damn!" He rose, startling Millie with the violence of his movements. "Johannes, you stupid fool!" With footfalls that shook the floor, he strode into Millie's bedroom.

"Sir, what are you doing? This is my room now. *What are you doing!?*"

The man acted like he didn't hear her. Instead, he grabbed her bed and dragged it out from the wall. Millie had never moved it. Its weight had been too much for her.

"Johannes found his blasted lode, didn't he? When I left, I thought he was onto something. That's why he ordered you. Fool! Blasted gold wasn't worth his life."

Millie stared, prepared at the least provocation to flee to Mary's cabin. Mr. D had cracked. Grief was one thing, losing one's mind another. She watched him crouch where the bed had been, striking the floor arbitrarily with his fist. "Mr. D, I did find your brother's poke. It was filled with gold nuggets. But it wasn't a fortune."

"What about his stash?"

"H-his stash?"

"This!" the man said, pounding the floor so hard a piece of it dislodged. To Millie's amazement, he lifted off a small, rectangular segment of the floor. "Well blast it!" He reached into the cavity and withdrew a rock. "That's it?"

He rose and stepped back, the rock in his hand. Millie crept forward and lowered her candle into the hole. It was empty, or almost empty, with only a couple rocks lying in the dirt. She was about to pull the candle out when something sparkling caught her eye. Reaching into a corner, she picked up several pinky-sized rocks. Before she could look at them, Mr. D started cursing, causing her to quickly stand and retreat from the hidey-hole.

"This is gold ore, but not particularly high grade." He angrily threw the ore at the wall. Millie dodged the rebound, feeling trapped. The crazy man stood between her and escape. Edging away as far as was possible in the tiny space, she watched as he picked up the ore and stared at it. "Low grade ore. Nothing to murder someone over." He prowled back and forth. "So how'd he pay for the blasted stove?"

"He used these." Millie extended her hand and opened her fist. The tear-shaped gold nuggets sparkled in the candlelight.

The man spun around, looking surprised to find Millie there. "What?" One stride brought him to her side. She quickly tossed one of the nuggets toward him and edged around his bulk. "Humm. Now we're talking gold." Fingering the gold, he followed Millie out of the bedroom. "Strange shape. Smooth. Almost looks like a teardrop. Only time I've ever seen gold like this was from a vug."

"A vug?" Millie asked.

"An underground geode. A hollow nodule lined with gold and other crystals." He rubbed the gold nugget between his fingers. "If Johannes found a vug and was spending nuggets like this…" His face darkened.

“No way Johannes died in a mining accident!” His booming voice cracked against the wall. Millie grabbed her boots and coat, jamming her feet into the shoes. She reached for the front door as Mr. D hollered, “My brother was murdered!”

EIGHTEEN

October 9, 1863
Murder?!?

Murdered? Millie spun around, one hand still on the door handle. She stared at the large man silhouetted in the fire's glow. His clasped fists and furious expression made him look dangerous. She should leave. Stay with Mary. But even as she had the thought, she heard herself say, "Mr. D, you are distraught. Why do you say your brother was murdered?"

Had he been? That might explain the knife. And the threats. Still, now was not the time to cause further distress. Who knew what this cracked mountain man might do? In a composed voice she said, "I understand, sir. Your brother's death is a shock. Please, return my room to order and let us retire to the front parlor."

He shot her a look of disgust. "Retire to the front parlor," he mimicked in a poor imitation of a Southern accent. Shaking his head, he disappeared back into Millie's room. She heard the scraping of the bedposts against the floor. Cautiously she waited until Mr. D strode back into the kitchen. When he paused and sliced another piece of bread from her loaf, Millie decided he'd calmed, at least a bit. She rehung her coat and left her boots handy by the door.

Returning to her chair, Millie cautiously picked up her darning. She kept an eye on Mr. D, watching him carry a new slice of bread to the rocking chair. He ate, rocked back and forth, and brooded as he stared at the tiny gold nugget in his large palm. Millie looked down at the two nuggets in her own hand. They were the size of her pinky and felt solid.

Would someone kill for them?

Oh, yes. In this wild country, she'd learned it took little to provoke one man to kill another. Almost every newspaper included some type of story about men killing for pride, greed, over a woman, or for some imagined slight. If this nugget was pure, it could keep a miner fed for months. But did it mean Mr. D was murdered?

Using her fingers—a technique she'd used to keep track of all the LeGrand children—she began listing off the facts she knew.

Fact one: Mr. D had found gold and Mr. D—

She paused. How to distinguish between two Mr. D's? Glad her unwelcome visitor couldn't read her thoughts, Millie dubbed her fiancé Mr. Pleasant D, and his rude brother, Mr. Impolite D. Not proper, but accurate.

Rearranging her thoughts, she pointed to her pinky.

Fact one: Mr. Pleasant D was dead. Was it because he found a fortune in gold? Mr. Impolite D crazily thought so.

Fact two: Millie had been threatened, twice. Well, three times actually, but surely Mr. Gould and his treasure had nothing to do with Mr. D and his mine. She shook her head, trying to clear it.

"What's the matter?"

Millie ignored him and went back to the facts on her fingers.

Fact three: the person who threatened her had Mr. Pleasant D's knife. Or could the knife have belonged to Mr. Impolite D? She'd have to find out.

Fact four: every man in Idaho Springs, and many in the surrounding towns, wanted to buy Mr. Pleasant D's mine.

"Why are you shaking your head and pointing at your fingers? Makes you look a bit deranged."

"I'm thinking," Millie said, trying to ignore him. Blast it, he'd derailed her train of thought. Was Mr. Pleasant D murdered? Surely if someone had wanted the mine bad enough to kill for it, they would have done more than threaten her. A sudden chill ran up Millie's spine.

Maybe someone was just waiting for the right time.

Looking up, Millie found Mr. Impolite D staring at her, a worried expression on his face. Perhaps he wasn't cracked. At least not about his brother's death. The galoot definitely had an irrational streak, but maybe her fiancé's death hadn't been an accident. "I would appreciate if you could explain once more why you think your brother was murdered."

"You done doing whatever with your fingers?"

Millie rolled her eyes. "Just explain again, please."

He nodded and looked into the fire. In a surprisingly quiet tone, he began. "You said it was a mining accident. A cave-in. Yet his hat was hanging here, in the cabin, where he always left it. No blood stains, no sign of damage. Candle bracket isn't even bent. Johannes would *never* go into a mine without his hat. Thus, someone forced him. Either killing him outright or killing him with the cave-in. Knowing my brother, he wouldn't wait like a sheep to be slaughtered, so I'd guess the former."

"Mr. D, you're accusing someone of murder based on a *hat*? Why in the world wouldn't he enter the mine without that hat?"

Muttering under his breath, Millie thought she heard "redheads" and "fool woman" before he snarled, "Dom. My name is Dom. This isn't a high society ball."

"I'm a Southern lady, Mr. D," Millie said. "Using your given name would be highly improper."

"You're a woman who answered a wife-wanted advertisement." His blue eyes flashed. "Any tart who does that can consent to call me by my name."

"Tart!" Millie jumped to her feet. "You impolite, impossible…" she stuttered. She was so angry she couldn't think of the right insult for the man. "I want you to leave, immediately!"

"No!" Dom crossed his beefy arms and glared at her. Then, like the flip of a coin, his defiance turned to melancholy. "You're stuck with me," he sighed. "At least until I find my brother's killer. To answer your question, a miner, one like my brother, would never enter a mine without his hat. This metal bracket," he picked up the hat and tapped the gold nugget against the twisted metal bracket, "holds either a lard oil lamp or a candle. It lets a miner's hands remain free. Johannes would never go into the mine without a light. He'd never be so stupid."

"Maybe he bought a new hat," Millie said, sitting back down, annoyed by his refusal to leave. "Mr. D had the means. He found these gold nuggets and used them to buy the stove and numerous other items. Mr. Tappan said he—"

"Mr. Tappan," Dom barked out, making Millie jump. The man's voice could be as loud as a cannon blast. "Old Shakespeare. Bet he noticed my brother's newfound wealth. The scoundrel probably recognized the purity in these nuggets too. Did Shakespeare offer to buy the mine?" Before she could respond his eyes narrowed. "It's been over two months. Why aren't you married? A man could get a wife and not have to pay for the mine."

"Is that a proposal?" Millie asked dryly. "I've received more romantic proposals from half dead Yankee soldiers."

He grinned, startling Millie with his white teeth beneath his thick beard. "No proposal. I'm not partial to strong-willed redheads with annoying Southern accents. Although ownership of the mine is tempting."

"My hair is auburn with a few red streaks!"

"Right, and I'm a clean-shaven English remittance man with a title."

He didn't have a title, did he? With this man, she'd believe anything! He was incorrigible. Smiling through gritted teeth, she responded, "Mr. D, I believe you would look much better clean-shaven. The beard and other facial hair make you look…" she paused. She was going to say dangerous, but decided "unkempt" the safer option.

"Unkempt, huh? Well, huh." He tried to run his fingers through his beard, but they got stuck in the tangle. Jerking them free, he said, "Tell me about Old Shakespeare. Did he try to buy the mine? I'd like to narrow down my suspect list."

"Suspect list? Mr. D, I—"

"Dom!"

Millie shook her head and took a deep breath. "Sir. I believe the most logical solution is your brother bought a new mining hat."

"No way. This one was Pa's. Ma gave it to Johannes on her deathbed and made him promise to always wear it while in a mine. No way he'd replace it. Johannes was too sentimental. *And* superstitious." He shook his head, his tangled beard twisting with the movement. "The hat was hanging by his bed. There's no blood or stains on it so it weren't put there by whoever dug him out. Someone knew Johannes struck it rich and murdered him. Now, who's proposed to you? Who wants to buy the mine?"

Millie threw up her hands. "Every eligible man in town, Mr. Drouillard. Plus numerous from adjacent towns. Most married men just offered to buy the mine, although we do have a couple Mormons in the area."

"Huh." He scratched his head. "Who made the highest offer?"

"Mr. Ferris offered eight hundred and fifty dollars a week ago."

"Ferris. Never liked that man. Why didn't you sell? You obviously didn't know about the gold. For that matter, why haven't you married? You answered a wife-wanted advertisement. You can't be picky." His bushy eyebrows rose, emphasizing his glittering blue eyes. "Couldn't forget me, huh, after our meeting at the stagecoach?"

Millie rolled her eyes. Just when she thought the man might have one or two redeeming qualities, he'd say something to confirm he was a total, unrefined galoot. "Do you try to be rude, Mr. D, or does it come naturally?" Before he could answer, she continued. "Just to be clear, I do *not* wish to marry any man, and if I did, you'd be at the bottom of the list. No. *You* I'd remove from the list entirely! My reasons are none of your business. As for selling the mine, I decided yesterday to sell it to Mr. Ferris, when he comes back from Denver City."

"Don't."

It was a command, not a request. Millie wanted to strangle him. "Don't tell me what to do."

"Don't sell the mine. *Please.*" It still sounded like a command. "I want to use it to catch the killer."

"Fine. *I* won't sell the mine if *you* leave and go live somewhere else. You can live in Mary's cabin, and Mary can come live with me."

He rose, tossed the gold nugget to her, and disappeared into his bedroom, returning minutes later with a pile of clothes.

Millie tried not to show too much elation at his departure.

She'd celebrate after he was gone.

Her delight turned to confusion when he set the clothes on the table and filled every pot she owned with water. When he placed the pots on the stove, Millie quickly asked, "What are you doing?"

"Heating water for my bath."

"No!" Millie squeaked. "You can't take a bath. You're leaving, or I'll sell the mine to Mr. Ferris."

He looked at her, his expression bland. "I am *not* leaving and you are *not* selling the mine." He disappeared back into his bedroom and returned carrying her washtub. "Now, being a gentle Southern lady, I expect you'll be heading to your room for the night." He unbuttoned the top button of his shirt, his eyebrows lifting. "Or do you plan to watch?"

Millie felt her face heat. He had to leave. He couldn't take a bath with her in the cabin. What would people say? When he unbuttoned a second button, Millie blurted out, "Where have you been since I last saw you?"

He tilted his head to one side and looked confused. "Why?"

"Just answer my question." Millie prayed he'd stop undressing.

He shrugged. "You heard what happened in Mountain City. Sheriff asked me to join his posse. Took a week to track down one bandit. Found him near Gold Dirt. Searched for the other one but never did find him. The two had split up almost immediately. Unfortunately, first one gave us a fight and ended up riddled with bullets, so he couldn't tell us anything.

"The second outlaw was Mr. Gould."

"What? Who's Mr. Gould? How do *you* know?"

"He came to visit me. I'll explain later."

The big man shook his head, his rough beard swaying. "You just attract trouble, woman!"

"Apparently," Millie said, glumly staring at her guest. "What did you do after you caught the first outlaw?"

"I returned to Mountain City and picked up Columbine. You remember Columbine? My poor burro you almost ran over."

"I did *not* almost run over Columbine!" Could the man not keep a single strand of conversation going without twisting it in knots? "I stopped the runaway stagecoach. I saved Columbine's life."

"Sure," he said dismissively. "So why'd you ask where I've been?"

To distract you from taking a bath, Millie thought, but to him she said, "I wanted to know if you were near Idaho Springs during the first week I was here."

"Course I wasn't. I was heading here when I ran into you. Thought I'd make up with Johannes and come to his wedding. But…" His shoulders sagged. "But that didn't work out, did it?"

Unless he was lying, he couldn't be the one who threatened her. But could she trust him?

He pinched the bridge of his nose with two fingers, as if he had a headache, and absently undid the third button on his shirt.

Millie had no choice. How else could she stop him from taking a bath? "Do *not* take off your clothes, Mr. D. I have something to show you." She rose and hurried into her room.

When she returned, she was relieved to find him sitting in his rocking chair, staring sullenly at the fire, his big hand resting on Buttercup's head. Unfortunately, the top three buttons of his shirt were still undone. Without a word, Millie handed him the threatening note.

"What's this?"

"My second night here, someone broke into the cabin and left this note. The intruder pinned it to the table under this knife." She handed him the knife. "I found the sheath in Mr. D's bedroom. I think it belongs to the knife."

"It does," he said, his voice gruff. "This is Johannes' buck knife. I gave it to him for Christmas last year." His eyes darted from the knife to the note. As he read, all expression left his face and his eyes turned flat.

"You stayed here, alone, after someone broke in and left this note pinned under Johannes' buck knife?"

"Yes," Millie said slowly.

"You're either very brave, or very stupid. Why in the world did you stay?"

Millie hesitated then shrugged her shoulders. "This is my home. Where else would I have gone?"

He gave her a queer look before asking, "Was this the only threat you received?"

Millie shook her head and summarized her visit from Mr. Gould. His eyes widened in disbelief so she shortened her description of the intruder's second visit and the dead chicken.

"Blast it, woman. This is serious. A frying pan. Really? And you closed your eyes when you shot at the chicken coop?" He shook his head and turned his attention to the knife and note.

After several minutes of silence, Millie began feeling uneasy. She thought taking a bath was the worst threat he could make, but this dark silence unnerved her. When he finally spoke, she jumped in surprise.

"Who found Johannes' body?"

"Mr. Shumate, the blacksmith. Mr. D missed their Friday night poker game, so Mr. Shumate went looking for him. He found him at the mine."

"Tomorrow I'll track down Johannes' murderer, and when I do…" He crumpled the threatening note in his fist and rose. "Go to bed, Millie."

"Miss Virginia, please!" When he just glared at her, she quickly added, "Are you leaving?"

"No," he said, unbuttoning his fourth button. "I smell worse than Columbine. I'm taking a bath."

NINETEEN

October 10, 1863
Gold Assay

Millie kneaded her sourdough and thought of the day ahead. This morning she'd woken and been surprised to find the washtub put away, the kitchen clean, and a path in the fresh snow cleared to the privy. The man was neither a slob nor was he lazy. Too bad he was offensive and pigheaded.

On her way back from the privy, she paused to let Buttercup dig through the snow and heard Dom in the small barn, feeding Columbine. He was carrying on a one-sided conversation—his voice actually sounding friendly—explaining to his burro why she wouldn't be seeing Johannes. The simple heartbreak in his words had Millie hurrying back to the house, tears flowing down her cheeks. Not wanting him to see how upset she was, Millie busied herself with making breakfast and cooking two sourdough loaves. If he stayed for the day, she'd need extra.

The bread was just coming out when Dom entered through the back door. As he slammed the door, a knock sounded at the front door. Millie sighed. She could have done without a morning visitor. Wiping her hands on her apron, she opened the door.

"Mr. Turck," she said, wishing it had been any other man. Forcing herself to remain polite, she added, "What a pleasure to see you. Won't you come in?"

He stomped in, sending snow everywhere and after removing his winter clothing, he grasped his beard braids and began squeezing them. Water dripped off their ends as he glowered at Millie. "Widow D," he snarled, "I've decided you're done with this mourning stuff. It's been long enough. We'll marry today. I spoke with Brother Bunce and he's available after we eat."

"Don't marry him, Red. He just wants your mine."

Millie pursed her lips. Mr. D might be right, but such rudeness would not to be tolerated in her home. It was time her unwanted guest learned the proper way to address her, along with some manners. Fisting her hands on her hips, she turned to reprimand him.

No words came out of her mouth.

Dumbfounded, Millie stared at a stranger. He sat, eating her hot bread with gusto, his face clean-shaven, his short hair curling around a broad forehead.

"Mr. D. You have dimples!"

He choked on his bread and swore. "Blast it woman! I knew shaving was a bad idea." His face darkened. "*I do not have dimples!*"

"Hey, Dom," Mr. Turck said, scooting around Millie. "Heard you were in town." He moved to the table and sat down. "Good thing she made two loaves. If I can't get her to marry me, do you have time to assay some ore?"

Millie wanted to scream. One undisciplined galoot was bad. Two was giving her a headache.

"She ain't marrying today," Dom said. "She's still mourning my brother." He paused to slice another piece of bread.

"I thought you only panned placer gold, Titus. Don't you work up near Fall Creek?"

"Mostly." Mr. Turck released one of his beard braids and patted his poke affectionately. "But I been exploring Chicago Creek and found this near an outcropping." He pulled out a fist-size rock and handed it across the table. Millie stepped closer, despite herself. Could she recognize gold ore if she found some? The rock in Dom's hand was white, or maybe opaque, with yellow and gold spots dotting the surface. Even as she glanced at the rock, Millie had trouble keeping her eyes from straying to Dom's face. Without the beard and long, straggly hair, the man was actually pleasant to look at. He had a strong jaw, intelligent blue eyes, and the cutest dimples Millie had ever seen on a man.

As if hearing her thoughts, Dom scowled. Millie wisely transferred her attention to the rock.

"This here is quartz with some crystalline gold imbedded into it." He held it out so Millie could see as he turned the sample over in his hand. "It has potential. Was there more like this?"

"Some." Mr. Turck turned to look at Millie. "We marrying this morning?"

"No, Mr. Turck," Millie said, between clenched teeth. "We are not."

With a grunt, Mr. Turck returned his attention to Dom. "You have time to do the assay?" He opened his poke and withdrew a brown rock the size of a large marble, handing it to Dom. "I found this and thought you might want it for your collection. It can be payment, for the assay."

Dom pulled a magnifying glass from his pocket and held it up to the sample. "Interesting piece of gold wire poking out the top. Never seen one curved like this. Looks like a miniature ram's horn."

Millie inched behind Dom, wondering what gold wire looked like. Before she realized his intent, Dom took her hand, turned it over, and dropped the sample and magnifying glass into her palm. The rock was the size of a Liberty dollar, and on the top a gold wire strand twisted out from the surface. It was tiny, barely visible even with the magnifying glass, but after Millie handed it back, Dom pocketed it and said, "Titus and I will finish eating before I do the assay. What about more coffee?"

He turned, as if dismissing her, and sliced another piece of bread. "Man, this bread is almost worth marrying Red," he said conversationally. "I haven't eaten warm bread since I was a kid. When Johannes and I lived in Jefferson County, Kentucky, Ma made fresh bread every morning."

"Red," Titus responded, chuckling. "I like it."

Millie picked up the kettle and carried it to the table. "More coffee?" she asked politely. Dom's mouth was stuffed full of bread but he grunted and nodded. Millie reached over and refilled his cup, but as she withdrew the kettle, she spilled a thimbleful of the steaming liquid on to his lap.

Bread sprayed across the table as he cried out and jumped to his feet, swiping at the spot.

"How clumsy of me," Millie said. "My apology, Mr. D." She turned to her second guest and smiled. "More coffee Mr. Turck? Oh, and by the way, I don't *ever* wish to be called Red." She lifted her eyebrows. "Is that clear?"

His head bobbed up and down in agreement, his eyes wide. In some instances, Millie decided, ladylike behavior was not effective.

She refilled Mr. Turck's coffee and wiped the table of Mr. D's spittle and bread. He returned to his seat by the time she placed bacon, scrambled eggs, and beans on the table. Taking her seat, she served Mr. Turck and herself before settling down to eat.

If Dom noticed the slight, he said nothing. Instead, he filled his plate and began devouring everything as if he hadn't eaten in months. Millie watched in disbelief as every scrap of food on the table disappeared, including both loaves of bread. After belching loudly and wiping his face with the back of his hand, Dom rose and looked down at Millie. "Red, if you cook like this every morning, maybe I can overlook your temper and flaming red hair." He glanced at Mr. Turck. "You say Brother Bunce is available?"

Millie stood and picked up the kettle, but before she could bring it anywhere near him, Dom grabbed her arm. "Lord, woman," he said, keeping her and the coffee at armslength, "you need to develop a sense of humor. Didn't anyone tell you spilling coffee on your guests is unladylike?"

"Don't *you* dare remind *me* about proper behavior, you uncouth, unkempt, vulgar man." Millie shook she was so angry, but the galoot just released her and quickly walked toward his room.

"I want you out of my home, immediately!" Millie yelled at his retreating form.

"Can't," he said without turning around. "Titus needs an assay on his ore. He paid me with this interesting sample, so I got to do it. You'll need to clear the table." He disappeared, shutting his door behind him.

"That, that…"

"If you marry me, Widow D, I'll make him leave." Mr. Turck pulled out his gun. "I can shoot him."

If Dom was going to get shot, Millie wanted to do the shooting. Picking up a plate, she glared at the bedroom door and over at Mr. Turck. Mr. Turck must have seen murder in her eyes because he quickly rose and retreated near the fire, his hands fisting around his beard braids as he glanced in disgust at Buttercup. The goat lay curled up in her quilt, like a pet dog. Huffing out a breath, Millie turned and put the plate in the washbasin.

The dishes were half done by the time Dom dared return. He glanced at Millie as he set several packages where his plate had been, giving Millie another furtive glance before he carefully began unwrapping each package. One contained an enameled tin case protecting a pocket scale with weights. Another held a heavy-looking mortar and pestle, and the third was a small box filled with individual containers of powders, all well organized and labeled. He returned to his room and brought out three more items: two thick ceramic pots, one of which he placed on the stove and the other on the table. The third item, a dirty, porous cup, he placed beside the scale.

Despite her irritation, Millie's curiosity was aroused. She left the dishes, refreshed her tea, and sat down to watch.

"You gonna do a fire assay?" Mr. Turck asked, returning to the table.

"Course." Dom glanced up as he removed the pestle from the mortar and placed Mr. Turck's white rock inside. "Where'd you say you found the sample?"

"I didn't."

"Of course. But you understand the assay may not represent all the ore in your find."

"Yes," Mr. Turck said as Millie asked, "Why?"

"This is a single sample," Dom said without looking up. He used the pestle and pounded the ore sample into smaller pieces. "The assay is just for this rock. It might have fallen from a higher shelf, or been swept to that location during high rains. A single sample, no matter how good it assays, doesn't mean the area is filled with other high grade ore."

"But it's a damn good indication," said Mr. Turck, his eyes bright. "Begging your pardon for the language, Widow D."

"Thank you kindly for the apology, sir," Millie said, staring pointedly at Dom. He used impolite language all the time and *he* never apologized. Dom just stared back with complete understanding and grinned, making his dimples more prominent. Millie rolled her eyes. "What makes an area high in gold?" she asked. "For that matter, where do you find gold?"

"If we knew the answer to that," Dom responded, lifting his pestle to check the material. "We'd all be rich."

"Okay," Millie said. "How does a prospector decide where to dig?"

"Some, like Titus, find ore and get it assayed. If this assays high, he'll dig out more ore from the area." Dom rechecked the ore in the mortar, mixing it around with his finger.

"Other prospectors pan for placer gold and—"

"Placer gold?" Millie had heard the term from the men she washed for. When they pinched out her payment, they said it was placer gold, but she didn't really know what it meant.

"Gold flakes found loose in a river," Dom said. "It usually flakes loose from a gold vein so if you follow it upstream, you can sometimes find its source." Dom continued to grind the material, occasionally picking up the pestle and tapping it against a larger chunk. "Experienced miners look for rock formations formed in conditions conducive to gold, such as quartz with pyrite, mica, or tourmaline." He stopped his grinding and looked down at the table. Quietly he added, "Johannes followed placer gold upstream till it disappeared and then tossed his hat. He dug where it landed, calling his mine the Lucky Hat Mine." He put down the pestle and rubbed his face. "I thought he was crazy."

In silence, Dom picked up the pestle and continued to grind the ore, checking it from time to time. Finally, he moved the mortar close to the scale and spooned the pulverized material into a dish, carefully adding more powder until the scale was balanced.

"Now what are you doing?" Millie asked, hoping her questions diverted his thoughts from his brother.

"First I crush the sample into a powder and measure out a precise quantity. Next I'll melt it with the flock in my crucible." He took the powder ore from the scale and poured it into the pot on the stove.

"What's a crucible? And flock?"

"A crucible is a type of pot made of special clay so it can withstand the high temperatures needed to melt the ore. Flock is a mixture of chemicals. It's used to get the gold and silver to separate from the other minerals. Each flock mixture is different, depending on the mineral content of the ore."

"That's why most miners round here want Dom," said Mr. Turck. "He's magic at picking out the right flock. His assays are golden." He grinned, showing brown teeth. "Course, it don't hurt none Dom's willing to accept unusual rocks, like my gold wire, as payment."

Golden, huh. Meaning the man had a brain, but why accept strange rocks for pay? Millie remembered the labeled samples in his room, but Dom began selecting jars from his case before she could ask. Like Monsieur Dufilho, the proprietor of the apothecary in New Orleans' French Quarter that Millie had frequented, Dom used his scale to measure precise quantities of each chemical, adding them to the ore powder. He lowered the crucible into the stove's fire chamber, keeping an eye on it until the contents glowed red. Using tongs, he carefully poured the top layer from the hot crucible into the cold crucible on the table. Finally, he poured the bottom of the molten stone into the gray, porous cup.

Without prompting—Millie suspected he was showing off—Dom continued his explanation. "The top mixture holds all the minerals and contaminants we don't care about, but this little button," he pointed at the molten material in the cup, "contains all the gold and silver in the sample."

"Is the gray cup special?" It looked to Millie like something dug out of a trash heap.

"Yep. It's made from bone ash, which absorbs the lead, leaving the gold and silver for me to weigh." He swirled the gray porous cup until he was left with a tiny bead of material. After it cooled he removed it, weighed it with his scale, and it handed to Mr. Turck. "Not bad, but still fairly low grade. You'd need a lot to strike it rich."

Mr. Turck looked at the small gold nugget. "If I dig out several pieces, I'll have enough for a wedding ring." He looked at Millie. "How about marrying tomorrow?"

Before Millie could answer, Dom's voice boomed out. "She ain't marrying you, Titus! She's got more sense! Now, what do you know about my brother's death?"

"I don't know nothing," Mr. Turck answered sullenly, his hands once again fisting around his beard braids. "Heard a landslide hit his mine entrance, snapping some of his support logs. We found him under the rock and timber."

"You found him?" Dom asked, his voice low. Mr. Turck would have to be a fool not to hear the implied threat.

"No. *I* didn't find him. Sooty did. He come back to town and a bunch of us went back up to dig him out."

"Was he found lying face up or face down?"

What a gruesome question. Millie wondered why Dom cared.

"Face down, maybe."

Millie noticed Mr. Turck didn't look at Dom as he answered.

"With his feet facing into the mine or out?"

"Out," Mr. Turck said immediately. "That's how Sooty knew he was under the pile. His foot and boot was sticking out. It weren't pretty."

Millie shuddered, seeing the scene in her mind all too clearly. Dom grunted and reached up to pull his whiskers, realized they were gone and scowled at Millie. Rubbing his bare chin, he asked, "You hear anything about Johannes finding gold nuggets?"

"Course. He didn't say nothing, but you know how he was. He started buying things. Like her and the stove." He nodded toward Millie. "Even bought some new clothes. Said he wanted to look sharp for his wife when she come. A couple weeks before he died, during a card game, I asked if he found a lode. He just grinned, said he couldn't say. Next hand he set a tiny tear-drop shaped nugget on the table for his stake."

Dom scowled and shook his head. "How many people knew he discovered something?"

"You know what kind of town this is," Mr. Turck said, standing up and reaching for his coat. "Ain't nobody who didn't know."

TWENTY

October 10, 1863
Mr. D's Mine

Dom rose and put away his instruments as Millie returned to her breakfast dishes and set beans in a pot to soak. The mundane work let her mind focus on more important things, and she mentally rehearsed her side of the dialogue she planned to have with Mr. D. Along with his deplorable manners, Millie also needed to discuss how long he would remain in her cabin. In New Orleans, a single man *never* stayed alone in the home of a single woman, but this was the Colorado Territory. Rules of social etiquette tended to gray here. Therefore, he could remain a week—a reasonable amount of time considering he was mourning—but any longer would be improper. And no more baths!

"I'm going to take a look at our mine."

"Our mine?" Millie had been so absorbed in her thoughts she hadn't heard him return to the room.

"I'll be back before dark." He sat down to lace his boots.

"One moment. I'm coming with you," Millie said, curious to see the mine she'd heard so much about. She hurried to her room, ignoring Dom's blustering, and slipped on her hat, scarf, and gloves, pausing to look at her revolver. Normally she'd bring it with her, but Mr. D had a way of riling her up. If it was handy, she just might shoot him. Deciding it would be safe in her apron tucked under her coat, she slipped it in and returned to the main room.

"You are not going with me!" he shouted, standing with his hands on his hips, blocking the door.

"Of course we are," Millie said, pulling her heavy coat from a nail and slipping into it. Unlike her unwanted guest, she did not need to raise her voice. She had no doubt she would win the argument.

His clean-shaven face turned a dark purple as he sputtered out, "W-we?"

"I'm sure Buttercup would like to stretch her legs." Without waiting for a response, Millie turned and walked to the back door, calling for the goat. "We'll wait outside."

His expletive was rather creative as he stomped out into the snow, reminding Millie she needed to add his unfortunate habit of using inappropriate language to her growing list. Ignoring his rude insinuation that she wouldn't be able to make the climb, Millie followed him past his brother's grave and into the woods, Buttercup romping happily behind.

"Blasted goat's going to be eaten by a wild critter. There's wolverines, bruins, even lions in these mountains."

Millie wasn't sure what a wolverine was, but there were other, more pressing items, to discuss. Clearing her throat, she said, "Mr. D, I believe we need to discuss—"

"Dom, woman. My name is *Dom*! Mr. D was my Pa."

"Well, yes. As I was saying sir, we need to discuss your language. The cursing hasta stop. It's simply not acceptable. And no more nicknames. Miss Virginia, if you please." He didn't respond, although he did flap his arms in a strange way. Millie wasn't sure the movement indicated agreement, but she chose to interpret it as such. Perhaps she should wait a bit before tackling other items on her list. Taking a deep breath of the cold air, Millie turned her attention to the path and her surroundings.

The scenery was stunning. The flowers and colors of fall were gone, replaced by clean, sparkling white. Fresh snow covered the evergreens, their boughs sagging slightly under the weight. They walked in silence, the blanket of white muffling their footsteps. Millie recognized the trail they were following beside Spring Gulch; she and Mary had picked strawberries and raspberries here in the fall. They entered unfamiliar terrain when Dom turned and headed uphill along a smaller tributary.

"Just as I thought," Dom said, stopping and squatting in the snow.

"What's that?" Millie asked, relieved for a moment's rest, hoping Dom hadn't noticed her heavy breathing.

"Footprints in the snow."

"You believe someone's been exploring my mine?"

"Yep."

"Who?"

"That ass, Titus."

Millie hid a smile behind her hand but didn't correct the improper language. She couldn't agree more. Still, until they determined it was Mr. Turck, she felt it prudent to change the subject. "What are your views on the war, sir? Are you a Copperhead?"

"A what?"

"A Yankee opposed to the war effort?"

"A Copperhead," Dom said. "Sounds like a goldarn snake. I am not opposed to the war. I just find the whole mess a terrible waste of life."

"Is that why you stay here instead of returning to the States? You don't want to fight?"

"I've fought in this war," he said, sounding defensive. "Because of our gold, both sides have been recruiting in the Colorado Territory. They want us to *finance* the darned war."

Millie hadn't heard about this, but she wasn't surprised. Several newspapers she'd read—on both sides—had mentioned the huge monetary cost of the war. "Which side does the territory support?"

"The Colorado Territory is Union land. We've fought to keep it that way."

"Fought? There have been no battles here."

"Maybe not in the Colorado Territory, but in '61 Johannes and I joined the 1st Colorado Volunteers to support the Union after the Rebs organized the Confederate Arizona Territory. Last spring we fought in a battle near Apache Pass under Captain Wynkoop."

"A battle in the Colorado Territory?" Newspapers had never mentioned battles out West. "When did this battle take place? Who was fighting whom?"

"Apache Pass is in the New Mexico Territory, but the battle was in defense of Colorado gold. Texas rebels under the command of Walking Whisky Keg captured Albuquerque and Santa Fe. They were headed to Fort Union to capture its go—"

"Walking Whisky Keg?" Millie asked with a touch of sarcasm. "Really, Mr. D. Do you assume I'm uneducated or just uninformed? There isn't a confederate leader with such a name."

He turned and glared down at her. "You're a pain in the ass, Red. Walking Whisky Keg is the nickname for rebel General Sibley—it's said the man is never sober. The nickname comes from his own men."

"Language," Millie said. "And I'm Miss Virginia to you!"

Dom grinned and reached out, surprising Millie when he tugged on her braid. "Yes, ma'am. Miss Millie Virginia."

Millie slapped his hand away. The man was impossible.

"The fight at the pass, Mr. D. Please explain what happened?"

"The 1st Colorado Volunteers, led by Col. John Slough, joined the New Mexico Volunteers and went to stop old Whisky Keg and his men. We met in Apache Canyon in March of '62." He paused and gazed at the mountains, his expression distant. "Johannes and I were part of an advanced unit that surprised the rebels. That first fight raged most of the day, but we pushed them back."

Millie heard the pride in his voice. She couldn't imagine fighting a war, killing, and seeing your friends killed.

"The next day we gathered our wounded and buried our dead," Dom continued. "Not sure why we waited for the next battle—guess they wanted the entire force there. Anyway, when Col. Slough arrived, he sent the Fighting Parson…" Dom paused and scowled down at Millie. "That'd be Col. Chivington." He hesitated, daring Millie to comment. She wisely refrained.

"Anyway, he took a couple hundred of us around to attack the rear flank. After marching all night, we couldn't find the blasted rebel army. Luckily, we accidently came across their supply train instead. Fool rebels left it poorly guarded—much to our elation. As I'm sure you know," he added with a touch of sarcasm, "an army can't survive without its supply train. Johannes and I wanted to rush down and destroy it, but for whatever reason, it took over an hour for Chivington to decide to attack." He shook his head. "We were lucky the main rebel army didn't reappear. Course at the time, we didn't know they were engaged in attacking Slough's forces at the pass." He shrugged. "Eventually we did destroy it, forcing the rebels to retreat back to Santa Fe. Good thing, since Col. Slough's day of battle didn't go so well."

"Have there been other battles?"

"The 1st Colorado Infantry got reorganized into the 1st Colorado Cavalry. They're charged with guarding the Colorado Territory but thus far, they've only fought a couple skirmishes with some Utes, Kiowas, and Comanches."

"Why aren't you still fighting with them?"

His clean-shaven face reddened. "Got injured and discharged," he grunted. Spinning around, he stomped up the trail. Millie wondered what kind of injury would cause such embarrassment. On the *Sultana*, she'd changed bandages on numerous gruesome injuries, amputations, and infected wounds. Her patients had been in too much pain to be embarrassed. Millie looked up and down the man's sturdy frame. She didn't see any obvious damage.

"With your Southern accent," he said, not even breathing hard as he climbed, "I'd expect you to support the rebels, but after seeing you with Mary, I'm not so sure. Which side are you on?"

"Does it matter, Mr. D?" Millie asked, her own breathing ragged. "Women can't vote. We have no say in the politics that kill our husbands and sons."

"But you do have an opinion."

"Of course. Although I doubt men will ever allow a woman to voice her opinion. Much less give us the vote." She shaded her face and looked up at his broad back. He climbed effortlessly, his movements confident. "Why do *you* support the Union?"

"I support the United States' lawfully elected president, Mr. Lincoln. Even if I didn't, I've never believed one person should own another. I've met both Indians and colored folks with more integrity than..." He paused and pointed. "Than a white scoundrel like that."

In the clearing ahead, Millie saw Mr. Turck dumping a bucket of tailings from a mine in the side of the hill. Not twenty feet away she spotted the tailings and crushed lumber from another mine. "Mr. D's?"

"Yep. I thought Turck's ore looked familiar." In a booming voice he yelled, "Titus, you ass, did you murder my brother so you could jump his claim?"

TWENTY-ONE

October 10, 1863

The Dangerous Rocky Mountains

I didn't kill nobody," Mr. Turck yelled, dropping his bucket of tailings as Dom charged him. Mr. Turck raised his fists and ran forward, his braided beard flapping as he met Dom head-on.

Their bodies collided with an echoing thud. Millie cringed, watching them grapple, their fists swinging wildly. They twisted and turned, so close it almost looked like they were engaged in some strange, exotic dance. Suddenly Mr. Turck stepped back and swung hard, his fist connecting with Dom's face. Dom's head snapped up, and he tottered backwards.

"Dom! Watch out!" Millie's warning was too late. Dom's foot struck a timber and he stumbled backward, landing hard on his back. Mr. Turck let out a triumphant yell, jumped forward and kicked Dom in the side. He pulled his foot back to kick again and Millie let out a furious cry. She charged forward, but only took a couple steps before Dom grabbed Mr. Turck's boot and twisted hard. In an instant, Turck was on the ground and Dom was on top of him.

Dom pummeled the smaller man until he yelped for mercy. With a final blow, Dom stood up and stepped back. Bloodied and beaten, Mr. Turck scrambled to his feet and stumbled past Millie, sending her an evil look.

"Come on back," Dom shouted, "if you want a little more. Next time I catch you at our mine, I won't let you walk away."

Below her, Mr. Turck stopped and spun around. "I'll get even with you, Dom." Blood and spittle accompanied his words. He glared at Millie. "You too, Widow D. I'll make sure you're sorry you chose him over me."

"You ever touch her," Dom said, his voice dangerously low as he walked over and stood beside Millie. "And I'll kill you. Now get."

Mr. Turck's eyes blazed, but Millie saw fear as well as rage. She'd never cared for Mr. Turck but, until today, she'd never believed he was a killer. He turned and lurched down the trail.

"He could have murdered your brother. I saw it in his eyes."

"Could have." Dom wiped his bloody lip with his sleeve. "Knocking someone out and using a landslide to kill is the act of a coward. Turck fits the bill."

"You believe your brother was buried alive?" Millie shuddered, looking at the rubble pile blocking Mr. D's mine. She couldn't imagine a worse way to die.

"They found him face down with his feet pointing out of the mine. Way I see it, someone struck him from behind before burying him." His words were harsh, but also slightly garbled.

"Mr. D, you look awful." Dom's lip was beginning to swell, his knuckles were bloody, and his woolens poked through a rip in his trousers. "Are you hurt?"

He grunted in response.

"Perhaps we should head back to the cabin."

"No," he said gruffly. "I'm fine. Just a scratch. I want to look around." He took a step, winced, and rubbed the side where Mr. Turck had kicked him. "I knew Turck was a coward, but who'd have thought he'd resort to kicking a downed man?" Suddenly, his annoyed expression lightened and he grinned at Millie, looking a bit loopy.

"What?"

"You called me Dom." He looked like a kid who'd swiped a handful of cookies.

Millie shook her head. "Mr. Drouillard, I think your head struck a rock when you fell."

His grinned disappeared. "You are one stubborn redhead."

"May I remind you, my hair is auburn with a few red streaks," Millie responded tartly.

"Your hair is as flaming red as a good sunrise. I like it. What do you have against redheads?"

Millie blushed but then scowled. "Everyone considers them stubborn and temperamental."

"That doesn't describe you at all," he said, laughing as he turned his attention to the mine.

Millie followed his gaze, taking in the broken timbers and boulders that completely blocked the mine's entrance. Dom stepped closer and Millie followed, her unease increasing the closer she got. How could anyone work underground in a cold, dark cave? As far as she was concerned, it wasn't natural to spend any time beneath the cold ground, at least not while one was alive.

"Stay back," Dom said, walking around the landslide and scrambling through the snow up the slope to the right. "And mind the goat."

Millie quickly herded Buttercup back until they stood near Mr. Turck's digging. Dom scaled the hillside above the mine, climbing high enough that if he fell, he'd break his ornery neck. Thirty feet above the mine, he stopped and kicked at a large boulder. On his third kick, the boulder tumbled free, knocking loose other stones and snow as it crashed down the hill.

"That's how he buried the body," Dom yelled as the noise from the rockslide quieted. "The landslide would have killed Johannes, if he wasn't already dead."

Millie shivered. She hoped Mr. D had been unconscious or dead before the rocks crushed his body.

Dom, agile as a goat despite his injuries, scrambled down the rocky hillside and once again approached the mine entrance. He stood and stared at the rock pile, his face unreadable.

"I'm going to open it."

Millie shook her head. Leave it to a *man* to come up with such an absurd idea. Even though *she* owned the mine and hadn't given him permission, she knew Dom would do whatever he wanted. She doubted logic would help, but she could at least try. "If you open it, sir, others can get in and find whatever Mr. D found."

"Nobody'll bother the mine now. Not after Titus starts drinking and tells the townsfolk of his beating. Plus, I'll be here daily to work the claim."

"But Mr. D. You'll only be staying a we—" Her words were lost as Dom picked up a small boulder and sent it crashing down the tailing pile. Other rocks and debris soon followed, making conversation impossible.

Millie knew she'd lost the argument, even though there hadn't been a discussion, but for now she let it go. Later she would address his notion of opening and working her mine, not to mention his implied assumption of living with her indefinitely.

Millie looked down and rubbed Buttercup's ears. "Shall we go exploring, Miss Buttercup, and let the idiot man throw rocks down the hill?"

Buttercup bleated.

They scrambled over the tailing pile—skirting around Dom—and followed a hint of a trail past a boulder the size of a cabin. The trail came out above a steep meadow surrounded by dwarf, twisted evergreens. Pausing to catch her breath, Millie admired the breathtaking view. Below was Spring Gulch and her cabin, although Millie couldn't see it. Beyond was Idaho Springs where Fall River broke up the ridgeline and Clear Creek wound through the wide valley. Far to the right, steam rose from the hot springs up Soda

Creek. Everywhere she looked, tailing piles cascaded down from individual mining claims.

The Sweet Water Mountains surrounded the valley, their jagged ledges cutting through the deep blue sky. Once these towering mountains had made her feel closed in and trapped, but sometime during the past two months she'd come to love the wild beauty of her adopted home.

Buttercup edged around her and walked several feet along the steep incline, her head cocked to one side. She bleated and climbed down lower. Alarmed, Millie hurried after her, catching sight of the long-haired mountain goats at the same time she caught hold of Buttercup's bandana collar.

"Silly girl, they're three times your size." The goat strained against her hold. "Are you lonely, sweet pea? I'm sorry. But you can't join them. Still, we can sit and watch a bit." Knocking snow off a nearby rock, Millie sat down, pulling Buttercup onto her lap. Together they watched the wild goats scurry across the uneven footing, leaping down onto narrow ledges and dangerous precipices with the grace of dancers.

Buttercup tried to pull free, but Millie held tight. Her little goat wouldn't have a chance in the wilderness. As the mountain goats disappeared, Millie rose and placed Buttercup in front of her, nudging her toward Dom and the mine.

Buttercup planted her feet and refused to take a single step. After a minute-long battle, Millie stopped and frowned down at the goat. "Dom's the one making all the racket. He won't hurt you."

She urged the goat forward, but Buttercup remained immobile, her eyes focused on the large rock they'd passed. Millie wiped the sweat from her brow and followed the goat's gaze.

The glittering eyes of a Rocky Mountain lion met her gaze.

The tawny cat crouched on the boulder in front of them, its tail twitching, its yellow eyes fixed on Buttercup.

"Oh, Lor'," Millie said, carefully skirting around Buttercup so she stood between the goat and the lion. "Go away. Shoo!" She waved her arms at the large animal.

The cat's hindquarters rose, its tail suddenly quiet. Without warning it let out a bone-chilling cry and leapt from the rock. Millie screamed and jumped back, her heel striking Buttercup.

The Rocky Mountain lion crashed into her and together they tumbled backward and rolled down the hill. The cat snarled and twisted, biting and scratching as they rolled over rocks and crashed through branches of twisted evergreen trees.

Millie shoved the snarling animal away, frantic to break free, but their motion held them together like lovers. Pain exploded in her shoulder when the cat bit through her coat and ripped open her skin. Millie cried out, but her shriek was cut short when the cat's body struck a rock and their motion came to an abrupt stop. Millie slammed into the animal, her breath knocked out of her. The cat snarled, twisted out from beneath her and bounded down the valley.

Millie lay still, struggling to breathe, too stunned to move. Was she dead? Surely death wouldn't hurt this much. Her hip and back ached and one ankle felt like someone was twisting it, but it was the fiery pain in her left shoulder that numbed her mind. She felt blood running down her arm and could see red staining the white snow. Taking shallow breaths, she tried to fill her aching lungs.

"Millie! Oh my God." Dom's big hands gently rolled her onto her back. "Oh, God. Millie, you're a mess. Where are you hurt?" His hands gently probed her body.

Despite the pain, Millie was mortified. Gasping in a half-breath, she whispered. "Stop. Don't touch me. It isn't proper." She batted weakly at his hands, trying to use her one good arm to stop his roving fingers.

"Thank goodness! If you still insist on proper behavior, you can't be hurt too bad, can you? I need to get you to the cabin." He carefully slid his hands under her and lifted. The movement caused new pain to shoot through her shoulder and back. Millie cried out, the impropriety of his actions forgotten.

"It's okay, honey. We'll get you back to the cabin and have Doc Noxon take care of you. Just hold on." He pulled her against his chest, resting her head on his big shoulder. "I'll get you home." He carefully carried her over rocks and around trees toward the trail.

With each jarring step, new aches and pains shot through Millie's body. In a haze, she remembered and whispered, "Buttercup?"

"Blasted goat is following right behind me." As if in reply, Buttercup bleated. "Next time, let the lion eat the goat. It wouldn't have bothered you."

"I couldn't let it eat Buttercup," Millie said slowly, her voice cracking as tears streaked her face.

"Course you couldn't, honey. Don't you worry. I'll get you back to our cabin. Mary can tend you while I get Doc Noxon."

"Don't call me honey," Millie slurred, "I'm Miss Virginia to you."

TWENTY-TWO

October 13, 1863
You—You Miscreant

Millie opened her eyes to find Dom's face so close she could see the texture of his skin and feel his warm breath on her cheek. She jerked back, but a pillow stopped her movement, forcing her to take a close look at his swollen, purple lip. It was quite unpleasant. She tried to push away, but gasped as pain shot through her shoulder. What had Dom done to her? Groaning, she closed her eyes.

"Easy, honey," he said.

"I told you…not to…call me *honey*," Millie said slowly, her voice sounding uneven and husky, her throat parched. Why were her lips dry and cracked? In a whisper, she opened one eye and added, "It's Miss Virginia."

The ends of his mouth twisted up, although she noticed he had shadowy rings under his eyes and dark stubble covered his face. The man did not look good.

"I never thought I'd be so happy to hear you gripe at me." He gently touched her cheek. "Welcome back, Red." Before Millie could respond, he stood up and stretched. "I'll fetch you some hot tea with honey. You sound terrible."

Millie watched him leave, trying to remember why she felt so awful. How had she come to be in bed? She was in bed! What was Dom doing in her bedroom? Her thoughts wouldn't quite solidify. The mountain lion. That's right. Dom picked her up, but after, it was like a dream filled with images and half-remembered words. Doc Noxon. Yes, his face and his voice. Mary. Had Mary been crying? She tried to remember.

Like a repeating nightmare, she opened her eyes to find Dom's face once again hovering inches above hers. Jerking away, she groaned as new spikes of pain radiated out from her shoulder. "Don't do that." She meant to yell it in her crossest voice, but instead it came out in a croaked whisper.

"Let's see if we can get some tea down you before you drift off again." Gently he lifted her head with one big hand and held the cup to her lips with the other. "Doc Noxon says to feed you chicken soup and sweet tea."

Millie opened her mouth to object and Dom poured the liquid down her throat. She coughed, spilling some of the tea, but as soon as her coughing fit stopped, he continued pouring. "I hate cold tea," she grumbled when he put the empty cup on the floor. He nodded and set her head back down before picking up a corner of her quilt to dab at the spills on her face and neck.

"Don't do that! It takes half the morning to wash this quilt." At least her voice sounded almost normal.

"That's my Red. I'll make some more."

"Make it hot!" she called to his retreating back, deciding it was too much work to reprimand him on the blasted nickname.

Next time she opened her eyes, she found Dom rocking quietly, his head resting on the hard wooden back of his rocking chair, his eyes closed. He looked dreadful. Besides the fat lip and scruffy growth of beard, his knuckles were bruised and scabbed. He reminded Millie of the time she'd stayed with Carissa during Carnival, and Coilen, Carissa's husband, had staggered in the door supported by his "mates," smelling of Bourbon Street. That was the only time she ever saw her friend lose her temper.

"Mr. Drouillard. Have you been drinking at Mr. Diefendorf's saloon?" Millie asked crossly.

He opened one eye and surveyed her. Millie couldn't help but admire the color of his eye; it reminded her of a cloudless Colorado sky. "Dom," he admonished quietly. "And no, I haven't been drinking." He sounded tired. "But I will, soon. More tea?"

"Drinking is despicable. Is the tea hot?"

"It was two hours ago when I brought it in." Without asking permission, he again lifted Millie's head, careful not to disturb her injured shoulder, and poured the liquid down her throat. This time Millie managed to drink more than she spilled, but she could feel a bit dripping down the side of her neck. He removed the cup and used a dishrag to dry her throat. At least the man could be trained.

Through the thin rag, Millie felt the warmth of his fingers and when he finished, she felt those fingers brush her collar bone. Her skin! She shivered, mortified, realizing she was no longer wearing her dress. Was she wearing anything?

"Where are my clothes?" She blushed all the way down to her toes. "What have *you* done? Take your hand away, immediately!"

He grinned and removed his hand, very, very slowly. His fingers brushed against her throat and cheek, and his eyes sparkled at his devilment. Feeling both furious and embarrassed, Millie used her good hand to pull the blanket up over her chin. The slight motion caused her eyes to water from the pain. "You hafta leave, immediately! Mr. Drouillard. This is…It's entirely improper…I—"

She froze, too shocked for words. Someone had undressed her! "Did *you* remove my clothes? You—you—miscreant!"

Dom stood and rolled his shoulders, looking not the least perturbed by her discomfort or insults. "Honey, when I take off your clothes, it'll be something you remember." He smiled and his tired expression changed to something mischievous. "Don't worry your head none this time. I got Mary as soon as we got back. She undressed you and put you to bed while I ran, and I mean ran, and got Doc Noxon. I'm still tending the blisters on my toes."

Millie felt marginally better, but still…she *was* in bed. In the presence of a man. This was a situation definitely not covered in the *Ladies' Book of Etiquette*. It was a position no lady would permit! "Mr. D, I insist you leave. At once. And you must not return. A man should never be in the bed-chamber of a lady while she is in…I mean…It's not proper! I'm not…" She struggled to find a polite way to refer to her state of undress.

Instead of heeding her words, the insolent man bent down and kissed her!

On the mouth!

The kiss was fleeting, just a brief touch, but his warm lips made Millie feel quiet peculiar.

"Mr. Drouillard!" she stuttered, when he lifted his face. "How dare you!? Taking advantage of a helpless lady is cowardly. You are no gentleman!" Her voice shook with confused indignation. "I insist you leave my cabin and never return!"

He grinned, looking not the least repentant. Whistling, he picked up her teacup and swaggered from the room, glancing back at Millie. "You sure are cute when you get riled. I'll go make some hot soup." He laughed and left the room.

Cute when riled? How dare he? The degenerate, uncouth…She was so rattled she couldn't decide what she should call him. Why had he kissed her? She could still feel the warmth of his lips on hers.

Once, in New Orleans, she'd been kissed, but Dom's kiss felt different. Working for the LeGrands, she'd never been permitted to go out walking, much less have a beau, but the butcher's son had offered a batch of fresh shrimp for a kiss. It'd been highly improper—no lady would have agreed—

but Millie loved shrimp and could never afford if for herself. Plus, she'd been curious. Carissa told her Coilen's kisses made her tingle all the way down to her toes. Millie didn't believe it. She'd permitted the butcher's son's forwardness, although he had to climb two stairs in order to reach. He'd dragged her face to his by tugging on her braid and planted his wide, wet lips against hers, making a loud slapping noise. His lips had felt soft and squishy, sort of like a fish left too long in the sun, but without the smell. Fortunately, all she had to do was stand up straight to end the unfortunate encounter. She'd found the kiss disappointing, but the shrimp had been excellent.

Her face heated as she remembered Dom's kiss. His lips had felt neither soft nor squishy, but warm and firm. She blushed and felt a tingle all the way down to her toes! What was wrong with her? Her thoughts continued to churn uncomfortably until she heard Mary rush into the cabin.

Flushed, Mary shook snow from her hair as she skidded into Millie's bedroom. "Mr. Dom say you awake and be bossin' him round." She dropped to her knees beside Millie's bed. "Oh Miss Millie, you scare me bad! You all right?"

"I was not bossing him around! The man is an uncouth oaf. A cad with no manners. I want him out of my home immediately. He's, he's…" Millie trailed off as she noticed tears streaming down Mary's face. "Whatever's the matter, Miss Mary?"

"Doc Noxon say you might die." Mary swiped at a tear and grasped Millie's hand. "Mr. Dom and me, we be scared. For two day you thrash 'bout. Talk fever crazy." More tears streamed down her face. Squeezing Millie's hand, she took a deep breath and smiled slightly. "In your crazy talk, you describe Mrs. LeGrand and how she pretend faint. She really faint every week? And what 'bout little Mr. Rufus. What that little boy do with them grits? Even half crazed, you blush bad."

Millie cursed as she felt a blush working its way up her face. She hadn't thought of Rufus LeGrand and his grits in years. Carissa had laughed until tears streamed down her eyes when Millie asked for advice on how to stop the one-year old from taking his warm grits and squishing them into the front of his diaper. The look he got as he squirted the warm grits around his little boy parts was unnatural!

Not willing to discuss such things, Millie asked instead, "I was unconscious for two days? What do you mean I almost died? Surely you exaggerate."

Mary shook her head from side to side, so violently her wiry hair whipped across her face. "You shoulder turn red and streaky. You start burning up with fever. Mr. D and me. We take turns. For two day and two night we clean you shoulder. Keep cold rag on you forehead. We both exhausted when you fever finally broke. Thank the Lord!" she said in one long, heartfelt exhalation, using Millie's quilt to wipe away her tears. "After you fever break, I head home. Need sleep."

Millie's mortification deepened. "Dom tended my shoulder? My bare shoulder?"

"That man never leave you side. After he bring back Doc Noxon, he fret like a miner protecting he gold. For two day he not sleep. He drip water in your mouth. Try to make you drink. Tend you shoulder. He *never* leave you."

Why had Dom worried about her? Surely the uncouth man didn't wish to become a suitor. But he'd kissed her. Oh, Lor', what if he did? He might propose! Just the thought made her queasy.

"You okay?" Mary asked, looking suddenly concerned. "You face just lose color."

"Here's some chicken broth for our patient," Dom said, carrying in a bowl. "It's hot. Shall I feed it to you, Red?" His eyes twinkled.

Red? Millie narrowed her eyes. No way Dom gave a whit about her. He just enjoyed tormenting her. Riling her, as he put it. The man obtained a perverse pleasure from her reactions to his improper actions and words.

"Out! Leave now!" Millie tried to lift her hand and point her finger, but gave up after a short struggle. Even moving her good arm hurt. "Give Miss Mary the soup and get out."

He handed Mary the soup, but his eyes sparkled. He blew Millie a kiss and left the room.

"That man. He's evil. He delights in tormenting me. Is amused by acting improper."

"Miss Millie. You too hard on him." Mary spooned soup into Millie's mouth. "Mr. Dom worry 'bout you." She grinned and rolled back on her heels. "I think he sweet on you."

Millie choked on her soup.

TWENTY-THREE

October 16, 1863

An Indian Scalping

Millie woke to find Dom sitting in his rocker, the October 1 *Weekly Commonwealth* spread open, blocking his face. She sighed. When Mary wasn't around, Dom was, spooning soup down her throat and forcing her to drink cold tea, perfectly at home in her bedroom. She'd given up being mortified. No matter what she said, the man wouldn't leave. She sighed again, and he lowered the newspaper.

"How was your afternoon nap?" he asked, standing to stretch.

"Fine," Millie grumbled, her throat dry.

"I'll get some hot soup and tea, but first I want a quote from The American Lady." He rubbed his bare chin thoughtfully. "I really liked that one about proper dress, what was it?" He lifted a finger and pressed it against his forehead, as if in deep thought. "Oh yes. 'If your stature is short, you shouldn't allow a superfluity of flounces upon your skirt,' or something like that. Superfluity. What a word. Next time I join the boys at Diefendorf's saloon, I'm going to tell Old Shakespeare, 'A superfluity of Shakespeare quotes makes you a bore.' What do you think?"

Millie glowered. She truly regretted using quotes from *True Politeness, A Hand-Book of Etiquette for Ladies* to try to convince him to leave her bedroom. He thought The American Lady's advice hilarious. "No more quotes, Mr. Drouillard."

His eyebrows rose. "Do you want cold tea?"

Fuming and frustrated, hating her dependence on the man, Millie considered her options. "If you wish to avoid the company of a gentleman who has been properly introduced," she said in as haughty a tone as she could muster. "Treat him with respect, at the same time shunning his company."

"Ouch!"

He returned with hot soup and lukewarm tea.

After she'd eaten, he cleared away the dishes and handed her a cup of hot tea before settling back down in his rocking chair. "While you were sick, you kept moaning about being scalped alive. It sounded like a bad dream except you blamed it on Captain Budge. Wasn't he the Mormon leader of the wagon train? Did something happen when you crossed the plains?"

"You mean besides Captain Budge wanting me to become his fifth wife and a band of Sioux wanting to trade ponies for women?"

Dom smiled. "Yes, something unusual. Like almost being scalped alive."

What kind of a world did Millie now live in? Here she was, in her bed, in an improper state of undress, casually having a conversation with a man about being scalped. She sighed. If she ignored him, she knew he would pester her until she answered. "Did you cross the plains with a wagon train?"

"Johannes and I crossed together, but we took the south route by Fort Wise, Fort Lyon now. The Indians we met were friendly."

"The Indian who almost scalped me was *very* friendly."

Dom pushed his rocker into motion and waited, his eyes glittering. "So why'd he try and scalp you?"

Millie shook her head, winced at the pain from the movement, and thought back to that afternoon. There had been so many difficulties while crossing the plains, but the merciless wind and dangerous river crossings had been the worst. On the day of the near scalping, they'd come to an especially nasty looking creek. Water splashed into the wagon as they lumbered through the swift current, but Millie had hardly noticed. Her eyes had been glued on the girl. A tiny thing, only twelve or thirteen years old, she'd seen the girl hurrying ahead every day with her milk cow, getting to camp early so she could begin chores before her sick mother in their wagon arrived.

Now the girl stood on the far side of the river, staring unhappily at the swift current. Millie yelled for her to wait and cross with the next wagon, but river noise drowned out her voice. With a sour expression, the girl lashed her bag, milk bucket, and lead rope around the cow's neck. Leading the animal into the water, she urged it forward and let go, grabbing its tail as it passed. The cow led her into the river, and the current buffeted her legs, instantly soaking her already heavy shot-filled skirt.

Oh, Lor', Millie thought, *she won't make it. The force of the current and weight of her skirt will drown her!*

The Ouellette wagon reached the far side and Millie jumped out, Sarah and the goats forgotten. Anxiously she paced beside the river and watched the girl's progress. The cow crossed the first heavy current area, the river pounded the girl's thighs. She tottered unsteadily, each step taking her into swifter water. Suddenly, she stumbled and the current knocked her legs out from underneath her. Yelling, Millie waved her arms, feeling horribly helpless.

The cow continued to plod forward until Millie caught sight of the girl's hands and head. She was holding onto the cow's tail, being dragged behind it. The cow didn't look like it was struggling, but it was only half-way across. Could the girl hold on? Millie paced along the shore impatiently, never taking her eyes from the girl.

They reached the center of the crossing where a giant boulder upstream blocked the flow, reducing the current. The girl struggled and got her feet under her, taking three or four steps before the heavier current rammed against her.

With barely a splash she went under and her head disappeared.

Millie watched, horrified, as the girl's hands slipped down the tail, out of sight. The cow drew closer, but as its tail rose above the water, the girl was nowhere to be seen.

Running downstream, Millie yelled for help. Occasionally she caught a glimpse of the girl's green bonnet and blond braid. They tumbled in the current like a rag doll. Millie knew the girl would drown if someone didn't rescue her, but there was no way Millie could reach her in that current.

Suddenly a painted pony streaked past and charged into the water. Long, black braids flew out behind the rider and water exploded around the horse's legs. The man leaned off his horse, his head, arm, and torso disappearing into the foaming rapids. When he reemerged, he dragged the limp form of the girl out of the water and laid her across his horse's neck. Over the din of the current, Millie heard the Indian's wild whoop as he turned the horse and splashed back to shore. The painted pony skidded to a stop in front of Millie, its eyes wide, breathing heavily through flared its nostrils.

Millie backed away into the river, but the horse just followed her, splashing water as it snorted and reared. The Indian jumped from the animal, dropping the limp girl's body on the ground between them. Millie should have immediately tended to the girl, but she'd never been this close to a native. He stood just a bit taller than her, his black eyes glinting down at her, guttural, harsh sounds emitting from his mouth.

What did he want?

Millie had no idea until he pointed at the girl. Gathering her wits, Millie splashed from the water and knelt at the girl's side. Wide eyes stared up at her.

"Did an Injun rescue me?" asked the girl. She coughed a couple times. "Is he gonna take me way an make me live in a tepee?" From the tone of the girl's voice, Millie couldn't tell if this was an appealing or horrifying idea.

"He saved your life, young lady. Be grateful." Millie wrapped her arm around the girl's waist and lifted her to her feet. No wonder the current swept her off—Sarah's male goat weighed more than the child.

"He don't have no britches on."

Millie automatically looked. The Indian did not, in fact, have trousers on. Only a few leather strips covered the Indian's lower body, and these were wet and molded to his skin. Millie quickly raised her eyes, feeling heat spread up her neck and face. Flustered, she said, "Ah. Thank you, sir. You, ah. You saved this girl's life."

The Indian lowered his head until his eyes were at the same level as hers. His long braids fell between them and he uttered more guttural sounds Millie couldn't understand.

The sound of hoof beats caused Millie to look around. Captain Budge's horse splashed across the river and the leader of their wagon train jumped down and stepped in front of the Indian. He said something using strange guttural words and even odder hand movements. The Indian grunted and the two men carried on a loud, animated conversation, hands and arms moving wildly. When the Indian pointed at Millie, Captain Budge stepped back and sighed.

"W-what does he want?" Millie asked, afraid she already knew. She hadn't understood a word, but the Indian had gestured toward her numerous times.

Captain Budge responded dryly, confirming her worst fears. "He wants payment for saving Miss Emma. He says he has never seen hair on fire like yours."

Millie wanted to respond that her hair was *not* on fire, but couldn't find the words. What kind of payment had the Indian demanded?

"Miss Emma. Retrieve your cow and go stand by Mr. Ouellette's wagon."

"Yes, sir." The girl fled without looking back. Millie wanted to follow, but Captain Budge's warning look kept her frozen in place.

Her heartbeat thundered as the two men commenced to shout at each other. Finally, after what was obviously a heated argument, Captain Budge turned to Millie. "I'm sorry, Miss Virginia. I can't dissuade him. If I don't do as he asks, he'll lead a war party and take what he wants, but only after killing most of my men. Forgive me, ma'am, for this violation on your person."

This violation on your person. What exactly did that mean? She took several deep breaths, trying to calm her terror. Was there was no other choice? If Indians killed the men in their party, all the women would suffer. Millie raised her head and stumbled closer to the Indian. "I…understand."

The Indian tilted his head to one side and Millie fought to swallow her scream. She would behave like a lady, even when confronted by a savage. However, her thoughts about ladylike behavior disappeared when the Indian drew out an ugly looking bowie knife. Millie squealed and would have turned and run if Captain Budge hadn't grasped her shoulders and held her in place.

The blade, longer than her extended hand, glistened in the sunshine as the Indian stepped closer and reached around Millie, grabbing her braid. He was going to scalp her. Alive! Millie swayed unsteadily and would have fallen if Captain Budge hadn't been holding her.

The wagon train leader, a supposedly honorable gentleman, was holding her up so an Indian could scalp her. Millie felt furious. How could any white man—gentleman or not—hold her steady at a time like this? When he reached

Heaven, assuming Mormon heaven was the same as wherever she was about to go, she'd give the Captain a piece of her mind. Anger had her pulling free of his grip and standing on her own, taking deep breaths as the Indian brought his knife under her bonnet, close to her ear.

This was it. Millie couldn't scream. Her vocal cords had stopped working. She couldn't run. Her feet felt like they were planted in the mud. Closing her eyes, praying to a God she wasn't sure she believed in, she waited for the end. The savage wrapped her braid around his fist, obviously getting a good grip to rip off her scalp. Millie felt light-headed as he tugged on her braid.

Strangely, being scalped wasn't painful, or maybe she was already dead. Opening one eye, she saw the Indian watching her, the bottom half of her braid swinging from his hand. Millie's knees gave out and she dropped like a stone into the mud. The Indian patted her head, said something to Captain Budge, and vaulted gracefully onto his horse. The horse spun to one side and with a wild "Ye! Ye! Ye!" the savage galloped away.

Dom laughed until tears streamed from his eyes. "Captain Budge didn't explain the Indian only wanted part of your braid?"

"No," Millie said sourly.

"With your temper, I'm surprised you didn't shoot him." Dom stared at her. "Did he really propose afterwards?"

"Can you imagine he actually had the gall to believe I would consent to become his fifth wife?"

Four days later, Dom sauntered into Millie's room, a letter in one hand, a newspaper in the other. "Old Shakespeare delivered this," he said, handing it to Millie. "He wanted to bring it in here and recite sonnets, but I told him you were not yet well enough."

"Of course he shouldn't come into my bedroom. In my current state of undress, it would be highly improper."

"But you've gotten used to me," Dom said, rocking back on his heels.

Millie glared at him. "I've had no choice."

"I think you like it." He laughed and showed her the newspaper. "Old Shakespeare also brought us this. It's the October 8 *Weekly Commonwealth*. There's an interesting article about the circular Mr. Seward has addressed to all foreign Ministers about, let me quote: 'giving a comprehensive history of the progress of the war against the rebellion during the last twelve months.'" He sat in his rocker, shaking his head. "Comprehensive history. It's been a bloodbath. Read your letter and afterwards, I'll read you the news."

Hating the fact that she had to ask, Millie handed him the letter. She didn't want to wait until Mary arrived. "I am unable to open this with one hand."

"Did I hear a please?"

Millie just glared at him. He grinned and glanced at the letter in his hand. "Miss Permelia Abingdon Virginia. Quite the name." Carefully, he tore the envelope and handed it back. "Who's it from?"

Millie eagerly pulled out the letter. "My friend, Mrs. Ouellette."

"The farmer's wife you traveled with across the prairie? The one who gave you Buttercup. Didn't she settle on a potato farm east of Denver City?"

Millie nodded absently, trying to decipher Sarah's rough handwriting. In the middle of the letter Millie stopped and reread a sentence. "Where's Buttercup?"

Dom rolled his eyes. "By the fire, sleeping on the quilt Mary made her. I swear, I have to shoo her out a couple times a day, just to get her to move. Laziest animal I've ever met."

"Buttercup," Millie yelled. "Buttercup, come here!"

The goat ambled into the room.

"She's fat," Dom said with disgust. "I swear I haven't been giving her extra vittles."

The goat did look fatter. Millie glanced at the letter and back at the goat.

"What?" Dom asked, suspiciously.

"Sarah says Buttercup's kid should be born in January."

Dom choked on his coffee, spilling it down his shirt. "Her kid?" He stared at the goat. "I didn't sign up for kids."

TWENTY-FOUR

October 27, 1863

Beef A La Mode

Millie's recovery felt as slow as molasses. The wounds on her shoulder were healing cleanly, causing her less discomfort, but regaining her strength was a lesson in patience. She had never spent so much time piddling around doing nothing and as the days passed, a new and rather distressing rhythm developed in her home. Dom spent less time hovering in her bedroom like a distressed mother hen, and instead began working as if Millie's cabin belonged to him. He fed critters, cut and stacked firewood, fixed shutter hinges, replaced broken floor slats, and chinked and daubed log joints.

When he wasn't treating her home like his own, he was doing ore assays and working at the mine. Millie soon learned rocks—the stranger looking the better—were the man's love and passion. She might have guessed it based on his hard head, but she couldn't help being amused by his almost childlike fascination of miner's discards. Excited as a kid, he showed her a black rock—payment for his latest assay—and insisted it was microcline feldspar. With another sample, he used his magnifying glass to point out smoky quartz crystals and spent a half hour theorizing how they had formed. Millie remembered the books she'd found in his room and couldn't help being impressed, although usually the conversation ended with a sarcastic statement or him calling her Red, and she'd shout him out of her room.

He drove her crazy!

Of course, when she was in a fairer mood—when the man wasn't being irritable or teasing her—Millie had to admit she couldn't have survived without him. Still, it was now late October. Dom had been living with her for two and a half weeks and he appeared to be settling in, not planning his departure. Worse, he'd taken two more baths since his arrival!

At least this morning, after a loud argument she finally won, Millie rose from her bed and resumed her cooking duties. Insisting it was too early for her to be out and about, Dom stomped off, mumbling about stubborn redheads and Southern belles. Despite his complaints, Millie thought he was secretly relieved—his cooking, or more accurately, his warming of food made by Mary, was palatable, but only just. Plus the man couldn't steep a decent cup of hot tea if his life depended on it. It was either watery, tasteless, cold, or all three.

Alone in her cabin and on her feet, Millie sighed contentedly and began preparations for cooking Beef A La Mode, a new recipe from the *Great Western Cookbook*. The recipe called for cutting holes in her round of beef—something she'd never done before—and pulling strips of salted pork rolled in curry powder through the holes. The result produced a fancy roast that Millie rather admired, looking like a dish served at an elegant restaurant. Further down, the recipe called for orange peel and Millie just shook her head; she hadn't seen an orange since leaving New Orleans. Still, she made spice substitutions and as the cabin filled with savory smells, she couldn't help but smile. The cabin hadn't smelled this good since her accident.

Dom stomped in, spreading snow across the floor as he removed his coat, mumbling about a non-existent vug. He'd cleared enough rubble to enter the mine, but after several days of exploring, he'd found nothing. No vug. No gold vein. Not even high-grade ore. Suddenly his mumbling stopped, one glove still on, the other dangling from cold fingers. He sniffed the air.

"God that smells good." He grinned at Millie. "Red, I might have to marry you. I'll never find another woman who can cook gourmet meals in the wilds of the Colorado Territory."

"As I have asked before, Mr. Drouillard, do not call me Red. Or honey. Or sweetheart. Or darling." Millie used her sternest voice. She was back on her feet. It was time to set the man straight about endearments, his manners, and their living arrangements, although she wasn't sure what to do about the latter. He couldn't continue to live with her. She didn't even want to think what the townswomen were saying. Still, she felt a bit guilty. She knew Dom cared for her, in his own way.

Dom eyed her and finished removing his gloves and boots. His swollen lip was gone and his blue eyes sparkled with mischief. "Glad you're feeling better, Red. Where's Mary?"

Mary had left early in the afternoon, the coward. Millie had asked for advice on how to address Dom and his impending departure from Millie's cabin. Mary had ducked her head with a sudden "coughing fit" and insisted she had chores to tend to.

"Mary is at her cabin, which gives us a chance to discuss some things."

Dom took the morning bread down and sliced himself a piece. After helping himself to the strawberry preserves, he asked, "Things? Like you calling me Dom?"

Millie rolled her eyes. They were about to eat supper yet the man was making himself a snack. Another reason to get him to leave: the man never stopped eating.

"I wish to discuss our living arrangements." She paused, expecting an explosion; but instead, Dom nodded.

"I've been thinking about that myself."

"You have?"

"Yes. I'm a gentleman and you—well most of the time—are a lady. My kiss may have swept you off your feet, but I could never move into your bedroom. I'm sorry, it's out of the question. What would the neighbors say?" He shook his head sadly. "No, I couldn't. It just wouldn't be proper unless we were married."

"Married? That's…I mean…I want…" She choked on her tea and broke into a coughing fit. Her eyes began to water.

"Okay. Okay," he said, lifting his hands in resignation. "I hate watching a lady cry." He sighed and handed her a dish towel. "If you insist, I'll marry you. We can go to town and find Brother Bunce, but first I want to eat. The smell of whatever you made is driving me crazy."

"Marry you?" Millie cried, finally finding her voice. She flung the dish towel at him. "I don't want to marry you. I want you out. To leave my cabin. Immediately!"

He casually took his plate and fork from the shelf and sat down at the table. "Can I eat first?"

Millie seethed. She bent down and jerked the meat from the oven. Glaring at him, she spun around and marched over to the fireplace.

"No you can not!"

She dumped the fancy roast into the flames. "Find someplace else to eat."

Dom's face twisted from an expression of horror to fury to disgust. He uttered several colorful curses before shouting, "You are *such* a redhead." Stomping to the door, he threw on his boots, coat, hat, and gloves. "Mr. Diefendorf's saloon sounds like a fine idea. At least it has decent company."

TWENTY-FIVE

October 28, 1863

Outlaws

Dom didn't emerge from his room until late afternoon of the following day—his eyes red and his expression haggard. Millie didn't comment on his appearance. In fact neither of them spoke at all, although Millie gained immense satisfaction watching him grab his head every time she slammed a door or accidently dropped something. That evening she was unusually clumsy.

Days passed and their interactions returned to normal, although Dom did seem to control his tongue, just a bit. Millie never again broached the subject of his leaving; just imagining another conversation about marriage mortified her. Instead she cooked, cleaned, and washed clothes, pleased to feel more like herself. She visited Mary regularly, but her former suitors did not resume their visits. Millie actually missed them.

She considered hiking into town to visit the ladies and refresh her newspapers, but didn't. At first, she told herself she didn't have the energy and the snow was too deep, but as days passed and her energy returned, Millie still hesitated. The mountain lion wouldn't have attacked except for Buttercup. The trail was safe. Still, Millie couldn't shake her unease.

She jumped at shadows and glanced over her shoulder, unsure and frustrated by her jitteriness. At one point she almost decided to tell Dom her fears, but she didn't. He'd probably call her an irrational female and he'd be right.

On November 8, a month after the mountain lion attack, Millie felt so restless and out of sorts she thought she might scream. Outside, the sun glistened on a feathery layer of new snow and inside, Millie paced in front of her cookstove.

Dom, oblivious to her mood, described the mineral specimen in front of him, commenting on color, streak, hardness, and fracture. When he made a comment about the rock's cleavage, Millie snapped.

"Mr. Drouillard. Such language. The sample does not have…What you just said."

"Cleavage?" he asked, raising an eyebrow. "It most certainly does. I could describe how it cleaves along its curvature, or would you prefer a comparison of its cleavage to yours?"

"Mr. Drouillard!" Millie kicked the table's leg, cried out in pain, and grabbed her foot, hopping on one leg.

Both of Dom's thick eyebrows shot up. "You seem a bit cranky, Red. You up for going to town? Maybe hike to the hot springs and afterwards take in a meal at the Beebee house?"

"Yes," Millie said quickly, not even reprimanding him on the nickname. Before he could change his mind, she slipped into her coat, gloves, and boots and looked at him expectantly. "I've never been to the sulfur hot springs. What are they like?"

"They're a great place to get naked and take a hot bath."

Millie narrowed her eyes. By now she had experienced enough of Dom's twisted sense of humor to know when to ignore him. She usually could, but this was…it was…well, it could not be ignored. The man needed to learn what was proper and what should never be said. She retrieved Florence Hartley's book of etiquette and began flipping through the pages.

"Oh, no," groaned Dom, "not another quote from Mrs. Hartley. She's not nearly as amusing as the American Lady."

Millie glared at him. "Get ready while I find…Ah yes, here in Chapter XVI, Polite Deportment, and Good Habits." She cleared her throat and began to read. "Lord Chesterfield says, 'Good sense and good nature suggest civility in general; but in good breeding there are a thousand little delicacies which are established only by custom.'"

Dom rolled his eyes heavenward and asked, "Meaning what?"

"Meaning cleavage is never mentioned in mixed company and bathing should be done in the privacy of one's own home!"

He grinned. "We can do that, too."

Millie slammed the book and returned to lacing her boot. Not even a saint could teach this man manners.

"We'll ask Miss Mary to come with us," Millie said, rising. Dom tended to behave better when Mary was around, but when they stopped by, her friend demurely refused, offering instead to watch Buttercup for the day.

"Maybe you should keep her," Dom grumbled. "Did you know she's going to have a kid? Can you imagine a little Buttercup?" He shuddered. "I'll walk into the cabin and both of them will faint."

Mary just laughed and held the door open. Buttercup waddled in.

It was a clear, cold morning and Millie had trouble with her long skirt in the fresh snow as she followed Dom down the snowy path. When they reached the valley, they paused to watch hot steam billow in the chilly air above Soda Creek. Millie had never taken the time to visit the springs, but the townswomen spoke of effervescing pools and vapor caves surrounded by mountain goats and other wildlife.

"Do you think Miss Mary refused because she was worried she wouldn't be allowed in the Beebee House?" Millie asked suddenly.

"They'd let her in. I'd make sure of it."

Millie didn't doubt it. "So why do you think she didn't come?"

"She was being polite," he said, turning to face her.

Millie fisted both hands on her hips. When she could see Dom's dimples, she knew trouble was coming. "Polite?"

"Polite. So we had some time alone. For my courting."

"Courting?" Millie felt a wave of panic. "Who?"

He frowned. "You, of course."

Millie swallowed. Surely the man was jesting. Since her accident, he'd delighted in riling her and had become quite versed at it. Regardless, this wasn't funny. Regaining some composure, she said tartly, "We are *not* courting, Mr. Drouillard. You wouldn't know *how* to court a woman. You'd probably act like those oversized mountain sheep rams I watched in the fall. They chased their wide-eyed ewes until the poor girls collapsed in exhaustion." She eyed him speculatively. "You are not courting me. What do you really want?"

"Why can't I court you?" he asked. "Your other suitors do."

"This is not amusing, Mr. Drouillard." Millie glared at him, feeling her face redden. She shook her head. "Of course. You want the mine, just like the other men."

He frowned. "Is that what you think?"

"You can have it."

"What?"

"The mine. You can have it."

He raised a bushy eyebrow. "You're just giving it to me? I don't even have to pay for it? Or marry you?"

"It's yours." Oh, Lor', she could use the money. Still, Mr. Drouillard would have wanted his brother to have it. "But you hafta find another cabin to live in," she said, trying to get something out of the deal.

"I like yours."

Millie threw up her hands. How did one get rid of an unwanted male guest? At this rate, he'd be staying all winter. Her supplies would be gone by Christmas.

"You okay? You look a bit pale."

"I'm fine."

He nodded, turned, and trudged down the trail. "I'm a bit cold. How about we stop at Payne's Bar House for something hot to drink and maybe a slice of Mrs. Gardner's berry pie? If Mrs. Gardner learns we went to the Beebee House for a meal but didn't stop by her establishment, there'll be hell to pay."

"Language," Millie said automatically, although with little force. She knew Dom's suggestion was his way of offering her a rest. Sometimes he could be thoughtful. She might even admit, if only to herself, every once in a blue moon he was actually considerate.

Payne's Bar House was busy with people dressed in their finest, and Millie realized it was Sunday. She blushed. Every person in the restaurant knew she was not only sharing a cabin with a single man, but also not attending church. She didn't even want to imagine the gossip.

They settled into a table and Millie sipped her tea, watching Dom enjoy coffee and pie, pleased at how many townsfolk and former suitors took turns stopping by to greet them. Many of her neighbors had visited the cabin while she was recovering, bringing gifts of food, supplies, and good wishes. Millie greeted each person, thanking them again for their kindness. She knew how hard it was to survive here—especially in winter—but the townsfolk took care of their own. It warmed Millie to think they considered her one of them.

"Och aye the noo! Did you really wrestle a Rocky Mountain lion?" asked Mr. Shumate, leaving a smudge of soot where he touched Millie's hand.

"What a tall tale it is," added Mr. Tappan. "A wild scene even the great Bard couldn't have dreamed up."

"Are you all right, dear," asked Mrs. Gilson, gently patting Millie on her good arm. "Did you get the cheese I sent up, or did Mr. D eat it?"

"Why aren't you carrying your Colt?" insisted Charlotte Card, her hands on her hips. "You can't depend on nobody—especially not a man. I thought you had better sense."

"You're right," Millie said, feeling her apron pocket. Her pocket watch was there, but she'd forgotten to bring her loaded Colt. "Thank you for the reminder."

Mr. Poor stopped by, eyed Dom without enthusiasm, and turned to Millie. "Are you still in mourning?"

Dom answered "*Yes*!" in a loud, booming voice before Millie could respond.

"Will you sell your mine to me?" was Mr. Turck's gruff question, his fists squeezing his beard braids. He refused to look at Dom as he added, "I'll add fifty dollars to my last offer."

"She sold it to me," Dom said, silencing the entire room. Millie rolled her eyes heavenward. The man hadn't paid a Liberty half-dollar. Still, she held her tongue. It was a relief to be rid of it.

"I've been mining my new mine," he added boastfully. He reached into his pocket and pulled out a tear-shaped nugget. He held it to the light to admire it. Every eye in the restaurant locked on it.

Millie suddenly felt very uneasy. She knew exactly what he was up to, but did he really think the killer was in the room? She guessed it didn't matter. By early afternoon, everyone in town would know Dom owned the mine and assume he had found his brother's gold. Then whoever killed his brother would go after him. The killer might have hesitated to kill Millie, a lone woman, but there'd be no such reservations with Dom. Millie felt a shiver of fear and pulled her coat tighter around her shoulders.

Casually he tossed the nugget to Mrs. Gardner. "This should pay for our drinks and pie."

Mrs. Gardner put the nugget between her teeth and bit down. She glanced at her teeth marks and nodded. "This'll pay for your fare and a month's worth of additional meals."

"Well then," Dom said lazily. "Use it to pay for my good friend, Mr. Turck's meal."

Millie had been in the high country long enough to understand Dom's insult. To jump a claim, that was expected, even admired at times, but charity was something else.

Millie remembered a story Elder Griswold had told about a miner, Mr. H.A.W. Tabor. Mr. Tabor had come to prospect Idaho Springs in its early days. He'd arrived with his wife, Augusta, and son, Max, and built a rough cabin near their claim. Actually, according to the story, Mrs. Tabor—the first white woman in Idaho Springs—had built the cabin and used their tent for a roof. Either way, in the fall, a kind old miner warned them high snow or avalanches would wipe them out. Mr. Tabor took his family to Denver City for the winter, only to return the next spring to find the kindly old miner had jumped his claim and his cabin.

"I don't need my meal paid for," spat Mr. Turck. He pulled out his poke. "I've plenty of my own gold." Millie noticed Mr. Turck's poke looked mostly empty. Winter was hard on prospectors.

"As you like," Dom said casually. He turned to Mrs. Gardner. "Please keep a tab for us."

A stocky man Millie didn't recognize hurried in, looked around, and headed in their direction. Dom stood up and extended his hand. "Sheriff Reynolds, I hear congratulations are in order." The two men shook hands like they were old friends. "Heard you were in the party that tracked down Felipe Espinosa and his nephew, José Vicente."

"Yep. Tom Tobin hunted them down. Man's as good a tracker as an Indian." He turned to Millie and tipped his hat. "You must be Miss Virginia. I've heard all about you. Did I just hear you sold the mine to Dom?"

"It's a pleasure to make your acquaintance, Sheriff Reynolds and, yes, Mr. Drouillard now owns the mine." Millie couldn't bring herself to say Dom had bought it. "I think it's what his brother would have wanted."

"I'm sure you're right, although I was hoping to make a bid on it." The lawman frowned, removed his hat, and scratched his head. "Unfortunately, I have some bad news."

Had something happened to Sarah Ouellette and her husband? "What is it," she whispered.

"While I was on the Espinosas' trail, Mr. Gould escaped from the jail in Denver City."

"Mr. Gould escaped, but....but how?" Millie rose her to feet. "When?"

"Don't know. All I heard is someone assisted his escape."

TWENTY-SIX

November 8, 1863

Soda Creek Hot Springs

The room erupted. Millie slowly dropped into her seat, stunned.

Mr. Gould was free.

And he had an accomplice. Where was he? When would he come to Idaho Springs? A man like that didn't give up. He'd be back for the map. And for her. He'd never believe she had no idea about the location of the town. She blinked back tears and felt Dom squeeze her hand. She looked up at him and some of the coldness left her. Dom wouldn't let Mr. Gould hurt her. For the first time, Millie was glad for her unwanted guest.

"When did he escape?" Dom asked quietly.

"A week last Wednesday. I heard they tracked him south, as far as Pikes Peak, but then lost the trail."

Dom rubbed his chin. "Miss Virginia and I were thinking of visiting the Soda Creek hot springs. Do you think Mr. Gould could be in the area?"

Miss Virginia? Millie started despite her distress. Dom never addressed her properly.

"I think you're safe, Dom. I doubt Mr. Gould will come back here. He knows we're watching for him. Plus, with the snow, there's little chance of him making his way north without being seen, not to mention he'd have to find a place to stay." The sheriff accepted a tin cup filled with black coffee and sipped thoughtfully. "What about the other business? James told me about the threats Widow D received. You still think your brother was murdered?"

"Johannes was murdered. I think it was his killer who threatened Miss Virginia. Now the mine belongs to me, I don't think he'll bother *her* anymore."

A crowd had formed around them, unabashedly listening to the conversation. "That may be true," said Mr. Ferris, "but Widow D is still weak from her injury. Are you sure it's wise to take her to the hot springs? The exercise might not be beneficial." Murmurs of agreement followed. Dom glanced at Millie and raised an eyebrow in question.

Millie looked from her neighbors—the women who'd become friends and her many suitors—to Dom. Touched by their concern and still reeling from the news about Mr. Gould, she felt a tear spill down her cheek. She swiped at it and coughed. "Thank you. I'll be fine. Dom—Mr. Drouillard—will assist me." It took a bit more convincing, but eventually she and Dom left, following a trail toward Soda Creek.

They walked through town and despite her worries, Millie felt warmed by her neighbors' concern. She'd lived in New Orleans her entire life, but after a few short months, the Rocky Mountains and this town had become her home. Her neighbors were friends. Friends who worried about her.

Dom, in a rare gentlemanly move, slipped his arm through hers. "Don't worry, Millie. I know you didn't want a houseguest, but Mr. Gould won't dare come near you. Not while I'm here."

It was typical of Dom to leave open the suggestion he'd be around indefinitely, but Millie couldn't argue. Right now, his company felt safe. They walked in companionable silence until they passed Miss Marble, the school mistress.

"You ever hear about the first school in Idaho Springs?"

"No," Millie said absently.

"It was started by Mrs. Doud, a miner's wife, in '61. She had ten or eleven students, each paying seventy-five cents in gold dust. Wasn't much of a school-house, not like now. We just put four posts in the ground and covered them with pine boughs. But children were getting an education. At least they were until Mrs. Doud ran off with a handsome stranger. It's said she disappeared one night, was seen riding into the moonlight behind her new lover, and the first seeds of immorality were planted in Idaho Springs."

Millie stopped and glared. "Mr. Drouillard, just when I think you have one or two redeeming qualities, you make up such a story. You're incorrigible!"

"A few redeeming qualities?" He grinned, a devilish expression she knew meant trouble. "That mean you like me, just a little?"

Shaking her head, she released his arm and strode purposefully in the direction of the steam clouds. He caught up with her and took hold of her hand, swinging it like a schoolboy. "Actually, the story about Mrs. Doud is true. Course immorality in the form of Tit Bit's crib may have been here before Mrs. Doud ran off."

Millie scowled at him and tried to pull her hand free. He held it tightly, refusing to release it. "You know Tit Bit?"

"Depends on your definition of *know*."

Millie decided it was best to stop asking questions. She gave up trying to pull free of his grasp and walked in silence beside him. The billowing steam over Soda Creek grew closer. Snow sparkled in the bright sunlight and ice magically captured cascading streams into a frozen mirage. Pine boughs hunched under the weight of the fresh snow and when Millie ducked under an especially loaded branch, Dom released her hand and playfully knocked it.

Snow rained down.

Millie let out a surprised yelp as the cold chilled her bare neck. Dom's laughter ended abruptly when Millie scooped up a handful of snow and threw it. Their snowball fight was short. Millie's hands quickly chilled and Dom had collapsed in the snow, laughing at her miserable aim. While he lay helpless, Millie scooped up a pile of snow and dumped it on his exposed face. As he blustered in surprise, she turned, lifted her skirt, and hurried away.

Rounding a corner, Millie stopped short, not quite believing her eyes. In the valley before her, the snow still clung to the higher walls, but lower down, green grass peeked through a haze of mist. Steaming pools of iridescent green and blue dotted the landscape, their boiling water trickling into the river that meandered around them. Millie walked forward, trying to look everywhere at once. The green grass was spotted with elk and whitetail deer. A couple long-haired mountain goats grazed peacefully beside curved-horned mountain sheep. Between two of the strange pools, a massive moose stood in the river, his head completely underwater. As she watched, he looked up and water streamed off his antlers, sparkling in the sunlight.

"It's remarkable, huh?" Dom took her hand again and squeezed. "Before the miners arrived, Soda Creek here was the dividing line between the Ute and Arapaho territories. The two tribes fought, well, like Indians, except at the hot springs. Both tribes considered this sacred."

Millie nodded, understanding the emotion.

"Over there, the river's so warm you can bathe in it, but never put any part of your body in the pools themselves. They're hot enough to burn the skin down to the bone." As if to emphasize his warning, he led her near one pool where bubbles broke the smooth surface. "See the bones?"

The crystal clear, steaming water allowed Millie to easily see the unnatural green, yellow, and blue plants swaying in the liquid's movement. On top of the plants was a perfectly preserved white skeleton. She wasn't sure what it was, but it looked as big as the moose.

They settled on a rock near the stream and Millie felt like a lady visiting an expensive spa as she slipped out of her boots and stockings and dipped her bare feet into deliciously warm water. If Dom hadn't been there, she might have been tempted to lift her skirt and soak her entire shin. As if reading her mind—the man could be so annoying—Dom pointed up the hill behind them. "Those are steam caves." His grin made Millie blush. "That one has hot pools inside, providing a more private place to bathe."

"No caves!"

His eyebrows rose and Millie knew her response had been too immediate and shrill. Blasted man. He was way too perceptive.

"You don't bathe in caves? Or you don't bathe with me?"

"I don't go into caves." Millie shuddered at the thought. "And I'd never bathe with a man."

"Here I thought you weren't afraid of anything."

"I'm not afraid," Millie lied. "I just don't like caves."

"Too bad. I'd happily bathe with you."

He scrambled away before she could strike him and began drying his feet with his stockings. "I think we should start back. The sun will go down in a couple hours. With Mr. Gould on the loose, I want to be safe at home before it gets dark."

Millie sighed, disappointed to have thoughts of Mr. Gould intrude their peaceful interlude. Dom rose and after Millie dried her feet and put on her stockings and boots, he reached down and lifted her to her feet. "Shall we walk back on the high trail?" He pointed to a faint trail below the caves. "The view from above is impressive."

Millie eyed the caves as she silently scrambled up the incline. Dom might tease her, but she trusted he'd never force her to do anything she didn't want. The climb to the trail was steep and rocky and when they finally reached the top, Millie paused to catch her breath and look around.

Dom was right. The view was magical. The steam transformed the landscape and animals into something unearthly.

"Wish we could admire it all day," Dom said after a moment, "but we need to get going."

Millie nodded and followed him along the trail, careful of her footing. An unusual twisted red and white rock caught her attention and she bent to pick it up, hoping Dom might like it for his collection.

Crack!

Millie jumped at the loud noise and stumbled, feeling gravel from the slope behind pummel her back. She scrambled to regain her balance and another crack broke the stillness. A puff of stones and dirt exploded near her foot.

Someone was shooting at them!

TWENTY-SEVEN

November 8, 1863

The Vapor Caves

Dom knocked Millie's breath out when he seized her around the waist, lifted her off the ground, and charged down the trail. Another shot shattered the quiet afternoon. Dom grunted, stumbled, and scraped Millie's leg against a rocky outcropping.

"Ouch!" Millie cried and grabbed at the injury. Her hands were knocked aside as Dom heaved her from one arm to the other and crushed her against his body.

Darkness suddenly enveloped them.

Millie looked up and screamed, her cry echoing against the cave's walls as Dom carried her deeper into the darkness.

She struggled against his hold, her injured leg forgotten. Another gunshot reverberated in the dark confines, but Millie didn't care—she had to get out. She twisted and thrashed against Dom's hold, but he just tightened his grip, his pace slowing.

"No," Millie managed, the shrill word not sounding like her voice. Wildly she kicked at Dom and struggled against his hold, unable to draw in enough air. Feeling light-headed, her vision tunneled and she hoped she might pass out.

Her fear wouldn't let her.

"Easy, honey," Dom gasped out. He slowed to a walk, his chest heaving as he struggled to catch his breath. Millie redoubled her efforts to break his hold, but he simply repositioned her and wrapped both arms around her, hugging her tight as he stopped and slowly lowered her to the ground.

"Shush," he whispered. "It's okay."

It wasn't okay. They were in a cave. A dark, closed-in, suffocating underground tomb. Her heart beat so hard she could barely hear Dom.

"You have to calm down, Millie. Now. The shooter won't dare come after us. He knows I'm armed. But we can't leave. Not until we figure out where he is."

"No! He might. Bury us. Alive. Got to get. Out!" Millie's panic blinded all other emotions. She kicked Dom's shin. He grunted as she screamed. "Now!"

Another bullet exploded in the rocks at the front of the cave.

"Stop it, Millie!"

Dom roughly twisted her around and crushed her back against his chest, pinning her arms under his. "I know you're afraid," he added more quietly. "I'm sorry. We can't leave. Not with someone shooting at us. Focus on the light. See. At the mouth of the tunnel." He scooted back, leaning against a boulder, and pulled her onto his lap, capturing her thrashing legs under his thigh. "Easy." He rested his forehead in her hair, his breathing still ragged, but his voice quiet. "Hush. Look at the light. See, it's just in front of us."

Millie's struggles lessened. Sweat poured down her face. She felt drenched in it. No matter what she did or said, Dom continued to hold her and whisper quiet words in her ear. His grip never loosened. Finally, exhausted, Millie slumped against him, her body trembling. She stared at the entrance, noticing steam glittering in the shadows, creating rainbows in the light.

"That's my girl. Just take deep breaths. Focus on the light." He cautiously lifted his leg, unpinning hers. Millie didn't move, she didn't have the energy. Slowly he unwrapped one of his arms. "That's it."

Millie felt the darkness like an evil presence. Her breath scorched her lungs; the wild beating of her heart ripped through her chest. Her eyes bore into the small circle of light. A scream gurgled up, but only a harsh hiss came out of her mouth. Oh, Lor', she had to get out. A bullet couldn't possibly be this agonizing. She tensed and Dom's arm tightened.

"Did I ever tell you about Mountain Charley?" Dom's tone was casual, as if they were settling down for an evening meal.

Rainbows of colored light twirled in front of the cave entrance. Steam billowed, blurring the light's edges. "No," Millie said shakily.

"When Johannes and I first came to Denver City, old Mountain Charley was running the Mountain Boy's Saloon. Charley was quite the businessman. Swore like a double-crossed cowboy, gambled like a swindler, always had a lit cigar between his teeth. He could down Taos Lightning like an outlaw."

"You. You don't gamble. Do you?"

"Not anymore. You've reformed me. If I stick around much longer, you'll be dragging me to church, although if anyone called me Elder Drouillard, I might have to shoot 'em."

Millie laughed weakly. Her eyes had begun to adjust. She could see shadowy details of the tunnel walls and rock-strewn floor. The circle of light at the entrance appeared brighter.

"Mountain Charley. He was a legend among men, until we found out he wasn't actually a man. He was Elsa Jane Forest. A woman. Turns out Miss Elsa Jane was pretending to be a man to survive. Years ago, one of her husband's men, a man named Jamieson, shot and killed her husband. Becoming a man was the only way she could find work."

"A lady? Dressed like a man. Wouldn't someone have recognized her?"

"I guess we see what we expect to see. I never suspected it, and I met her several times. Anyway, she acted like a man to find work that paid enough to feed her kids. Later, we heard she'd worked as a cabin boy on a New Orleans steamer, became a brakeman on the Illinois Central Railroad, hauled provisions to California gold camps, and eventually moved to Denver City and opened the Mountain Boy's Saloon. She might have continued her masquerade indefinitely, she certainly had everyone fooled."

He paused and slowly loosened his hold. Millie didn't move. She felt him use his sleeve to wipe perspiration off his face.

"Why?" asked Millie slowly, her mind dully considering a woman in the guise of a man. It was appalling, but not as dreadful as how war widows in New Orleans had been forced to survive.

One—a farmer's wife Millie had bought vegetables from before the war—had been in the French Quarter just before Millie left. The young woman had stared at Millie—her eyes defeated and shallow—and allowed a Northern soldier to wrap his beefy arm around her. As they passed, she'd whispered, "My husband's dead. My children are starving."

"Why did Mountain Charley let anyone know about her deception?" Millie asked, not wanting to remember the widow's desperate face.

"As luck would have it, poor Miss Elsa Jane ran into Jamieson. The lady recognized him and emptied her revolver into his retreating hide. Unfortunately, he survived long enough to reveal Elsa Jane's secret."

"What…what'd she do?"

"Sold her saloon, married her former bartender, and moved to St. Joe."

Millie was almost breathing normally. Well, as normal as was possible in this hot, steamy darkness. Then she noticed the shadows at the end of the cave lengthening, the light fading.

"No," she whimpered, sucking in a deep breath. If the light disappeared, she'd lose her mind.

"Easy, Millie. We're going to stand up and move closer to the front. In the darkness, the shooter won't be able to see us. But I need you to be quiet. Can you do that?"

Millie nodded, realized he couldn't see her, and whispered, "Yes."

"That's my girl." He unwrapped his arm, but laced his fingers through hers and tightly gripped her hand. "Stand up, honey."

Millie tried. She pushed against Dom and felt her feet press against the ground but as she added her weight, her limbs felt loose and unstable. Dom released her hand and grabbed her waist, catching her before she fell. He pulled her snugly against his solid side and held her steady. Millie's legs shook, but she remained on her feet.

"Put your arm around me," he said. "You're still weak from the mountain lion attack. Between that and your fear, your muscles have froze up."

Millie wrapped her arm around his broad shoulder and limped beside him toward the front of the cave. He froze after a couple steps. In the silence, Millie heard an owl hoot and felt Dom's heart beat against her. The steam twirled around them, twisting the dimming light. She glanced at Dom, wondering why he'd stopped, and saw his six-shooter gripped in his free hand.

They moved again, only to stop after a couple steps.

Finally, cool night air brushed against Millie's wet cheeks. "Ahh," she sighed.

"Feels good," Dom agreed. "It was hot and steamy back there."

"Can we go out? Please." She hated the pleading sound she heard in her own voice.

"Sorry," Dom said, squeezing her against him. "We can't leave until its full dark. Even then, you'll have to stay hidden here while I search for the shooter." He lowered her to the ground and slowly sat down beside her.

Through the fresh, cool air, Millie could see stars and a hazy cloud cover. The breeze made her shiver, but she felt her fear fade. "I'm okay. As long as I don't hafta go back in—"

"It'd be safer to spend the night in the cave."

"Spend the night?" Millie stared at him. In the fading light, his eyes looked bruised and haggard. His fist still gripped the six-shooter, but it rested on his thigh.

"You're too sore to walk home, Millie. Even with my help, we wouldn't make it. No way I can carry you if you go down. Plus, there's the shooter to worry about. He might be gone, but who knows if he's waiting along the trail. At least here in the cave, we don't have to worry about freezing to death."

"You want me to spend the night here? With you?"

He squeezed her arm. "Don't worry, Red. I'll let you snuggle."

TWENTY-EIGHT

November 8, 1863
Blizzard!

After his inappropriate comment, Dom hurried out in search of their assailant, leaving Millie silently brooding. *Snuggle with him indeed!* She'd just as soon snuggle with a wet fish. The man was impossible. Of course they'd walk home tonight. Just as soon as he returned. Determined to show she could make the walk, Millie pushed herself onto her knees and climbed up the wall. The exertion caused her legs and arms to shake violently and she swayed unsteadily, like a tree about to fall. She stood for only a minute before sinking back to the floor.

Anger turned to humiliation and tears burned her eyes. The long days after the mountain lion attack had made her feel dependent—vulnerable and helpless—emotions she learned to hate in the orphanage. When she left the orphanage, Millie had vowed never again to be helpless and scared, yet here she was, so weak she could barely stand up. Damn the shooter. Damn Dom. But mostly, damn her unreasonable fear of dark, closed-in places.

This minute, she decided, she'd no longer let her fear rule her. *Caves are not so scary!* Pulling her legs up against her chest, she wrapped her arms around them, and laid her head on her knees. *Caves are not scary!* Silently, she repeated the mantra.

Rocks clattered down the slope outside. Millie jumped, startled and frightened. Her heart hammered as a dark form appeared just outside the entrance. Millie wasn't certain if it was Dom or someone else, but whoever was outside would see her as soon as they stepped into the cave. Carefully, she felt the ground around her until her fingers wrapped around a fist-sized rock. Tensing, she waited.

"We've got a problem."

Millie dropped the rock as Dom stepped into the cave and slowly lowered himself down beside her.

Millie let out her breath and asked in a shaky voice, "Is the shooter still out there?" If the shooter had entered the cave instead of Dom, she'd be dead. Immediately she made another resolution. Never, ever, would she leave the cabin without her six-shooter. Like Charlotte Card said, Millie needed to protect herself and not depend on anyone else.

"I think the shooter's gone, but a storm's brewing. Temperature's dropping fast. Wind's picking up. We're in for a bad one. I can feel it."

Millie stared at Dom. It was too dark to see his face clearly, but if she didn't know better, she'd say he was scared. "Then we'll hafta walk home. Tonight."

"It'll be safer to stay here. The cave will keep us warm and protected. Problem is, if the storm's as bad as I fear, the snow might block the entrance or be too deep to get through for several days. We'd have water but no food."

Millie shuddered. Forget food or water. Only too clearly could she imagine the cave's entrance blocked by snow. They'd be trapped inside. "No!" She scrambled to her feet. "See, I'm fine. I can walk."

Dom sighed and slowly stood up, wrapping his arm around her. "I think that's best, but can you really walk?"

"Of course," she lied.

"Let's go."

Millie bit her lip, trying to smother her moan as Dom guided her from the cave. They headed down the steep incline and her entire body began to shake. Dom didn't say a word, but he tightened his grip. If he hadn't, Millie would have fallen and tumbled down the incline. His sturdy arm kept her upright, but by the time they reached the grass near the river, Millie's body was coated in perspiration and her legs felt like tapioca pudding. Dom released her and she sank into the grass.

"Millie." Dom took her face in his hands and made her look at him. "We've got a long walk home. A really bad storm is coming. If you can't walk, we have to stay here, in the shelter of the cave. The shooter might be out there. If he gets lucky…" His expression turned grim. "You'd be rid of an unwanted guest, but you'd have to get home on your own."

"The shooter is *not* going to get lucky!"

Dom's expression softened. "If anyone gets to shoot me, it'll be you. Right?"

Millie nodded uncertainly. She couldn't imagine what she'd do if anything happened to Dom.

"Ten minutes soaking here in the river, here where the water's hot, will loosen your muscles. It'll help you walk by yourself."

Millie's softening thoughts disappeared.

"You want me to bathe!? Now? Mr. Drouillard, you are a degenerate. You keep hinting I should take off my clothes. Of course I won't bathe here!"

He released her face and stepped back so shadows hid his face. "I need to check the trail, Millie. To make sure the shooter isn't waiting down valley. You'll have fifteen, maybe twenty minutes of privacy. Do what you think's best, but you can't get your hair or underpinnings wet." He lifted his hand and ran a finger down her cheek. "You *have* to be able to walk on your own, Red. Either that, or we stay here tonight." His hand dropped to his side and he turned and stumbled away, disappearing into the darkness.

Shocked, Millie stared after him. She'd seen Dom arrogant, humorous, even angry, but never scared. Not until tonight. For a moment she wavered. She didn't even want to think what Florence Hartley or The American Lady might say. And what if Dom wasn't searching for the shooter but hiding in the shadows, watching? Oh, Lor'!

Bathe in the hot springs or chance being snowed into a cave? There was no decision. No way would she spend the night underground. New resolution or not.

Reaching down, she untied her boots and pulled off her stockings. As quickly as she could, she removed the outer layers of her garments, the steam from the pool keeping her warm. When she was down to her chemise, she nervously glanced around at the darkness.

Was Dom out there, watching?

Ignoring the thought, she slipped the chemise over her head and quickly removed her underpinnings. Her legs shook as she lowered herself into the hot water.

Heat enveloped her and she sighed out loud. Her shaking muscles relaxed and she moved into the hotter water, marveling how it massaged and caressed her bare skin. She closed her eyes and felt the heat flow around her. Spending the night suspended in the warmth sounded heavenly. Unless Dom returned. The thought caused her to flounder back toward her clothing.

Reluctantly she climbed out and used her apron to dry her wet skin. Glancing uneasily at the surrounding darkness, Millie quickly slipped back into her underpinnings and chemise. If Dom was out there somewhere, watching, she'd kill him.

She reached for her bodice and paused. How did Dom, an unmarried man, know about underpinnings? Just the thought made Millie blush. Hurriedly she donned the layers of her clothes and had just finished buttoning her coat when Dom emerged from the shadows.

His timing was suspicious.

"I didn't see anyone," he said. "You ready?"

Millie took a couple steps. He'd been right. Soaking in the hot water had loosened and relaxed her muscles. Not that she'd ever admit it to him.

"If I ever find out you sneaked a peek, Mr. Drouillard, you'll be sleeping in the barn with your burro, Columbine."

He grinned, his white teeth remarkably visible in the darkness. "Glad you're feeling better, Red. Let's go."

He stepped beside her and slipped an arm around her waist. Millie considered objecting to his forward gesture, but his warmth took the chill from the air and his closeness reassured her. In silence, they left the hot springs and slowly trudged down the valley. They entered the darkness under the trees and Dom paused to listen. A snowflake floated down, joined by a second and a third. They continued on and soon the air was thick with falling snow, graying Dom's black wool hat and covering their path. Within minutes, the gentle snowfall had turned into a blizzard. Snow, driven by an icy wind, pelted their faces.

"I can't see the trail," Millie yelled into Dom's ear.

"We're on it," he said, tightening his grip around her.

"Are you sure?" If they lost the trail, Millie knew they were dead.

"Me? Lost?" Dom's breath warmed her ear but his attempt at humor did not hearten Millie. His bravado was gone. The man was worried, but trying not to show it. Was he afraid she would break down if she knew the truth? Remembering she'd done just that in the cave, she sighed, bit the inside of her cheek, and forced one foot in front of the other.

The wind began to howl, ripping their clothing and blasting their exposed skin. Dom wrapped his bandana around his face like a bandit and encouraged Millie to cover her face with her apron. She did so, although her fingers were too cold to tie it tightly and it kept slipping down.

They staggered onward until the trail opened up into the Clear Creek valley where blowing snow blurred the line between the ground and sky. Although town was on the far side of the valley, Millie couldn't see it.

"Should we head to town?" Millie hollered, her teeth chattering.

"No. The blizzard will worsen in the open valley. We'd also have to cross Clear Creek. Good chance the bridge is drifted over and impassable. Our best hope is reaching our cabin."

Millie lowered her head and clutched Dom's waist. They stumbled on, reaching the trail up Spring Gulch. Millie had traversed this trail forty or fifty times yet she barely recognized a single familiar landmark. The steep hill with its many switchbacks disoriented her, and she prayed Dom knew where he was.

They were rounding a corner when Millie lost her footing and slipped, dragging them both to the ground. They rolled down the hill, stopping in an explosion of snow, Dom sprawled atop Millie.

"Another time," Dom gasped, breathing hard, "and I would take advantage of this position." His cold lips pressed against hers before he dragged himself back onto his feet and pulled her up beside him.

Millie didn't respond. She didn't have the energy to shiver anymore, much less chastise Dom for his improper words and actions. Mechanically she wrapped an arm around him, snuggling against him as she fought to keep as little skin as possible exposed to the bitter elements.

They climbed higher, the wind and snow scouring their frozen skin. A buried log caught Millie's foot, knocking her off balance. She fell, Dom collapsing beside her. For a long moment they just lay there, panting. All Millie wanted was to close her eyes, curl up in a ball, and sleep.

"Up!" Dom stood and dragged Millie to her feet. "We'll freeze if we stop."

Millie nodded and wearily staggered forward. They fell again, and again. Each time it took just a bit longer for Dom to struggle back onto his feet and pull Millie up beside him. Finally Millie stumbled, knocking Dom over and landing on top of him. She heard him groan, but otherwise he didn't move. Wind howled around them, ripping out their ragged breaths. Snow pelted down.

Slowly, it began to bury them.

TWENTY-NINE

November 8, 1863
Columbine's in My Kitchen?

Somehow, Dom dragged them back onto their feet and kept them moving. He never gave up. Millie couldn't have said how long they struggled through the blizzard, nor did she have any idea how Dom managed to find their cabin. By the time they stumbled through the door, Millie's hands and feet were frozen, her cheeks numb, and when Dom let her go, she collapsed in a heap in front of a blazing fire, too exhausted to crawl closer to the warmth.

"You be a sight for sore eyes," Mary said, lifting Millie's face and pouring warm tea down her throat.

"Miss Mary?" Millie said weakly, looking at her friend.

"I come over. Once I see how bad it get. Me an' Buttercup. We tend the chicks and Columbine."

When the tea was gone, Mary gently set Millie's face again on the floor and hurried away. Millie closed her eyes and felt Buttercup nibble on her frozen braid, but she didn't have the energy to lift a hand to reassure the goat. She lay there, her body numb, her mind blank.

Unable to move until her hands began to tingle.

Pain, like the stinging of a bee, brought her out of her stupor. Clumsily Millie sat up and shook her hands, only to find her discomfort increase. Mary tipped a second cup of tea down Millie's throat, muttering about "warming you insides." Some tea spilled down her face but Millie barely noticed. Her fingers felt like someone was chewing on them. Someone with sharp teeth.

"Hands be hurting?" Mary asked, removing Millie's coat and boots, tending to her as if she were a child.

"Good," Dom grunted. Millie squinted over to find him slumped on the floor nearby, a puddle of water forming around him as the snow and ice melted off his coat. "That means her hands aren't frostbit too bad. Can you feel your feet, Millie?"

Millie couldn't answer. Instead of improving as they warmed, her fingers burned like they'd been forced into the fire. Tears spilled down her cheeks. Neither moving nor tucking them close to her skin eased her torment.

"Here. Put 'em here," Mary said, returning to Millie's side with a large pot of water. "It ain't too hot. Will warm 'em slow." When Millie hesitated, Mary grabbed Millie's wrists and forced both their hands into the water. Pain, more excruciating than anything Millie had ever experienced struck her like a slap across the face. She tried to jerk her hands free, but Mary held them submerged.

"Let go," Millie screamed, calling Mary several impolite names.

"I knows," said Mary, unhappily. "I sorry. It be better soon."

Gradually the shooting pain reduced to a dull ache. That's when Millie realized her feet had begun to sting. She bit her lip, not wanting to say anything, but it didn't matter. Mary released Millie's hands and knelt to remove Millie's wool stockings. Once her feet were bare, Mary sat on her and forced them into the tub of water.

Millie screamed.

Like her hands, the agony in her feet eventually subsided, but by then Millie could only lie on her side and watch as Mary repeated the same procedure on Dom. He didn't cry out or need to be subdued, but his inventive cursing would have made an outlaw proud. Millie couldn't even blush. She didn't have the energy. Closing her eyes, she gave in as exhaustion washed over her.

She awoke in a cocoon of warmth, utter darkness, and an unfortunate need to answer the call of nature. She could hear the wind shriek, the fire crackle, and someone snoring. Nature's call intensified, bringing Millie fully awake.

Why was someone breathing down her neck? She tried to squirm away and realized an arm was pressed snugly over her waist. Her senses kicked into gear as she felt a hand cradling her breast. A hand that did *not* belong to her!

Struggling wildly, she shoved it away, hearing Dom grunt as her elbow careened into his belly. Mary groaned. Millie sat up and used an extremely vulgar expletive—one she'd learned from Dom. How had she come to be sleeping in front of the fire, sardined between Mary and Dom? In her haste to escape Dom's hand, Millie had knocked the quilts and coats off all of them.

Frigid air bit into her warm skin.

"Millie awake," Mary said sleepily, pulling the quilts back over her head. Buttercup bleated, complaining about the movement of her own quilt.

"Using language that would make the American Lady blush," Dom added, yawning as he sat up. "You shouldn't swear, Red. It isn't ladylike. Plus, it makes Columbine uncomfortable."

"Columbine? Why would…" Her words petered out. From the light of the dying fire, Millie saw Columbine's silhouette near her cookstove, munching on hay. "Why? I mean…Columbine's in my kitchen!"

"Mary brought her in. She thought poor Columbine might freeze outside." Before Millie could think of a response, he added, "The chickens are in the box near her feet."

Millie looked down and saw not only the box with the chickens, but also several long, narrow snowdrifts. They formed ridges out from the walls as snow crystals swirled in the air. Her breath produced steamy eddies in the icy air. They were inside her cabin, but it was freezing and snow hazed the air.

"Hurry up and do what you need to do," Dom growled, grumpily getting to his feet. "Use the privy pot in your bedroom. I'll add wood to the fire in the stove and fireplace."

Millie slipped into her coat and hurried to her room. *Privy pots are disgusting*, she thought, as she squatted uncomfortably over the frozen crock. Oh, Lor'! It was freezing. The pot's edge brushed against her thigh and Millie shivered. Finishing her business, she began to stand, only to feel the pot move with her. Grabbing out to keep it from spilling, she caught the half-filled pot as it ripped a strip of skin off her thigh.

Biting back a curse, Millie squatted back down, her underpinnings and drawers tangled around her stockings, her hands and the privy pot trapped beneath her skirts. She lowered the pot to the ground and let go.

Nothing happened.

Her fingertips were frozen to the pot! Groaning, she awkwardly stepped through her arms, trying to keep her loose clothes from dipping into the foul liquid. Finally she set the privy pot on the floor in front of her and carefully began ripping each finger free. By the time she'd freed them all, she was shaking from the cold and blood oozed down each bloody fingertip.

Her hands shook as she readjusted her clothing, leaving spots of blood on each garment she touched. Finally she slipped her hands into her apron and hurried out of the room. She didn't want to think what Dom would say if he saw her bloody fingertips.

The warmth of the fire drew her like a moth to light. Dom had added fresh wood and it blazed bright, but its warmth barely penetrated into the cold room. Millie's teeth chattered, and her whole body shook as she hurried over to stand as close to the warmth as she could without stepping on Mary or Buttercup.

She stopped as she noticed Dom stretched out beside Mary, holding the quilt up for her to crawl under.

He expected her to sleep under the quilt with him!

"I cannot," Millie said crossing her shaking arms over her chest. "It is completely improper. Mr. Drouillard, you—"

"I's right," Mary said, laughing.

"I will to return to my bedroom and sleep in my own bed," Millie said, the dignity of her tone diminished by the chattering of her teeth.

"Of all the stupid, impossible, unbelievable." Dom shook his head. "Redheads! I ought to let her freeze to death." With that he grabbed Millie's ankles and jerked her off her feet, catching her and tucking her under the quilts. "Now take off your coat and lay still."

"I cannot sleep here! It's entirely inappropriate."

He ignored her and pulled the quilts up over them. Millie felt warmth envelope her. "Be still, Red, else I'll show you improper."

Millie wiggled away from him, bumping into Mary. "Keep your hands to yourself!" Quickly she buried her head beneath the layers.

Dom grunted and Millie felt him tuck the quilts around them. He even reached down and checked on Buttercup. By the time he finished, he was so close Millie could feel the heat radiating from him. Whispering just loud enough for him to hear, she added, "And as I've told you numerous times, Mr. Drouillard, my hair is auburn with a few red streaks!"

Behind her, Dom's body shook with laughter.

Buttercup's cold nose pressed into Millie's warm neck, waking her. The goat had dislodged the quilt from Millie's head and frigid air immediately chilled her face. Millie wanted nothing more than to pull the quilt back over her head, but Buttercup insisted. The goat didn't have a privy pot.

Crawling from the cocoon of quilts, blankets, and coats, Millie tried not to kick Dom or Mary, but they were packed so close it was difficult to avoid. Freezing air chilled her as she quickly donned her coat and gloves, taking stock of the cabin as she laced her boots.

Outside, wind howled and snow pelted the roof and walls. Inside, light from the fire cast strange shadows. Everywhere Millie looked was gray or white. Everything, including poor Columbine, was covered in a thin dusting of snow and several large snowdrifts curved out from the walls. Dom's chinking had obviously not filled all the cracks.

Buttercup bleated, waddling toward the back door, but Millie took a moment to add fresh wood to the fire and cookstove. Unfortunately, she refreshed them with the last of their wood supply.

Joining Buttercup at the back door, Millie removed the bar and cracked open the door. Snow blasted her face and the snowdrift blocking the door tumbled inside. Millie quickly slammed the door and looked down at the goat. "You don't want to go out there."

"No choice," said Dom, limping slightly as he approached. "We need wood." He turned to slip his hand into his coat and Millie gasped.

Dom's hip and left leg were coated in dried blood.

THIRTY

November 9, 1863
Just a Scratch?

"You're hurt," Millie cried, rushing over and brushing Dom's coat back. "What happened?"

"It's fine," Dom said gruffly. "Just a scratch." He knocked her hand away, letting his coat cover the injury. Millie roughly grabbed the coat and jerked it back, bending down for a closer look. Two small holes pierced the bloody area.

"You were shot?" she asked, her stomach lurching.

"Just nicked. Now hold the door while I go for wood." Brushing her hands away, he pulled the door open, forced his way through a waist-high snowdrift, and disappeared into the blowing snow. Buttercup gave Millie a sour look and waddled after him.

Keeping the door ajar, Millie waited impatiently, relieved when both Dom and Buttercup lurched back inside. Snow caked every inch of them, making Buttercup look like a four-legged snow monster and Dom a giant snowman.

Millie slammed and barred the door as Dom dropped his armload of wood and shook his head, sending snow everywhere. He removed his heavy coat, giving Millie a glimpse of his injured leg—blood stained most of his hip.

"I want to look at your injury," Millie insisted. "Right now."

"No! I'm starving." He picked up some logs and carried them toward the fireplace, favoring his injured leg. "Leave me alone, Red. I'm fine. I need food."

The man was as stubborn as his burro, but Millie hadn't kept four of the five LeGrand children alive by being timid about tending injuries. Sneaking into her room, she dug out a bottle from the medicines she'd brought from New Orleans and slipped it into her pocket.

Mary stood by the cookstove, Columbine beside her, and her sourdough pot clutched in her hand. She held up the pot and grinned. "Sleeped with it. Them sourdoughies ain't froze. How 'bout hotcakes?"

Hotcakes sounded fast and easy. Millie was freezing. She stepped over a smelly pile of dung and lifted the lid of the chicken box. They huddled together, shivering and clucking unhappily. None had graced them with a fresh egg.

In the bowl above the cookstove, Millie retrieved an older egg and tried to crack it. It was frozen solid. Fingers stiff from the cold, Millie pealed the egg as Mary freshened the sourdough and put aside a starter. As they worked, Dom slowly brought the rest of the firewood into the room, definitely favoring the injured leg.

"Dom," Millie said, "You—"

"I'm fine, woman." Settling on the quilts, he turned his back on her and lifted his hands toward the fire.

Irritated, Millie did her best to ignore him. "Miss Mary, do you think the other townsfolk are okay? Some of them live in awful clapboard cabins."

"They be fine," Mary said. "It storm like this every winter."

They chatted casually as the wind rattled the shutters and their pile of hotcakes grew. Finally Millie carried the overflowing plate to the fireplace, and they settled on their sleeping quilts to eat. The first stack disappeared without a word said, but as Millie made and brought over a second stack, Dom broke the silence.

"It was a storm like this, during the winter of '59, caused Jackson to find the first gold here in Idaho Springs." Dom dragged another hotcake onto his plate. As always, eating improved his temperament.

"A blizzard was the reason he found gold?" Millie asked, heaping jam over her hotcake, one eye on Dom. His injury did not appear to affect his appetite. Knowing Dom, he could be dying and still eat.

Dom cleaned his plate before answering. "Mr. Jackson was just exploring when he camped at the Chicago diggings. He—"

"Chicago diggin'?" Mary interrupted.

"The mining operation on Clear Creek near Old Shakespeare's place. When he found color, Jackson named the site the Chicago diggings."

"He was searching for gold in the middle of the winter?"

"He was exploring, but he was a miner. Miner's always have one eye open for color. It seems like most find it when they give up and do something else. In '58, Green Russell and his party of Georgians found gold in the bed of Little Dry Creek. Their party started almost a hundred strong, but after twenty days of fruitless searching, most quit and headed back to the States. Russell didn't and when he stumbled on shining sand, the Pikes Peak gold rush was born."

He pulled another hotcake onto his plate. Millie wondered if it was his sixth or seventh. She sighed. She really didn't want to get up and leave the relative warmth of the fireplace to make more. Maybe if he was distracted…

"What about Mr. Jackson?" she asked.

"Mr. Jackson. Well, back in '59 there used to be a geyser at the hot pools we visited. The Indians say it threw up a beautiful bluish spray that billowed into the cold winter—"

"Mr. Updike, the stagecoach driver, said the Arapahoe called the geyser Edanhau or maybe Edauhoe," Millie said. "He said it translated into something like "Gem in the Mountain" which is where the word Idahoe came from."

"Naw." Dom forked another hotcake onto his plate. "Idaho Springs was first called Chicago Diggings, then Jackson's Bar and Spanish Bar, and finally Idahoe, an Anglicized version of the Ute's word for columbines. It means 'flower of the beautiful head.' After mail started getting lost and heading to Idaho territory, the town changed its name to Idaho Springs."

"I wondered, when I answered that ad, if I was coming to Idaho or Colorado Territory. Not that I knew anything about either." She paused, thinking of her previous life. When her ink unfroze, she'd write Carissa and tell her about this snowstorm. Maybe even send details about her bath in the hot springs. Carissa would find that deliciously scandalizing.

"I think it was January of '59," Dom said, helping himself to another hotcake. "Mr. Jackson had been exploring, hiking up the Vasquez River. Clear Creek now. He saw this strange blue spray. Headed toward it to investigate, and found the geyser. Unfortunately, soon afterward, a storm hit. He—"

"He was traveling alone? In Indian territory? In the winter?"

Dom laughed. "Lots of folks explore these mountains alone."

"Do you?"

"At times. Johannes was the one who wanted to settle. He's the reason we homesteaded here and built the cabins. But I like to explore. I usually spend most of the year traveling to mining towns, earning my keep doing assays and filling my pockets with unusual rock and mineral samples."

"Like the ones in your room?"

"Yep."

"Why?"

"Why what?"

"Finish your story Mr. Dom!" huffed Mary. "You're worse than Old Shakespeare. Forget your fancy rocks. Tell us 'bout Mr. Jackson and gold."

"Women! How'd I end up in a cabin with two of 'em?"

He pulled the last hotcake onto his plate and Millie decided he wasn't suffering too much. She gave him a severe look.

"Actually," Dom grumbled, "Mr. Jackson wasn't traveling alone. He had his dogs with him. But that don't matter none. It was a terrible winter blizzard that caused Mr. Jackson to hunker down. Way he told it, a blizzard like the one outside forced him to camp. He built a roaring fire at the junction where Chicago Creek met Clear Creek and when the fire thawed the ground, being a miner, Mr. Jackson used his hunting knife to dig up some dirt. He panned it using his cup. Told me he discovered nine dollars in gold dust, just from the area under his fire."

Mary whistled. "Nine dollars, just panning with his cup. Musta been lots of color."

"Water's boiling," Millie said, picking up their cups. "I'll make some hot coffee and tea. My fingers are freezing."

She made the hot drinks and came to a decision. The consequences wouldn't be pleasant, but his injury needed attention. She'd lost a LeGrand child to an infection she'd initially assumed was a minor scratch. She'd been young and hadn't realized how serious the injury had become until it was too late. Dom, being a stubborn male, wouldn't let her examine the wound even if his leg was striped red with infection.

Glancing over, she made sure Mary and Dom weren't paying her any mind before she removed the bottle from her pocket. A couple drops in Dom's coffee was all she needed.

Scurrying back to the fire, she handed Dom his coffee and Mary her tea. "I don't remember meeting Mr. Jackson."

"You haven't," he said, sipping the hot liquid. "Mr. Jackson made his claim and came back the following spring with twenty-some-odd men. It's said they prospected almost two thousand dollars in gold dust their first week. Just before Mr. Jackson left Idaho Springs for good, he told me his story." Shaking his head, he yawned. "Said Cannibal Phil was in the initial party, but that might have been a stretch, something to liven up the yarn."

"Cannibal Phil?" Mary asked. "You make this up, Mr. Dom?"

"Maybe," Dom said, grinning. "Not sure if Old Phil really was part of the Jackson party. The scoundrel used to hang out in Apollo Hall, a Denver saloon I frequented. If—"

"How often *did* you frequent Denver saloons, Mr. Drouillard?" asked Millie, noting Dom's eyelids appeared to be drooping. She moved to sit beside him. "In the vapor cave you told me about Mountain Charley. Now Cannibal Phil? You must have spent significant time in those Denver saloons."

Dom's eyes glassed over and he spoke slowly, pausing often. "It's hot in Denver. During the summer. A man needs. A man needs...a drink. Every now and then." He set down his empty coffee cup and rubbed his face. "Old Cannibal Phil. He was an ugly cuss. Hung out at saloos. S-saloons. W-with his giant dog." His words slurred and Millie put her arm around him. He didn't seem to notice. "I-if you paid for his drink. He'd. He'd tell you about...about eating his squaw." He shook his head and leaned on Millie, looking at her with a loopy expression. "He was. Trapping for Mr. K-Kit Carson. Got caught. I-in a blizzard. Said. Said he ate her." A wide yawn interrupted his words. They became more slurred and hesitant. "Her name. Was. Was Kloock. H-he returned. To camp. In spring...Said her leg. Was packed. O-on his mule." Dom slumped against Millie, his head dropping onto her shoulder. In slow, slurred words he said, "Wonder. What. She. Tasted. Like?"

"That awful," said Mary, jumping to her feet. "What wrong with him?"

"Help me lay him down," Millie said, but she was too slow. Dom went limp and his weight knocked her over. He sprawled on top of her, his face cradled between her breasts. His drool dampened her bodice.

“Get him off me!”

Millie squirmed and with Mary’s help, they managed to roll him off and onto his back. Millie dragged his limp legs out in front of him and untangled his arms. Panting, she glanced at Mary. “Don’t worry. I put laudanum in his coffee.”

“You drug Mr. Dom?”

“He wasn’t going to let me look at his injured hip. This way, I don’t hafta listen to him bellow.”

“When he wake up,” Mary said, shaking her head, “He gonna kill you.”

THIRTY-ONE

November 9, 1863
Dom on the Warpath

Dom might kill me, Millie thought as she stared at the blood caked on his hip and leg. But would he kill her because she drugged him, or because she removed his pants while he was unconscious? Blushing all the way down to her toes, Millie looked bleakly at Mary. "Help me remove his trousers."

"No way!" Mary said, backing away. "I ain't taking the britches off no white man! I rather be lynched. I heat water." She turned her back on Millie and hurried to the stove.

Rolling her eyes, Millie knelt down and probed the injury. The bullet had ripped two holes in his trousers, but she couldn't see how deep it had penetrated his hip. She had to remove his trousers. There was simply no other way. Surely he'd understand.

Her hands shook as she reached for the buttons at the front of his pants. She froze. What if he was no longer wearing drawers or his woolens? Rising, Millie paced around, adding wood to the fire before draping a quilt over Dom's torso.

Maybe she didn't need to check. He said he was fine.

The blood on his hip and leg said otherwise.

Oh, Lor'. *What should I do?* This situation was definitely not covered in her books on etiquette. He could die if the wound fouled. She took a deep breath. Cleaning and bandaging Dom's injury was no different than the numerous times she'd bandaged the injured soldiers on the *Sultana* or tended the cuts, bruises, and injuries of the LeGrand children. Indeed.

Millie looked at the unconscious man. Indeed not! None of the soldier's injuries had been on their lower anatomy, and the LeGrand children were just that, *children*.

Flinching, Millie knelt and quickly unbuttoned the top button of Dom's trousers. Despite the freezing temperatures, Millie felt perspiration bead on her forehead. The second button popped open and Millie caught a glimpse of skin and dark hair. Oh, Lor'! She looked away and felt for the third button. Her shaking fingers missed the button and brushed against Dom's warm skin. She jerked her hand back.

Just a month ago, she'd thought Dom's bathing in the cabin was the worst thing she could imagine. Removing his pants had never entered her imagination! Fortifying herself with several deep breaths, she quickly unhooked the last button, relieved to see his rough, woolen underdrawers.

The unbuttoning process had been mortifying. Dragging the pants off his inert form was worse. Twice she'd had to stop to pull up his drawers as they slid low on his hips. They were the simple type, thick homespun wool that fell half way to his knees, held in place by a drawstring. Millie finally managed to wrestle the trousers off, falling as she jerked them free. She paused to catch her breath and heard muffled snorts beside her. Turning, she found Mary doubled over, tears streaming down her face, her laughter muffled.

"Traitor," Millie uttered, turning her attention to the unconscious man clothed only in light drawers and coarse stockings. Like his pants, the side of his drawers were also encrusted in blood. Too bad. No way would she remove another layer of clothing. She cleaned the blood off the rough material and widened the rip in his drawers for a better view of the wound. The bullet had grazed his hip, leaving a gash that gaped open and still oozed blood.

How had he walked through the blizzard and gotten her home?

Millie cleaned and washed the wound, satisfied the surrounding skin was still pink and healthy. Patting the wound dry with a clean cloth, she moved slightly and caught a glimpse of the rounded curve of his buttocks and a long red scar. She jerked away, embarrassed. Thank the Lor' Dom was unconscious!

From her sewing kit she retrieved thread and needle, wondering about the nasty scar. Was that his keepsake from the battle at Glorieta Pass? Dom had been discharged from military service because he'd been shot in the buttock.

Millie used her darning thread to close the wound before putting a clean rag over it. It would be best to secure the rag with bandages, but Millie stood up and looked down at Dom in his loose drawers. She shook her head. She was done.

The storm raged on, but when Dom awoke, it was his booming shouts that shook the cabin. He modestly wrapped a quilt around him and hurried to his room, calling Millie names she didn't recognize, although his tone made it clear they were not complimentary. She slipped a fresh loaf of sourdough into the oven, hoping food might appease him, although this time, she doubted it.

"How dare you?" fumed Dom as he stomped back into the room, now dressed in new trousers. He raged in front of her, crowding her, and poked her in the shoulder. "You removed my pants! You, you…" words failed him.

"Your injury needed tending," Millie shouted back, "I—"

"I can tend my own injuries. Don't you ever…Where is it? What did you use to knock me out?"

"I used Laudanum. It—"

He spun around, almost losing his balance in his haste, and stomped into Millie's room. She could hear him moving boxes and slamming her things about, searching for the drug. His actions were insulting, but not surprising. Millie expected something of the sort and had hidden the Laudanum and her other medications in the kitchen near the stove. If he discovered them there, she'd put up a fight.

"He steaming mad," Mary whispered, giggling.

"Do you think food will help?"

Mary shook her head, her eyes dancing. "Nope. You in for a rampage. He bellow like a buffalo. Maybe all winter."

"Lovely," Millie said sarcastically and braced herself as Dom tore back into the kitchen.

"Where is it? Where have you hidden it?"

"You will *not* destroy my medications, Mr. Drouillard," Millie said severely. "Now quit acting like a spoiled child."

"A spoiled child?" Dom roared. "You've gone too far, Red!" He stamped over and looked down at her, his nose inches from her face. "If you ever drug me again, I'll take you over my knee and—"

"Of course you won't," Millie said icily, not positive he wasn't serious. "Now sit down. The bread is ready." She turned and pulled the hot loaf from the oven, placing it on the table.

Dom sniffed it suspiciously, his hands fisted on his hips. "You take a bite first. Prove it ain't drugged."

Fortunately, the storm abated as quickly as it had started. Millie sighed with relief when Dom took his ill temper—along with Columbine—outside. It took two days to clear a path through the deep snow, first to the barn and privy, next to Mary's cabin. Mary immediately fled, explaining she needed to tend to some things, but Millie knew she just wanted to escape Dom and his volatile temper.

The man continued to berate her and act suspicious, but Millie noticed with satisfaction his limp had almost disappeared.

On the fifth day after the storm, Dom stomped into the cabin, kicking snow everywhere. He'd developed several unpleasant new mannerisms since the storm—unsaid little punishments for Millie.

"Finally reached town. I raised some hell trying to find out who shot at us, but nobody knew nothing."

"Was everyone okay?" Millie felt a bit guilty, but she was relieved his fury was now directed at someone else.

"The ones I dug out were. No one's seen any of the prospectors up Virginia Canyon or Fall River, including that rascal Turck. Tomorrow I'll go looking. I'm going to find out who tried to kill us and when I do—" His voice trailed off as he headed back outside, slamming the door in his wake.

THIRTY-TWO

November 15, 1863
Thanksgiving

Dom raised hell as he dug out prospectors, bullying and threatening each one, but obtaining a confession from none. The heavy blanket of snow covered tracks and buried secrets, providing no clue to the shooter who'd almost cost them their lives. Millie suggested their assailant might have been Mr. Gould, but Dom was certain his brother's killer had struck again. He reasoned it was mid-winter. Gould couldn't survive in Idaho Springs without having been seen.

Days passed. With no new clues to follow, Dom's attention turned from digging out neighbors to cutting a trail to his mine. Millie admired his determination—the path was totally snowed under—and a part of her was relieved when he finally reached the mine and resumed his search for his brother's gold. She'd had quite enough of his temper and insinuations.

On the other hand, Millie couldn't help but worry. Dom was working alone, just as his brother had, and while digging out the town, she had no doubt Dom had goaded each man with reminders of his brother's discovery. The killer was out there somewhere, and sooner or later he'd go after Dom.

Worries about Dom filled her days, but at night Millie tossed and turned as worries about Mr. Gould filled her head. There'd been no word about the fugitive, but with each passing day, Millie felt an urgency she couldn't explain. Perhaps the shooting at the hot springs had set her on edge, or more likely, it was Dom's continued temper.

Either way, Millie felt like time was running out.

Eventually Mr. Gould would return or Mr. D's killer would strike again. She could do little but practice with her six-shooter to prepare for Mr. Gould, but surely she could uncover Mr. D's killer before he struck again. The only question was how.

It was a newspaper article that gave her the perfect idea. She'd been reading President Lincoln's latest proclamation on Thanksgiving and it hit her: the perfect trap to catch a killer was a Thanksgiving dinner party.

For reasons Millie would never understand, in the midst of this terribly bloody war, President Lincoln had proclaimed the last Thursday in November to be Thanksgiving, a day to give thanks for all the country's blessings. Of course there had been other Thanksgivings. They'd started when the pilgrims first arrived, and sometimes occurred twice or three times in a year. In 1789, George Washington declared two nationwide Thanksgiving days—one in November and one in February—and even President Davis had declared his country's day of Thanksgiving in September of '62.

Still, Millie had seen firsthand the death and horror from the war and she had trouble understanding the President's timing. Probably the industrious Miss Josepha Hale, the editor of *Godey's Lady's Book*, had convinced Lincoln a day devoted to thanks and memories might heal some of the country's wounds. Millie doubted that was possible. After all the terrible battles and loss of life, she questioned if the country could ever heal, no matter the outcome of the war.

Nonetheless, the proclamation gave her the opportunity to put a dinner plan into action. She'd host a Thanksgiving supper, invite her list of suspects, and discreetly question them during the meal. When the killer made a mistake, Millie would have him.

With her plan formulated, Millie settled at the table, steaming tea in hand, and considered her invitation list. Since her arrival, at least fifty men had offered to buy the mine. Too many suspects. Maybe she needed to focus on the men who persisted. There were her four main suitors: Mr. Poor, Mr. Shumate, Mr. Tappan, and Mr. Turck. Only Mr. Turck seemed a likely suspect. Still, Millie wrote down all four names. She didn't want to hurt anyone's feelings.

Tapping her pencil against the table, she considered who else wanted the mine. Brother Bunce and Mr. Ferris had continued to add fifty dollars to their offers every couple of weeks, as had Elder Griswold, and the Grouse—James Whitlatch. Come to think of it, so had Charlotte Card, but the voice she'd heard cursing in her chicken coop had been a man's, hadn't it?

She looked around the small cabin. With Mary—and Mary would be coming even if her guests objected—there would be fourteen. That many people would barely fit and she'd have to borrow chairs and dishes. Still, the tiny space would force close, intimate conversations—tête-à-têtes—where she could get to the bottom of this mystery, find the killer, and send Dom packing.

Millie wrote down each guest's name before jotting down ideas for her menu. Food was no problem—she would enjoy making it—but how did one throw a formal party? Or write an official Thanksgiving dinner invitation? Trusting Florence Hartley, Millie searched her book and was rewarded with both hints on planning the party and an example of a proper invitation. On a clean sheet of paper, Millie wrote her first invitation.

Miss Permelia Abingdon Virginia requests the favor of Miss Mary Randolph's company to a

Thanksgiving dinner, on Thursday, November 26th, at 1 o'clock.

Invitation in hand, Millie followed the narrow path to Mary's cabin. Her friend opened the door on the second knock and Millie formally handed her the invitation before she and Buttercup hurried inside.

"What this?" Mary asked, looking at the folded sheet of paper.

"Read it," Millie said, belatedly realizing the invitations might provide a clue themselves. Mary enjoyed reading the newspaper as much as Millie, but she suspected not all of her suitors and neighbors were educated. Whoever threatened her was literate.

"A Thanksgiving dinner?" Mary huffed. Suspiciously she stared at Millie. "This be some proper invite. I's the only guest?"

"Of course not," Millie said. She read the other names on her list.

"You want me and Elder Griswold eatin' together?" Mary asked, her eyebrows shooting up. "And Titus Turck? You crazy, girl? You know how proper folks feel 'bout colored folk." She shook her head. "You just as well invite Tit Bit and Smooth Bore."

"Don't be foolish. It's time you were brought into society. Or at least Idaho Springs society."

Mary grumbled but agreed to help with the cooking, dishes, and chairs. When Millie mentioned she planned to use the meal to flush out the killer, Mary laughed. "What Dom say?"

Millie couldn't answer. She hadn't yet told Dom. It wasn't a conversation she was particularly looking forward to.

That evening Millie cooked a potato pie, one of Dom's favorite dishes, managing to hold her tongue when he sniffed and asked, "Is it drugged?" After he'd devoured half the dish, Millie casually mentioned her plan, bracing for the explosion.

"A Thanksgiving meal, huh?" He rubbed Buttercup's head, his expression thoughtful. "Thinking of doing some detecting, are you? Who's on the invite list?"

Millie listed her guests, surprised to see him nod in agreement.

"I think it's got to be someone local, too. After the gold in the mine, that is. I don't think the shooting had anything to do with Gould."

Millie agreed. Mr. Gould was a future problem. One she'd have to deal with alone, after Dom left.

Dom paused and helped himself to another portion of the potato pie. "Problem is, any of them could have done it. Lord knows most folks up here are just scraping by, although I can't see Elder Griswold. He cares too much about his reputation and Idaho Springs."

"Who do you suspect?" Millie asked. He'd talked of a suspect list when he first arrived, but once he got busy clearing the mine, he seemed to have lost interest.

"Your list includes my top suspects. Asa Poor and Titus Turck both been struggling. Gold ain't as easy to find, like in the past. Plus, both of them have a sneaky streak. For a preacher, Brother Bunce is all right, but never heard much about the Arkansas Traveler before he come out this way. Course that's true for most of the miners 'round here. Lots came here to make a new start, but some are hiding from something in their pasts."

"Mr. Shumate's told me about his past. He's not hiding anything."

"Are you sure?" Dom asked, giving Millie a hard look. "Willing to bet your life on it?"

Millie swallowed. She liked Mr. Shumate. Still. What did she really know about the man? What did she know about any of them, including Dom? She glanced at him, wondering what secrets he might be hiding.

"Sooty, Old Shakespeare, Mr. Whitlatch, even Mr. Ferris. They all appear respectable. Well, as respectable as you get in a mining town like Idaho Springs, but they could have done anything before they come here. You ever seen anything to prove Mr. Ferris really is a solicitor?"

Millie shook her head. She hated suspecting any of them. They were her neighbors. They'd helped her survive and been kind to her, making her feel like she fit in and had a home. "You're too skeptical. Most folks in this town are good, honest, hardworking folk."

"Maybe," Dom said, scraping the last of the potato pie onto his plate, "but at least one of those honest folk tried to kill us. Add the Gardners, Beebees, and Gilsons to your list."

"You suspect them?" Millie asked, surprised. The Gardners, Beebees, and Gilsons—along with the Griswolds—were the founding families of Idaho Springs.

"Not really," Dom said, finishing off his meal. "But more ladies will make our meal feel legit. Plus, you're going to cause quite a stir. Insult anyone not invited."

Millie shook her head. "We can't add three couples. We'd be twenty, plus some kids. We'd never fit."

"It'll work."

Millie just shook her head. Only a man would add six more dinner guests so casually. Millie opened her mouth to object, but Dom spoke first. "You still have some of those teardrop nuggets we found in Johannes' hidey-hole?"

"A couple," Millie answered cautiously. She'd been coveting her small fortune, knowing with Dom's eating habits, her food wouldn't last the winter.

"Spend two or three of 'em. Act like we're rolling in nuggets. Splurge and buy some lemons, dried fruit, and chestnuts." His eyebrows lifted and his expression turned soft. "Get some peppermint candy too."

"Peppermint candy?"

Dom blushed and stood up, strolling to the fire. "I like it," he said gruffly. As if deliberately changing the subject, he added, "Maybe we should take a trip to Denver City. Try to buy us a turkey. In June, the *Rocky Mountain News* said a man drove around 500 turkeys from Missouri to Denver. Maybe we could still find one. That'd be sure to make the shooter think we found the mother lode."

"But we haven't found the mother lode…or any gold to speak of," Millie said. She approved of his idea to flaunt some wealth—to draw out the killer—but a stagecoach ride to Denver, not to mention the cost of a turkey if they could find one, would easily use up a full nugget. She only had two left. "We don't need a turkey. Mary and I have agreed to a menu of mince and chicken pies. But I'll use one of the nuggets to purchase delicacies."

"Use two. I want the shooter hungry, and not just for your gourmet food." He rubbed his chin thoughtfully. "Maybe I'll plan a turkey shoot."

"A turkey shoot?" Millie asked, alarmed. "What's that?"

"A shooting contest. Traditionally the best shot won a turkey, but I'm sure one of Mary's fruit pies will suffice."

"But why?" The thought of Dom shooting his six-shooter in the same place as the killer alarmed her.

"To figure out who's a crack shot. Determine who shot at us."

THIRTY-THREE

November 26, 1863
A Turkey Shoot

On the morning of November 26, Millie wasn't thinking about the killer, the gold, or even Mr. Gould. Her thoughts were focused strictly on food. She rushed to finish two more mince pies and slipped three mountain cakes into her warmer. She definitely had a lapse of good sense when she made this plan. Her guests had received their invitations and exuberantly accepted, causing such a fuss Millie had actually heard grumblings from those not invited. Not that she'd tell Dom he'd been right.

Food that could be made early—the fruit pies, pickled cabbage, keg tomato pickles and such—were made, but the meat pies and the Canada goose that Dom had shot needed to wait until the night before. Millie loved to cook, but after working by candlelight most of the night, she was ready to forget the whole thing. At least she was almost done.

Dom stomped into the room, shaking the floor. Millie braced herself. If the man asked her for something to eat, she'd scream. Looking up from her dishes, she dropped her skillet back into the water.

"What?" Dom snarled at her astonished expression. "You think I only own one set of clothes?"

Well, yes. Until today, Millie had never seen him in anything but his patched wool britches and faded flannel shirts.

With his face freshly shaved, his hair brushed back, wearing a clean linen shirt, matching waistcoat, trousers, and a wide necktie, he looked civilized. And handsome. Almost. His scowl hadn't changed.

"I'd better go dress," Millie said, leaving the dishes for later. "Folks should be arriving soon."

A knock at the door punctuated her words.

She watched as Dom opened the door and helped Mary remove her winter coat. Once again, Millie stared in shock. Mary wore a black and white linsey-woolsey dress with white lace around the neckline, highlighting her ebony skin and white teeth. A matching bonnet and a lovely knit shawl completed the ensemble. She looked beautiful, but nervous.

"Mary, I've never seen you in such finery," Dom said, taking her hand and causing Mary to blush as he kissed it. "You'll outshine all the white ladies. Please come in. I'll bring you some punch. Millie made it special with the lemons and sugar she bought, although I added a bit of rum for flavor."

Rum for flavor? How much? Millie glanced around for the bottle. They wanted folks talking freely, but rum in her lemonade?

Shaking her head, she went to her bedroom and struggled into a stiff corset before slipping on her new crinoline and an extra petticoat. Dom had insisted they should appear flush in gold and Millie had never owned a real crinoline, although ordering the unmentionable at Mr. Tappan's store had been mortifying. Smoothing her much-prized sprigged calico dress over the undergarments, Millie was pleased with her new shape, although breathing in the tight corset was restricted to shallow gasps.

Finally, Millie untied her braid and brushed out the kinks, pulling the thick mass into a tight chignon with the ends draping free down her neck in curled ringlets. It would be easier with a mirror, but Millie did the best she could, pulling it back and holding it in place with the only finery she owned: two silver hair clasps.

Dom whistled as Millie swept into the room, causing her to blush. He strode over and gently brushed a hand down the loose curls. "I've never seen it loose, Red." He grinned. "I like it. Reminds me of a wild bonfire."

"A bonfire?" Millie asked, swatting away his hand. The galoot might look like a gentleman, but he definitely didn't act like one. "Mr. Drouillard. How many times do I need to remind you, my hair is—"

Her words were interrupted by a knock at the door. Turning her back on Dom, Millie marched to the door and jerked it open. Mr. Tappan, wearing the same strange outfit he'd worn to Mr. D's funeral, removed his straw top-hat and bowed low in greeting.

"Widow D, as the Bard might say, 'Thou art more lovely and more temperate than a summer's day.'" He glanced toward town. "Before the other gentlemen arrive, I'd like to take this opportunity to give you these fresh apples. They seemed appropriate after the fortune you spent at my store." He glanced down at Millie's figure, his eyes pausing as if to admire the new corset and crinoline. "I see some of your purchases have been put to good use."

Millie blushed and would have stepped to the side, but Mr. Tappan grabbed her hand and held her in place as he knelt. Clearing his throat, he pulled Millie closer.

"'Hear my soul speak. The very instant that I saw you, did my heart fly to your service.'" His deep baritone voice made the words sing.

Millie couldn't help smiling. When Mr. Tappan began quoting the Bard, he put his heart and soul into it.

"That's from Shakespeare's *The Tempest*," he said. "Widow D, you've mourned long enough. It's time you married me."

Millie paused, expecting an outcry from Dom, but the room behind her was strangely silent. "You want to marry me, Mr. Tappan, even though I don't own the mine?"

"Selling it to Dom is a darn shame," Mr. Tappan said, using her hand to pull himself up from his knee, "but this cabin's better built than mine and I froze during that last storm."

"Thank you, Mr. Tappan, but I hafta refuse."

He glanced to Millie's side. "Because he's living with you?"

"No!" Millie said sharply. "As I've told you on numerous occasions, Mr. Drouillard is my guest. He'll be leaving soon."

"Uh-huh."

"If you're done proposing," Dom said solicitously, "may I offer you a bit of punch, Old Shakespeare?"

Millie turned to stare. Where was the Dom she knew? Before she could ask, Mr. Poor walked up and pushed Mr. Tappan from his spot. Mr. Poor had changed out of his black and white overalls and even brushed his hair and beard. Unfortunately, somehow during the grooming his thick left eyebrow had been brushed up and the right one down, making him look slightly out of kilter.

"Mr. Poor, what a pleasure to see you." When Millie had given her invitation to Mr. Poor, he'd glanced at it and asked, "What's this?" After she'd explained, he'd tossed the invitation unopened on his table, leaving Millie to curse her own stupidity. Was the man illiterate, or sly?

"Widow D." He dropped to one knee and Millie almost sighed. Coughing to clear his throat, he said, "Widow D, you need a husband to protect you. To hunt and provide for you. You unfortunately don't need a miner no more to tend to your mine, but you need a husband to chop and carry wood. And do other chores you can't do. I need a wife to cook for me. Plus, Tit Bit raised her rates and my poke's starting to sag, so I could use a wife, if you knows what I mean." He looked down at Buttercup and back up at Millie. "How about we get hitched and roast the goat. She's fat enough to feed most of the townsfolk."

Millie politely refused and Mr. Poor scooted around her and accepted a glass of punch from Dom. Looking back outside, Millie watched Mr. Shumate and Mr. Turck approach. They were together, so maybe she'd escape a proposal. When they reached the door, Mr. Turck scowled, squeezed his beard braids, and growled, "Me and Sooty tossed a Gruber twenty and he won, so he gets to propose. But you don't have to accept."

Mr. Turck stepped into the cabin and Mr. Shumate knelt at her feet. His big hands closed over Millie's, causing hers to disappear. "I'd be mighty pleased, lassie, if you'd consent to marry me." He looked up expectantly. It was the first time Millie had seen his face without soot on it. Of all her suitors, he was her favorite, but she didn't want to marry him. As kindly as she could, she refused.

"Thought not," he said, getting back on his feet and sniffing the air. "So when do we get to eat your bevy of delectables?"

So much for breaking the man's heart.

Within an hour, guests filled every inch of Millie's cabin, all happily devouring dish after dish. Conversations were shouted, with only the loudest ones being heard. Making her way through the crowd with her full skirts was almost impossible. Millie wondered how she could have been so stupid to wear such a garment or to imagine she might have intimate conversations in this crowd.

"Dom, you really gonna have a turkey shoot?" called Brother Bunce.

"Course. Just as soon as we're finished eating."

"Will it be like the California Gulch Turkey shoot of '60?" Elder Griswold asked. The room instantly quieted. Elder Griswold's stories had that effect.

"I've never heard about any such turkey shoot," said Millie, encouragingly. Between serving food, getting jostled as she moved about the room, and talking politely with her guests, she was exhausted. One of Elder Griswold's stories sounded like a godsend.

"It was back during the Christmas of '60," Elder Griswold began in his calm, slow voice. "I was in Oro City and Old Newt, the cuss who ran the town boardinghouse and saloon, started putting up placards proclaiming:

SHUTIN FOR TURKEYS
NEWT'S SALOON CHRISMUS EVE

"We all thought it was Old Newt having some fun. There ain't *no* wild turkeys anywhere near there. Still, a few days 'fore Christmas, a group of us from the Tarryall camp were curious, so we asked Old Newt to see them birds. We was surprised when he obliged and took us back to his dusky storeroom. To our amazement, there in the back were a bunch of crates and inside were featherless red heads and eyes that reflected the candlelight. Somehow Old Newt had got hold of a dozen turkeys. That's when the excitement started." He paused and helped himself to another slice of mince pie. As he ate, the room remained silent. He picked up his punch to wet his whistle, and Charlotte Card expressed the suspense they all felt.

"You gonna keep us waiting all evening? What happened?"

He laughed. Elder Griswold knew timing was everything in a good story. "Well, on Christmas Eve, a long line formed in front of Newt's Saloon, each of us wanting to shoot a bird and take it to our sweetheart—or more likely to the boardinghouse woman—for supper. Old Newt met us outside and announced his rules. Each turkey would be set in a bulletproof box with only their ugly heads sticking out. For five dollars, a competitor got three shots from a distance of twenty feet. He had to hit its head to get the bird and only one shooter—"

"The poor birds were locked in a crate with their heads sticking out? Just waiting to be shot?" Millie asked. "That's terrible."

Everyone in the room turned to stare. Millie had butchered her share of chickens but the thought of a turkey locked in a box with his head sticking out just seemed cruel. Or maybe, after the shooting at the hot springs, she understood too well the terror the turkey might have felt. Unfortunately, her neighbors' expressions indicated they thought her sympathy a bit dull-witted.

"I'm sorry. Please continue with your story, Elder Griswold."

"That's fine, Widow D. This here's an excellent meal. Do you think I could trouble you for a piece of Miss Mary's fine-looking berry pie?"

Millie rose and struggled to reach the stove. After slicing and serving the pie, Millie stood by the stove, unwilling to attempt the journey back to her seat.

"As I was saying," Elder Griswold said, patting his stomach. "Each shooter got three chances and only one shooter at a time was allowed inside. Them's were Old Newt's rules.

"We all watched the first shooter head inside. Old Newt closed the door but when we heard a shot and a curse, we cheered. Mind you, there were only so many turkeys. His second shot brought a cry of triumph, only, just after, we heard curses and Newt's voice. Wasn't too long after that when Old Newt came for the next shooter.

"We all wondered where the first shooter had got to, but then we heard the second shooter's shot. This time he was successful with his first volley. Once again there were his triumphant cry, some cursing, and then laughter. It was a mite confusing. Especially since it went on like that as a third, fourth, and fifth shooter took his turn.

"After the tenth one went in with none coming out—and lots of curses and laughter following each shooter—we all got a mite bit suspicious. When Old Newt come for the eleventh shooter, we rushed the door and pushed our way in. Any guesses what we found?"

"A turkey with his head shot off!"

"Old Newt with his head shot off."

"The shooters holding their turkeys?"

"The shooters sitting around drinking whiskey!"

"What did you see?"

Elder Griswold chuckled. "Sticking out of the box was an ugly red head, but it weren't no turkey. It was a darn turkey buzzard. And there was Old Newt and the first ten shooters, slapping their knees and laughing so hard tears streamed down their faces." The Elder's eyes took on a faraway look and he began laughing. "We were none too pleased to be missing our turkey dinner, but we appreciated Old Newt's fun."

As the laughter in the room subsided, Dom rose and stretched. "We don't have a turkey prize, but Miss Mary made us one of her famous strawberry rhubarb pies. I've built wooden X's and marked thirty paces distance so the shoot can be fair." He placed his hand on the bulge of the six-shooter in his pocket. "Shall we go, gentlemen?"

"Gentlemen?" asked Charlotte Card indignantly. "Ain't this turkey shoot open to anyone?"

THIRTY-FOUR

December 19, 1863
An Accident?

Three weeks after the Thanksgiving celebration, Millie still had no new clues pointing to the killer's identity. Charlotte Card won the turkey shoot, with Titus Turck coming in a close second. Mr. Ferris and Old Shakespeare had the honor of being the worst shots, but the information did little good. At the hot springs, the shooter had missed, mostly, but whether that was the deliberate action of a crack shot or the result of a lousy shot, Millie didn't know.

Dom headed off to the mine and Millie poured a fresh cup of tea and settled down at the table to think. Things had been quiet, too quiet, but last week while walking to town, Millie swore someone was watching her. She didn't see anyone and couldn't imagine hiking off the trail…Still, the feeling hadn't gone away. And yesterday, when she'd returned to the cabin after visiting Mary, she was certain someone had searched her bedroom. A shiver ran down her spine.

Was Mr. Gould back, searching for the map? Or was it the killer?

Worse, what would Dom do if she told him her worries? The man's reactions tended to be explosive and unpredictable. Shaking her head, Millie wondered how it had come to this. A man who was not her husband lived with her. An unknown assailant had killed Mr. D for a gold lode Dom couldn't find, and a criminal believed she knew the location of his stolen loot.

Millie knew she had to discover the killer before Mr. Gould started causing trouble. There had to be something—something she'd missed—that identified the killer. If he was local, he had to have made a mistake. Which of her neighbors wanted the mine bad enough to kill for it?

She thought back on all that had happened. Her initial intruder merely insisted she leave. His scare tactics were unpleasant, but they hadn't actually hurt her. Maybe he wasn't a murderer and Mr. D's death *had* been an accident. But the shots at the hot springs were no accident—of course they'd been aimed at Dom. Millie understood. Dom could drive even a gentle lady like herself to violence. What Millie couldn't understand was why there'd been no more threats since the hot springs. Why had the killer initially insisted she leave Idaho Springs?

What would have happened to the mine if she'd left?

The thought gave her moment to pause. As long as she remained here, the miners' court protected her ownership of the mine. Sure, Mr. Turck tried to jump the claim, but at Millie's request the miners' court would have driven him off. But what if she left town? Would there have been a violent scramble between the men who wanted the claim? Who would legally win? Or would violence win? Millie had no idea.

Rising, she went into her bedroom and searched through her belongings. The letter she'd received from Mr. D with his holographic will was nowhere to be found. Sitting back on her heels, Millie held the remains of Mr. D's first correspondence. It was half gone, a large, familiar bite mark in the center. She stared at her extremely obese goat. "Did you eat those legal documents Buttercup?"

Buttercup just looked up and bleated. The poor goat waddled out of the room and lay down on her quilt by the fire. When Mrs. LeGrand started waddling the way Buttercup now moved, Millie knew a baby was imminent. She wondered how Dom would deal with a Christmas kid. She'd given up hope he'd leave, so she guessed she'd find out.

Leaving Buttercup by the fire, Millie stepped outside and breathed in the fresh, crisp air. The sky was blue, the sun shone, and the temperature was surprisingly warm for mid-December. Would Mr. Ferris have copies of the documents? The only way to find out was to ask. She donned her coat, gloves, hat, and boots—since the blizzard Millie never went outside without proper clothing. Her Colt rested securely in her apron and she checked to make sure it was loaded. With someone sneaking around, Millie wanted to be prepared.

Buttercup rose and waddled over, bumping her head into Millie's thigh. "Think you can make the walk?" Millie asked doubtfully, rubbing the goat behind her ears. It appeared Buttercup wasn't going to stay home alone. Hopefully, her baby would wait. Mrs. Ferris tended to be nervous and prone to tears—she'd make a terrible midwife and probably just as bad a nursemaid.

Mrs. Ferris answered Millie's knock and announced that Mr. Ferris was in Denver City and not due back until the afternoon stagecoach. "Course with the snow," she said grumbling, "He might not make it back till tomorrow or the day after. Won't you come in?" She eyed Buttercup. "Maybe you can tie her just inside the door."

Over tea and an extremely bland bread pudding, Millie explained her dilemma.

"That's what happens when farm animals live in your home," said Mrs. Ferris sourly, glancing at Buttercup. "I'll look through Mr. Ferris' papers, but I don't attend to his business." She rose and headed to his desk, adding, "You'll probably have to wait until he returns."

Much to Millie's surprise, it took less than a minute for Mrs. Ferris to find papers with Mr. D's name on them. "Is this what you wanted?" She handed Millie a stack of folded papers.

Millie glanced through the documents and smiled. "Thank you so much, Mrs. Ferris. They look just like the ones Buttercup ate. Please tell Mr. Ferris I've taken them to read through. When he returns we can discuss how to make another copy."

"Make sure to keep them out of the goat's reach," said Mrs. Ferris, giving Buttercup another critical glance. "She's looking awful hungry."

Millie thanked the woman again, choked down the last of her tasteless pudding, and headed out. Since she was in town, she stopped by Old Shakespeare's store for a newspaper, flour, coffee, and some peppermint candy. Dom had eaten all the peppermints before the Thanksgiving meal and she'd noticed him looking forlornly at the empty jar as of late.

After bidding Mr. Tappan goodbye, Millie hurried out to find Mr. Poor standing over Buttercup, his eyes sad, his expression hungry.

"Mr. Poor, what a surprise," Millie said uneasily.

"I never ate goat," said Mr. Poor, his eyes glued to Buttercup, "Till I visited the Navajo Injuns living in Mormon land." He licked his lips. "Not sure what them squaws did to the meat—boiled it with some berries and spices—but I never tasted anything better." He sighed and wandered off, muttering about fry bread, pumpkins, and goat meat.

Troubled, Millie quickly untied Buttercup and hurried out of town. They climbed through the deep snow back up toward the cabin, but suddenly Millie felt the hairs on the back of her neck rise. Someone was out there, watching. She was sure of it. Nervously, she stopped and glanced around.

For just an instant, the sun glinted off something on the far hill. The reflection disappeared, but Millie knew something had been there. Nervously she pulled her gun from her apron and held it firmly as she continued up the path, hurrying Buttercup along in front of her. When they reached her cabin, Millie immediately barred the front and back doors and closed and barred all the shutters.

Tonight she would tell Dom her fears.

Tomorrow she'd make him hike to the location where she'd seen the reflection and see if there were fresh prints in the snow.

Still feeling unsettled, Millie prepared the saddle of venison she'd set out for dinner, trying a new recipe. They'd been eating venison almost every night since Dom shot the deer, and Millie was running short of new ideas. She basted the meat and left it to roast, adding some potatoes to the bottom of the dish.

Once all was ready, Millie turned her attention to Mr. Ferris' documents. On top was a handwritten homestead claim, dated September 21, 1860. Millie glanced through it, finding an accurate description of her meadow and its location. The document was signed by both J. W. Drouillard and D. A. Drouillard.

Idly, Millie wondered what the A stood for.

Setting the homestead document aside, Millie looked at the next sheet. It was Mr. D's mining claim, handwritten in a script Millie had difficulty reading.

Notice of location of a quartz claim.
Notice is hereby given to all whom it may concern that I, the undersigned J. W. Drouillard, a citizen of the United States, having complied with the revised statutes of the United States and the local Land Customs and Regulations, have this day located 1500 feet along the course of this vein, lode, ledge, or deposit of mineral bearing rock, together with 600 feet of surface ground in width, 600 feet running easterly, and 900 feet running westerly, and 300 feet in width on each side of center line and more particularly described as follows…

Millie yawned. How did lawyers stay awake long enough to write something so monotonous?

Refreshing her tea, she forced herself to read the rest of the document. It went on to describe how the claim ran six-hundred feet easterly of one stake, three-hundred feet northerly and such. Next it described the overall location in relation to the local valleys and rivers. Mr. D had named his claim the Lucky Hat Mine, presumably in reference to his locating the mine where his hat landed. The claim was signed September 10, 1861. Mr. Ferris had witnessed it.

Nothing looked amiss as far as Millie could tell, so she set the claim aside and looked at the final document. It was written in handwriting Millie recognized from Mr. D's letters and said simply,

If anything should happen to me, my mining claim and my homestead will be passed on to my future wife, Miss Permelia Abingdon Virginia. If she does not claim it, everything will be passed on to my brother, Mr. D. A. Drouillard.

This was signed and dated April 5, 1863, but it was the line between Mr. D's final words and his signature that caught and held Millie's attention.

If neither claims the properties, both will go to my solicitor, Mr. Ferris, as payment for his $50 grubstake.

Mr. Ferris' grubstake? Millie had no idea what a grubstake was, but she did understand the meaning of the words. If she left and Dom wasn't around to make the claim, the mine went to Mr. Ferris.

A shiver ran down her spine.

This couldn't wait until Dom got home. Millie slipped the paper into her apron and hurried to the door, donning her coat, boots, hat, and gloves. Feeling safer leaving the front door barred, Mille unbarred the back door and stepped into the snow.

Mr. Ferris stood waiting, his face set in an unpleasant scowl.

"Too bad Mrs. Ferris found those documents," he said. "It puts me in a rather difficult position."

THIRTY-FIVE

December 19th, 1863
Into the Mine

Mr. Ferris, what a surprise. I—"

"Don't bother with pleasantries, Widow D." He stepped forward and pulled his revolver from its holster. "We're both beyond that, aren't we?" He stared at Millie. "I assume you read the will?" He lifted his eyebrows. "Heading to the mine to tell Dom?"

Millie swallowed and nodded, her eyes glued to his gun. Taking a shaky breath, she realized she didn't feel so good. Looking into the action end of a six-shooter was quite unpleasant. As if trying to comfort her, Buttercup stepped outside and butted Millie in the leg.

Mr. Ferris waved the gun to the side. "Why don't we visit him together?" He emphasized his words by pushing her past him and slamming the cabin door shut.

Millie took a deep breath and kneed Buttercup out in front. Visiting Dom sounded like a really bad idea. Dom was irrational most of the time, and Millie didn't especially want to see his reaction to his brother's murderer. Since she had little choice, she slowly headed up the narrow trail.

"Don't think of doing anything stupid, Widow D," said Mr. Ferris behind her. "I don't really want to shoot you."

Millie felt a moment of relief. He didn't want to shoot her. The emotion disappeared as she realized there were many ways to kill someone without shooting them. "Did you shoot Mr. D?" she asked hesitantly.

"Of course not. He died accidently."

Millie's heart lifted. Maybe there really had been a landslide. She turned to face the solicitor and hesitated. His six-shooter remained pointed at her chest and the man didn't look particularly nervous. Quickly she spun back around and stumbled up the trail. "What happened to Mr. D?" she asked, not really expecting an answer.

"Mr. D was a fool. I visited and asked where he found all those tear-drop shaped nuggets he'd been spending. Seemed fair, since I'd given him the grubstake."

"Grubstake?" The conversation felt unreal. Still, talking made Millie feel less vulnerable.

"A grubstake. Money for provisions. Gear. In exchange for a share of the profit. Way I saw it that made me part owner of the mine, but he didn't see it my way. He paid me five of those little nuggets. Said that was my share. Wouldn't give me more." His voice turned boastful. "Least not 'til I pulled out my six-shooter. I convinced him to take me to the mine, but for some fool reason, he refused to go in when we got there. I tried to knock some sense into him. Unfortunately, I hit him too hard."

That was an accident? Millie kept her thoughts to herself. "The landslide. It was a cover-up?"

"The landslide was a stroke of genius. Unfortunately, I just wanted to justify his death, not close off the mine. Damn rocks were unstable. I twisted my ankle and almost tumbled down myself."

Millie stopped and turned to face Mr. Ferris. "No one will believe this was an accident. Not after you tried to shoot us at the hot springs."

"Maybe," he said, waving her back into motion with his gun. "But only one person knows I'm here. He won't say anything. Plus, this is the Colorado Territory. Accidents happen all the time. You read the news. Ute and Arapahoe

Indians are getting restless, hostile. They're killing settlers. Mountain men. Even miners."

"Are you planning on scalping us?"

Mr. Ferris gagged. "Of course not. I'm not a killer." His face twisted. "This is your fault Widow D! Entirely your fault. If you'd just scared off like any normal woman, I wouldn't have to do this. Now shut up and keep walking." He emphasized his words by giving Millie a hard shove.

In silence they climbed the steep slope to the mine, both of them panting in the cold air and high altitude. Buttercup, who'd fallen behind, bleated unhappily.

Millie tried to think of something to do, some way to stop what was coming. Her gun was in her apron. If she could reach it, maybe she could shoot him. Her hands shook slightly as she unbuttoned the top button on her coat.

"Keep your hands by your side, where I can see them," Mr. Ferris said, emphasizing his words by pushing the muzzle of his gun into her back.

Slowly Millie let her hands drop to her side. Now what? Cold bit her exposed skin, but Millie hardly noticed. Her fear grew as she led Mr. Ferris closer to the mine. Closer to Dom.

They climbed the steep incline and the Lucky Hat Mine came into sight. Mr. Ferris grabbed Millie's arm and roughly pulled her to a stop. The gun's frozen muzzle dug into Millie's jaw. "Call Dom out," Mr. Ferris whispered hoarsely. "If you're stupid, I'll do something neither one of us will enjoy."

Millie didn't want to call Dom. To endanger him. She hesitated and Mr. Ferris jerked his gun from below her jaw and rapped it sharply against her temple. Millie saw stars. The muzzle returned to her jaw, pressing so hard Millie had to lift her head.

"Call him!" Mr. Ferris hissed.

Heart racing, head spinning, Millie squeaked out a weak "Dom."

"Louder. He'll never hear you."

"Millie? That you and Buttercup? That goat sounds like she's lost her best friend." The light from the candle in his hat twinkled as he stepped from the darkness. "What in tarna—" Dom's voice petered out. His eyes narrowed at Millie and Mr. Ferris.

"That's right," said Mr. Ferris. "The only movement I want to see is you slowly removing your peacemaker and tossing it out into the snow." Ferris pressed the muzzle deeper into Millie's jaw, causing her to cry out. "You do anything stupid, Dom, and I'll kill the woman you love."

Woman he loved? The knock on her head had affected her hearing. Dom didn't love her, did he? Millie was too confused and scared to think.

"I should have known it was you," Dom snarled, looking like a furious bear. Using two fingers, he slowly pulled his Colt from his coat pocket. "Never trust a lawyer," he added, tossing the gun into the snow. "Okay. I did what you want. Let her go."

Mr. Ferris shoved Millie closer to the mine, using her body as a shield. "You so much as twitch, Dom, and I'll kill her." He gave Millie a shove, forcing her a step closer. "I'm a lousy shot, but even I can't miss at this distance." He stopped well out of Dom's reach and thrust Millie forward. "Go on. Join your lover."

"But," Millie squealed, stumbling two steps closer. Dom was standing in the shadow of the mine entrance. The gaping black hole loomed behind him like an opening into hell. She tried to take a step closer, but couldn't move.

"It's okay, honey," Dom said, his voice tight. "Look at my face." He smiled, although it looked more like a grimace. "Forget the mine and focus on my cute dimples."

Millie choked, unable to laugh or cry. Dom hated those dimples. She tried to step toward him, but her feet refused to move.

"Widow D, don't play with me. If I have to I'll shoot you. Or would you prefer I start with your goat?"

Millie looked down at Buttercup and felt tears stream down her cheeks. She didn't want anyone shot, especially not Buttercup. Biting her lip, she took a tiny step forward and then a second. She tried to take a third, but the mine entrance filled her vision and her body refused to obey.

"Millie, honey," Dom said, sounding almost frantic. "You have to come to me. Try to think about something else."

She stared at Dom's tense face. Behind her she could hear Mr. Ferris muttering about stubborn redheads and obese goats. What else did Dom expect her to think about?

"Widow D," Mr. Ferris yelled, his voice high and agitated. "Go to your lover or I'll shoot you!"

Anxiously, Dom lifted his hand toward her. "Come here, Millie. Please, sweetheart. I can't lose you."

The desperation in his voice burned through Millie's terror. She looked up at him and saw dread etched in his deep blue eyes. In a whisper she asked, "You don't love me, do you?"

His expression softened. "I do, Millie. I just couldn't figure out how to get you to marry me."

"Marry?" Millie choked on the word and stumbled a step forward.

"What do you say to a long, exciting life together? We can explore the wonders of this territory. How'd you like to see the Petrified Forest near Pike's Peak? Or maybe even climb Pikes Peak? I've heard about sand dunes down South. Imagine that! I want to explore it all with you, but first you need to come to me." His hand extended toward her, reaching as far as he could.

"Your declaration of love is touching, Dom," Mr. Ferris said snidely. "But I don't have all day." He stepped forward and kicked Millie in the back. She stumbled, staying on her feet for three or four steps before tumbling into the snow, landing at Dom's feet.

Dom quickly reached down, picked her up, and dragged her behind him, wrapping her arms around his solid waist. "I got you, honey," he whispered. "Close your eyes and just hold on to me."

Millie closed her eyes, leaned her cheek against his sturdy back, and breathed in his scent, trying to calm her racing heart.

"I'm sure you lovebirds would like some time alone," said Mr. Ferris mockingly. "Back up. Go deep enough into the mine so I can't see you. Take the goat with you. I'll shoot anything near the entrance that moves."

Millie whimpered and felt Dom's hands tighten on hers. "Just breathe," Dom said quietly. Slowly he began backing up. "I'll take care of you."

Millie's eyes flew open and she struggled as Dom forced her to step back. His grip just tightened and he pushed her backward. Dark walls closed in around them. Step by step, his bulk forced her deeper into the mine. "You have to do this, Millie. I know you can."

Millie tried not to think. She tried not to notice how the daylight grew dimmer, and the candlelight formed grotesque shadows on the dark walls. She wanted to stop, fought to stop, but Dom overpowered her and continued to slowly back up. Pressing her forehead into Dom's back, she shuddered. His steady breathing did nothing to calm her fright.

They were completely surrounded by darkness when a rock smashed down in front of the entrance. Millie jumped, but Dom refused to release her hands.

"He's going to bury us alive," Millie cried, her voice shrill.

"He's going to try." Dom pulled her around and hugged her tight. "After the slide, we'll dig ourselves out."

That sounded like a terrible plan.

"I-if I had my druthers, you'd shoot him *before* he buries us alive!"

Dom squeezed her tighter. "I'd like to, but he made me toss my gun away."

"Use mine." Millie pulled away until Dom released her. Quickly she unbuttoned her coat, slipped her hand inside, and pulled out her revolver. Dom's eyes widened in the flickering candlelight.

"God I love you!" he said, giving her a quick kiss as he took the gun. The kiss was hurried, but nice. It made her forget her fear for a moment.

"I'm gonna sneak out," he explained, gripping her shoulder with one hand. "Hopefully, Ferris is having trouble climbing the bank. It won't be easy in the deep snow. He'll need to focus on his footing and may not notice me until it's too late." Dom pulled Millie in for another quick kiss. "You stay here until it's safe."

The kiss lingered on her lips nicely, but no way was Millie going to remain alone in this black hole.

THIRTY-SIX

December 19, 1863

Landslide

Dom slowly crept forward and Millie quietly followed. They'd only gone a couple of steps when Dom turned and frowned. "Millie, you have to stay in the mine. If Ferris starts a landslide when I'm anywhere near the entrance, it'll get tricky. A falling rock can kill as quick as a bullet." He kissed her. This time the kiss lasted longer and Dom sighed when he raised his head. His voice sounded hoarse as he said, "Now, stay here."

Millie remembered in New Orleans how Carissa's face lit up and her smile turned dreamy whenever Coilen kissed her. She finally understood. Dom's kisses were addicting. They dulled her brain like a drug, making her warm all over. He better not get hurt. After three kisses, she had plans for the man. Still, no way she was staying in this mine! Quietly she followed the flickering candlelight, stopping when Dom turned to face her. In the poor light, his dark expression looked dangerous.

"Damn it, Millie, you can't come with me. Start acting like a wife and obey me."

"A wife doesn't hafta obey her husband. Not if he's being unreasonable."

"I am *not* being unreasonable!" Dom shouted, his shout punctuated by the sound of more falling rocks. "I'm trying to save our lives."

"Okay. But I'm *not* your wife."

"You would be," Dom said, running a finger down her cheek. "If I could have figured out a way to make you marry me. You drive me crazy. I've actually considered behaving improperly, just to force my hand."

"We've been living improperly for months, what else—"

"We've been living in the same cabin for months. That's not improper."

"I'm sure Florence Hartley would call our living arrangements improper. She'd say—"

Dom grabbed Millie and pulled her hard against him, giving her a kiss that sent her head spinning. "Don't quote that woman," he snarled. "I hate her book. I'll demonstrate improper later, but for now, I have to get out of here before Ferris starts a serious landslide." He held her away from him. "You're not going to stay in here, are you?"

"No."

He shook his head, making the flame on the candle flicker unsteadily. "Why'd I have to fall for a stubborn redhead?" He touched her face. "Stay close." Turning, he took her hand and led her toward the circle of light and white snow.

Millie felt cold air brush against her cheeks, and the sunlight brightened until she could almost touch it. She jumped when a mixture of snow, dirt, and rocks crashed down in front of them, shattering and flying out in all directions. The noise echoed through the cave, deafening them. A sharp stone struck Millie's arm, ripping through her coat and into her skin.

"Come on," Dom cried, dragging her forward. Falling rubble darkened the light as they rushed toward the entrance. "Stay as close to the wall as possible."

Millie could barely hear him over the thunderous roar. Covering her head and face with her free arm, she held tight to Dom's hand. The thick, grimy air was difficult to breathe. Falling debris bit into her shoulder and back. For a moment, all Millie could see was the dirty snow pouring down around them. *We're not going to make it,* she thought. Moments later, the air cleared slightly and Millie caught a glimpse of white snow and blue sky.

A rock struck Dom and he stumbled, almost pulling Millie off her feet. He balanced unsteadily on one knee, looking like a suitor proposing marriage. He made a poor prospect with his dazed look, hat cocked almost off his head, and blood spilling down his forehead. Millie bent over, wrapped her arms around him, and heaved with all her strength. He struggled to his feet, and they stumbled toward the snow as rubble continued to pummel them.

Millie dragged him out into the snow, but after two or three steps, she tripped over his feet and they both fell. Millie landed on top of his broad back. Tensely, she waited for a boulder to crush them. Instead, the thunder of the landslide quieted, replaced by the hysterical screaming of Mr. Ferris. His words were incoherent, but the bullet that exploded in the snow near Dom's shoulder clearly demonstrated his intent.

Millie scrambled over Dom's inert back and ran her hand down his arm, trying to locate her six-shooter. Another shot rang out. Mr. Ferris was a lousy shot, but even the worst shooter got lucky once in a while.

Frantically, Mille felt down Dom's arm, digging in the snow until her fingers contacted the cold butt of the gun. Pulling it from his limp fingers, she spun around.

Mr. Ferris stood thirty feet above the mine entrance. Below him, the snow and loose rocks lay churned and disrupted in a twisted path, a stark contrast to the white around it. The lawyer kicked wildly at a large boulder as he aimed to take another shot.

Millie raised her gun and steadied her hands. Remembering Charlotte's instructions, Millie took a deep breath, looked down the barrel, and gently squeezed the trigger. The recoil knocked her back, but as she scrambled to regain her balance, she heard Mr. Ferris howl.

Shading her eyes, she watched Mr. Ferris scream obscenities as he grabbed his leg, blood spurting between his fingers. His cries became screams of terror and he released his leg, his arms windmilling wildly. Like a tree being felled, the lawyer slowly tipped forward. A cry like that of a pig being slaughtered mingled with the crash of stone. Ferris cartwheeled down the slope, his body creating a landslide of flesh, stone, and snow.

Millie threw herself over Dom's body and waited for this new slide to bury them. Instead, the air quieted and the dust cleared. Slowly Millie sat up and looked around. Behind, a foot from where they lay, a fresh pile of dirt, snow, and stone once again closed off the mine entrance. Mr. Ferris was nowhere to be seen.

Beneath her, Dom groaned.

Millie dropped the gun, scrambled off his back, grabbed his arm, and rolled him over. The gash on his head was bleeding profusely, forming rivulets of red down his face. His blue eyes looked at her dully. "You. Okay?"

Millie nodded. She pulled the will and her pocket watch from her apron and slipped them into her coat before reaching behind and jerking on her apron's ties. When it was free, she rolled the material into a long strip and wrapped it gently around Dom's head. The thick material covered his injury, stemming the bleeding.

"How do you feel?" Her voice shook as bad as her hands.

"Not great. Head's killing me." He gingerly sat up and looked behind her. "Where's Ferris?"

Millie stared at the landslide, not yet ready to consider her part in its creation. "He fell," she said hesitantly. "I think he's somewhere under the rocks." She glanced around, but not too closely. If Mr. Ferris was still alive, she'd hear his cries of pain. All she heard was Dom's labored breathing.

"Some justice there, I guess." Dom grunted as he pushed himself off the ground. With Millie's help, he rose unsteadily to his feet. "Let's go back to the cabin. I'll get the Grouse and Sheriff Reynolds to help dig him out."

Millie nodded and put her arm around him. With her help, he limped toward the trail.

Suddenly Millie froze.

"Where's Buttercup?"

THIRTY-SEVEN

December 19, 1863

Buried Alive

Buttercup was nowhere to be seen. Millie released Dom and turned, listening for the goat's distinctive bleating. Everything was deathly silent. Had the goat followed them into the mine? Was she buried alive? Shuddering, Millie imagined Buttercup crushed under the cold rubble.

"We hafta dig her out."

"Millie, honey. I'm sorry." Dom took her hand and squeezed. "I don't think she made it. She probably got caught in the landslide and—"

"No!" Millie yelled, tossing Dom's hand aside and hurrying to the pile of rubble. The landslide appeared to have once again closed off the mine's entrance, but Millie rushed to the far side, hoping to find an opening there. Instead, she stopped and gagged.

Mr. Ferris had not survived. His blood stained the dirty snow and parts of his body protruded from the rubble. His hand, with a single finger extended to the sky, pointed toward heaven. Turning away, Millie doubled over and was sick.

Dom was instantly beside her, holding her steady, brushing her loose hair back as he kept her braid and bonnet from falling onto her face. "It's okay, honey. It's okay. Let's go home."

Once her stomach quieted, Millie used her handkerchief to wipe around her mouth. To avoid looking at the bloody hand, she buried her face against Dom's chest and let him lead her back around to the trail. Only when she was sure Mr. Ferris' remains were no longer in sight did she look up. Blood dripped down Dom's pale face. With her apron wrapped haphazardly around his head, he looked like a character in one of Edgar Allan Poe's dreadful poems. Still, his blue eyes were steady.

"I'm okay. I just wasn't expecting—" Millie gestured.

"We need to go. We'll get some of the miners' court out here. They'll dig him out." He put his arm around Millie and rested some of his weight on her. "Let's go home."

Millie knew he was right, knew she needed to get Dom to the cabin, and to find him medical help. Buttercup was gone. Her tears created tracks down her filthy face. It was silly, but the floppy-eared, ridiculous fainting goat had become something she loved. She already missed her terribly. Wrapping her arm around Dom's waist, she helped him stumble around the rubble that blocked the mine. They were on the far side of the talus slope, heading down the trail, when Millie heard something.

"D-did you hear that?"

"What?" Dom sounded dazed.

"Shush."

They both stopped moving and Millie strained to hear. A weak bleat reverberated through the still air. Millie released Dom and spun around, running back toward the landslide. At the top of the pile, near the side where they'd escaped, she spotted a small black hole.

"There!" She pointed. "That's why we can hear her. She's alive, but trapped inside. We hafta get her out."

The hole was tiny, but it still looked dark and forboding. Buttercup's weak bleat floated out. Firming her resolve, Millie sucked in a deep breath, glad her stomach was empty. Just the thought of climbing up to the hole made her queasy.

Fisting her shaking hands and thinking only of Buttercup, she began to scramble up the loose rubble. The gravel and snow gave beneath her and Millie slipped backward, falling to her knees. Refusing to give up, Millie again crawled up the unstable incline.

"Don't stand below me," she called out as she knocked loose a head-sized boulder. It tumbled down, creating a small landslide below her. Carefully, she crept two steps higher only to slip and fall, landing hard on her belly and scraping her face in the rubble.

She couldn't do this.

What about Buttercup? She *had* to rescue Buttercup.

Taking a deep breath, she squirmed up the incline with her hands, knees, and belly pressed into the loose earth. The cold bit her wet skin, but Millie refused to let it slow her down. The opening appeared above her head. A bit further. When she finally reached it, her arms and legs were shaking so badly she was forced to remain on her belly. Shuddering, she closed her eyes and put her head near the empty darkness.

"Buttercup?" she croaked.

A familiar bleat answered her.

Millie squirmed up higher until she could roll over and sit up. Her hands were numb as she began clearing away loose debris, trying to enlarge the hole. Dom scrambled up beside her, falling twice before he reached her. Millie knew he needed to see Doc Noxon, and soon, yet when he sat down beside her and helped clear gravel and snow, she felt only relief. She couldn't leave Buttercup in the mine, buried alive.

Dirt, snow, and gravel were shoved aside, but larger boulders limited how much they could increase the opening. As they worked, they were occasionally rewarded with Buttercup's bleating, but something about the sound wasn't quite right.

Millie bit her lip but didn't say anything. She didn't want to worry Dom.

Buttercup's cries became more persistent, making Millie cringe. The goat sounded like she was in terrible pain. Had she been struck by a falling rock?

They paused to catch their breath, and Millie looked up and gasped. Under the filth, Dom's face was as white as the snow, accentuating the rivulets of blood still flowing from his head wound. His eyes were bloodshot and his cheeks sunken. He too was in pain. A lot of it. His clenched jaw and tightly pressed lips indicated he was trying, unsuccessfully, to hide just how much he hurt. Glancing at the small hole, Millie knew she had to do something. Soon Dom would be too weak to make it back to the cabin.

"It's big enough for me to slip through," she said, shivering, but not from the cold.

"No! No way in tarnation I'm letting you go back into the mine. We just need to make it a bit bigger and I'll retrieve the blasted goat." He began digging around a larger stone that blocked one side of the hole, but Millie placed a shaky hand on his.

"I'll be okay," she said, firming her resolve. "Give me your hat. Do you have flint and an extra candle?"

"You hate going into dark places Millie. You—"

"Please. Don't remind me!" Millie smiled weakly. Her heart raced, sounding as loud as the earlier landslide. Nervous sweat drenched her face and dripped down her back. "Give me your hat," she commanded, her voice shaking, "and light a candle for me."

Dom's swearing sounded more exhausted than angry as he pulled the hat from his pocket and removed two candles. "This is my tin. It's got flint and char cloth," he said through clenched teeth. He slipped the candle snuggly into the candle holder and handed her the hat, clearly unhappy.

Millie slipped it on her head but it fell over her eyes.

Without a word, Dom took the hat back and tightened the head strap until it fit snuggly. After slipping it gently on her again, he lit the candle mounted in the hat's bracket.

"You have to move slowly or you'll blow out the candle," Dom explained, his expression haggard. "Keep this flint box handy in your pocket. You'll need your hands free to climb down, but once you reach the mine floor, light the second candle." He slipped the extra candle in the flint box and handed it to her. "You can hold the second candle in your hand." He looked at her, his head drooping. "You shouldn't be doing this. The supports in the mine may no longer be stable. Is it worth risking your life for the goat?"

Millie didn't need to know she was entering a mine that might not be safe. Going into the darkness was enough of a terror. Buttercup bleated and Millie firmed her resolve.

"I'll be careful. I promise." Dom's fear radiated out like heat. Millie knew he'd be devastated if anything happened to her. She touched his face gently. "I'll be careful, but I can't leave her buried alive in there."

Dom nodded, looking miserable. "Just find her and bring her out. If she's hurt, we'll have Doc Noxon tend her in the cabin."

With a nod, Millie took a deep breath and swallowed hard. She balanced on hands and knees and lowered her face into the hole. Head first. It was the only way.

"Millie!" The anguish in Dom's voice caused Millie to pull back and look up. Dom pulled her to him and kissed her roughly. "You be careful and come back to me. Understand? I've got plans for you. Don't do anything stupid."

Millie nodded and he reluctantly released her. She wanted to say something to ease his fear but could think of nothing. Turning back to the tiny, dark opening, she once again put her face inside. The air was thick with grime and dirt, coating her mouth with each breath she took. Her hat's candlelight illuminated the black walls and the rocky incline that she needed to crawl down. Suddenly Dom's fear seemed insignificant to the terror churning in her stomach.

As if to remind her, a weak bleat penetrated the thick air. Buttercup. She had to find Buttercup.

Forcing herself, Millie put both arms into the mine and squeezed her shoulders through the narrow opening, scraping her back and right shoulder as she wormed inside. Her breathing became so ragged it echoed in the confined space. Her hands shook and her muscles felt cold and stiff. Even focusing all her thoughts on Buttercup, Millie could barely force herself to inch forward. Buttercup gave another desperate bleat, and Millie squirmed deeper into the blackness.

The opening was so tiny that she had to pull herself through with her arms and push with her toes. Her waist slid through easily, but her hips got stuck. For a terrible instant, Millie thought she wouldn't get through. The darkness closed in around her and she felt dizzy. Wildly wiggling her hips, she slowly slid through the opening.

That was when she realized Dom was outside, watching. As soon as her hips came all the way through, her legs and feet would be forced up into the air.

"Dom," she yelled, her voice unsteady. "Turn around this instant. If my dress comes up, you are not to look."

In response, she felt Dom's hand squeeze her leg.

Above her stocking!

"Dominic Drouillard, you vulgar galoot. Remove your hand from my thigh immediately!"

THIRTY-EIGHT

December 19, 1863
Deplorable Man

Millie couldn't believe it. After all his words of endearment, the depraved man was taking advantage of the situation. She hurriedly dragged her legs into the cave, scraping her hip and thigh on the sharp rocks. Even after she was sure her legs were safely inside the mine, she could still feel his warm hand on her ankle. Twisting around, she looked back to see Dom's face and shoulders blocking the hole, his blue eyes glinting in the candlelight.

"Dom. Remove your hand, immediately!" She angrily stretched the word immediately into five long syllables.

"My hand was cold," he said, sighing. "Your leg was nice and warm."

Millie shook with anger. "You are a deplorable man! When I get out, we're going to have a long discussion about proper, gentlemanly behavior. Now remove your hand."

Dom squeezed her ankle and released her. "I couldn't help myself, Millie. The way you were wiggling your hips was driving me crazy. When your legs went up and your skirt fell back. No mountain man could resist taking a peek. And my hand just snuck out on its own accord. I couldn't—"

"I do *not* wish to hear more, Mr. Drouillard. I am going to find Buttercup." Putting words into action, Millie gingerly crawled down the debris pile. When she reached the mine floor, she cautiously stood up.

"How are you doing, Millie?" Dom's voice reverberated in the narrow chamber.

"I am *not* talking to you, Mr. Drouillard. Your appalling actions are beyond words." She lit the second candle and held it out in front of her. The mine floor was littered with large and small boulders, but she couldn't see Buttercup. Carefully, she stepped over the rubble and headed deeper into the mine.

"Be careful," Dom said. Millie heard fear in his voice. "I love you."

Millie stopped and looked back. "How can you say that after what you just did?"

"You don't sound scared anymore."

Millie realized she wasn't scared. She was mad as a wet hen. Surely Dom hadn't acted disgracefully just to drive away her fear. "We'll discuss this later, Mr. Drouillard. Perhaps a nightly reading of Mrs. Hartley's chapter on—" Millie faltered. Her book contained rules of etiquette for ballroom parties, visiting, conduct in church, handling servants, and even proper conduct for a young lady contemplating marriage. None of it applied.

"If you insist," Dom groaned. "Just keep talking now. You can even quote me those ridiculous rules from the American Lady. Anything, just so I know you're okay. It keeps my panic in check."

His panic? Millie wasn't sure what to say. Instead, she turned and walked deeper into the mine.

"Buttercup," she called. The tunnel was too narrow to miss a goat, but she was still relieved when she heard Buttercup's bleat in front of her. Walking as quickly as she dared, she descended past a wooden support.

The candlelight finally reflected on a set of eyes Millie recognized.

"Buttercup! Are you okay?" The goat bleated and Millie stepped closer and stopped. A second set of eyes appeared.

And then a third. Millie swallowed. "Buttercup. Come here."

The goat didn't move.

"Dom," she called out. "Does anything live in this mine?"

"No...What do you see?"

"Two extra sets of eyes. Buttercup won't come to me. I think. Maybe." One set of eyes disappeared and Millie distinctly heard sucking sounds. "Oh Dom. I think some creature is devouring Buttercup." The goat bleated. "Alive!"

"Millie," Dom's voice was unnaturally high pitched. "You sound cra— You're not making sense. Gasses sometimes fill a mine. They're released from the surrounding rocks. These gasses can make you see things. Tommyknockers. Gnomes. Things that aren't there. Come back to the entrance where the air is fresh. Now! While you still can."

Millie heard the panic in his voice, but she couldn't leave. Buttercup's bright eyes indicated she was alive, even if partially devoured. Slowly Millie stepped forward. "Go away," she yelled, waving her arms. The third set of eyes reappeared. They didn't move. After another step, light from the candles began to illuminate Buttercup and Millie caught sight of a hoof and leg protruding out at an odd angle.

"Oh Buttercup, what have they done to you?" She took two more steps and froze.

Maybe she *was* breathing poor air. She was definitely seeing things that couldn't be real.

"Dom. Buttercup has two heads."

"Millie. Millie, honey. Come back here! Please. Now, before it's too late."

She heard the sound of him digging, trying to enlarge the hole, but despite his obvious fear Millie couldn't move. She stared at Buttercup's two heads and started when a third appeared. Rubbing her eyes, she tried to make the illusion go away. It didn't. What exactly was she seeing? She took a step closer and gasped.

"Dom. We've got twins!"

"Twins?" The noise from his digging stopped. "Twin what? Millie, are you crazy?"

"Buttercup had her baby. Or babies."

"Babies? But…but…you said she wouldn't have her kid until January. I'm not ready for kids!"

Millie hurried over and bent down, reaching out to touch the wet fur of the newborn goats. In the background, Dom kept up a steady stream of questions, sounding more frantic than before. "Millie, answer me. Are our kids okay? Do they have the right number of, uh, hoofs and ears? Do we have boys or girls?"

Millie sat down and gently lifted one of the babies into her lap, rubbing it dry with her skirt. The baby looked up at her with trusting brown eyes. "This one has her mama's ears and eyes, but is brown and white like the he-goat." She leaned forward to pick up the second baby, but something sparkled behind Buttercup's head.

Scooting forward, Millie gently pushed Buttercup's head aside and brought her candle near the wall. In the flickering light, Millie discovered a narrow crack just inches off the floor, blocked by a flat rock. The crack was only six to eight inches tall, wide enough for a hand to slip inside. Millie pushed the rock aside and held a candle to the opening.

Soft light sparkled off the ruby-red gemstones, milky white quartz, and tiny stalactites of tear-shaped gold. "Well bless my soul!" she whispered.

She'd found Mr. D's vug!

Mesmerized, Millie slipped her hand inside and picked up a handful of loose debris from the floor. Three of the tear-drop shaped gold nuggets sparkled in her palm.

"What about the other one. Do I have a son?"

Shaking her head, Millie slipped the gold nuggets into her coat pocket and replaced the rock to hide the crack. She picked up the second baby and dried it with her skirt. "Sorry, Dom, but I'm afraid you're doomed to be surrounded by females."

Dom groaned. "And these ones can't even cook. They'll probably faint when they meet me."

After making sure Buttercup was okay, Millie rose and picked up the babies, cradling them as she made her way back to the entrance. Buttercup followed docilely but became irate when Millie climbed the debris field and handed Dom the babies. Bounding up to the tiny opening, Buttercup head-butted Millie out of the way, knocking her over and sending her rolling down the incline. The goat squirmed out of the hole, her feet kicking out and pelting Millie with sharp stones.

"You're welcome," Millie muttered to Buttercup's disappearing rear end.

Gently rubbing several new bruises, Millie climbed back up to the opening and wormed her way out. She struggled to extricate her hips, looking for a helping hand from Dom.

"Hurry up," he yelled from below. "I don't want the kids getting cold."

"You're welcome," Millie muttered again as she dragged her legs free. When she finally crawled off the rock pile and stood up, she found Dom cradling a baby goat in each arm, looking like he was closer to death than life. Blood stained his clothing and streaked his face. One eye was swollen shut. The other gleamed like a madman.

Millie's heart skipped a beat. Unkempt, uncouth, and with the manners of a galoot. But a heart of gold. How could Millie *not* love him?

THIRTY-NINE

December 19, 1863
Boone Dogs' Cave?

By the time they reached their cabin, the sun was dropping behind the mountain peaks, the baby goats were walking behind their mama, and Millie was struggling to support Dom. He sagged against her, both eyes closed, his feet dragging. Worse, his gray pallor made Millie wonder if his next step would be his last. She prayed not. If Dom went down, she wouldn't be able to carry him. He'd freeze to death before she could return with help.

Somehow he kept on his feet, even when Millie propped him against the wall and pushed open the back door. The smell of roasted venison welcomed them, and Millie wrapped her arms around Dom and dragged him inside, finally letting him slump to the floor in front of the fireplace. He lay there unmoving, his breathing labored. Buttercup and her daughters came over and nibbled at the snow caking his filthy face.

"I'm so glad my partner didn't succeed in killing you. I would have been most displeased."

Millie spun around. Mr. Gould stood near her cookstove, his rat-tailed mustache twitching, a slice of sourdough bread in one hand, and his revolver in the other.

"You…your partner?"

"At least he had the good grace to incapacitate your lover." His cold eyes bored into Millie. "I assume Mr. Ferris is no longer amongst the living? Just as well. I would have killed him if he'd survived. Fool left me a panicked note, telling me you knew about him. Said he had to do something to stop you." Mr. Gould shook his head. "Man never did have any spine."

The goats' eyes bulged out and all three slumped to the floor, their heads lolling on top of Dom.

"Y-you and Mr. Ferris? You were partners?"

"He thought so. Initially he hired me to make sure you didn't make it to Idaho Springs." The man bit into his bread and spoke while he chewed. "Of course he failed to mention the gold nuggets found by your fiancé. After I saw your watch, I didn't care."

Mr. Ferris and Mr. Gould were in this together. Millie shook her head in disbelief.

Mr. Gould sniffed the air. "Once again the smell of dinner is driving me crazy. This time I intend to eat my fill. Shut the door, woman, and make me a plate of food." He waved his gun toward Dom. "If you leave, I'll kill your lover. Although from the looks of it, a bullet won't be needed. Best hurry."

His callous words struck Millie like a knife. She glanced at Dom and hurried toward the back door. Dom did look awful. He hadn't moved and the wrapping around his head was soaked in blood. She needed to fetch Doc Noxon, but if she ran, Mr. Gould would kill him. Feeling trapped, Millie returned to find Mr. Gould sitting expectantly at the table, like an invited guest.

"H-how long have you been in town?" she asked, the sudden silence unnerving her.

"Food woman!"

Millie turned and pulled the venison roast from the oven. It was crispy, but edible. Slicing off the least desirable, slightly blackened side, she placed a large chunk of meat on a plate. After adding a boiled potato, she spooned juices from the roast over everything.

"I've been here since I escaped from that Denver jail," Mr. Gould said, watching her preparation with interest. "I came back with Ferris, although the half-built cabin he found for me was draftier than the calaboose, not to mention Mrs. Ferris' cooking. Don't know how the good solicitor survived. Guess that's why he spent so much time in Denver with his mistress."

He grabbed the plate Millie set in front of him and speared the meat with his knife, using his teeth to rip off a chunk. Disgusted, Millie glanced at his gun-hand. It still gripped his six-shooter.

"When I leave," Mr. Gould said, spittle and food accompanying his words. "You're coming with me. Lord, this is good." He picked up the potato and bit off a hunk, giving Millie a good view of his half-eaten meat.

"It was you I spotted? Today in the trees?"

"Yes," he said, grease forming tears on the tips of his rat-tail mustache. His tongue wrapped around one side of the mustache and he sucked off the grease before repeating the procedure on the other side. "You forced me to take a detour. Wouldn't do to have my tracks lead back to my lodging. Unfortunately, I returned too late to catch the panicked solicitor."

Near the fire, Buttercup and her kids were reviving, but Dom hadn't moved. If anything, his face looked grayer. "I need to tend to Dom," Millie said, hoping she wasn't making it worse by drawing attention to him. Mr. Gould didn't object; he was too busy stuffing the last of his meat into his already full mouth.

Millie wet a rag and hurried to Dom's side. She wiped blood and dirt from his face, gasping when she removed the blood-soaked apron. The swelling was bad, but the dirt and pebbles embedded in the wound looked even worse. She cleaned it as best she could and rose. "He needs medicine. It's in my bedroom."

"Why bother? He's as dead as Mr. Ferris." Mr. Gould laughed. "He just doesn't know it yet."

Millie swallowed back tears. "I'll go with you and do what you want, but only if you let me tend Dom. *And* you leave him alive when we leave."

Mr. Gould rose and stalked menacingly toward Millie, swinging his gun in her face. She stood her ground, but it took all the courage she possessed. He grabbed her braid and dragged her face close to his. "You, sweet thing, will do whatever I want and come with me meekly. Understand?" To emphasize his point, he released her hair and back-handed her across the face.

Millie twisted and fell, landing beside Dom. She opened her eyes, her head spinning, and looked into Dom's open eye—the other was swollen shut. She touched his face, praying he was too weak to do anything stupid. Slowly she rose to her feet and faced Mr. Gould.

"Get me my map! I couldn't find it when I searched your room. And don't bother with medication for your lover. Why waste it on a dead man."

Shaking with fear and fury, Millie swiped at the grease and dirt smears he'd left on her face and hurried to the bed-room. She retrieved the map from its hiding place, donned a fresh apron, and slipped the bottle of laudanum out from her medical supplies and hid it in the apron's pocket. Hur-rying out, she found Mr. Gould back at the table, sopping up the meat sauce with a slice of bread. Her hands shook as she set the map in front of him.

"D-do you want coffee, too?"

"Yes. And more food." He shoved the plate in her direc-tion, his eyes on the map.

Millie did as she was bid, replenishing his plate be-fore filling the coffee pot and setting it on the stove. She glanced back. Mr. Gould appeared engrossed in the food and focused on the map. Hands shaking, Millie put cof-fee into the pot and slipped the bottle of laudanum out of her pocket. Carefully, she poured a dollop into the liquid.

"What's that?" Mr. Gould hissed.

Millie jumped, dropping the bottle into the coffee pot.

"What's what?" she asked, her voice trembling as she turned to face him.

"What's that?" Mr. Gould asked, using his pistol to point at the map. The muzzle touched the large X on the paper. "Boone Dogs' Cave. What's that mean?" He glared at Millie. "Where's my silver coins?"

Oh Lor'. Millie almost fainted with relief. He hadn't noticed the laudanum. Course, with the whole bottle now dumped in, the drink might be lethal. "I don't know," she said.

"Of course you do. Now who is Boone? Daniel Boone for God's sake? What town is this?"

"I don't know!"

Mr. Gould stood and grabbed Millie, digging his filthy fingers into her arm. "You're the daughter of my crooked partner." He slammed her into the wall before grabbing one shoulder and shaking her. Dazed, Millie tensed as he pulled his fist back. "You'll tell me or I'll—"

"I know," said a weak voice. Mr. Gould spun around, dragging Millie with him. Dom was sitting up. Unsteadily leaning against the big rocker, his single eye open. "I know what Boone Dogs' Cave means." Each word was slowly, painfully forced out. "I know where her Pa stashed the loot."

Mr. Gould flung Millie aside, knocking her into the table. She doubled over and tried to catch her breath, praying Dom's diversion wouldn't get him killed.

"How would *you* know?" Mr. Gould asked, striding over, his gun pointed at Dom's swollen forehead. Millie pushed herself from the table and glanced from the men to her frying pan. No way could she reach Gould before he noticed her. Before he pulled the trigger and killed Dom.

Cursing her stupidity for leaving her gun at the mine, Millie held her breath and watched.

"Why do you think I've been living here for three months? Just for her cooking?" Dom dragged himself into the rocking chair, so unsteady he almost tipped over. Finally he leaned back, his breathing ragged, and glared at Mr. Gould. "I heard about your visit and the silver coins. Decided I was sick of being poor. She was easy." He glanced at Millie. Gone was the warmth in his eye. Gone was any sign of affection. His expression made her shiver and step back. It was an act, Millie was sure of it, but it was a chillingly good act.

"Once she trusted me, I took a look at the map and started asking questions. Learned all about her stupid life in New Orleans. Figured she might not realize her dear daddy left her a clue. I was right."

"You're lying," Millie said. She wasn't sure why Dom was bluffing, but she could play along. Letting her anger at this whole insane situation show, she glared at Dom like she believed his betrayal. "You don't have any idea where the silver's hidden!" She punctuated her words by grabbing the tin bowl from the shelf and throwing it at him. Her aim was poor and Buttercup gave her a doleful look as the bowl clattered to a stop near her.

It felt good to throw something, to let her anger show. Millie seized more dishes and hurled them in Dom's direction, pleased when a tin cup struck Mr. Gould.

"Stop that," hissed the outlaw. He spun around, strode over, and grabbed Millie's arm. Millie yelped and dropped the second tin cup she'd picked up. "If you throw anything else, I'll shoot your goat."

"Bring me some food, Red," said Dom harshly, "And some coffee."

Mr. Gould shoved her toward the cookstove. "Do it," he hissed. "But bring *me* coffee first!"

Did Dom know about the coffee? Millie poured Mr. Gould's coffee into the tin cup, careful not to cause the laudanum bottle to roll and make noise. She handed it to Mr. Gould and was relieved when he raised it to his lips.

Mentally willing the man to drink, Millie prepared a second plate of food and carried it over to Dom. He took it without even glancing at her.

"Prove you're not bluffing," said Mr. Gould, his cold eyes burning Dom's face. "What does Boone Dogs' Cave mean?"

"I want half."

"And the woman, I suppose," Mr. Gould said dryly, taking a sip of coffee.

"And the woman. After the past three months, I've got a score to settle." Dom shot Millie a look that made her shiver. It was hard, ugly, indifferent. He grabbed the meat with his fingers, imitating Gould, and bit off a chunk. "But when I'm done, she's yours."

"I'm not fond of seconds," growled Mr. Gould, taking another sip of coffee. "Prove you're useful and we can have a discussion. Where are my silver coins?"

Dom nodded. The food seemed to have energized him. He leaned back, closed his eye, and shoved the last of the meat into his mouth. After a long pause he spoke. "Boone Dogs' Cave is a reference to a place called Wolff Hills."

"How do you know that?" Millie blurted out, stepping toward him.

"If your brain was half as sharp as your tongue, Red, you'd have figured it out."

"Explain Wolff Hills," Mr. Gould demanded, shoving Millie aside and spilling some of his coffee.

"Wolff Hills is a cave where Daniel Boone's dogs were attacked by wolves. Boone Dogs' Cave. The map spells it out clearly."

"Daniel Boone was a man? A real man?" Millie had heard the name, but assumed he was a fictional character like James Fenimore Cooper's hero, Natty Bumppo.

"Of course he was real," Dom snarled. "Bring me more food!"

Millie refilled his plate. After handing it to him, she glanced over and saw Mr. Gould's coffee was almost gone.

The barrel of his gun had dropped and no longer pointed at Dom.

"Where. Where is this Wolff Hills?" Mr. Gould's speech slurred slightly.

"In Virginia," Dom said. He looked up at Millie, exhaustion clouding his eyes. "Abingdon, Virginia."

FORTY

December 19, 1863
Vigilante Law

Abingdon, Virginia? Millie felt absurdly stupid. Her daddy hadn't named her. "How long have you known?" she asked, her voice barely a whisper.

Dom's silence was her only answer.

"Abingggdonnn Virrginnnia," said Mr. Gould, slurring each word. "Gooood tooo knowwww." He took an unsteady step forward, lifting the muzzle of his gun. "Guessss I don'ttt neeedddd yaaa nowww." Hand swaying, he pointed the gun in Dom's direction.

"No you don't," Millie said, grabbing his hand and jerking the gun free. Mr. Gould looked at her stupidly, his eyes unfocused. He swayed uneasily. "If anyone gets to shoot Dom, it'll be me. But first I get to do this."

Swinging the gun as hard as she could, Millie slammed the cold metal into Mr. Gould's drooping face. He dropped to the floor and lay sprawled like a comatose drunk. The gentle rise and fall of his chest were his only movements.

Turning, she hurried over to Dom, slipping Mr. Gould's gun into her apron. Dom sat with his head resting against the back of the rocking chair, his eyes closed. "Are you okay?"

The swelling on his head was worse. He half-opened one eye, his pain evident. "You and laudanum are dangerous," he said very slowly. Closing his eye, he haltingly continued.

"Go...go on. Get some help. Gould should be out. For a bit."

"I'll get Doc Noxon too. Just hold on." She considered giving him Gould's six-shooter, but worried he might take justice into his own hands. The laudanum would keep Gould unconscious for quite a while. Jerking on her coat, she fled the cabin.

Millie only managed to relate a slightly coherent summary of her wretched story, but it was enough for Mary to grasp. "Go tend Mr. Dom. I find help."

Exhausted, Millie headed back toward her cabin, her limbs feeling uncoordinated and leaden. Her movements were slow and it felt like the snow clutched at her skirt with each step. She fell twice, but finally reached the bridge that crossed her creek. Voices in the woods caused her to pause and look around. Stars filled the heavens, brilliant in the cloudless night. The voices grew louder. Suddenly, Sheriff Reynolds, the Grouse, Doc Noxon, and several of her suitors charged from the trees, Mary trailing after them.

"Where is he?" yelled the sheriff as he spotted Millie.

"How did you find them so fast?" Millie gasped, glancing at Mary.

"Mrs. Ferris be worried," Mary said, trying to catch her breath. "She sent 'em."

Relief flooded through her as she hurried forward and grabbed Doc Noxon's arm. "Ferris is dead. Mr. Gould's in my cabin, unconscious, but Dom's hurt bad."

"Mr. Gould?" shouted voices at the same time other's cried, "What happened to Ferris?"

Sheriff Reynolds quieted the group and began asking questions. Millie's answers brought hoots of anger. She told them everything. Everything *but* Dom's discovery of the location of the silver coins.

Sheriff Reynolds insisted on leading the posse to Millie's cabin, but when he tried to make the women wait outside, Millie lost it. "Dom needs Doc Noxon's help now!" She squeezed past him and hurried inside. Boots clumped after her.

Millie froze when she saw the bodies.

Dom lay slumped on the floor, the goats cuddled around his inert form. Mr. Gould lay where Millie had left him, but his head was twisted at an odd angle. A trickle of blood stained his forehead.

"Looks like Gould's dead," said the sheriff.

"Smells delicious," said Mr. Poor, stepping over Mr. Gould's body. He circled the table and sliced off a chuck of Millie's roast. "Don't mind if I do."

Doc Noxon hurried over and rolled Dom onto his back. "Put some water on to boil," he instructed. "This head wound looks bad."

"Definitely dead," said Sheriff Reynolds, nudging Mr. Gould with his toe. "Must have broke his neck when he fell."

Millie didn't say a word. She filled pots with water and set them on the stove, hoping her shock at Mr. Gould's death didn't show. Mr. Gould hadn't broken his neck falling. And the overdose of laudanum hadn't killed him.

Dom had broken his neck!

FORTY-ONE

December 21, 1863
A Frontier Christmas

Two days after Mr. Gould's death, Dom was finally strong enough to venture from his bed. Despite his very visible injuries, Millie couldn't help the fury she felt at him for taking the law into his own hands. He'd murdered Mr. Gould! If the miners' court knew, they'd hang him. It scared her to death. She voiced her displeasure by slamming his plate of eggs and potatoes down so hard several potatoes bounced off the plate. Dom looked up and narrowed his eyes, although the swollen half of his face only allowed that eye to open a slit.

"Surely you didn't believe anything I said to Mr. Gould. I was trying to distract him. Stop him from striking you again."

"Of course." Millie kept her back to him and poured coffee. "How long had you known the map referred to Abingdon, Virginia? Why didn't you tell me?"

"I didn't know," Dom said, striking the table with his fist and causing Millie to spill the coffee on her hand. She thrust the injured member under cold water before spinning around to face him.

"So you figured it out when Gould hit me?"

"No! I wanted to kill Gould when he struck you."

"You did kill him. You broke his neck!"

"You bet! That bounder needed dying." He stood up, shoving his chair back so hard it fell over backwards and crashed to the floor. His whole body shook. Millie had never seen him so furious. "I can't even think about what he wanted to do to you without...without wishing I could kill him all over again." He leaned across the table.

Millie slammed his coffee down and leaned across her side. Dom had killed a man! How could he feel absolutely no remorse for this act of lawlessness? Fighting to hold her own temper and trying to keep her fear in check, she decided changing the subject might be best. "So when did you figure out the map's location?"

"When Gould mentioned Boone Dogs' Cave and asked if it referred to Daniel Boone. His name made me remember the incident at Wolff Hills just outside Abingdon. Then I knew."

"I see," she said. "Will you be leaving now? Taking the map and retrieving the treasure?" She regretted her words as soon as she'd spoken them.

Dom recoiled, as if slapped. "You think it's the silver coins I want?"

"That and the gold from your brother's mine," Millie responded hotly. She reached into her apron and grabbed the three gold nuggets she'd found, shoving them under Dom's nose. "When you go back to search your mine, look for the bloodstains where Buttercup gave birth. You'll find your precious vug there. Then you'll have your brother's gold and the silver coins."

His furious expression wavered. "You found the vug?"

Millie threw the nuggets at him. "Take them, and the map. Treasure's all *you* care about!"

His misshapen face turned a bright red, highlighting the ugly bruise on his forehead. He leaned back over the table until they stood nose to nose. "Red, you are the most stubborn, impossible woman I've ever known. You make me so mad I want to take you over my knee. Unfortunately, I could never lay a hand on you! Instead I'll—"

A knock on the door interrupted him. Millie cursed. She was almost certain he planned to end the argument with a kiss. A kiss she desperately needed.

Instead, he spun around and stomped over to the door, flinging it open. Sheriff Reynolds touched his hat in greeting.

Millie froze. How much of the argument had the lawman heard? The window shutters on either side of the door were wide open. Had he heard Dom's murder confession?

"Dom, glad to see you up and about. Just stopped by to share the news."

"May I offer you breakfast, Sheriff Reynolds?" Millie asked, her palms suddenly damp.

"Don't mind if I do," said the lawman, taking a seat at the table. He picked up one of the gold nuggets on the table and admired it. "Found so much gold you're tossing nuggets around? Strange shape."

Millie turned to fix his plate, hoping he didn't see her fear.

"Not so many," Dom said casually. Millie turned with the full plate to see Dom scoop up the other two nuggets from the floor. "What's your news?"

"Yesterday, the boys and I managed to retrieve what we could find of Ferris," he said grimacing. "It weren't pretty. Afterwards, the miners' court met and discussed the incident. We ruled both deaths accidental. Ferris was killed by the landslide and Gould broke his neck when he fell. Anything you want to add?"

Millie handed Sheriff Reynolds his plate, feeling her shoulders sag. Dom shook his head. "Nope," he said gruffly.

"Thank you kindly, Widow D. Anything you have to add?"

"No," Millie said, her voice barely above a whisper.

"Good. Now that's done we can get on with the holiday season. Dom, you take it easy. I'm sure you wouldn't want to miss Idaho Spring's Christmas feast and ball. I hear the ladies are planning quite the celebration." His eyes sparkled and he took a bite from his potatoes and eggs. "As a single man, I can't wait to sample the food."

Christmas Day arrived. In the spirit of the season, neighbors began visiting Dom and Millie wishing them Season's Greetings. Mr. Poor, Mr. Shumate, and Mr. Tappan arrived together, smelling strongly of whiskey even though it was well before noon. Dom didn't help matters when he brought out a bottle—*how many*, Millie wondered, *were hidden in his bedroom*—and poured each man a gill.

"Merry Christmas," he said, clinking his glass with each man. "Bottoms up!"

After downing his drink, Mr. Poor approached Millie. "Widow D," he said, "it's time you learned about Kissing Day."

Millie took a step back. "Kissing Day?"

"Yup. See, the early Rocky Mountain trappers included Frenchmen, and they introduced their own Christmas customs." Without further preamble he grabbed Millie's shoulders and pulled her into a sloppy kiss. The kiss was wet and awful, leaving the taste of whiskey on her lips.

"Mr. Poor!" she said, stepping back after he released her. "I hardly think that's appropriate." She glanced at Dom, hoping to have him protest, or at least react, but he'd turned his attention to the baby goats. She felt like crying, but gasped instead as Mr. Shumate lumbered over, shoving Mr. Poor out of the way.

"Exchanging kisses, lassie, is how them French trappers celebrated the holiday," explained Mr. Shumate. Without another word he took his turn.

Millie was still reeling as Mr. Tappan stepped forward, grabbed Millie's braid, and pulled her head down. "I'm sure the Bard would approve of Kissing Day."

Slapping Dom on the back, each man wished him Season's Greetings and ambled unsteadily out the door. Head spinning, Millie looked over at Dom. He sat facing the fire, a baby goat asleep on his lap. Why hadn't he objected to the men's advances? Did he no longer love her? Since their argument the other morning and the sheriff's visit, he'd withdrawn and acted like a different man. Gone was his former stomping that shook the floor. Gone was the rude, loud galoot. Gone was his impolite sense of humor. And, worst of all, gone were the kisses.

Millie missed those kisses! Had Mr. Gould's death ended whatever future they might have shared? Millie couldn't stand the thought.

"Dom," she said, wiping her lips with her apron and coming away with a smudge of soot. "I understand about Mr. Gould. I don't like what you did, but I understand."

"Good," he said gruffly, keeping his back to her.

Millie didn't understand. She'd apologized! And it wasn't the first time. Why was he being so cold? He loved her, didn't he? Millie was no longer certain. She stared at his back but he refused to turn around.

The man was impossible! Still, planting her fists on her hips, she decided she would marry him! No way she'd let Mr. Gould ruin her future. She'd win Dom's love back somehow. But how?

Maybe *she* should kiss *him*! The boldness of such an action made her shiver with anticipation. Florence Hartley would wholeheartedly disapprove, but Millie was desperate. A life as a lady sounded boring compared to a life with Dom. She stepped toward Dom, intent on implementing this new plan, but froze at a new knock on the door. More men intent on celebrating Kissing Day? Millie glanced out a window, relieved to see Mary with two loaves of hot, yeasty smelling sourdough loafs wrapped in the apron of her Thanksgiving dress. Millie opened the door and ushered her friend inside.

"I not going," Mary said. "You take me bread."

"Of course you're going, Miss Mary." Dom gently placed the goat on a quilt, rose, and walked over. "Mrs. Beebee made a special trip to your cabin to invite you. She'll be insulted if you don't go."

"Maybe," Mary said uncertainly, "But they be lots of white miner men who ain't gonna be pleased to see me."

"That's true," Dom said, solicitously taking her arm. "But there are many of us who will be sad if you don't come." He guided Mary toward the door. "Shall we go?"

Millie was proud of him. With Dom as an escort, no one, not even a drunk miner like Mr. Turck, would dare question Mary's attendance. Retrieving her dish of hominy—made from the last of her precious dried corn—Millie followed them into town, her mind practicing different kissing plans.

They reached town and the noise exploding from Mrs. Beebee's establishment made Millie pause. Dom opened the door and led Mary inside, but Millie could only stand and stare in the open doorway.

In New Orleans Millie had experienced her share of raucous Christmas festivities. At home, merriment started with liberal imbibing of food, sweets, and of course spirits. They were followed by the shooting off of fireworks like flying pigeons, serpents, torpedoes, tourbillions, and various wheels. Millie couldn't imagine anything wilder until now.

Cautiously, she stepped into the room. It was full of extremely inebriated prospectors dancing and singing as Mr. Payne played his violin, accompanied by an enthusiastic Doc Noxon on a tin pan.

Dom grabbed Millie's dish as Mr. Shumate danced over and drew her into the fray, swinging her with such enthusiasm her feet left the floor. Before Millie could object, or even catch her breath, Mr. Shumate passed her over to the next dancer, a stranger who grabbed her around the waist and hollered as he swung her and gave her a kiss. He passed her on and each man took his turn, some giving her a whirl while others celebrated Kissing Day. Much to Millie's distress, it felt like every man took his turn. Every man but Dom.

She'd seen him dancing with Mary, Mrs. Beebee, Mrs. Gardner, and even the schoolmistress, Miss Marble. He danced and liberally celebrated Kissing Day with them, but every time he got near Millie, he turned away. If she hadn't been so occupied staying on her feet and avoiding kisses, Millie would have cried.

When Mr. Payne and Doc Noxon started the popular tune "New York Gals," the miners stopped dancing and began pounding their feet against the floor to the beat. Each time the chorus came around, they belted out their own words.

Hangtown gals are plump and rosy,
Hair in ringlets mighty cozy;
Painted cheeks and gassy bonnets;
Touch them and they'll sing like hornets.

After dancing to "Merrily Danced the Baker's Wife," "Jessie, the Flower o' Dumblane," and several songs Millie didn't know, she finally escaped and joined Mary and Mrs. Beebee, helping to set out the food. When Mrs. Beebee hollered it was time to eat, all dancing, singing, and music immediately stopped. Men—led by Dom—stampeded to the table, heaping their plates with wild venison, mashed potatoes, mince pies, and the other food.

As the food disappeared, Elder Griswold stood, patted his belly, and climbed onto the make-shift stage to begin the next phase of the evening's entertainment: the theater. He turned to face the rambunctious crowd.

"Which story you gonna tell?" yelled a miner.

"Tell about Idaho Spring's first death."

"Nah, I want the story of the rat cooked in the corn mush."

"How about the one about our first teacher, Mrs. Doud and her handsome stranger?"

"Tell us a fofarraw!" Dom hollered.

Elder Griswold raised his hand for silence.

"A fofarraw it is. For those new to the Rocky Mountains, early mountain men told fofarraw near roaring fires while the moon lolled in the sky and stars decorated the heavens. A fofarraw is a true Rocky Mountain yarn and since it's Christmas, a Christmas fofarraw is in order." He paused and Millie looked around. Every person in the room, including the drunken prospectors, waited impatiently.

"Back in '37, when mountain men hunted the Rockies, a group of them came together to celebrate Christmas at Fort William up north of here. Lots of Indians attended, celebrating "Big Eating," as they called the holiday, and of course those scarlet-capped French Canadian trappers were kissing everyone in sight. Trappers were enjoying their rum and whiskey, shooting off their guns, and having a good old time when suddenly one looks up and sees the fort's brass cannon. He decides the celebration needs a big bang."

He paused, took a drink of his whiskey, and smacked his lips. "Yep. All them dang mountain men agreed on it, but as they loaded the cannon, they decided they wanted an even louder blast. So, they stuffed a pair of buckskin pants and lots of old moccasins into the cannon's muzzle. When they touched it off, what do you think happened?"

"It didn't go off."

"Them clothes caught fire."

"There was a big bang!"

"Well, you're right. There was a big bang, but not what they was expecting. When they touched it off, the whole muzzle exploded, sending bits of britches, rawhide, and brass shards everywhere. Lots of folks was hurt, including the gunner when the big gun bucked backwards. Guess what them mountain men learned from this?"

"Stand back and let someone else light the blasted gun!" Dom yelled. The whole room erupted into laughter and Elder Griswold left the stage.

After Elder Griswold's story, a couple of miners acted out a short skit, which caused the room to roar when a rough, bearded miner turned to show off his lopsided, squash-sized breasts and said in a high-pitched voice, "I just love prospectors." Next came a series of miners who stood up to tell jokes followed by two men dressed in bison robes with bells on their arms and legs. Their faces were painted and they began dancing something they called "La Gineolet," a traditional French dance. Millie's amusement turned to shock when Dom let out a whoop and jumped up to join them.

She watched his enthusiastic movements, reminded again that he had refused to dance with her. Millie narrowed her eyes. When Dom sat back down, she was going to wish him a happy Kissing Day and remind him just how good their kisses were.

Dom returned to his seat and took a long draft on his beer as Mr. Tappan rose and took the stage. Everyone groaned. "He recites Shakespeare sonnets every year," Dom whispered. Millie twisted sideways, ready to implement her kissing plan, but Dom's face was already turned toward the stage. Millie wanted his mouth, not his cheek!

"I usually recite one of the Bard's great works, but this year, I must share with you the words of President Lincoln." He paused and a murmur rose in the audience. "As you know, in the first few days of July, a terrible battle was waged at Gettysburg in Pennsylvania. I've read more men—both Feds and Rebs—died in that battle, more than in any other battle of this terrible war. A few weeks ago, President Lincoln traveled to Gettysburg to dedicate a cemetery at the site of the battle. I'd like to read you the speech he gave, as reported in New York's newspaper, *The World*, on November 20 of this year." He paused and pulled out a worn and wrinkled newspaper. "I will attempt to read these words with the passion, I'm sure, spoken by the President." Clearing his voice, he began. He read with both a passion and eloquence that brought tears to Millie's eyes.

FOUR SCORE AND SEVEN YEARS AGO OUR FATHERS BROUGHT FORTH UPON THIS CONTINENT A NEW NATION, CONCEIVED IN LIBERTY, AND DEDICATED TO THE PROPOSITION THAT ALL MEN ARE CREATED EQUAL. NOW WE ARE ENGAGED IN A GREAT CIVIL WAR, TESTING WHETHER THAT NATION, OR ANY NATION SO CONCEIVED, AND SO DEDICATED, CAN LONG ENDURE. WE ARE MET ON A GREAT BATTLE-FIELD OF THAT WAR. WE ARE MET TO DEDICATE A PORTION OF IT AS THE FINAL RESTING PLACE OF THOSE WHO HERE GAVE THEIR LIVES THAT THAT NATION MIGHT LIVE. IT IS ALTOGETHER FITTING AND PROPER THAT WE SHOULD DO THIS. BUT IN A LARGER SENSE WE CANNOT DEDICATE, WE CANNOT CONSECRATE, WE CANNOT HALLOW THIS GROUND. THE BRAVE MEN, LIVING AND DEAD, WHO STRUGGLED HERE HAVE CONSECRATED IT FAR ABOVE OUR POWER TO ADD OR DETRACT. THE WORLD WILL LITTLE NOTE NOR LONG REMEMBER WHAT WE SAY HERE, BUT IT CAN NEVER FORGET WHAT THEY DID HERE. IT IS FOR US, THE LIVING, RATHER TO BE DEDICATED HERE TO THE REFINISHED WORK THAT THEY HAVE THUS SO FAR NOBLY CARRIED ON. IT IS RATHER FOR US TO BE HERE DEDICATED TO THE GREAT TASK REMAINING BEFORE US, THAT FROM THESE HONORED DEAD WE TAKE INCREASED DEVOTION TO THAT CAUSE FOR WHICH THEY HERE GAVE THE LAST FULL MEASURE OF DEVOTION; THAT WE HERE HIGHLY RESOLVE THAT THE DEAD SHALL NOT HAVE DIED IN VAIN; THAT THE NATION SHALL, UNDER GOD, HAVE A NEW BIRTH OF FREEDOM, AND THAT GOVERNMENTS OF THE PEOPLE, BY THE PEOPLE, AND FOR THE PEOPLE, SHALL NOT PERISH FROM THE EARTH.

The room exploded. Men jumped to their feet, yelling and stomping so loudly the building shook. Millie stood amongst them. She forgot about kissing Dom. More important feelings overwhelmed her. She'd been born and raised in the South, but President Lincoln's words resonated in her heart. This terrible war would rage on, but somehow the Union would stand.

They returned to the cabin well after midnight and Dom insisted he walk Mary to her cabin. Millie waited impatiently by the door, determined to successfully implement her kissing plan. And maybe even get him to propose. As if anticipating her, Dom returned through the back door and hurried to his room without so much as a "good night."

Tears stung her eyes as Millie hung her head and headed toward her room. She stopped when Dom opened his door and handed her a package.

"Thank you kindly," she said, confused. "But you gave me a gift earlier." Dom had presented both Millie and Mary with several colorful ribbons wrapped around bright yellow sunbonnets. For their part, Millie had knit Dom a new wool hat and Mary had sewed him a quilt. Millie looked at the package. She didn't want another gift. She wanted Dom to kiss her, to tell her he loved her, and to propose!

"Open it." Dom said, uncharacteristically keeping his eyes on his toes.

Feeling miserable, Millie carefully unwrapped the parcel and gasped. Slowly she ran her fingers over the most beautiful gown she had ever seen. The body was an unusual bluish-brown color that shimmered in the firelight. The neckline and bottom were trimmed in ornate, hand-tatted lace. A panel of shadowed lace about eighteen inches wide flowed loose from the waistline and the same lace was used for its sheer, flowing sleeves.

"Oh Dom," she whispered. "It's beautiful. Finer than anything I've ever owned. Where did you get it?"

"Mrs. Gardner helped me order it from the O.K. Store in Denver City," he said gruffly, still looking at the floor.

Millie stared at the top of his head, tears brimming in her eyes. This was a wedding dress, she was sure of it. "Why...why thank you. But why did you order it?"

"I thought..." he paused and glanced at her but quickly returned his eyes to the floor. "I thought you might like it."

Millie almost stomped on his foot to get him to look up, but decided that might not be the best way to get him to propose. She stepped forward, determined to thank him with a kiss, but he quickly backed into his room, either not noticing or deliberately avoiding her. She stopped, stunned and hurt, only to have him finally look up. He looked tired and unbelievably sad.

"I'm leaving. Tomorrow." Without another word, he shut the door.

FORTY-TWO

December 25, 1863

Leaving?!?

Millie looked down at the beautiful dress in her hands and backed up to Dom's closed bedroom door. She felt numb.

Dom was leaving? Why?

Surely he couldn't be leaving for good. He was supposed to marry her! Setting the dress out of Buttercup's reach, Millie marched over to Dom's bedroom door and pounded on it.

"Dominic A. Drouillard! You come out here this minute and explain yourself!"

"Gosh darn it, woman. We're in the same cabin." He opened the door and scowled at her. "You don't have to yell loud enough for Mary to hear."

Millie ignored his sarcasm and poked his chest with her finger. "What do you mean you're leaving?"

Dom shrugged. "I'm leaving. Going to Denver City. Maybe back to the States. To fight in the Union Army."

"But…but…" Millie threw up her arms in frustration, fear, and confusion. "You can't leave."

He narrowed his eyes. "Why not?"

"Because, you said…I mean, you told me…" Wiping a tear from her cheek Millie put her hands on her hips. "You said you loved me!" Her angry words sounded like an accusation.

Dom crossed his arms across his chest and scowled. "I do love you," he responded crossly.

"So why are you leaving? Why won't you marry me?"

Dom stepped forward and glared down at Millie, his nose almost touching the tip of her forehead. "I can't stay here or marry you. You think my killing of Mr. Gould was murder."

"I didn't like what you did," Millie yelled, "but I know you did it to protect me."

"Darn tooting. Had to be done. No way I'd risk him escaping and coming after you again."

"Okay."

"Okay?" His temper died, and he stepped back. "I still have to go."

Millie wanted to pull her hair out. Deciding his hair would hurt less, she grabbed both sides of his head and jerked him down for a kiss. She sighed when he finally lifted his head. "Happy Kissing Day."

"Why'd you do that?" he asked, his expression suspicious.

She frowned at him. "It's Kissing Day. It's tradition."

He nodded and pulled away from her, but he wasn't able to get far. She still had his hair grasped in each fist. "I'm still leaving."

Slowly Millie released his hair. "Why?"

"I told you I loved you. You never said nothing back." He deflated a bit, and his anger was replaced by sadness. His shoulders slumped as he turned toward his room. "It's okay. I know you want a refined man. A gentleman. Someone like Johannes."

"Dom," Millie said, flabbergasted at the man's ignorance. "A lady never says how she feels. Florence Hartley says it's not proper until after she's engaged."

"What?" he asked, spinning around so quickly he bumped into her. She would have fallen if he hadn't grabbed her arm. "What isn't proper?"

"According to Florence Hartley, a lady never shows or says how she feels until after she's engaged. It's in her chapter on a lady's conduct when contemplating marriage."

"Of all the stupid, idiotic…Where's that damn book?" He stormed around Millie, shaking the floors with his passage. Buttercup and her kids jumped to their feet and stared at him, eyes bulging.

"Blasted book!" He picked it up and glared at it.

All three goats fainted.

"Dom, don't!" Millie yelled, but she was too late. Dom had stepped over the goats and tossed Florence Hartley's *Manual of Politeness* into the fire. He turned to glare at Millie.

"Florence Hartley is an idiot," he said. His voice softened and he walked over and took Millie's hands. "Don't you know a man won't propose unless he knows how the woman's feeling?"

"I beg to disagree, Mr. Drouillard." Millie's voice hardened as she watched her book burn. "I've received numerous proposals—"

"I don't want to hear about your other proposals," he said, putting his fingers over her mouth. He stared at her, his blue eyes flashing. "So if I propose, are you going to tell me you love me?"

Millie just raised an eyebrow and tapped her foot against the floor.

"Damn you, woman. Why'd I have to fall for a stubborn redhead with idiotic ideas on ladylike behavior?"

"May I remind you, Mr. Drouillard, my hair is auburn with just a few red streaks."

He grinned and gently pulled the end of her braid between them, running his fingers over her hair. "I like them red streaks."

Millie's toe tapping increased in volume and cadence. The man was impossible. He got distracted by the stupidest things. Rising up on tip-toes Millie grasped his hair again and pulled his head to hers. She meant to give him just a quick kiss, but he wrapped his arms around her and pulled her in for a kiss that made her toes tingle. When he released her, Millie had to catch her breath.

"Thank you for the dress. It's beautiful."

"My kisses have ruined you. You're spoiled 'cause no other man can make your head spin. Plus, I spent all that money on your wedding dress. I guess I have to marry you."

"Mr. Drouillard, you have—"

He placed a finger on her lips, silencing her. "Hush. I have a question to ask." He took her hands in his and slowly knelt. "Miss Permelia Abingdon Virginia. I'm crazy about you. I can't imagine a life without you. I want to share my world with you." He lifted her hands and kissed each one. "We'll have amazing adventures together. Will you marry me?"

"Yes, Mr. Dominic A. Drouillard. I will marry you."

"And do you love me?"

"Of course I love you."

Dom jumped to his feet and gave a wild whoop. He picked Millie up and danced about the cabin, swinging her around, never letting her feet touch the floor. Buttercup and her babies, who'd risen from their first faint and were now huddled in front of the fire, fainted a second time.

Dom let go of Millie and she tumbled to the floor. She sat up and rubbed her knee as Dom hurried over to the babies. "One of these days they're going to faint into the fire." He carefully lifted one baby and set her on the quilt while Millie rose and rubbed her bruised posterior.

"Sorry," he said, laying the second baby by her sibling. "I didn't mean to drop you." He hurried over and gave her another kiss that made her forget about her new bruises.

"Tomorrow we'll find Brother Bunce and marry, okay?"

Millie smiled. She'd never felt so happy. Tomorrow she'd marry Dom and they'd spend their life arguing, laughing, and having adventures together.

A thought clouded her joy.

"Okay. But there's one thing."

Dom's elated expression turned cautious. "What's that?"

Millie could feel the blush reddening her face, but she forced herself to push on. "When we're married, we'll share a bed?"

Dom grinned. "Yep. Tomorrow I'll build one big enough for the both of us. It will barely fit in your room, but we'll make do."

"Okay." Millie felt shy and foolish, but she had to know. "My friend Carissa talked about marriage bliss, and, well, Sarah said something about a husband's right. Mrs. LeGrand referred to a cross a wife hadta bear." She could feel the heat from her face. "What…Well, what exactly is marriage bliss?"

Dom grinned and kissed her. "Just like it isn't proper for a lady to confess her love until she's engaged, I'm sure Florence Hartley would agree it isn't proper for a gentleman to explain marriage bliss until after he's married."

His smile faded and he looked at her with concern. "Millie, you know. When we're married, marriage bliss isn't improper."

Acknowledgements

Writing can be a lonely process, but publishing a book only occurs with the help and encouragement of a community. This book would not be what it is without the critique, encouragement, and assistance from numerous people. I wish to thank my daughters, Tess and Corrie, my friend Peggy Howell, and my parents, Joyce and Cleve, for their excellent comments, improvements, and encouragement. My beta readers, authors Tim Mahoney and HL Miller, provided invaluable insight into restructuring and improving the story flow. Finally, my critique group, 30th Street Fiction with Kate, Rick, Ian, Lezly, Tim, Mike, Jessica, Evan, and Caitlin, helped polish chapters and find scene errors.

As an author, I loved researching the history and historic stories incorporated into *The Lucky Hat Mine* almost as much as I enjoyed writing the book. I'd like to thank the librarians at the Denver Public Library, the Stephen H. Hart Library, and the Boulder Carnegie Library for their assistance in helping me locate historical information on anything from frontier clothing to washtub panning. I also want to give credit to the numerous books I've used for research, especially Ethel Morrow Gillette's *Idaho Springs Saratoga of the Rockies*, *A Pioneer History of Clear Creek County* published by the Pioneer Association in 1918, O.L. Baskin and Company's *History of Clear Creek and Boulder Valleys*, Henrietta Bromwell's *Fiftyniners' Directory*, Marilyn Lindenbaum's *Discovering Denver: Brick by Brick*, Robert Brown's *Colorado Ghost Towns*, Gayle Shirley's *More than Petticoats, Remarkable Colorado Women,* and of course *True Politeness. A Hand-Book of Etiquette for Ladies.*

Throughout the writing of this book, I've tried to be as accurate as possible, but historical fact is sometimes gray. I take full responsibility for any historical errors and offer my apology.

I'd like to thank the publishing professionals, editors, and cover designers, who turned the story from a manuscript to a published novel. My initial editors, Andrew McFadyen-Ketchum, Nicole Duggan, and Kara Duggan for cleaning up my writing and explaining when to use em-dashes, ellipses, and other confusing English grammar. My friend Mary George and other contributors who helped wordsmith my back cover blurb into something readable. Cover designer Jeffry A. DeCola was brilliant in his cover design and my artist friend, Annie Carter, who turned the picture in my head into a wonderful sketch.

Finally, I'd like to thank my husband, John, who supported me through years of writing and dreaming and my publisher, Hansen Publishing Group, for turning my dream into a published book.

Book Club Questions and Topics for Discussion

Thank you for reading *The Lucky Hat Mine*. This Book Club guide includes questions that are aimed at enriching your discussion and help your group find diverse topics of discussion.

Researching the history and stories in *The Lucky Hat Mine* was one of the author's favorite things to do. Because readers often want to know what is fact versus fiction, J.v.L. Bell will include a *Lucky Hat Mine* History Quiz on her website, listing answers to previous quizzes in her blog and adding a new quiz periodically. For book discussion groups, here is a quiz/discussion topic to start your meeting:

Millie Virginia recites quotes and includes information about proper lady's etiquette throughout the book. Only once has the author taken liberties and quoted proper etiquette that did not come from a lady's etiquette book. Can you guess which rule of etiquette is fabricated?

J.v.L. Bell would be glad to SKYPE in to your meeting if it can be arranged and provide you with the proper answer. Email her at Julie@jvlbell.com if you are interested in her attending your meeting.

Book Club Questions:

1. Millie chooses to answer a wife-wanted advertisement and leave everything and everyone she knows. Why would she do this? What would drive you to make this kind of change and sacrifice?

2. Millie arrives in Idaho Springs and is surprised by her modern cabin. The cabin is described as having uneven wooden board flooring, a river rock fireplace, and a Charter Oak cookstove. Is this an accurate description of the kind of cabin pioneers in the 1860s lived in? What do you think would be the hardest part of living in such a homestead?

3. When she first arrives in Idaho Springs, Millie describes how different the Colorado Territory and Idaho Springs are from New Orleans. Have you ever traveled somewhere that made you see your home differently? How? Has that travel changed your beliefs or behavior?

4. Millie has interesting adventures with her suitors. What fun adventures have you had on blind dates and with your suitors?

5. Millie wears traditional clothing of the day and is sometimes hindered by her long, full skirts. How have fashions changed over the years? What are your favorite fashions? Why?

6. Life in the Colorado Territory was difficult in 1863. This book makes light of those difficulties (hunger, sanitation, living rough) and the harsh living conditions. Does this make the book less enjoyable? Believable?

7. Because of Lincoln's proclamation, Millie celebrates Thanksgiving on the last Thursday of November. She writes out formal invitations and cooks traditional foods. How do you celebrate Thanksgiving? Are there any special foods you like to make or traditions you follow each year?

8. When Millie meets Mary, her colored neighbor, she is remarkably unprejudiced. Did you grow up with preju-

dices? How did these attitudes affect you? What kind of prejudices have you had to overcome?

9. Millie was raised as an orphan in New Orleans by Catholic nuns and later works as a servant for the LeGrand family. How does your upbringing affect the adult you became? What is a major event in your past that made you who you are?

10. Millie believes that to be a respectable lady, she must follow strict etiquette rules. Do you feel that is true in today's society? What societal rules do you feel a woman today must follow to earn respect? What rules today might cause her to lose that respect?

11. On Christmas day, Millie learns about the French trapper's tradition of "Kissing Day." What are your favorite traditions and why? What are some of the craziest holiday traditions you have ever encountered?

12. Elder Griswold tells historical stories throughout *The Lucky Hat Mine*. Share your favorite historical or family story. Why is it your favorite?

13. At the end of the story, Dom commits murder. Do you feel this murder is justified? Is killing ever justified? When and why or why not?

Meals to Enhance Your Meeting

• Try (at your own risk) a recipe from *The Great Western Cook Book*. Millie's meals of half a Calf's head and Beef A La Mode can be found at: http://jvlbell.com/1857-great-western-cookbook/#more-97.

• A digital copy of the entire cookbook can be found at: http://digital.lib.msu.edu/projects/cookbooks/html/books/book_20.cfm

About the Author

J.v.L. Bell is a Colorado native who was raised climbing Colorado's 14,000 foot mountains, exploring old ghost towns, and reading stories about life in the early frontier days. She enjoys hiking with friends and family, visiting new places and meeting new people, rafting the rivers of Utah and Colorado, and reading great historical fiction. She lives in Louisville, Colorado with her two daughters and her husband.

Curious what is fact versus fiction in *The Lucky Hat Mine*? Visit the author's web page at www.JvLBell.com and read her blogs about the historical topics she researched while writing *The Lucky Hat Mine.*

CPSIA information can be obtained
at www.ICGtesting.com
Printed in the USA
LVOW10s1513060217
523343LV00001B/165/P